TYCHE'S CROWN

A SPACE OPERA ADVENTURE EPIC

RICHARD PARRY

CONTENTS

Stay Primed	vii
Recruitment	1
Chapter 1	8
Chapter 2	14
Chapter 3	20
Chapter 4	31
Chapter 5	42
Chapter 6	54
Chapter 7	60
Chapter 8	63
Chapter 9	65
Chapter 10	67
Chapter 11	73
Chapter 12	82
Chapter 13	91
Chapter 14	101
Chapter 15	107
Chapter 16	120
Chapter 17	132
Chapter 18	137
Chapter 19	142
Chapter 20	152
Chapter 21	159
Chapter 22	164
Chapter 23	169
Chapter 24	173
Chapter 25	187
Chapter 26	192
Chapter 27	197
Chapter 28	206
Chapter 29	224

Chapter 30	226
Chapter 31	238
Chapter 32	243
Chapter 33	251
Chapter 34	255
Chapter 35	264
Chapter 36	268
Chapter 37	273
Chapter 38	277
Chapter 39	283
Chapter 40	288
About the Author	297
Also by Richard Parry	299
Glossary	302
Acknowledgments	311
EXCERPT: TYCHE'S DEMONS	313
Something Wicked	314
Chapter One	329

TYCHE'S CROWN copyright © 2017 Richard Parry.
Cover design copyright © 2020 Vivid Covers.

All rights reserved.
ISBN-13 paperback: 978-0-9951041-6-7
ISBN-13 ebook: 978-0-9951041-7-4

Second printing.

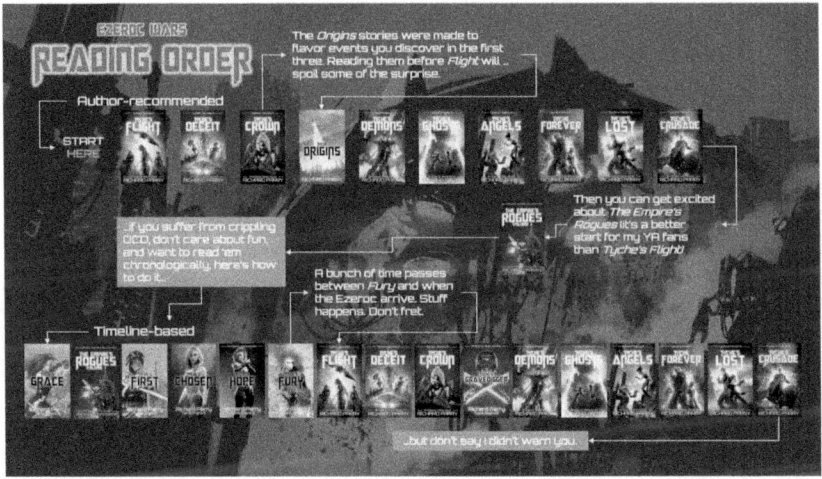

No parts of this book may be reproduced, scanned, or distributed in any form without permission. Piracy, much as it sounds like a cool thing done at sea with a lot of, "Me hearties!" commentary, is a dick move. It gives nothing back to the people who made this book, so don't do it. Support original works: purchase only authorized editions.

While we're here, what you're holding is a work of fiction created by a professional liar. It is not done in an edgy documentary style with recovered footage. Pretty much everything in here was made up by the author so you could enjoy a story about the world being saved through action scenes and clever dialog. No people were used as templates, serial numbers filed off for anonymity: let's be honest, October Kohl couldn't be based on anyone *real*. Any resemblance to humans you know (alive) or have known (dead) is coincidental.

Published by Mondegreen, New Zealand.

STAY PRIMED

Get updates from Richard Parry:
https://www.mondegreen.co/get-on-the-list/

You can find out more about him at:
mondegreen.co

For Greg, who always finds a way to make me think about the universe's limitless possibilities without making me feel stupid at the same time.

RECRUITMENT

"KOHL? KOHL, *NO*."

October Kohl looked at the bartender — same glowing green braids, same pissed off expression — and then around the bar. He kept on turning until he arrived back at the bartender — *yep, definitely pissed off* — and then kept on walking forward anyway. He put his empty glass on the bar. "Joni? I ain't working today." Kohl figured that was obvious, what with him in a plain grey jacket rather than a ship suit. He figured his dreads and fitted shirt made him look a little more shoreside too.

She eyed him with what he figured for a high level of suspicion. It was hard to tell, on account of him being drunk. "What are you doing then?"

He gave that some thought. "I'm recruiting." He frowned at his empty glass. "I *was* drinking."

"Which is it?" she said. "I can fill your glass. Hell, I'll give you a whole damn bottle. But if you're working, you can ... Kohl? Look at me." She reached across the bar top, raising his chin with her hand. "If you're working, you can get the fuck out of my bar."

He spent a little more time processing that. It gave him time to take in the grime level of the place while he did it. The place had seen a lick of paint since they were last in town. More than a lick: the bar had seen more love than Kohl himself in any given week. Which made sense, because last time he'd been in here a whole mess of Republic troops had come in and set fire to everything.

Technically, they'd shot the place up with plasma weapons, but the secondary effect of a good plasma volley was *fire*. This particular *spacer bar* — that's what the captain would have called the place — had been given a good facelift. Knocked twenty years off, maybe thirty. Then someone had gone around putting the dirt back in. Grime in the corners. Sticky floors. A holo stage was flickering its life away behind the bar. He squinted at it, trying to focus on the words imprisoned in the light. "Earth beer?"

"You want one?" said Joni, almost hopeful.

"Naw," said Kohl. "Beer gets you full, not drunk."

"So, you're drinking?" said Joni. "You want the good stuff or the cheap stuff?"

Kohl massaged a pocket, teasing out a stack of good Republic coins. He put them on the bar top. "Good stuff," said Kohl.

She looked at the pile of coins, not taking any of them. "I have to wonder, Kohl. I came on shift not two minutes ago. You're already listing. Sheets torn, flapping to the winds. How'd you get so drunk? Tommy doesn't like you."

"You don't like me either." Kohl sniffed. "I mean, I don't know. I guess I can live with Tommy not liking me."

"Answer the question."

"Oh, hell," said Kohl. He jerked a thumb over his shoulder in the general direction of *behind him*. "There was this asshole over there who got in my way. So I took his drink." He looked at the empty glass. "Before that, I was drinking on the ship. Before that, I said I'd go recruiting. Problem with these Resistance types is they're all soft. They're, how do you say it? *Trimmed fingernails*. That's it."

Joni looked at him, then picked a couple coins off the top of his stack. They disappeared, a kind of magic trick Kohl had never managed to work out, and a fresh glass — *waste of time, old glass was fine* — appeared on the bar in front of him. A chunk of ice as big as a fist — not one of Kohl's fists, because he grew them at a *proper* size, but maybe one of Joni's fists — entered the glass. A generous pour of amber liquid followed. Kohl watched in silence, then looked at the pile of coins. "Y'all not going to take the rest?"

"Not if you're drinking," she said. "That's more than you need for even the good stuff."

"Huh," said Kohl. "I tell you what. You hold on to 'em for me."

"Kohl? *No.*" Her eyes widened at something behind him, and Kohl let himself smile. Hell, he didn't even have to work at this recruiting business. The work did itself.

He felt a hand on his shoulder. Strong, big. Familiar in a way that said *I own you* rather than *I am your friend and here for a good time*. A touch like that would have put Kohl's teeth on edge if he hadn't been so well lubricated before setting out today. He let himself be turned around, leaving his drink on the bar. Kohl'd get back to it in good time. He stared at a man. Large. Muscles everywhere, and not dirty bulk. Lean like a tiger. Angry as one too. "*Asshole*," said the man. "Did you beat up my buddy and take his drink?"

"Might have," said Kohl. "Which one of these fuckers is your buddy?"

"Say," said Tiger. "Don't I know you?"

"I sure hope so," said Kohl. "It'll go easier on both of us if you do."

Tiger's eyes narrowed, lips tightening. "You held a gun to my head. Last time."

"Might have," agreed Kohl.

Tiger laid three punches into Kohl's gut, *bam-bam-bam*. They were hard and fast. If Kohl had been sober, he might have done something useful about them, but things being as they were he let them come. He wasn't in much of a position to do anything, on account of the liquor. Also, this guy would ease up faster when he worked out that Kohl was a bigger bear.

Both men stood still. Kohl heard Joni say something like *fuck all this shit* and the emergency shutters slid down over the bar behind him. Neither man moved at the rattle and clang as they locked into place. Kohl rubbed a hand over his gut. "That's not a bad right you've got there."

Tiger looked at Kohl's gut, then at his right hand. Then up at Kohl. "I ... hit you. I hit you *hard*."

"Naw," said Kohl. "*This* is hard." He swung, giving it a good seventy percent. Enough force in the punch to lift Tiger up off his feet, push the air out of his lungs, and leave his eyes wide, mouth wider, trying to suck in a tiny spoonful of air through a paralyzed diaphragm. "See what I'm saying?"

Tiger nodded, but that was about it. *Gracie would know what to say here. Course, Gracie wouldn't be in this situation. Gracie doesn't know how to drink proper.* "Look," said Kohl. "You're a Marine. I get it. You've been through the training. Used to having big guns and a whole bunch of other assholes with you. Right?" Tiger gave a nod, sucking in some air. A knife appeared out from behind him, held in an angry fist, which Kohl more or less expected, so he took the knife away — short block, grab the wrist, and *twist*, but not *too* much, because he was *recruiting*. The knife dropped out of Tiger's hand to clatter on the floor of the bar. "Nah," said Kohl. "Let's not do that. Where was I? Marines, check. Big guns ... oh right. Yeah. So, you're out of work, is where I'm going." Kohl frowned, because that was about the most words he used in a given day, and he was out of runway. What usually helped was alcohol, but his drink was on the other side of the emergency shutters. Kohl became aware — gradually, like the coming of a new dawn — that the entire bar had gone silent. Nothing from the jukebox, because it shut off in emergency situations. But the other patrons, if you could use a polite word like that to describe them, were all staring at Kohl and the Marine. A couple had gone towards the exit, and those were the kind Kohl wouldn't have wanted to recruit anyway. Probably didn't grin when they fought. *You need to get recruiting, October Kohl. Like you said you would.* He cleared his throat. "Say. If I get Joni to lift these shutters and offer to buy you a drink, will you at least hear me out?"

The Marine looked at him, rubbing his own gut in an absent-minded way that said *I am hurt, but I am more curious than hurt.* Which was good. He looked at the shutters behind the bar. "I don't think they'll open 'em up for us."

"Sure they will," said Kohl. He reached behind him, not turning away from the Marine, and rapped the back of his hand against the shutters. *Clang clang clang.* "Joni! Joni, it's all good out here. I need a round of beers. Or something."

Her voice came back, muffled by the shutters. "No way, Kohl. No way."

"No, we're good," said Tiger. He gave Kohl a look that said, *may I?* Kohl nodded for him to go on. "We … just want to talk."

"Uh huh."

"Joni," said Kohl. "If I wanted to mess the place up, it'd be messed up." He winced. Not the best approach. "I mean, uh…"

The shutters rolled back with a clatter, and Kohl turned to see Joni. Hair still green, face still pissed off. She pushed his drink across the bar at him. "Here."

"And one for all my new friends," said Kohl, his arm encompassing the entire bar. "Anyone who wants to sit and listen."

THAT SENIOR OFFICER guy Evans was still behaving like an asshole, even without his uniform and stripes. Kohl leaned on the table between them. "Hey, Evans."

The man looked like he wanted to twitch at that, because he was used to *Lieutenant* coming before his name. There'd be a lot of things he'd need to get used to. "What is it?"

"Stop being an asshole," said Kohl. "Drink your drink."

Evans made to rise. "I don't have to listen to this," he said. "I came here as a *courtesy.*" Kohl had to admit, the guy sure wore casual clothes like they were officer's finery. Pressed shirt. Nice black jacket, if that's your thing. Bit scrawny, but officers tended to that general direction. It was, Kohl figured, all the hand-waving and pointing rather than the actual soldiering. Not that Kohl thought much of soldiering either. It was a good way to get paid poorly while wasting a lot of time. Plenty of better ways to do the same work for more money.

The Marine — Sib — put a hand on Evans' arm. "It's okay, sir." He cleared his throat, remembering he wasn't a Marine anymore, and this asshole wasn't no Lieutenant neither. "Evans."

"See," said Kohl, "I know how it is."

"You do?" said Evans, leaning forward. There was real anger there. Anger Kohl might have responded to if he hadn't already been so drunk. "How can you know?"

"Well," said Kohl, "I figure the way it is, is kind of based on how my captain blew up the moon."

The circle of watchers — all holding their free drinks, all a rough and ready lot — leaned in closer. Kohl took a sip of his whiskey, frowned at the glass — too much ice melt, not enough strong liquor — and continued. "We had all these aliens. Which you sent us to go find, if I remember it rightly. You sent us out there — 'downed transmitter' my ass — and hoped we wouldn't die. Or we would. Hell if I know. Don't care. What I know is that we blew up a moon, and it was because you started something."

Evans sat down, like he was a mechanical construct, hissing back into place. "Okay," he said.

"And the thing you started was the downfall of the Republic," said Kohl. "There's a real Resistance and everything—"

"There's always been a Resistance," said Evans.

"I know," said Kohl, then took another drink. It was okay if you guzzled it. "This time your people are on the team. Hang on. One of them said to say something to you. Uh. Lieutenant Karkoski? You know a Karkoski?"

"I know *Captain* Karkoski," said Evans.

"Whatever," said Kohl. "She said she sends her regards."

"Any special messages? Code words?"

"Naw," said Kohl. "She said you and her never had time for that bullshit."

Evans nodded at that. "That sounds like Karkoski. What about her?"

"She's fixing to overthrow the Senate, on account of ninety percent of them being alien scum," said Kohl. "I dunno. She figures a new broom? Sweep 'em clean. Keep the same structure. I'm all for it. I *like* the Republic. What I don't like is fucking mind bugs that get in your skull and eat you out." He shuddered, remembering the one that had clawed inside him. How Gracie had saved him from doing something horrible. "But you know all this. It's why you've been busted out. Republic's shut down here on Enia Alpha. Office has closed. Discharged your sorry asses. The time for fighting's come, Evans. And we're needing people to do the fighting."

"While you're in charge?" said Evans. "No thanks."

"Me?" said Kohl. "Hell no. I don't want to be in charge. I guess you could say I don't have the temperament for it." There was a snigger from one of the men around them, and Kohl looked at the man. "What? You got a fucking *problem*? No? Didn't *think so*."

"Who's in charge?" said Evans. "Who's footing the bill for this merry escapade to rebuild our Republic?"

"Bills, I dunno," said Kohl. "That's Karkoski's area."

"Okay," said Evans. "Who's in charge?"

"Karkoski," said Kohl.

"No," said Evans. "I don't think so. Who is it *really*?"

CHAPTER ONE

GRACE STOOD in front of the Intelligencers, arms crossed, sword at her back. "You've got to decide if you want to live or die," she said. The sun of Enia Alpha was a balm on her skin. She liked the feel of its kiss, almost as much as she liked the feel of Nate's kisses. Grace had shucked her usual leather jacket just to feel its touch on her arms. She shook her head. *Not now. Focus.* "Do you want to live?"

There was a general round of nodding from the Intelligencers, some of it more enthusiastic than the others. Chad shuffled his feet. He was still too damn slim for someone about to go to war. "I think that's a given, Grace." They were at a place Chad claimed to own but probably didn't. The house was square, constructed around a large open area in the centre. There was real grass underfoot.

"Then you need to act like it," she said. She sighed, not sure why she felt angry. "We ... just don't have—"

"Chad," said Nate, walking up behind him, and clapping the esper on the shoulder, "what Grace is saying, if I can ... *paraphrase* ... is that we don't have time for you to get your shit together. What we've got here is a basic time-meets-opportunity problem. We've got no time, and plenty of opportunities."

"Sure," said a woman's voice from somewhere near the back. "We've got the opportunity to get killed."

"You want this one?" said Nate, cocking his head at Grace.

"I'll take it, sure," she said, wanting more time herself. More time to be alone with him. To talk, or dance, or fly among the stars without being shot at. Instead, here she was, trying to teach a bunch of people used to giving orders how to prepare themselves for being on the front line. She looked out over the crowd, not sure who'd spoken. That was the problem with this lot. Her usual gifts could pick out people's emotions. But the Old Empire's Intelligencers were all strong espers, pick of the crop, top shelf to the last. They could shield their thoughts like most people walked and talked at the same time. They'd been teaching Grace the trick, and it was working. But it made singling out people in the crowd difficult. *So don't bother.* "You'll get killed either way," she said. She waited for the gathering to stop their nervous shuffling. "You're either going to die on your feet or on your knees. The Ezeroc are coming. Sure, we blew a hole in Earth's moon. Took their Queen out. But that was just one. They'll send more. We need to be ready. And we need you for that." She paced, realized it was her nerves — because she wasn't used to being front and center, her role was always *behind* someone, *hiding* from something — but went with it. "Normals against these things? They can't compete. It's our time to do what we were made for. We need to save the human race. If we don't, then everyone will die."

"There's only a handful of us," said Chad.

"Eh," said Nate. "A hundred and fifty isn't a handful."

"Against an entire alien race, it's a rounding error."

"It's an important rounding error," said Grace. "Because we can learn to fight. Beat them. Lead humans to victory. I know it's different to order people to their deaths from the comfort of your executive lounge." That might not have been fair — not all of them were assholes. A great many of them were here because they didn't tow the party line of the Intelligencer leadership. They didn't want to rule humans as mind-controlling overlords. Neither did they want to be hunted to extinction by their previous comrades who led the Republic. "So, I'll teach you how to fight." She nodded at Nate. "And he's going to help."

"I am?" said Nate, brow furrowed.

"Yes," said Grace, wanting to reach out and smooth his confusion away, but now wasn't the time. "And after that—"

"You'll sail off," said the woman's voice, "leaving us to the dying."

Ah. That one. Grace managed to single the woman out. Blonde hair. Angular face, strong, used to giving orders, not taking them. Certainly not used to the possibility of dying that came with taking orders. Grace walked towards her, pushing through the rest of them. "You think I'm walking away?"

"You've got the ship," said the woman, giving her hair a toss. "You're going to leave us."

"Yes," said Grace.

"What?" said the woman.

"Because," said Grace, "we're going to find them."

"You're what?" said Chad.

Grace looked at Chad over her shoulder, then turned back to the blonde woman. "We're going to find them," said Grace. "In our ship. Then we'll call for your help, and you must be ready."

There was quiet. Total quiet.

"You're going to go out there *after* them," said Chad. "You. The one they've been so interested in."

"Yes," said Grace. "I don't think I want to wait for them to come to me. And it'll take some of the heat off of you. While you get ready."

The blonde woman watched her. Scrutinizing her, like she was a bug. Grace could imagine what was going through her mind. *You're not even a real esper* or *why should we do what you say* or *maybe they've already got to you*. None of it mattered, because Grace was going. She and Nate had already talked about it. Step one. Build the Resistance up. Step two. Find the bugs. Step three. Fangs out.

Still no one spoke, which was unusual. This crowd could have been talking mind-to-mind, but Grace didn't think so. There was none of the usual *noise* she'd picked up, the metal whispering as people talked just outside her mental hearing. It was just another way she was different. Broken. Damaged.

Nate's hand was on her arm, jerking her out of that little internal death spiral. She could smell him, the scent heady, familiar. Like the joy of being in sunlight outside. A reminder of how he made her feel when they were alone in his cabin. Someone who had her back. *Together.*

"So," said Nate, his voice bright. "Who wants to get shot first?"

GRACE STOOD in front of the Intelligencers, Nate and Chad behind her. Nate had a taser out, one he'd borrowed from Kohl. Or maybe Hope had made it for him. Not that it mattered. It would shoot its payload at Chad, and Chad would either dodge the shot or he wouldn't. And that was all a part of the lesson. The crowd of Intelligencers was like many other crowds, noses keen from the smell of promised blood that hung in the air. They were eager to see what would happen. The great Nathan Chevell, captain of the starship that had led the Resistance to victory. Not just against the Ezeroc, but against the might of the Republic.

What they missed was that it was *with* not *against* the might of the Republic. A hard thing for Nate, who'd worn the Emperor's Black back before the war. Nate, who'd fought against the corrupt Intelligencers, and lost. Who hated espers. Yet he had to work with them, and with the Republic they'd made, to fight insects that wanted to use humans as calories to power their ships. A more jaundiced, younger Grace would have given even odds that Nate would sell out his own species just to see the Intelligencers burn.

But that wasn't what he was like. She wanted to kick herself, to shake herself, to scream, because there wasn't *time* for this. No time for love, for her and Nate. Not *now*. Not with what was coming. She addressed the group. "Here's what'll happen," she said. "Nate's sword is ... special. It was a gift. As long as he holds it, no one can see into his mind. Or control it."

"A princely gift," said the blonde woman. "Also, bullshit."

"How do you figure that?" said Grace.

"No object can do that," she said. "Our power is over minds, and the tech hasn't been *invented* yet that will—" There was a *zzzzzcrack* and the woman gave a tight scream. She shook like she was taking on fifty thousand volts — which she was, the taser's launched payload embedded in her shoulder — then toppled like a felled tree.

Grace turned to Nate. "What the hell," she said. She saw he had his flesh hand on his sword's hilt, the taser extended from his metal one.

He lowered the taser. "Huh," he said, looking at the weapon. "I figured on it being a more effective demonstration this way." He slipped another cartridge into the taser. "Who wants some of this?"

"I'll take it," said Chad. "This time, hand off the sword."

Nate shrugged, let go of his sword, and readied the taser. He did a fast-draw — quick, like a cobra; if Grace hadn't been looking for it, she would have missed the raise-and-fire of the weapon. Chad side-stepped, like he was just out for a stroll.

Grace turned back to the Intelligencers. "We're working on getting more of these swords made," she said. "Once we have them, the Ezeroc won't be able to get in your minds. Other Intelligencers won't be able to either. Any questions?"

The blonde woman was getting to her feet, looking terrible. Grace wanted to smile, pushed the feeling down, and waited. "You've only got one of those swords?" said the blonde woman.

"For now," said Nate, from behind them. "But we're not training you for *now*. We're training you for the future. Because fighting humans is one thing. But fighting the Ezeroc? They give nothing away. You'll be just like me."

"Hardly," said Chad. "Half as handsome and twice as slow."

Grace smiled. "Get your practice weapons," she said. "It's time to get to work."

NATE HELD a practice sword between them, a simple piece of wood that would do nothing but bruise. He held it in his right hand, flesh and blood around the hilt like he was gripping a lifeline. "I hate this," he said.

Grace circled him, slow and steady. Her feet barely left the surface of the practice mat. "You'll thank me for it."

"It's unfair," he said. "You can read my mind."

"It's not about fair," she said, lashing out with her own weapon. He tried to get his sword up, gaining a partial success — Grace's blow was diverted a little, but he still wore some of it on the side of his head. She wanted to wince, but kept a clamp on it. This wasn't about her not hurting her lover. This was about her lover not dying when she wasn't there. "It's about you learning to use that hand to hold a sword." Nate was left-handed, and he'd always held a sword on that side, at least until the fire had left him with metal on the stump of his arm. Even before that, he'd not been — by his own admission — the universe's best swordsman. Gunslinger, sure. Swordsman, no.

He swung at her, an ugly motion with no finesse in it. She tilted her body out of the way, the wood humming past her with light years of space to spare. She sighed. "Chad?"

Chad came jogging over. "Sup."

"Chad, I need you to beat Nate. I mean, leave him bloody."

"Hey," said Nate.

"Because he's pulling his swings with me, and that's not okay."

"It's a little okay," said Nate, "isn't it?"

"It'd be my pleasure," said Chad.

Grace hid her smile as she walked away, leaving them to it. She'd make Nate a swordsman again if it was the last thing she did. He'd probably be ready before her new sword was, anyway.

CHAPTER TWO

HOPE WAS IN ENGINEERING. It smelled of grease, smoke, ozone, and home. She was listening to the fabricator, the machine humming away as it printed what felt like the hundredth sword blade. The *Tyche* was mostly powered down, the reactor running low — a shiny new reactor, courtesy of the *Torrington*. The *Torrington's* Engineers had offered Hope a reactor fit for a ship of the *Tyche's* size, and she'd stared at them and said, *it's not the size of the dog in the fight*. And because they'd looked confused, she'd said, *the* Tyche *thinks she has a big heart, so give her one*. While the *Ravana's* reactor was burned out and gone, the new one was fancy new Republic tech. Oversize for a ship like the *Tyche*. And that was just fine.

The tiniest trickle of juice fed the machines around Hope. Life support was powered down, the ship slumbering for the most part. Just the fabricator. That, and Hope's console, where she was reading more about the Ezeroc. There were a few files she'd scraped together. She had her holo up, and was flipping between two things: the first was a report on the Ezeroc compiled by the Republic facility on Absalom Delta. The second? A picture of Rei-Rei. Those beautiful eyes. The curve of her face. Gone now. And so that's where Hope sat, torn between the picture of her dead wife and a report about the insects that would kill them all. *If I don't get an edge on these roaches, they'll kill the rest of my family too.* Sure, sure: it wasn't like Hope owned the problem. She was just better suited to solving it. El was good at flying ships, and Kohl was good at lifting heavy things and sometimes saving Hope from certain death. Nate was good at being a person whom she could trust to look after her, and sometimes at being a captain, too. And Grace was good at being a friend, that person she felt she could talk to if there was anything worth talking about.

Flip. Reiko's face. *Flip.* The report.

The fabricator chimed, and Hope's eyes left the report for a second to look at it. She turned back to the console. *Flip.* Reiko looked out at her. *Flip.* The report with answers, probably. She sighed, ran a dirty hand through dirtier pink hair, and got out of her acceleration couch. The fabricator's door opened, and the smell of hot metal came to her. There: Grace's sword. Or, if there was any justice, it would be this time. She picked up the metal, already cool enough to touch. She'd told the fab to bead metal on metal, a nanometer at a time, each layer hot as it was laid, but the overall blade cool by the time she got her hands on it. The metal gleamed in the low light of Engineering, just the console's holo working to lift the mood. And that report? Not a mood-lifter.

Hope swung the flat of the blade against the side of a drive cowl. It clanged, harsh and loud. Didn't break. Good.

The problem here was Grace was used to using a nice curved edge. She'd had an ancient sword she'd broken while slicing open Ezeroc, so Hope had made her another. The second version, no longer ancient, Grace had also broken after fighting Republic troops using nano-edged weapons. That was a thing Hope hadn't planned for, and she'd felt so stupid when Grace had shown her the sheared stump of metal that used to be a sword. Stupid, because Hope Baedeker was the best damn Guild Engineer there'd ever been, Shingle or no, and good Engineers knew to plan for how things were used. You didn't build a drive that couldn't give a lot of joules when under heavy thrust, because that was the only time you'd need a lot of joules. Likewise, you didn't make a sword that couldn't stand a little blade-on-blade action with modern weapons.

So, this was v3.0. She'd got the idea from the Republic swords Grace had tangled with. This weapon had a straight edge — not Grace's style — that was sharpened to a molecule's width at the finest point. Perfect for slicing apart pretty much anything. Difficult to know quite how it'd end up if you fought another sword just like it though. Would they cut each other? Would they shatter? Hope didn't know, because she only had the sample Grace had brought her, and besides Grace didn't want her to break her one remaining good blade. But here in Engineering, she had what she needed: a little time to work, a little space to think, and a project worthy of her time. If she got it right, Grace wouldn't die — or at least, Grace wouldn't die because Hope had screwed up.

This third edition was built layer on layer. The edge was very sharp. Not a monoblade, not like the Republic weapon, but near enough. No one would argue about how sharp it was. But Hope had built the blade so it was strong all the way through. She'd learned a lot about sword making in the past three days. Back before fabs, they'd folded metal. *Like anyone has time for that.* But it had given her the idea of layers. What was old was new again.

The fab didn't agree. It kept printing new swords where the layers weren't cohesive. It was like trying to teach an idiot child. But she'd kept at it, and now? Progress, because the sword hadn't shattered when she'd struck it.

Good enough for a test run.

Hope picked up Grace's hilt, fitting it to the sword blade. She wasn't paying good enough attention, and some of her hair fell against the blade's edge. It sheared with no resistance at all, pink strands falling past her face to the floor of Engineering. Hope took better care after that. Standing tall, she held the sword in what she felt was the right way — two hands on the hilt, blade out. She raised it, swung it down against her practice dummy — a block of metal and ceramicrete that used to be an insulator for a high-power capacitor. The sword hit the edge of the block, and kept on going, straight through and out the other side. Hope overbalanced, the sword hitting the decking, biting into the *Tyche's* floor. She paused, shaking a little, because the sword blade had halted close to her foot. She would have felt stupid calling for help while she was bleeding to death.

But the sword? It worked. Hope would need to find out whether Grace liked the way it felt, but from an Engineer's perspective, it seemed to do the job. Functional requirements all in the green. Just the non-functionals to go, the user testing phase. She hoped she hadn't forgotten anything this time.

Time to get back to the report. She paused, looking at the sword, her eyes moving back towards Grace's scabbard. Sword, scabbard, sword, scabbard. Hope realized two things then. First, she would need to make a scabbard the sword wouldn't cut through when it was sheathed. Second, she was very tired, because that was another stupid thing to miss. Hope laid the sword down by the *Tyche's* new reactor, and went back to her acceleration couch. She pulled a fresh stim from the pile by the console. Plenty of time for sleep later.

THE PROBLEM with the science geeks on Absalom Delta was they had been trying to build themselves a weapon. They'd found themselves a nice new alien race that could take human bodies and convert them into fuels or organic building blocks. A ready-made army for use against whatever army you didn't like very much. The real problem with their geeks — aside from them being sociopaths, as near as Hope could tell — was they had thought they could control the Ezeroc. Like the Ezeroc didn't have a commanding presence of their own. Like the Ezeroc hadn't set the whole thing up, seeding greedy humanity with the weapons of its own destruction.

With a series of reports written from the perspective of *we're going to control everything*, it was hard to glean useful intelligence. There were a couple of things Hope managed to get from the reports though.

Most important was the Ezeroc did, as everyone figured, communicate mind-to-mind. There didn't seem to be any pesky speed of light issues to contend with, which was a worrying facet that would give someone who cared about military strategy nightmares. Not Hope's problem.

Second, and high on the list, was that their Endless tech was different. Ships like the *Tyche* used an Endless Drive to go to various locations, but you use one of those too close to a gravity well you'd fry the system. Oh, you could use it to generate a little vertical lift, maybe take the load off your cargo or your hull, but if you tried to jump? Boom. Dead drive. The Ezeroc didn't have that problem. But that wasn't the real gravy in the reports. The high-value sauce was that the Ezeroc had worked out how to make an Endless jump instantaneously. Humans used Guild Bridges to open wormholes for the same purpose, but you needed endpoints to make a tunnel through space. Endless Drives didn't need endpoints but didn't move instantly from point A to Point B: if you got an Endless ship to go too fast it screwed with a human's perspective of linear time. Whole crews would go crazy, and if you pushed it too much, their consciousness would wink out like a reactor in emergency shutdown. Either the Ezeroc didn't have a similar view of linear time, or their tech was better. Hope made notes in the file: *Ezeroc do not experience linear time*. It felt kind of right, because it made her so worried. Plan for the worst, right?

Third, and this was a bit of a problem too, was humans had in fact picked up transmissions out there on the silky edge of human space. Absalom Delta was constructed as a colony world, but the great conceit was it had been chosen because the Republic geeks had heard signals from 'out that way.' Hope checked the report again. Yep, Ezeroc spoke mind-to-mind. Also yep, transmissions on the electromagnetic spectrum.

Why would a bunch of bugs that communicated mind-to-mind need radio?

Hope tugged another stim from the pile. They made her teeth hurt, but they also gave her a little more clarity.

The reason was obvious: humans hadn't heard the Ezeroc. They'd heard something else — *someone* else — entirely. Not only were humans not alone, but there was more than one alien intelligence out there.

Nate would pitch a fit.

CHAPTER THREE

WHEN EL WOKE, it was with a man's warm arms around her. Warm, *strong* arms. Connected to a chest that, even in sleep, looked purpose-built. The smell of sweat and sex and after alcohol was around her, holding her tighter than his embrace.

What the fuck was his name again?

Johnson. Davison. Mendleson. Something-son. She was sure of it.

El gave a lazy blink, taking in the room. Nice enough as far as these things went. Rented by the night rather than by the hour. Not attached to a bar — that was up the street aways. They'd navigated here like sailors of old, using the light of the stars to guide them in. Enia Alpha didn't have crickets like Earth, but it had something that chirped out in the trees or weeds or whatever crust-huggers called 'em, and that was just fine as far as El was concerned. She and the strong-arms-attached-to-the-chest had rented a room. Two floors up in a short-rise hotel. Cozy, done in an old style. Red roses on the table as they entered, like the proprietor knew the kind of customers he'd be getting.

Coins on the counter. Not hers. He'd paid, right? She was sure of it. She'd giggled, drunk and happy about it. No need to fly tonight, leastways not in the sky. But she went to heaven anyway.

Smithson. That was it. David Smithson, not John Davison or some other bullshit combination. David Smithson, a strong name to go with those strong arms and chest. He was a little younger than her, but not by a lot. Kept himself in good trim, not a sheet or a rope stowed out of place. She lifted the covers, glimpsing that torso, the abs you could play checkers on, the inviting V leading to his groin. El realized she wanted another round, but she'd been raised polite: let him sleep a little. She could snare them both some breakfast. Be back before he woke, surprise him with kisses and cake. She knew the path to a man's heart; any decent Helm knew how to fly those skies.

She slipped from the covers, something in her back giving a small pop. Then something in her neck. El knew she wasn't getting any younger. The only thing keeping her lean and trim was constant stress ... although last night had removed that nagging itch she'd been carrying for days.

Weeks. Months.

Might have been a year.

Bare feet padded her over to the mixed pile of clothes on the floor by the door. They hadn't made it far at all before the action started. She pulled on her pants, tucked in her shirt a little half-heartedly, tugged a jacket on over the top, and then checked her sidearm. Good to go. A-grade and ready to fly. Not even a hangover.

Not that she'd admit it either way. If Kohl didn't get hangovers, neither did she.

The door cycled open with a quiet hum, Smithson not even moving a muscle in bed. Out to it. At least he didn't snore. Maybe he'd be a keeper for a while longer. A dalliance while on shore leave. She kept that thought close, trying it on for size as she tugged hair into a ponytail that wouldn't pass muster on a Navy ship, but would get her by just fine on a colony world. She hit the lobby at a brisk walk, putting a little more saunter in it as she gated the main doors and into the bright light of Enia Alpha's yellow star.

Who'd have thought paradise would also be the home of the Resistance?

There was a bakery across the way, a place that sold nothing but carbohydrates topped with more carbohydrates. Sure, they had a Danish or two, some mock fruit thrown in to make you feel like it was a health food, but El had been on a starship for too long to turn down any kind of real fare. Reconstituted protein synthetics made you yearn for a little daily bread grown under a real sun. Something that didn't come out of a factory. She looked through the cabinets, her own personal gateway into obesity. That was a good way to spend a morning: having sex and trying to get fat at the same time.

Studying the cabinets made her miss the figure slipping into the hotel behind her.

El dropped good Republic coins on the counter, snaring what felt like four of everything. Big bags. Two cups of coffee, one white, one black, because she didn't know how Smithson took his and she didn't care how she took hers. She turned back to the street in time to see the wall of the hotel above her explode outward in a shower of ceramicrete, the plasma blasts from inside tearing at the side of the building with thunder and fire.

She paused. Didn't run — the Cap had always said that got you shot, and besides, she was confused. Was that *her* room? She was pretty sure it was. If she ran up, sidearm out, she'd probably get shot. She wasn't good at groundwork, not a crust-hugger like Kohl. Didn't want to get that dirty, and — let's be clear, crystal like the dawn here — she was still terrified of being killed. It was a fear she figured a lot more people should have. It was with this thought she saw Smithson tumble from the now open wall, arms pinwheeling as he fell to impact the ceramicrete below.

Screaming. Smoke. People running. Those were the sights and sounds that filtered to her now as she stood, breakfast in hand for a man who'd just impacted pavement four meters from her. She should probably panic too. El should probably run. She should probably do *something*. Instead of doing any of those things, El looked up at the hole in the hotel. She saw a man standing there, hands on hips, looking down at her.

El wanted to be angry. She wanted to yell. She gritted her teeth. "Captain," she said. "Did you shoot up my hotel room and toss my date out a window?"

"No," said Nate, from the open wall above her. "I—"

"Because that was my first decent lay in longer than I feel comfortable discussing on the street!" El looked around, saw people still running and yelling and doing the usual things people who led a quiet life did when things got unquiet. "Why the hell did you shoot up that room? I bought *breakfast!*"

"Didn't shoot," said Nate. "He did."

"I mean, you ... what?" she said.

"He shot," said Nate. "Didn't even get my weapon out. Just laid about him with a mean shooter, all kinds of righteous anger in his eyes."

"Do you think it's because you broke into our room and surprised him while he was asleep?" said El.

"No," said Nate. "I think it's because he's a Republic spy."

El thought about that for a few cycles. "Hell," she said. "I'm coming up."

"Don't bother," said Nate. "I'm coming down. Nothing else up here."

He had that right.

"DAVID SMITHSON," said Nate. "Seriously?" They sat at a table outside, a few blocks away. They'd both figured on it being unwise to hang loose around a Republic spy, if the Republic police would turn up. It'd get uncomfortable, no matter the official government situation of Enia Alpha.

El was sure that no one knew what that situation was. The Republic were shutting down services, bugging out. Laying off the help. The spaceport wasn't staffed by the usual people. She could tell: they were a lot more reasonable these days. Maybe revolution had a few upsides. She pushed a Danish around the brown paper bag she was using as a plate. "That's what he said."

"It's the most generic name in the universe," said Nate. "Next to John Smith, I mean. But it's *close*." He held the white coffee.

She'd taken the black but hadn't touched it. "If you could have waited," she said. "Like, just another *hour*."

"In an hour he'd have cored your mind out like a Halloween pumpkin," said Nate.

El felt a shiver walk down her spine. "He was *that* kind of Republic spy?"

"I reckon so," said Nate. "Mostly on account of how he acted when I turned up with my sword." He patted the hilt of his black blade. "Also, he didn't want to talk. He just shot at me."

"What did you do?"

"I hit him in the face, then threw him out the hole in the wall." Nate held up his metal hand. "It's got its uses. I never thought that before, but it's growing on me."

El thought while she nibbled Danish. "Don't we want to question him?"

"We will," said Nate. "Later. For now, we've got to get the ship prepped. We're leaving."

At least I got laid. At least that. "What? Now?"

"Not now-now, but soon-now," he said. "Got a solid lead. Hope's found a beacon. Or, well, the Republic did. She just bothered to read the report."

"The Ezeroc have a beacon?"

"Not the Ezeroc," said Nate.

"Then who ... oh. *Oh*."

"Yeah," said Nate. "Might be allies. Might be something we can use out there. El, we might just get through this."

El thought about that for a couple minutes. The trouble with fighting an alien race that bred like cockroaches and used your species as fuel? They were tough opponents. Their Endless tech was better than the human's. The only thing going for humanity right now was that the Ezeroc seemed content to throw rocks, whereas humans were used to energy weapons, nukes, and harsh language. Having bigger guns helped. Having to make starships was a problem though; one small Ezeroc base on the moon had been a close call against four human ships — three destroyers and a carrier wasn't a fuck-around option, either. That was what you'd take to subdue a whole planet from orbit. "Okay," she said. "Then we've got to try, right?"

"Right," said Nate.

"Out of interest, what if he hadn't been a spy?"

"Then he wouldn't have shot at me," said Nate. "Probably. I get shot at a lot these days. Speaking of which."

"You want me to go prep the ship so we can get shot at some more?"

"Yeah."

"Can I finish my breakfast first?"

"Yeah. I'm off to see an old friend anyway. And we need to extract a few morsels of intel from Smithson's brain. If that's even his name."

El gave a sigh filled with regret. "You know? I don't think his name was the important part."

EL WANTED to do more than finish her breakfast. Sure, that was important. If they were about to haul ass for the sky, it'd mean a lot of time eating reconstituted food again. Best to not let the little things slip on by. But there was something more important than prepping the ship. A trained monkey could do that. Anyone of a higher skill level than Kohl, say.

No. She needed to pick up a present for someone who needed it. She'd have liked a shower too, but that could wait for the 'prep the ship' phase of the day. The *Tyche* had great showers, and there wouldn't be anyone likely to unload plasma on her while she got clean. Besides, Smithson might have been a spy, but a little of the smell of him still clung to her clothes, and that was just fine.

Back to the present she needed to collect: it was something simple. El couldn't match the fancy levels of the gift's recipient, so why try?

She walked into the jeweler, some of the swagger back in her stride after about five kilos of pastries and another coffee. She marched up to the counter, leaning an elbow on it.

No one here.

She rang the bell. A quaint bell — it's why she'd chosen this place. They did all their work by hand, no machines more advanced than a lathe anywhere to be found. The *ding ding* rang through the store, and a man — short, gray hair, a little stooped — came out from the back room. "Help you?" he said. Thick glasses, that's right. El remembered the thick glasses, a weird oddity in a universe where new eyes could be bought in the unlikely chance your old eyes couldn't be fixed. It was probably marketing, back to the handmade thing.

"Yeah," said El. "Elspeth Roussel. Here to pick up a commission."

"Ah, that's right," said the man. "It's ... very simple."

"That's the point," she said, counting good Republic coins onto the counter. Good for a while, at least. No telling how much longer that currency would be buoyant. Long enough to get the gift, though.

He nodded to her, ignoring the coins, and hobbling out the back again. He returned with a thin rectangle, wrapped in cloth. He placed it on the counter, a *clunk* as he set it down. Thin, but heavy, exactly what she wanted. "Thanks," she said.

"Come back again," said the shopkeeper.

"I hope not," said El. "I mean, this is a once in a lifetime thing, you know?"

"I figured," said the man, turning away and going back to his work. It'd be nice to have work where you weren't being shot at. Sure, but it'd also be boring, right? A shop like this, you'd never get a chance to see the stars.

EL WALKED up the ramp to the *Tyche's* cargo bay. Wide open, because the crew's reputation was out there. You didn't want to mess with this crew. There was a captain who had taken them headlong into a fight with an alien race. An Assessor who could read minds, or close enough it didn't matter. An Engineer who knew how to fix most anything, and if she couldn't fix it, she'd make a new one for you from spare parts. And a sociopath trying to be … less sociopathic, with mixed results.

And let's not forget the amazing Helm, capable of flying an old military heavy lifter through the eye of a needle in a hurricane.

Her boots clanged against the decking as she hit the cargo bay. Lights off. Clean air around, like the *Tyche* had been dusted, waxed, and polished. No dirt anywhere. No blood stains, no scuffs. Someone had been busy. Might have been Hope. Might have been the Intelligencers. They seemed thankful to be alive and not in a reprogramming facility.

El climbed the ladder to the crew deck, then walked aft to Engineering. She paused at the small ladder leading to the airlock. Closed. She knocked. The door slid open with a hiss, and El caught site of Hope in her acceleration couch, holo display on. She caught sight of an image of the betrayer Reiko being toggled away, lines of text — some kind of Republic report by the looks — replacing it. Hope was facing away from El, but waved. "Heya."

"Hey, Hope. Bad time?"

"No," said Hope. She turned, and El saw the dark circles under her eyes. *How many stims has she had? All of them, probably.* "We got to be ready to go."

"Which brings me to this," said El, holding the rectangle aloft.

"What's that?"

"Present," said El.

"For who?"

"You," said El.

"Why?" Hope blinked. "I don't think … I don't know. It's not my birthday."

"How long have you been working, Hope?" El walked into Engineering, perching herself on the side of a drive cowling. The place smelled of … *clean* grease, which was … *unusual*. Not that Hope didn't keep it shipshape, everything in the right place. It's just … she seemed to like the smell of *old* grease.

"Uh," said Hope. "How long have we been here?"

"In this room?"

"On Enia Alpha."

"Two, almost three weeks."

"I guess," said Hope, counting on her fingers, "about two weeks then."

El looked down at the gift she held. It was a shitty idea. A stupid present, while here was Hope trying to … get *by*. Doing the work to save the human race, while everything she cared about was gone. Reiko might have betrayed her wife, but that wasn't any of El's business. She stood up to go. "I'm sorry," she said. "I … didn't think."

"It's cool," said Hope, pushing away a strand of pink hair. "Well, go on. Show me." Some of the old Hope shone through, a glimmer of the eager, inquisitive person El had met years ago. Even being in jail hadn't beaten that out of her. But, you know, being betrayed to the long arm of the law by your wife, who it turned out was the one who got you in trouble in the first place? Yeah, that'd alter your worldview.

"It's … just something small," said El. She handed over the wrapped rectangle.

Hope almost dropped it. "It's heavy."

"Yeah."

Hope unwrapped the fabric around it, El noticing the telltale shakes in her hands. *How many stims? Two weeks, let's say five a day at least ... that's way more than a safe dose.* The fabric fell away, the dim lighting of Engineering reflecting off what was inside. Gold. A plaque, solid gold, with laser etching.

"You see," said El. "I ... I've been on to the Guild. Your pardon came down from the Republic, so, you know."

"I know," said Hope, turning it over. Just staring at it, not really seeing it.

"You're an Engineer again," said El. "Not that you weren't, but ... I figured. It'd be nice to be reminded."

Hope looked up at El. "It's beautiful," she said. She pushed her weary body up from the acceleration couch, grabbing a power tool from a bench. She set the Shingle against a wall, screwing it in place. El got a look at the finished product for the first time.

THE GUILD PRESENTS

HOPE BAEDEKER

ENTRY INTO OUR RANKS. WELCOME, ENGINEER.

DO GREAT THINGS.

IT WAS as close as El could get to the real thing. It had a Guild emblem and all. A hand-etched Shingle, like the old man guaranteed.

Hope's old Shingle had been lost or taken, but El had it on authority that this was right. "I ... wanted you to remember," said El.

Hope laughed, a tired, thin sound. "It's so hard," she said.

"Yes," said El. "Why don't you get some sleep?"

"Got to get the *Tyche* ready," said Hope. "Cap said."

"Cap can wait," said El. "C'mon. Let's go."

CHAPTER FOUR

ENIA ALPHA WAS A NICE WORLD. Gravity was nice and light and it was warm. Dry when it needed to be, wet when it counted. Nate could stand to settle down here, maybe retire one day. There were two things standing in the way of that pleasant little dream: first up, aliens wanted to kill all humans. Second, this world was the de facto Resistance High Command. Why? Because it's where Nate had brought all the Resistance leaders.

You should have taken them to a shitty mudball.

It'd been weird, Amedea's tip about that spy. But she was good. Had always been good *at* it. She wasn't great at being a decent human being, but she was trying. It had only been a few weeks since her number one lieutenant had hit her on the back of the head because she wanted to rule humans before saving them. Hard road to hoe, that. Hard road to come back from, for either party.

Nate looked up at the entrance to the bar. It was the kind that said, real polite like, that spacers weren't welcome. Genuine fire lamps outside. Tables with fresh cut flowers. Fabric napkins. Nate was a spacer, through and through, but he used to be something else before that, and it had taught him manners. He walked inside, not like he owned the place, but like he wanted a drink with nice people. It was mostly true.

Harlow was behind the bar. His hair was a little thinner, his gut a little thicker. But that smile? He was looking happier than Nate remembered seeing him in a while. "Hey, Nate." Aside from Harlow, the bar was empty. Unless you were a spacer, keeping odd hours with odd people, you probably wouldn't want to go to a bar mid-morning.

"Harlow," said Nate. "You're looking well."

"Retirement suits me," said Harlow.

"You're working at a bar," said Nate.

"It's not work if you love it," said Harlow. "You hear to see her?"

"Might be here to see you."

"Both things can be true. Ain't a crime."

"I hear you." Nate pulled up a chair at the bar — a little higher than he liked, what with his metal leg, but he was getting comfortable with the prosthetic. *Finally*. "What do you recommend?"

"Got whiskey from Io," said Harlow. "It's got an interesting bite, like it wants to be an angry dog, but also wants to lay down and show you its belly."

"I'll take a bottle," said Nate.

"Going to be that kind of session with her?"

"Might be."

"Fair enough." Harlow turned, *hmmm*'d to himself while he selected a bottle, then placed it in front of Nate. "Here."

"Let's try it first, hey?" Nate set a few coins on the bar, and at Harlow's look, a few more. "That enough?"

"Keep going."

"You trying to retire on this one sale?" But Nate counted out a few more coins, the rich clink of Republic currency something sure to make Harlow even happier. Nate figured he owed him, on account of some of the ruckus that went down on Earth. Both back in the old days, and more recently. Harlow owed him some too, what with trying to stitch him up with Resistance High Command. Still, friends were hard to find, and old friends harder still, because most of Nate's were dead. Good friends were harder still. A few coins didn't matter much in the grand scheme of things.

"She's had a rough night," said Harlow. "I think she's working herself too hard."

"I think she's trying to make up for lost time," said Nate. He caught Harlow's expression. "Okay, okay. Let me talk to her. But first, we need to test this drink."

"Thought you'd never ask," said Harlow, setting a couple of chunky glasses on the counter.

Nate opened the whiskey, closed his eyes while he smelled the aroma, then poured a generous splash in each glass. He raised his glass. "To friendship."

"To not fucking dying," said Harlow. They clinked, each taking a sip.

"I don't know about the show-you-the-belly part," said Nate, "but I think I like it."

"Me too," said Harlow. "And I don't mean about this particular drink. I mean about you and me, here, in this bar, not shouting at each other. Not running, or trying to hustle. Why don't you ... stop? Just settle down? You could open a business. Hell, with the coin you hauled from the last jobs, you don't need to work. Sell the *Tyche*. Make a home."

Nate took another hit from the glass. "I've got a home, Harlow. I don't aim to sell her, either. She's a part of me, and I figure we'll die together." He looked at his metal hand. It was likely because he was part machine, and the *Tyche* just a little human now. She'd looked after them so well. "Besides, the universe ain't going to save itself."

"You've done enough."

"Not yet," said Nate. "But soon." He got off the stool, snaring the bottle and his glass. He gave Harlow a nod, then walked out back.

'OUT BACK' was dim, another real fire burning in a hearth. Vertical column heaters were placed at the back of the room, keeping the whole place warm. A little too warm, but if all you did was sit around staring into space, Nate figured you could use the extra heat. There was a figure hunched before the fire, hair a little messy but not lank. Clothes a little looser than they should, because eating was important if you wanted to keep up your strength, and Nate wasn't sure this one did much of that. She was on a bench, leather, overstuffed, no back. Two chairs were on either side of her — for holding court, or maybe for when Harlow had the time to come sit a while. "Amedea," he said.

She turned, offering him a tired smile. Amedea still looked poorly handled by time, but her smile seemed genuine. "Captain." Nate settled himself into a chair. He held up the bottle, waggling it in the air. "Sure. Why not?"

The small table in front of her held a few knick-knacks. A comm. A portable console. An empty glass. He splashed some of the whiskey into her glass, then held his own up. "Cheers."

"What's the occasion?" she said, taking a sip. "Oh, this is nice. The new stuff?"

"So Harlow claims," said Nate. "Middle of a war with aliens and a revolution in our own government, and he still finds ways to import."

"The Guild won't shut down the Bridges," said Amedea. "They don't need government to run 'em."

"They do not," agreed Nate. "We're shipping out."

Amedea hesitated, her glass caught half-way to her lips, then she completed the motion, taking a sip. "So soon?"

"Found something. Found something big."

"And you're telling me?" She gave a low chuckle. "I didn't think I was in your trusted circle."

"Sure you are," said Nate. "You just got to stop being an asshole all the time."

"I'm ... trying," she said. "Do you know what it's like to be better than everyone?"

"No," said Nate.

"Yes, you do," she said. "You're the head of a starship. Leader of people. Pulled hurting folks into a healthy whole. Got everyone moving in the right direction. Blew alien insects out of a moon. *Our* moon. Even got the Republic to come to heel. Stopped me cold, right when I thought we would win. You're better at that than anyone I've ever met."

Nate didn't know what to say to that. "I ... guess I did what needed doing."

"Which makes you better than everyone else," she said. "Like me."

"Not really," said Nate. "I don't want to crush the rest of humanity under my heel."

"Neither do I. I just ... know what's good for them." She held up her free hand. "No, I don't mean that in an evil dictator way. I mean I can see in their heads. Pry out their thoughts. I can see what will make them really happy. Help them get there. Is that so wrong?"

"Only if they don't get a say-so," said Nate. "But I figure most people work their shit out. I expect you will too." He stood to go. "The lead was good, by the way. He'd made a move on El. Called himself David Smithson."

"That was his name."

"He was born with that name and didn't change it?" Nate frowned. "You sure he was Republic? They're usually smarter than that." He sighed, then set the bottle down beside her. "Here. Something to remember me by."

"That's it?" She straightened. "No lectures. No 'play nice or else?'"

"Hell," said Nate. "I ain't your priest. But if you think you need to play nice, then maybe you should."

He was almost out of the room when she spoke again. "Nate? Thank you."

"What for?" He didn't turn.

"For not killing me when you should have."

"Huh," said Nate. "Maybe you should play that forward." He left Amedea in the gloom of her room, to continue reaching out with her mind, combing the streets of Enia Alpha. Looking for the humans who would hurt them. Working at it until she burned herself out.

THE *TYCHE*. His ship. He stood outside, hands on his hips, smile on his face. There was carbon scoring in plentiful amounts on the outside of the hull, new shiny metal next to old metal where repairs had been made. But she was whole. She'd fly true. The ship was online, steam escaping from underneath, lights on outside the hull. She looked ready to fly. The winking woman painted on her hull smiled down at him.

He walked up the gangway to the cargo bay, laying a hand on the ship's skin as he entered. Familiar. Old, but not older than him. It'd been made to fly in a war that lasted the blink of an eye, the Old Emperor cast down, the new Republic and its Senate rising in the wake. The Old Emperor — Dom, the line between friend and family so blurred as to be indistinct — had made the tools of his own destruction. The Intelligencers, humans who could read, and often change, the minds of other humans.

One of them was Amedea. She'd helped to lead the Resistance. Starting a movement, breaking away from the others of her kind. Living a life of the hunted. Her ideals were still to rule. She thought she was made as a god, and walked among mortals.

Another of the Intelligencers was in the *Tyche's* hold, talking with Kohl. Chad. A reasonable man. Took his gifts like they were no particular thing of value or benefit. A little like Grace, but less good with a sword. Still good enough to beat Nate like a carpet. Nate had entered part-way through a conversation that sounded jovial enough, although with the slurring of Kohl's words you could never tell when a squall might hit.

Kohl was holding out a laser carbine to Chad. "It's a beauty, innit?"

Chad took the offered weapon. Shouldered it, sighted down the barrel. Lowered it, like he was feeling the weight. "Sure is," he said. "Sure you don't want to sell it?"

"Nah," said Kohl. "Hope fixed it for me. Said the targeting matrix computer didn't know what Ezeroc looked like. So now it does. I don't know. What's a targeting matrix computer?"

Chad handed the weapon back. "Real collector's piece, that one. I don't know where you got it. Rare. What with AI being outlawed. That one's got to circle real close to the drain."

"Ain't AI," said Kohl. "It doesn't talk back."

"Captain," said Chad, like he'd only just noticed Nate standing there. Maybe he had; Nate's sword did a fine job of hiding him from Intelligencers. But Chad still had two good eyes. "We were just talking shop."

"So I see," said Nate. "How'd today's recruiting go, Kohl?"

"Well enough," said Kohl. "I mean," and here, he counted on his fingers, moving his lips silently, "I guess we got about a couple hundred new bodies for the grinder."

"Uh," said Chad. "I think of them as cohorts of the cause."

"Sure, that," said Kohl. "Anyway, you pay 'em, they'll turn up for war."

"Pay?"

"Pay." Kohl nodded. "Wars don't get fought on an empty stomach."

"Okay," said Chad, looking ill. "Captain, if I might have a word?"

"It's okay, Chad," said Kohl. "I was just going to grab some chow. See you 'round." He clasped Chad in a big hug, and Nate was surprised to see Chad return the embrace. "Be safe, you hear? I won't be around to pull your ass out of another insect nest."

"Sure, Kohl," said Chad. "Try not to get yourself killed before I get the chance to win my coins back at cards."

"Keep dreaming," said Kohl. He cocked his gaze at Nate. "You know these guys can't read minds for shit when you're drunk?" And with that, he lumbered off, pulling himself up the ladder to the crew deck.

Nate watched him go, waiting. No need to fill a silence with noise when dealing with an Intelligencer. Some were good, or trying to be. But when you were dealing with people who could read your mind, see your intent, sometimes before you did? Well, those encounters were best to freestyle a little.

"So," said Chad. "You've been to see Amedea?"

"Yeah," said Nate. "She's ... coming along."

"She'll get there," said Chad. "We all will. It's ... hard, Nate. To be on top, and then just be one of the team. A small part. A tiny part. You know what I mean?"

"I've got a ship with five souls against the universe," said Nate. "Against a new Empire in all but name. Against an alien race that wants to suck out our brains. I figure I got some idea."

Chad laughed. "I guess you do, at that. I'm just not used to it."

"You know what, Chad?" said Nate. "I think you'll do just fine. I'd have tossed you out an airlock otherwise."

"Uh," said Chad, shifting his weight. "Thanks?"

"Also," said Nate, "you did your part. Stayed on the *Tyche*. Rode the storm with us. Put yourself in the way of harm. Stood against the mighty, when you were weak. So, if you ever need a berth? There's one here for you."

Chad looked down, contemplating his feet, the deck, or the universe in general. "Thank you," he said. "Grace said you were ... different. I didn't believe."

"I'm not different," said Nate. "I'm the same. You've just been looking in all the wrong places." He offered Chad a smile. "You going to be ready? When we call, Chad, we need you to be ready. There's a lot riding on you answering the comm. My skin, that and my crew. Not to mention the whole human race."

"We'll be ready," said Chad. "We've got a lot to do, but we'll be ready." He offered a hand, which Nate took. "Godspeed, Captain."

Nate watched him leave the *Tyche*. Chad didn't look back,

because this wasn't *goodbye* as much as *until next time*. Nate breathed a little easier, and spoke to no one in particular. "Hear that, *Tyche*? Someone's getting it. We're flying with the Goddess of Luck."

NATE SAT on the acceleration couch next to El. She was looking pissed off, her hands on the comm. "Dock control?"

"This is Dock Control. You are not cleared for launch, *Tyche*." They said it *tai chi*, not *tai kee*.

"Two things," said El. "First, there ain't no *tai chi* here. This ship is not named after an ancient fighting art. It's *Tyche*. Say it. Say the ship's name."

"Uh."

"Say. The fucking. Name," said El.

"*Tyche*," said the comm.

"Better," said El. "Second thing, why the fuck are we not cleared for launch?"

"Random inspection," said the voice at the end of the comm.

"How about randomly choosing not to?" said El. "We're on the clock. You know, alien invaders. Whole human-race-might-die thing." Nate watched as she cocked her head. "You guys get the memo on that? About Earth? The moon? The whole—"

"We heard, *Tyche*. Still. That's what makes the Republic run so well. Random inspections."

"Random inspections, the very thing that delay departures, keep the Republic running well?" El frowned. "Look, I'll make it simple for you. We're leaving in five. If you've got us chained to the ground, we're just going to tear a piece of your pretty space port out."

"*Tyche*, may I remind you—"

"You can do whatever you like as long as that lockdown's lifted." She clicked the comm to the ship channel. "Hope?"

"You've got Hope."

"We're on lockdown." El tapped her fingers. "Can you do

anything about that? I don't want Kohl to murder any pencil necks who come onboard with an attitude. We just got the ship clean."

There was a pause. "What lockdown?"

"My girl," said El, then changed back to the Dock Control channel. "Thank you, Dock Control."

"Uh," said the voice.

"Much obliged. Thanks for lifting the lockdown."

"We haven't. I mean—"

"Have a great day," said El, clicking the comm off. She looked at Nate. "Good to go?"

"You know I love watching you work," said Nate. He waved a hand out the window. "Do your thing."

"Thing being done," said El. She worked the console, the ship rumbling around them. "Let's see. Endless systems are go. Let's take a walk." She grabbed the sticks, turning on the negative mass generator, and the *Tyche* rose from the ground. Nate felt the ship move under him as it pointed its nose to the stars. "And, walking." El pushed forward on the throttle, and the *Tyche's* fusion drives roared, clearing their dual throats, building a pillar of fire under them. Nate was pressed back into his seat, the force of the thrust holding him there like the hand of God. Or, the hand of a Goddess.

"Thought you said 'walk,'" said Nate.

"This is a walk," said El. "Barely moving." But she gave him a smile. Because she was a Helm, and Helms loved to fly.

"LAST STOP before we breeze on out of here," said Nate. "There's a fair wind at our backs, but we need to leave a message."

They were navigating towards the Guild Bridge, the massive ring still running to time. Wars or insects, it didn't matter. The Guild didn't tolerate a disruption to revenue. That was one thing you could always count on, rain or shine, war or peacetime: coin still talked.

El brought the ship close to the Bridge, and Nate could see the automated maintenance drones working. Arcs of electricity as they welded spars and struts into place according to their plan. Small flares of drives as they bussed materials from place to place. All silent, a beautiful dance in space. Nate tapped his console, entering a message. Short, simple, to the point:

KARKOSKI. WE HAVE A TRAIL AT THESE COORDINATES. DON'T BE LATE.

He pressed send, then leaned back. "Well," he said. "Let's not keep everyone waiting." He clicked his own comm. "Captain to *Tyche*. Captain to *Tyche*. Helm is clear for jump. Confirm readiness."

Grace's voice came first. The voice he most wanted to hear. "Assessor ready, *Tyche*."

Hope: "Hope is ready to fly, Cap."

Kohl's voice, cheerful through the alcohol, came last. "I don't think I've jumped drunk before. I'll let you know what it's like."

Nate turned to El. "Helm, you have control."

"Aye, Captain," said El. Nate felt the grumble of the *Tyche's* Endless Drive. The holo stage shifted from pure delta-v to Endless math, plots, charts, and entry points. The fusion drives were working hard, the pressure of thrust like a foot on his chest. "Burn is good, 3Gs. Negative space bow wave forming. All hands, bow wave is stable. Route is green. In three." The countdown started on the holo stage, a big 3 hanging between them. "Two." The number shifted to a big 2, this time flashing. "One," said El. "Jumping."

Space in front of the window stretched, pulled, and Nate felt—

The presence of his crew, all the souls under his care. Not running towards a war, but running to save their race. His skin, tight and loose at the same time. His arm and leg, metal but whole, a part of him. And the pure thrill of acceleration, impossible, unbelievable acceleration. He couldn't feel it. He was it. He was everything. He was the universe.

Stars stretched, made points of light that streaked past the *Tyche's* cockpit.

They jumped.

CHAPTER FIVE

GRACE HAD a shoulder against the airlock sill between the ready room and the flight deck. Nate and El were in the flight deck, doing their flying-the-ship thing. They were focused on delta-v, orbital entry, and trying not to make the ship fall apart as they entered the atmosphere. Which meant they were ignoring a salient point: the atmosphere they were entering was burned. Not a lot of anything out there that wasn't a poison. Lots of carbon, like the universe's worst global warming problem. Grace didn't need instruments to see that: she needed her eyes. Because the planet underneath them was a uniform brown-gray color. No green. No blue. None of the tones that said *life is here*. All the shades were necrotic, the uniform muddy texture of something that had been dead a long, long time.

The holo stage was charting a course into the gravity well, a signal coming from down there. Lifeless it might be now, but it had had life once. Something had come here, dropped a beacon, and then gone. Whether they'd been shucked out of their planet by evil space insects or this had never been their planet was something the *Tyche* needed to find out. Also they needed to find out who 'they' was.

"I'm not seeing anything alive down there," said El, her voice thoughtful, almost distracted.

"If it's alien, we might not notice it as life," said Nate.

"No lights, nothing that looks like machines. Couple sandstorms," said El, pointing at the holo stage. "That sucker there is a mean one."

"We going to be okay to land?"

"We're in a starship," said El. "We can land just about anywhere we like."

"It's just that you get jumpy when we fly into bad situations," said Nate.

"Bad situations involve people shooting at us," said El. "Or dropping rocks on us from orbit. This is none of those things. What we've got here is a planet, third from a sun in an unremarkable system. Nothing here. No satellites in orbit. Nothing made of metal anywhere around us. Just a spitball spinning around a star. It's cold, it's miserable, and I'll bet there's no beer down there."

"At least it's not raining," said Grace. That earned her a glance. "The bright side is that there's nothing with a mind down there either. Not that I can ... *feel*." Not the hissing of the Ezeroc's mind-speech, or the emotional torrent of humans. Just ... nothing. A few weeks ago, she'd have struggled to pick a single person out of a crowd, or follow someone at a distance of more than a klick. But with some coaching from Chad and his team, her talents were coming along. Range for one. Insulation for another, because having range just meant more noise unless you could shut it out. They'd taught her mantras of a sort to keep her mind to herself.

She still couldn't read thoughts. That was okay — those assholes couldn't read emotions. There wasn't a rulebook, but Grace felt it was like the difference between arms and legs. Both useful, but for different purposes. Tricky to run a marathon on your arms. Tricky to open a beer with your feet.

"You sure?" said Nate.

"No," said Grace. "But I'm as sure as we'll get." She tapped the side of her head. "I'm the best esper for a hundred light years in any direction." *There.* She'd said it. *Esper.* Owning what you were was a part of the journey. Chad had told her that as they'd sat alone with cups of tea between them. *You can't learn to be something you deny. Be complete.*

Good advice. Grace was used to being whatever it took to survive. Liar, thief, stowaway. Her eyes moved to Nate. *Lover.* Not all things she had to become were bad. Some were very, very good.

"Okay then," said Nate. "That's good enough for me."

"Me too," said Hope's voice, over the comm. "I can't wait to see what it is."

"Hell no," said Nate. "You're staying with the ship. It's dangerous out there, Hope."

"How do you know?"

"What?"

"That it's dangerous. There's a sandstorm and no life. How bad can it be? Besides, if you find alien tech, are you going to be able to do anything with it?"

"Uh—"

"Exactly," she said, the comm clicking off.

"One day, we'll get some privacy," said Nate, looking up.

"I don't know," said Grace. "It's like having a helpful angel always watching."

"A helpful annoying angel," said El, but with a smile. "Let's get the skids down and we can argue more when we're in suits." She turned to Nate. "Just FYI. You're not winning this argument."

"Are *you* staying with the ship?" he said.

"Of course," said El. "I don't want to get my boots dirty. They're new. But you kids have fun."

SAND SWIRLED around the open cargo bay doors. Grace had her helmet on, sword at her back, letting her mind range ahead. She wasn't getting *anything*. Nothing with a recognizable brain was out there. Not a dog. Not a cat. Not a gnat. Nothing but sand and wind and freezing, poisonous air.

"Well, shit," said Kohl over the comm. He was in his power armor, big gun slung on its mounts at his back. "It looked better in the brochure."

Hope jumped over the sill of the cargo bay doors, turning to face them. "Come *on*. We've got a whole alien race to discover."

"Hope, this could just be … another Republic site," said Nate. "Encrypted comms. You know the drill."

"No," said Hope. "There was nothing human in that signal. Encrypted comms look a certain way. They're usually a wrapped packet that … never mind. It wasn't us, Cap." She turned, rig in place, sandstorm swallowing her as she walked ahead.

Grace jumped down from the *Tyche*. While there was *probably* nothing here that would kill them, the universe was a bad and nasty place. It wouldn't do for their Engineer to get killed, right after she'd just had her first four hours' sleep in two weeks. While there might not be any life here, there could be sinkholes, or hell, sharp rocks. Hope had a curious mind, and curiosity could get you killed in a hundred unpleasant ways.

As her boots hit sand, Grace thought: *I am the second human to ever put boots on this rock*. Hope being the first. Then she thought: *This sand is just like any other sand. It might be on the shores of a foreign land, but it's just tiny rocks.* She bent over, sifting some through her gloves. It was whisked away by the storm, streaming away to be lost in the flow of a million other pieces of particulate. Grace stood, her HUD showing her Hope's position ahead of her. She leaned into the wind and set off after her friend.

El had set the *Tyche* down close to the beacon. Electromagnetic radiation coming from the ground. Nothing as obvious as a dish, nothing made by human hands for human eyes. Just drifts of sand, big hills of it. And underneath it, the signal. That signal would have to have been strong to broadcast out over space once upon a time to make the march a hundred light years to humanity. The attenuation of distance alone was a thing to consider, although a lot could have happened in a hundred years. The signal wasn't that strong anymore, not according to the *Tyche*. Weak now, an older power source run down by time. And, no doubt, a huge amount of sand over the top of whatever passed as an alien transmitter.

"Hey," said Hope. "I've got something."

Something turned out to be more sand. Or that's what it looked like at first. Grace's footsteps — *crunch, crunch* as she walked, the sand dragging the energy from her, starving her stride of purpose — brought Grace closer to a big hill. Or sand drift. Or ... *something*, like Hope said. A big shadow emerging from the storm in front of them. "I would bet," said Nate, coming up behind her, his voice clear over the comm, "that there is a building. Under all the sand."

"Like I said, Cap," said Hope. "I've found something. Over here." She was beckoning them over. Grace trudged towards Hope, the structure's shadow taking on form and substance, a big construct rearing out of the sand around it. It was pyramidal in shape, or the view that Grace had made it look that way — could be round at the back end for all she knew. There was a huge aperture in the side facing them, filled with sand. Hope was sliding down the slope into the pyramid's interior.

Hell. It looked like fun. Grace sat herself down and drifted along after Hope, feeling the rush of sand under her suit, fingers trailing through the material as she slid. The rush was over too soon, her boots *crunching* as the sand gave way to a stone floor. The pyramid's roof was lost high above them, the interior dark. Her suit lights didn't reach the top.

"Hey," said Kohl. "Maybe I should go first. In case there's something heavy that needs lifting." He'd made the bottom of the sand drift, and his plasma cannon was out on its mounts. He was swinging it around like he was looking for something to shoot, which — based on his *fear/fear/uncertainty* — was almost a hundred percent what was going on.

"No one's been here in a long time," said Hope. "Nobody's home. Nothing to shoot, Kohl." But she wasn't being harsh. She almost sounded ... *delighted*. "There's just a signal. *The* signal."

"What's it saying, Hope?" said Kohl.

"Beats me," she said. "Ain't it cool?"

Grace was walking, looking up, trying to find where the end of her lights *might just* hit something up there, when Nate's hand grabbed her elbow. She paused, one foot raised. He nodded down, and she looked where her foot was poised over an opening in the ground. Perfectly circular, despite the sand dusted around the lip, and a perfect drop to broken bones or death. "Thanks," she said.

"Hey," he said. "Of course. Just try not to die when I'm not around, yeah?"

"What are you guys talking about?" said Hope, coming over. "Oh. Hey. *Cool*."

"Is everything cool?" said Grace.

"For the moment," said Hope. "You found the way in."

"It's a hole in the ground," said Kohl. "No elevator. Stairs. How do you know it's not an accident?"

"It's a perfect accident," said Hope, kneeling down next to the edge. Her rig articulated a limb out, green light lazing to touch the sides of the circle. "Let's see. It's, uh, yeah. A perfect circle."

"I can see that," said Nate.

"No," said Hope. "You see a round thing in the ground. I'm telling you, this is a *perfect* circle. Oh, there's burring around the edges—"

"Hope?" said Nate.

"Sure. Right, so the sides? The burring damage. I don't know. Might have been the sand."

"Hope."

"Okay. Anyway, it's not just a circle. It's a perfect circle. Radius 2 meters. Exactly 2. Meters. With our machines? Our tech? Yeah, we could do a circle like this with a lot of practice and a little swearing. If you were the kind of person who swore," she said, looking at Kohl, "but also with the intelligence to make a perfect circle. And how would it be meters? Our units of measurement? Feels like a big coincidence."

"Uh," said Kohl. "What?"

"I'm saying it's no accident," said Hope. "It's *perfect*. Anyway, it goes down."

"But," said Kohl, point at the hole, "no elevator."

"Oh," said Hope, "it's a gravity lift."

"A what now?" said Nate. "Like an Endless Drive? Negative space field?"

"C'mon, Cap," said Hope. "How would I know?"

"But—"

"Use your imagination," she said, standing up. "Alien pyramid. Hole in the ground going to a *cool* place. No obvious way in or out. But there's like a missing piece, right? A thing that used to be here," and she gestured with both hands, the rig's claw joining in, "is no longer here. Must have been a gravity lift."

Grace grinned. Hope's enthusiasm was ... downright infectious. Not just because of the *joy/joy/discovery/joy* she was getting from the Engineer, like she was in the universe's biggest amusement park, but for the sheer size of the smile splitting the young woman's face, visible through her visor. "So we go in, is what you're saying," she said.

"Well, hey," said Nate. "I—"

"This isn't captaining stuff," said Hope. "This is Engineering stuff."

"I reckon we need to go in," said Kohl, "if only because it'll make the comm channel nice and quiet."

"I'm not sure that's a certainty," said Grace. "But I think it sounds ... cool."

"I know, right?" said Hope. She looked down. "Radius two, diameter is four... Drop looks like the same as the diameter. Good news is there's a sand pile here. We can just kind of slip on in." And with that, she swung herself into the darkness below, the lights on her rig dropping like a glowing snowflake.

Grace realized she still had a grin on her face. Nate's face mirrored it. "C'mon, lover," she said. "Let's go play."

THE BASE of the sand pile — four meters, as Hope had said — was just a floor. No spikes, alien death traps, or obvious machines. The walls, still stone, were marred by a circular portal in the wall. It had no blockage, just an opening leading down a ... tunnel. Corridor? Tunnel? It was smooth to Grace's touch, machined out of the rock with no obvious flaws. The ... tunnel ... was round, not square like a human construct.

"I'm going to call this a tunnel," said Grace. "I can't find another word for it and it's doing my head in."

"Yeah," agreed Kohl. "Why's it so round?" He stepped inside, his feet firm and solid on it. "It's weird to stand on a floor that slopes up."

"Aliens," said Hope.

"You ... okay," said Kohl. "I know you're smarter than me, Hope."

"I was just—"

"Because you're an Engineer," he said. "But when you say 'aliens' like it's an explanation, I figure on you missing a few steps there for those of us at the back of the class."

"Okay," said Hope. She was agitating from foot to foot, eager to head on off. "Look, life on Earth is familiar to us all because it's like us. A lot of it has a skeleton, so it's balanced around the middle. Legs. Walking. With me?"

"What about running?" said Kohl, his eyes narrowing through his visor.

"If you like," said Hope.

"I don't like to run," said Kohl. "Rhinos don't run."

"You're saying," said Grace, "that these things might not have legs. Don't need a flat surface to walk on?"

"Exactly," said Hope. She looked at Kohl. "See?"

There was a grumble without words over the comm, and Kohl turned to walk down the corridor. Tunnel. Tunnel thing. Grace shook her head. She took a look at Nate. "Actual aliens," she said.

"Yeah, and they don't want to kill us," said Nate.

"To be fair, they might all be dead," said Grace.

"There's a thought," said Nate. He set off after Kohl.

Hope looked at Grace. "This is *cool*, Grace. I'm ... I'm glad you're here too." *Joy/joy/joy.*

"Me too, Hope," said Grace. "C'mon. Let's see what's in this sand wonderland you've found."

THE TUNNEL WAS STRAIGHT, their lights bouncing off the sides as they continued down. There was an end ahead, lights reflecting at them off a wall. They hit a junction with the circular tunnel leading off in a Y pattern. "Left or right?" said Grace.

"Signal's coming from the right," said Hope.

"Yeah, but there's something moving down there," said Kohl, pointing to the left.

They all turned down the left leg of the Y. Nothing.

"You sure?"

Kohl's plasma cannon didn't waver. "I look like the practical joker type to you?"

"Not really," said Nate.

"Something moved," said Grace. "I can see it too. Right at the edge of the light."

"That's not creepy at all," said Nate.

"It's mechanical," said Grace.

"How do you know?" said Hope. "I can't tell."

"No brain," said Grace. She tapped her helmet. "Nothing coming in over the ol' esper channel."

"Okay," said Nate. "Hope? You're with me. Let's find the signal.

Grace? Kohl? Guard our six. Find out what that is. If it's alien robots, I don't want to be bottled up in here with them at our backs."

"I want to see the robot," said Hope.

"I'm sure there'll be plenty of time," said Nate. "Hope? C'mon."

"I AIN'T SO sure I like us splitting up," said Kohl as they walked slowly down the tunnel. Grace's sword was out, held low. The tunnel, while curved, was plenty wide for a swing of the weapon.

She sighed. "Me either, but I don't like us missing the signal or getting eaten by robots either."

"Signal's been here for a hundred years or more," said Kohl. *Stubborn/stubborn/grumpy.*

"Signal might be waiting for someone to trip the trap." Grace shrugged, realized Kohl couldn't see it, and said, "Anyway. Thrill of discovery, right?"

"Sure, Gracie," he said.

"Asshole."

She couldn't see his face, but she'd heard the smile in his voice. She smiled herself. *It's good to have friends. Who'd have thought all you had to do to find them was to have an alien menace threatening everything you know?*

Their lights picked out the movement in more detail as they got closer — an iris of sorts, no other word for it. Three pieces of metal making up a circular door in the tunnel were closing, opening, closing, getting caught and jammed on something on the ground. The 'something' turned out to be an Ezeroc claw, the right shape and size to come from one of the crab-sized aliens. Grace looked around the tunnel. "It doesn't make sense," she said.

"Fucking Ezeroc," said Kohl, like that explained everything.

"No," said Grace. "Look, this tunnel is fine and all, but those things? You know, the owner of the claw? They're big, Kohl. Too big to get down here." She keyed the comm. "Nate? Hope? Guard up. We've found the remains of an Ezeroc."

"Hardly remains," said Kohl. "Looks like just an arm."

"Copy that," said Nate's voice. "Where there's an arm, there's the rest of the insect."

Kohl's face brightened through his visor. "I was starting to miss shooting those fuckers," he said.

Grace clicked the comm off. "So I figure, behind this door? Will be a bigger room. Big enough to hold a crab Ezeroc. And there will be one of two other things."

Kohl cocked his head at her. "Spill."

"There will be an alternative route to the surface where this crab came down from," she said, "*or* this will be just like Absalom Delta. The alien version of the Republic, doing experiments on Ezeroc, and getting fucked over it. It'll be a closed room filled with aliens wanting to suck our insides out."

"I'm hoping for an ... alternative exit," admitted Kohl.

"Me too," she said. "Still. A hundred years is a long time for this door to be doing this." She walked closer, playing her light over the claw. Grace had no clue how long the organic material of an Ezeroc would last. It was *meat*, sure, but what it was made of was well outside her knowledge space. Smelled a little like crab when you cooked it with plasma, but that was about the only relationship she could draw. But she was certain that — this world being lifeless, with a poisonous atmosphere was well below zero — something should have happened to the claw. Some kind of perishing. Desiccation. Rot, maybe, if there were bacteria here at all.

Who was she kidding? There was bacteria everywhere. If for no other reason than the little bastards would have hitched a ride on the Ezeroc themselves.

This particular claw didn't look like it had seen much of the ravages of time. There wasn't any ... *liquid* ... around the end of the stump on the other side of the door. The planet they were on had an atmosphere (of sorts) so the alien's blood wouldn't have boiled off into a vacuum. So, let's say evaporation, the old-fashioned way. Which might have sucked more of the moisture out of the claw. Which didn't look the case.

"Uh," said Grace. "I think it's fresh."

"C'mon, Gracie," said Kohl. "I don't see how. You said yourself there was no life down here."

"I don't mean it's right off the shelf," said Grace. "I mean, it's not been here a hundred years."

"How long you reckon?"

"Less than a hundred," said Grace. "More than a day. I don't know."

"That's not super specific."

"No," she said. "That the door is working is good news. The aliens ... the *other* aliens ... made this place to last."

"Eh," said Kohl. "I'm more worried about it shutting after us after we remove the claw. Wait one." He walked forward, power armor clanking against the floor of the tunnel, and reached out for one of the three door seals. He was tugged off balance for a moment until he found the rhythm, then Grace watched with a little bit of horror mixed with awe as he leaned back. Kohl's armor *whined* for a moment, then the door seal bent, then tore free. He dropped the piece of material — some kind of metal — on the ground with a clank. "There."

"Kohl," said Grace. "That was a piece of alien tech. Priceless by any measure."

"It was in the way," said Kohl. "Let's go."

CHAPTER SIX

WHEN NATE HAD SET off away from Grace, he did it like he always did: with regret. It wasn't just that she was fine to look at, but he wanted her at his side. He'd known her for less than a couple of months, but it felt like he'd been missing her his whole life. It was the kind of sentimental nonsense he'd never bought into, the kind of thing Annemarie — the Emperor's sister — would have laughed at him for. She would have laid those cool fingers on his arm, like she had a hundred times before, and said *Nathan, you're doomed*. Or she might have said, *Nathan Chevell, you have found out what it means to be a king*.

She wouldn't say any of those things ever again though, because she was dead. She died after Nate had left the Emperor's Black. After he'd got his metal hand and metal leg. All of House Fergelic, heads of the Prirene Dynasty, were gone.

Nate shook himself. Annemarie was long dead, but Grace was alive. Alive, and she wanted him like he wanted her. And that was ... happiness. Like he hadn't felt in a long time, if ever.

"Cap," said Hope.

"Yeah, yo," said Nate.

"Lost you for a second," she said. "Did you hear what I said?"

Nate played back the last thirty seconds in his mind. Tunnels, check. A bunch of circles cut into the walls, an iris with three petals that sealed. Hope nattering over the comm. "Yes."

"What did I say?"

"Uh…"

"You weren't listening, were you?" She was leaning next to one iris, lights from her rig playing over it. "Doesn't matter. This is a door."

"They made you an Engineer because you can work things like that out? Wow."

She turned and gave him a glare through her visor. "I—"

"No, seriously," said Nate. "I'm glad we've got your hands on the fusion reactor that powers our home."

She made a sound that wasn't at all polite. "I was saying, what do you think is behind these doors? There's a few of 'em."

"Alien stuff," said Nate. "Is the signal back there?"

"No," said Hope.

"Then let's keep going," said Nate. "We're burning air here. We can come back and play with your dead alien friends when we've tracked down the *real* reason we're here."

CHAMBER, check. Round, check. Full of weird round gizmos, check. No lights, nothing that looked like power, just a big fucking room with round things arrayed in … yeah, a circle. "They got a whole sphere-slash-circle thing going on here, don't they?" said Nate.

"Aliens," said Hope, like it explained everything. Here, it probably did. "Anyway. This is where the signal is coming from. Near as I can determine, these round things," she pointed at the spherical objects on the floor, "are making it."

"All of them?"

"Maybe."

"That's not specific."

"We've been here less than thirty seconds," said Hope. "Give a girl a chance."

"Right you are," said Nate. They'd got the call from Grace and Kohl a few moments ago — remains of an Ezeroc, which was of moderate concern — and he felt like he needed to do a circuit to make sure nothing horrible would leap out to eat their faces. "You do your thing, Hope. I'm going to ... walk."

She waved a hand at him, not listening as she bent over one sphere. *There we go — the benefits of command. The respect and admiration of the people who serve under you.* He smiled though. It was good to see Hope working again, to see her *living* again. Reiko might have been a bitch, and a liar, and a traitor — to her own *wife*, which was a thing Nate could never countenance — but she'd been *Hope's* wife. You couldn't just turn those kinds of feelings off. Leastways, if you could then Nate didn't want you on his crew.

He started on his circuit of the room, careful to not touch anything. It wasn't so much a fear of upsetting Hope as a natural, healthy concern for being killed in ways he couldn't predict by alien technology. There had been no evidence of security here. No locked doors. Aside from the iris portals, but Nate figured on those just being out of power, not locked. A good pry bar and swearing would grunt one open without too much trouble. Hell, if he could get his metal fingers through the cracks of one he might worry it open himself. No, whoever had built this place had relied on something else for security. Something Nate couldn't see, feel, or touch, and that worried him.

It could have been that there were Ezeroc here. That kind of thing didn't need security: anyone walking into an Ezeroc lair, well, that was a problem that would solve itself.

More likely though, this place was different tech. Energy barriers, or some damn thing. The power ran out, like an old battery, a long time ago. Just a trickle of juice keeping the ... whatever it was ... broadcasting a signal to the stars. Hoping someone would hear. This planet had been spinning in space. Maybe there had been more broadcast sites a hundred years ago. Maybe this site had rotated like the dishes humans made. Maybe these particular aliens were just spraying noise into the hard black, hoping someone would hear.

If that last was the case, what were they saying? Something desperate. They had to know the odds of someone hearing them were a million, billion, even trillion to one. They had to know it would take a long time for help to arrive.

Nate shivered in his suit. He sure hoped the signal wasn't *stay away*. Old time mariners had put dragons at the edge of the map, and this place sure felt like dragons might have lived here, once. Dragons that looked like insects, that used people for fuel, and demolished worlds.

He made the back of the room, the curve of the wall heading into the black above. *Circles and pyramids.* There were pyramids on Earth still — although it was no great secret that large parts had been remade as the ravages of time continued. For architecture to be common across two species, that said something. Maybe these aliens had been to Earth. Maybe there were shapes all intelligent life liked. Maybe—

A cracking sound, like the shearing of an ice flow, interrupted his thoughts. Hope screamed, and Nate spun in place. His blaster cleared its holster before his brain even engaged. Nate's metal fingers had closed on the grip, and were already squeezing the trigger as the Ezeroc drone fell from above. His shots blew chunks off it, three good, clean hits before it hit the ground, smoldering. Not a lot of fire, because of the lack of oxygen and all, but plasma still gave its loving caress of heat.

Silence. Then a slow, low rumble.

"Hope," said Nate. She was huddling down, visor turned up. "Come on over here now."

"I..." said Hope. "It was, uh..." She pointed to one of the spheres. "And then it, uh."

"It's okay," said Nate, eyes up. There was light breaking in from above, the entire roof of the cavern irising open on three leaves. And then, with a *cruuuunch*, the roof stopped opening. Nate moved towards Hope, eyes still up, looking for more Ezeroc. No movement. Nothing. He got to Hope — eyes checking for a moment the fallen drone, lying still — and snared the back of her rig. He pulled her back, as gently as he dared, to stand with him against the curvature of the wall. Her breathing was loud over the comm, their shoes scuffing as they huddled together near the wall.

No movement. Nate's blaster moved across the space, seeking something, anything. The gloom was almost total, a thin, reedy light coming in along with drifts of sand from above. The chamber had opened to the outside. Then stalled, or locked up, or some damn thing. Nate relaxed a shade, stood a little taller, and said to Hope, "Wait here." He clicked the comm to Grace and Kohl. "It's Nate."

Nothing but a gentle hiss of static. Too much rock and stone between them and him. He clicked the channel back to Hope. "I'm just going to check it out."

"Cap," said Hope. "I ... I didn't mean to..."

"It's okay, Hope," said Nate, edging out into the cavern. Sand drifted low and slow, eddying around the floor. He approached the fallen Ezeroc drone. Nudged it with his boot. Nothing. He flipped it over, checking it. Plasma charring — score one for the home team — pocked its carapace. One of its claws was mangled, crushed like it had been through an industrial press. Nate looked up again, checking out the roof. "You know, I think it got stuck up there. I think you triggered something down here that opened the roof up, right, and that thing fell down. I think it might have been trying to get out when the roof closed."

"Out?" said Hope. "Why?"

"Beats me," said Nate. "Maybe everything down here was dead." He holstered his blaster, then grabbed the Ezeroc corpse, dragging it. It felt light enough, and he wanted it away from Hope so she could keep working without being terrified by the damn thing. At least it wasn't one of those crabs. He'd never be able to move one of those.

Light flickered, a low blue glow, and Nate paused. Vertical strips around the wall — eight in total, running floor to the edge of the roof's iris — were lighting up. "Uh," said Nate. "Hope?"

"I think I turned it on, Cap," said Hope. She was walking back towards the spherical gizmo she'd been next to. "I gave it a jolt with some EM radiation—"

"Hope?"

"I used a radio on it," she said. "Like it was using on us. And then the Ezeroc, and the roof, uh."

"Hmm," said Nate. "I figure these folks were waiting on a response from someone."

"Folks?"

Nate waved a hand. "Whatever. They were calling for help, or something like it."

"Or it was a trap," said Hope.

"Now why, for all the stars, would you say a thing like that?" said Nate. "That is an unpleasant thought."

"Guess we'll never know," said Hope. That was when the center of the ring of spheres flickered like a holo stage, and Nate saw his first glimpse of what these aliens looked like.

CHAPTER SEVEN

"HUH," said Kohl. "Now there's a thing." He had his plasma cannon pointed down the room, his armor's lights bright and clear in the gloom. They were in a good-sized spherical chamber, perhaps the same size as the *Tyche's* cargo hold. Arranged around the room were spheres set into the ground. The spheres had lids, the lids opened, the contents long gone.

Grace nodded. The room was also littered with ... *pods*. Like the pods Ezeroc encased humans in to use as a fuel. These were all flaccid, sacs empty and dry. The feeding pipes on the floor traced their lines back through a huge hole in the far wall. The hole wasn't manufactured, not the smooth, clean circular shapes used by this species. No, it'd been busted out, chunks of rock still lying on the ground. Inside the hole, visible from Kohl's lights, was the husk of an Ezeroc Queen. It was attached to the feeding pipes, head bowed, a coating of dust visible over the top of its carapace. Nate was right, the Queens looked like an armored locust, but with shorter legs. "I guess this was a party," she said. Around the Queen was a bunch of pale eggs, all sealed, waiting.

"Ain't no way this is a party," said Kohl. "There's no beer." He walked across the room, boots of his armor crunching over the flaccid, dry sacs on the ground. Dust puffed out in the wake of his steps. "Gracie?"

"Asshole."

"I think we missed whatever happened here."

"No, Kohl," she said. "We didn't miss anything." She walked over to one of the open spheres, shining her light inside. "Here."

"Uh," said Kohl. "What am I looking at?"

"You're looking at the alien version of Absalom Delta," said Grace. "I figure this room was a ... a farm."

"Like an ant farm?"

"Like," agreed Grace. "Put something in these pods. Put a Queen in here. Wait for the ... party to start."

"You saying they experimented on their own people?" said Kohl. "That's inhuman."

"That's entirely human," said Grace. "That's the point. Anyway, here." She pointed at the wall, one sac attached there large, torn open. "Here's your source of the crab."

"Huh," said Kohl. "Well, sure. That's where it came from." He turned around the room, light playing against the walls, the roof. "Where'd it go? I mean, sure, it tried to bust out. Someone shut the door on it. Cut off its arm, made it pissed off, whatever. But it was never getting out that way. No, too damn big to fit through. So it made a hole. Why?"

Grace looked around. There was no shell, no empty carapace of a large crab in here. It'd be hard to hide something like that. There was nowhere to hide it anyway. The Queen had made her nest in here, had done a bit of hatching, then ... died. The crab had ... done what? "Oh, no," said Grace, her heart skipping a beat. She looked again at the eggs.

"I don't like that tone," said Kohl. "What's going on?"

"Kohl," said Grace. "You know how they use us as food?"

"Sure," said Kohl. "I'm hoping to return the favor one day. They smell a lot like crab when they're roasting—"

"What if they can use anything as food? Like, themselves?" She nudged an empty sac. "There's this shit." She pointed at the eggs. "And ... those. A dead Queen over her brood, waiting. They, I don't know, the rest made an exit. One big crab to hold the door. And then the rest got out."

"Okay, I'll bite," said Kohl. "Where'd they go?"

Grace keyed her comm. "Nate?" A hiss of static, nothing else. She looked at Kohl. "Too much rock."

"Sure," he said. "That'll be it."

Grace closed her eyes, reaching out with her mind. Like Chad had shown her. She felt the warm solid *fight/confusion/anger* of Kohl next to her. It was like the man didn't know how to feel fear like he should, when he should. Farther out, she probed, finding the bright spots of light and color that were Nate and Hope. She knew the shape of their minds like she could tell their faces apart, a richness and a texture to each living creature. Chad — and Amedea, too — had shown her things her father never had.

When she touched their minds, she felt their *fear/panic/terror*. Her eyes snapped open. "Come on."

"Where we going?" Kohl stood next to the Queen's husk, looking up at it.

"Nate and Hope are in trouble," said Grace.

"You know what?" said Kohl. "I think we are too." He was reaching a hand up towards the dead Queen.

That made Grace pause, her gaze moving back to Kohl. "Kohl?"

"Because," said Kohl, "this fucker ain't dead." And he touched the Queen.

CHAPTER EIGHT

THE THING in the holo looked ... plain fucking ugly, no two ways about it. It was squat, with a shell on its back. Like a snail, if a snail also had limbs that came off its back near the shell. The picture was in low blue tones, which might have been the holo stage not working for shit after a hundred years sitting cold, or it could be an alien race of snails liking blue light. Who knew? The snail was waving claws and stalks all over the show in a rhythmic series of patterns.

"That is really gross," said Hope.

"Beauty's in the eye of the beholder, Hope," said Nate. "It's probably an attractive example of its species."

"Those stories from old holos, where people voyage across the galaxy to have relationships with aliens?" said Hope. "I don't see it. Not at all."

Nate's comm crackled, and he keyed it. "Yeah." Nothing, just more crackling. "Huh," he said. "Hope? You figure on working out what's going on here?"

"I'm recording it all," she said. "I don't think I can work it out here, Cap. This is an alien race. Best guess is they use sign language. Or something. But it'll take years for us to unpick that."

The holo stage flickered, and something else came to life next to it. It also looked like a super-ugly snail, but ... well, if Nate had to guess, it was some kind of stylized rendition. Like what an artist might draw. The articulation of the limbs — stalks and claws — was more rhythmic, or predictable, or some damn thing. He looked at it for a while, walking around the holo, then said, "What the fuck is that?"

"Beats me," said Hope. "Looks like another ugly alien."

"Not recorded, though," said Nate. "Like, it's ... manufactured."

"Cartoons. A computer, maybe," said Hope. "If we stay here a thousand years we'll still be discovering stuff."

There was another rumble, from back the way they came. Nate pointed his light in that direction. "You know what, Hope? I'm fixing for us to regroup. Check on the others. See what they've found. You've recorded this. We've found the signal. Everyone's dead, so maybe we go back to the ship, grab a burger and beer, and talk this over." He was expecting a little resistance, maybe a bit of static from Hope.

That didn't happen. "Good idea," she said.

Nate blinked. "Say what?"

"Great idea," she said. "Because I am pretty sure this whole thing is a trap. Nothing about it is warm, cozy, and welcoming."

"Okay then," said Nate. "With me. Stay on my six, Hope. Focus."

"You got it, Cap."

Nate led them back the way they came, exiting the big cavern with its space radio and weird alien recordings. They walked swift and sure down the long tunnel they'd entered by. It was dark, quiet, silent, just the same as when they'd come this way the first time. Except for one small, tiny detail. Tiny, yet crucial.

All the doors were open. The irises had slid wide, black and ominous space behind them. Nate slowed his pace as they approached, finding his blaster in his hand again. He poked a cautious head around the side of one iris. His eyes widened in shock, and he stumbled back. He turned to Hope, and said, *"Run."*

CHAPTER NINE

WHEN KOHL TOUCHED the carapace of the dead Queen, nothing happened. For about three seconds. Then the big head rose, dust sifting down, and Grace could hear — like tuning into a radio — that familiar static hiss of Ezeroc communication.

"Get back!" she hissed.

"No kidding," said Kohl, backing up.

"How'd you know it wasn't dead?" she said.

"Looked fine," said Kohl. "Not dried out or fucked up in any particular fashion. I figured it was just sleeping."

"So, you also figured on waking it up? Are you crazy?"

"Sometimes," admitted Kohl. "I always like to make sure what's dead is dead, and what's alive is alive."

The Ezeroc Queen was trying to rise, long years of somnolence making its movements sluggish. Grace drew her sword with a whisper of steel. She hadn't tested this version of the blade, and there was no time like the present. Grace took five quick steps towards the Queen then swung the blade. She never hit, because it whisked out a limb, much faster than Grace expected, and knocked her clear backward. She felt the bruising crush of the blow against her chest, the air leaving her chest in a rush, and she lay on the ground, trying to draw in a breath. Kohl grabbed her arm, and was dragging her backward, away from the Queen. Into the safety of the tunnel.

Kohl was watching where they were going, but she was watching where they were coming from. The Queen was still attached to its feeding pipes. It wasn't going anywhere. But its carapace flexed, bulging, and then cracked down the middle. The hissing in Grace's mind grew ... *louder* ... for a moment, then the Queen slumped forward, head dropping. Dead.

The carapace ruptured, and out of that rupture burst ... fluids. Food for a hundred smaller insects. The eggs started to rupture, cat-sized Ezeroc climbing free, bodies wet and slick with fluids. Grace knew what the claws promised, if they dug into your flesh. Larvae, under the skin. Bugs in your body that would eat your brain. Grace managed a breath, grabbing Kohl's arm. He turned, took in the sight, and unslung his plasma cannon. "It's time to get to work," he said.

She stood next to him. "It is." The first of the insects scampered forward. As it came at them, Grace stepped forward, her sword whisking out. She cut it in half, the two pieces flying past her to land on the ground. "One down."

"Ninety-nine to go," said Kohl, and opened up with his plasma cannon.

CHAPTER TEN

RUNNING WAS GETTING to be a habit. There were a lot of scary things in the universe. There was radiation, sure, that could kill silent and deadly, leaving you to bleed your internal organs dry, eyeballs leaking fluid and pus. It'd be a bad way to go. Then there was an accidental impact with a high-velocity object — say, an asteroid — that would crush the hull of your ship. If you were wiped out in the initial impact, that'd be a kindness, because dying from depressurization would just plain suck. The list went on, and on, and eventually arrived at the new dangers Nate had discovered: aliens.

Each of the rooms behind the irises were full of them. Ezeroc drones, insect-centaur forms lined up like soldiers on parade, silent. Waiting for something. The doors had opened, the air had rushed in, and the drones picked up movement. On waking up, they found that a hundred years or more of sleeping had left them hungry, and with hunger came a certain urgency Nate could relate to. The urgency gave speed, and those fucking bugs were boiling out of those damn rooms like roaches out from under a rock.

Nate and Hope were running — her rig lights leading the way as he held the rear — down the tunnel, boots slapping against the stone beneath them. The Ezeroc flowed out of the irises in their wake like water flowing out of pipes. They impacted each other, sometimes clawing over their comrades in the hunger that drove them mindless and mad. Where those claws hit, shells were cracked, limbs severed. Some of the aliens fell on their brethren, trying to get at the juicy interior. But far too many flowed on after Nate. He pointed his blaster, squeezing off shot after shot behind them, a steady salvo of bright light, plasma cracking with energy as it hit.

It'd be hard *not* to hit anything. There were *hundreds* of them.

They rounded a bend in the tunnel, and Nate saw lights ahead. Grace and Kohl, running back towards them. "Run!" said Nate.

"Already on it, Cap," said Kohl, his big power armor lumbering along with the enthusiasm of a tank. "You get on now."

Nate turned, dropped to one knee, and unloaded his blaster. He kept his finger on the trigger, the barrel glowing in the steady stream of plasma he was emptying down the tunnel. The weapon whined to silence, the spent battery falling from the bottom of the weapon.

"Stand back a second," said Kohl, and braced himself. His plasma cannon was pointed toward the horde of Ezeroc, and he pulled the trigger. The noise that erupted was staggering, the tunnel reflecting the bright flare of plasma. But Nate would take the noise and light any day over the alternative. Pieces of Ezeroc exploded in the tunnel, smoking, smoldering chitin thrown out and back like they'd been hit with … well, high yield plasma.

Nate slapped another battery in his gun, turning back the way Kohl had come. He realized he was still on one damn knee, figured it worked for the moment, and leaned around Kohl to fire down the tunnel. Bright flashes of plasma fire turned Ezeroc into floating ash.

He could hear Grace on the comm. "El! We need an evac. Get the ship warmed up."

"Situation?"

"Bugs."

"Get your own ride. Just kidding, on my way."

There was a brief lull in the firefight, and Nate rose to his feet,

Kohl chuckling beside him. He gave the big man a glance. "You okay?"

"I'm great, Cap. Just peachy. I figure, I don't know, we got to start keeping score. I want to make another visit to these assholes, make a short date of it." Kohl lifted his plasma cannon, ejecting the battery. It fell, contacts glowing white-hot, smoke trailing from it as it clattered against the tunnel floor. He slapped another battery in, the weapon ready lights blinking. "Most of my dates are short, you know? It's how I roll."

"That's not a good selling point," said Hope. She was ahead of them. "There may be a small problem."

Nate hurried after her, Grace ahead of him in the tunnel, Kohl behind. The big man was walking backward, the *whirr-clunk, whirr-clunk* of his power armor's steps somehow comforting. Human tech, under human control, in this alien death facility that had been constructed to trap them. Or someone like them, here, with the Ezeroc. And that human, using his human tech, was still going strong. Nate's good vibes didn't last long when he caught sight of Hope's face through her visor. Her expression was fearful. "What is it, Hope?"

"Well, it's a long way up," she said. "I figured, you know. We'd be able to winch Kohl out or something."

"You what?" said Kohl. "You'd best hurry, whatever you're planning. They're, I dunno, regrouping. They don't seem real smart, not like the regular ones."

"Hive mind," said Grace. "Queen's out. Until they elect a new one—"

"Elect?" said Nate.

"Elect," said Grace. "Until there's a new Queen, they're just animals. Hungry animals."

"How do they elect a Queen?" said Kohl.

"Usually it hatches right out of someone," said Grace.

"Get me the fuck out of this death hole," said Kohl. "I don't care if you need a winch or what, just get me out."

Nate looked at Kohl in his armor, and at the lip of the hole. They could boost out Hope, Grace could probably just fly out because she was like a gymnast, and Nate — with a bit of clawing and scrabbling — could get out if he stood on Kohl's shoulders. But that'd leave Kohl, with three hundred kilos of power armor, at the bottom of a pit of devils. That armor wasn't coming off either; it was his suit. It'd be a long run back though ice-cold poisonous air to the *Tyche*, and while Kohl was big, tough, and dumb, he wasn't indestructible. He just acted that way. "So," said Nate.

"So," agreed Kohl. "Why don't you get on?"

"Because," said Nate. "We don't leave people behind."

"What about if there's a bunch of space insects who will kill everyone if you don't?" said Kohl, glancing back at Nate.

"He makes a compelling argument," said Grace. But she was standing there, sword in hand, held low and ready. Her teeth were showing, not quite a grin, like she wanted to fight. Like she was ready for it.

Nate keyed the comm. "El?"

"I'm almost there. Hold on to your knitting."

"I need a winch or something," said Nate.

"What does the *Tyche* look like to you, Nate?" There was a pause. "Captain. Sir."

"A ship," said Nate.

"She look like a tractor to you, Cap?"

Nate sighed. He turned to Hope. "If we get you out of here, can you get a, I don't know, a rope or something?"

She blinked at him. "There's no rope on the *Tyche*, Cap. We don't keep rope on a starship. No rigging. Not the kind of boat that needs ropes."

Hell. "Okay, well. See what you can do."

"They're coming," said Kohl. He stood at the base of the sand pile, facing the tunnel's mouth. Feet braced against the tide that wanted to swallow them all. "Best get going."

"Sure," said Grace, not moving.

"Absolutely," said Nate, blaster in his hand. Somehow his sword had found its way to his other hand. It felt unfamiliar, wrong-handed, but comfortable with the touch of his fingers regardless. Like it wanted to be used. And it did. It was made for a better hand than his. It was made to kill the enemies of an Empire that fell long ago. Those enemies could be human or alien, didn't much matter to the sword. Kohl took point position, Grace and Nate flanking him.

The insects swarmed towards them, the tunnel clouding over with the sheer number of them. Kohl pulled the trigger of his plasma cannon, and Nate joined in, his smaller blaster firing down the hole. Then the insects were on them, too many Ezeroc, the sheer force of the crush pushing one or two out of the tunnel.

Grace moved like a liquid, like a dancer, beautiful like the dawn. Nate glimpsed her sword moving through the air, pieces of Ezeroc flying apart. He swung his own sword, the black blade biting into the side of an Ezeroc drone, the creature rearing back with those deadly claws to land on him. *Not today.* He raised his blaster and unloaded three rounds into the carapace, pieces flying away. A smaller bug made it past Nate, scuttling up and behind him. He turned to see it making straight for Hope. She was standing behind them, up the sand pile aways, her face a mask of concentration. The Ezeroc made it to her, claws outspread to drive them home. The arms of her rig snapped out, all four at once, laser light moving in a complex pattern. The Ezeroc separated into about fifty different smoking pieces.

Nate turned back to the melee, firing wild. He took out another two drones, catching another smaller one on a jump. His sword moved in an arc, like his body remembered how this dance was supposed to go, like it wanted to live. He didn't feel like it was going to get the chance.

Kohl's cannon ran dry, the weapon ejecting the battery in a spiral of smoke, the bright red points of the overheated contacts tracing lines through the gloom. The action paused — the Ezeroc noting that they weren't been mown down in great numbers, and the crew of the *Tyche* realizing that things were about to get worse. Kohl's hands let go of his cannon, and he seemed to sag a little as a sigh came over the comm. "Well," he said, "there's only one thing for it." The big man reached behind him, tugging at the clasps on his belt. The belt came free, a chain of grenades strung together. Black Ezeroc eyes followed the movement.

"Kohl," said Nate.

"It's okay, Cap. Ain't no way I'm going down as bug food," said Kohl, and tossed the belt into the tunnel. The big man turned, power armor *clanking* as he barged Grace to the ground. Nate took the hint, grabbing Hope — eliciting a yell over the comm — and tucking her under him. The blast, when it hit, took everything away.

CHAPTER ELEVEN

THERE WAS A HIGH-PITCHED NOISE, like a tiny angel screaming. It made Grace want to kill the angel, because whatever was mauling it wasn't working fast enough. There was a weight on her chest, a big weight that made it very hard to pull in air.

Something bad happened. You need to get up, Grace Gushiken.

Her eyes were heavy, though. That was a problem. And that noise went on forever. She tried to get an arm up to touch the side of her head. Clumsy fingers found the side of something hard, halting her touch. *Helmet. You're wearing a helmet. You're outside the ship. The* Tyche. *She's waiting for you.*

Another breath. She needed one little sip of O2, and she'd be good to go.

It felt like her father was standing above her. The weight of his regard, on her chest. His *presence*, pushing down like it always had. *You're weak. Half of what you need to be. You're no daughter of mine.*

But I am your little girl. She'd never said it, but she'd felt it a hundred times. Because fathers protected their daughters. Wasn't that the deal?

I don't have little girls. I have warriors. They stand tall and do what's needed. You ... you're a mongrel. Disfigured. She felt him turn away, like he had a hundred times before. *When you can stand tall, when you're not so weak that you stumble through the steps of kata that should be easy, come find me.*

Her fingers scrabbled on the ground, seeking something. Her sword. She had dropped it. Grace didn't know why she needed it. This new blade made it a better sword than it had ever been. The same familiar hilt enclosed future metal, forged in the heart of a Goddess. Made by a friend.

She needed air. Just a little bit of air.

Her eyes opened, like it was time for it to happen, like they'd been waiting for her all this time. Her vision went from blurry to clear. In front of her face were bright lines of a HUD, their usual cool amber marked in multiple bright spots of red. There was a paper doll — *I don't stand like that, I never stand like that, that figure does not dance* — of the suit, a point highlighted on her shoulder. A breach. All her precious air, going through the hole. The tiny angel was her suit alarm, warning her she had less than ten percent of her oxygen left.

Warriors fight whenever needed. You think air is an excuse? Her father snorted, arms crossed. *You should be able to fight blind. Without air. Without rest. Without friends, without love.*

I always fight without love, Father. Or she had, until ... now. Nathan Chevell. She loved that man. It was not a good time to realize it, lying here on the ground of an alien planet, a heavy weight on her, and running out of air. Nonetheless, she felt like it was the right thing to know, a truth that had been waiting for her to discover it. And if she died, she would die knowing love, a gentle hand, someone who had her back. Together.

Focus. She looked beyond her visor, to the weight lying across her. It was October Kohl. Her father would have called him *stupid* or perhaps *foolish*. Grace wanted to call him *brave*. And, if the stars aligned right, perhaps a friend. His helmet had collided with her chest as he'd knocked her over, the bulk of his armor taking the shrapnel from the explosion. She couldn't see around the helmet to the back of the armor, but she could tell he was dead weight. Not moving, three hundred kilos of armor and a hundred kilos of man lying on her. It'd be easier to do a push up under 3Gs of thrust than to get him off. But she needed to get him off, or she would die here. She'd die knowing love, but she'd still be dead.

Not a good deal is it, mongrel? Her father seemed to frown, Grace's eyes going out of focus. She didn't know why he called her mongrel. He had always done it, like she was diseased, like she wasn't his child. Like he was angry at her but angry at himself, too. It didn't matter now. *Of course it matters. To get off this rock, you need to fight without air. Without rest.* He seemed to shrug. *Or you will die. It doesn't matter to me. If you weren't such a failure ...* He left that trailing thought between them.

Failure? Father, I have defeated aliens. They wanted to break our world!

That was then. This is now. There is no success but what is in this moment. Anything else is history.

Grace gritted her teeth, pushing her hand against Kohl's bulk. His frame rocked a little, easing her breathing a whisker. A slight amount, only an extra thimbleful of air. But a thimble was more than she had a moment ago. She panted, then pushed again. The sand under them shifted, and Kohl's body slid away from her towards the bottom of the slope. She watched him go, the lights from his armor facing the ground, hidden from view. It was like watching a light fall into a pit. But as his bulk left her, her own suit's lights flickered, coming on. Showing her the chamber they were in. She killed the alarm in her suit — *thank God* — and took a look around.

Kohl: at the bottom of the slope, his frame being buried by sand.

Nate: off to one side, his body on top of Hope's. Neither of them moving. No lights. No sound on the comm.

She didn't want to look at the tunnel mouth. But she knew what her father would say, so she looked anyway. Where there had been a smooth, round opening leading into a den of horror, there was now crumbled stone. Big rocks, blocking the way. No more Ezeroc coming to kill them. Not until they cleared the stone, or found another way out. She didn't know if there was another way out. It didn't matter at the moment. Grace needed to get out of this pit. She needed to get out, with her friends. Her eyes moved to Kohl. *Even if they're dead.*

The suit's lights glinted against something in the gloom. Her sword. It was stuck into the wall of the chamber above where she'd been lying. She reached up, giving it a tug. The metal — a true edge, a gift from the gods — pulled free without resistance. Sword from stone, like it was made for her hand — which it had been. She clutched her free hand over the breach in her suit, air whistling past her fingers, and looked up the walls of the chamber. Grace might have monkeyed up there with a boost, but there was no one left down here to boost her up. She hefted the sword, looking at the wall again, then stabbed the blade into the rock at her shoulder height, the flat of the blade horizontal with the ground. It slid in like the stone was a fabrication of the mind, a mosaic over butter. *Thank you, Hope.* She tested the blade with a hand. Would it hold her weight? Hope had said it was strong, but what did that even mean?

Time to find out.

Grace released the breach on her suit. She put a hand on the hilt of the sword, resting weight there, then skipped her feet up the wall. Her weight transferred from her legs to her hand as her body went horizontal. Her knees bunched closer to her chest, the blade flexing under her, threatening to spill her off.

No child of mine would fall from such an easy perch.

"Fuck you, Dad," hissed Grace, holding herself in place — one hand on the sword, flexing under her, feet against the wall. The sword didn't break. Grace reached out her other hand to the wall, got her feet underneath her, and then rose — *nice and easy, nice and easy* — to look up over the edge of the pit.

Nothing there. Just the entrance room, the vaulted roof of the pyramid above her. She put hands on the edge and hauled herself out. She felt a pang — her sword was down there, and here she was on an alien world without even a blaster. Not that she was any good with a sidearm — even if she'd had a blaster it wouldn't have changed that displaced feeling. She needed her sword, but she couldn't have it until she got her friends out.

My friends. I have, for the first time, actual friends. One of them laid his life down for me.

The feeling coursed through her, a sense of belonging she had never known she needed. Even mongrels could find a pack. She keyed her comm. "El." Her voice cracked, and she tried again. "*Tyche*. This is Grace."

"I hear you, Assessor," said El. "I'm almost there. What's up? You're all very quiet." Grace left her fingers over her comm controls, not sure what to say, or even where to start. "Grace?"

"I'm here. I'm … the only one still up." She coughed, some stray external atmosphere in her suit through the breach. No time to worry about that now. "They're … stuck. We need a winch, or something to get them out. I … my suit's holed."

There was a rumble through the floor, in the air around her, and the sandstorm outside the pyramid was disturbed by the bright landing lights of the *Tyche*. Grace could see El in the flight deck, saw her wave. "I see you, Grace. Look, we don't have a winch. Like I told the Cap, this is a starship, not a tractor." There was a pause while the *Tyche* hovered on its Endless negative space field. "Idle Q though. If we had a hypothetic winch, what would you want it for?"

Grace pointed to the pit behind her. "They're down there. I guess about four meters. There's no ladder."

"How'd you figure on getting out in the first place?"

"Boost," said Grace, her fingers finding the breach in her suit, trying to keep a little more air inside. "Everyone was … awake then."

"Huh," said El. "Well, that's an easy problem to solve."

"It's … what?"

"Easy problem," said El. "The hard bit will be getting the *Tyche* in there. Tight fit, near as I can tell. Look, can you go find cover? I'm going to open the door up some."

"You're what?"

El's voice softened over the comm, and Grace could see the Helm hunching forward. "The door here. It's not big enough to get the ship inside. I figure I can fit in there if I hug the dirt, but I need to, I don't know, sort of remove this wall."

"The wall?"

"That's right."

"Won't the roof fall in?" said Grace.

"It might," agreed El. She shrugged up there in the flight deck. "But it's the solution I've got on hand."

"Do it," said Grace. She looked around for a place to hide, but there wasn't one. *Back down in the hole.* She'd been so pleased about getting out, but she didn't want to be flensed by flying debris. Keeping a hand on the breach in her suit, she moved to the edge of the pit, jumping in. "Good to go."

"Copy that. This will get a little loud."

A little loud was an understatement. Grace had heard — and felt — the *Tyche's* fury once before, when they'd been on the crust of Absalom Delta. There had been Ezeroc closing in all around, and the ship had come in, PDCs hot. A hundred rounds a second from each cannon had turned the Ezeroc into little more than airborne chum. Those same PDCs opened up now. Grace hunched down, the sound almost a physical presence, the hammering like a second heart. She felt a rumble as pieces of the pyramid broke away to fall on the ground above her. *Chunk, chunk, chunk.* Then, silence. "You done?"

"I'm done," said El. "Wait one, I need to get inside. Hell, I hate reversing."

Reversing? Grace was tired, and she was no doubt suffering from a concussion, but no one reversed a starship. She put her hand on the sword again, boosting herself up and over the edge of the pit. She saw the *Tyche* turn in space, presenting the twin fusion drives to her. The apertures were glowing with remembered heat, their fires were banked for the moment, the ship running on the Endless field alone. The ship came close to the deck, then moved backward. *Holy shit.*

She is reversing a starship into a cavern. A cavern that is so small any sane pilot would just laugh and fly away. The belly of the *Tyche* scraped a fallen rock or two, the grinding of metal loud, but nothing broke off. The ship continued to back until it hovered above the pit. Grace could see the stylized, winking face above her. That wink said *I've got you, Gushiken. I'll always come for you.* Grace wanted to laugh.

"Okay," said El. "This is where shit gets real. I've got a negative space field going above the ship so I'm floating, you with me?"

"Yeah," said Grace.

"I'll generate another one under the ship. I need to amp up the one above me so I don't get sucked onto the surface by it. Anyway. Doesn't matter. But that should lift everyone in the pit out. What I'll need you to do is kind of knock 'em so they float sideways."

"Sideways."

"Sure," said El. "Because then when I turn off the Endless field, they won't fall back into the pit. We'll do it a bit at a time. I figure enough joules through the field will lift the cap and Hope. I'll need a few more to get Kohl out, because he's a monster. Also, that armor's got to weigh some."

"It does," agreed Grace. "So should I...?"

"Y'all get in the pit, and I'll suck you out too. Then you can knock them aside, and I'll drop you back in. You with me?"

"This is crazy."

"I can leave again if you like. I mean, if you want to try hauling 'em out yourself."

"I said it was crazy, not that I didn't like it." Grace hopped into the pit, then moved to stand near Nate and Hope. "Go."

The feeling as the Endless field came on above her was like having two *downs*. The down *above* her wanted to make her fall ... *up*. But the planet below her didn't want to let go. The Endless field's strength increased until Grace floated. She giggled as her feet came off the ground. Sand particles in the pit had already swirled up past her to hug the belly of the *Tyche*. Nate and Hope's bodies drifted up, which stopped Grace's giggle dead in her throat. Kohl's form remained at the bottom, a free arm being tugged upward but that's all; there wasn't enough force to lift his heavy armor.

Grace and the other two cleared the edge of the pit. Grace put a foot against each of them and *pushed*. They floated away, just like zero G, as she went in the opposite direction. "Okay El, they're clear."

"Cool as ice," agreed the Helm. "I'll let you down nice and easy and we'll do the same thing with the bison."

El reversed the effect, Grace returning to the ground. She hopped back in the pit, then snared her sword from the wall, sliding it home into its sheath. It was a good sword, and she wouldn't surrender it to the grip of this world. She grabbed Kohl's armor, wincing as she saw the blood seeping from the back of it where chunks of shrapnel had impacted him. "We're good."

The pull of the field was stronger this time, hoisting her up. She held onto Kohl, then realized that trying to hold him was like trying to hold 300 kilos of weight under her. She scrambled around his form, gasping for breath, the Endless field holding them close. Her visor pressed against his. His eyes were closed. She couldn't tell if he was alive or dead. Either way, she wasn't leaving him here. Grace was sure that Nate wouldn't either. *Together*. They wouldn't leave anyone behind. Not today.

As they cleared the lip of the pit, Grace felt herself starting to breath heavy. The sensation was like having Kohl on top of her again, his weight pressing against her. Down was up, all over again. "I'm having trouble," she admitted over the comm.

"You should try flying a starship inside a pyramid while manipulating Endless fields," said El. "We can swap if you like."

Grace wanted to laugh, but it would have been too much effort. Instead she said, "No, I'm good. Boosting off." She bunched her feet under Kohl and kicked off. The big man drifted to the other side of the pit. Her, not so much — as she came out from underneath, she felt like she was a cork freed from a bottle. She popped out sideways, pinwheeling through the air and up towards the underside of the *Tyche*. She impacted with a painful outrush of breath.

"You good?" said El. "That last one didn't sound great."

"Fine," said Grace. "We're out."

"Dropping the field. Lights are green on the board. Let's get those layabouts onboard, hey?"

Grace was lowered to the ground, her feet touching the rock. The cargo bay door of the *Tyche* opened like a welcome into heaven. She stared at it for a while, then said, "I think I'm just going to sit down for a bit."

"Grace? You can sit when you're on the ship."

Grace looked at her O2 levels. Zero percent. That'd be why.

You don't need air to fight.

Shut up, Father.

"Grace?" El's voice seemed to be coming from a long way away. So near, in the warmth and light of the ship. So far, because she was out here on the surface of a dead world. And she was out of air.

CHAPTER TWELVE

SOMETHING PUSHED NATE AROUND. Zero G. A foot in his belly. It didn't feel great, but hitting the ground — which wasn't part of the deal with zero G — felt worse. He lay there for a while, listening to chatter on the comm. Something about Kohl. Something about Endless fields.

Then something about Grace. His eyes snapped open and he hauled himself to a sitting position. He took in the scene: the *Tyche* above him. *What the fuck?* Inside the pyramid. The pit to one side. Hope over there aways. Kohl's armored form slumped to the ground, face-first in the dirt. And Grace, beautiful, elegant Grace, sliding sideways to hit the ground like a dropped sack. Nate was on his feet before he'd thought much about it. He ran to her side, checking her over. Her suit holed. He clicked through the diagnostics with his suit, taking in the damage. O2 spent. She was out. She'd be dead soon.

"El?"

"Cap," said the Helm. "What's going on?"

"Need a little help," he said. "Everyone's down."

"I feel like I've just had this conversation—"

"Now!" barked Nate. "Grace is out of air. Get down here and

help me." He popped the repair pocket of his suit open, pulling out a tube of sealant. He sprayed it over the hole in her shoulder, watching it as it set. Then he pushed her over, exposing the air cycler on her back. He popped it free — not even a wisp of air coming from the ports — and tossed it aside. Then he reached behind him and yanked his own suit's cycler. He slotted it into place on her suit, then rolled her back over. Diagnostics from his own suit showed green from Grace's systems, air filling her suit.

Which left just one problem: the total lack of air in his own suit.

He stood up, jogging back to the *Tyche*, trying for a little mental math on the way. Air in his suit, enough for a couple of breaths, no problem. The real thing that would kill him wasn't so much the lack of oxygen — although that was a factor — but rather getting CO_2 poisoning and dropping like a cold beer on a hot day. Breathing was an illusion, trapped in the shell of his suit. *So, don't breathe, Chevell. You don't need to breathe, do you? You need to make it to the* Tyche, *grab some emergency air, and you'll be fine.*

Emergency air: hand-held canisters with a mouthpiece, attached to the wall inside the cargo bay's airlock.

Cargo bay: on the ship.

The ship: no more than fifteen meters away.

Easy job.

He reached up to his helmet's seal as he ran, working the ring around, feeling it pop. The biting cold of the planet's air rushed inside, and he resisted the urge to take a huff. Sure, it felt like cold air, but it was full of poison, and it'd kill him faster than almost anything. On his way to the bright lights of the *Tyche*, he caught movement against movement: the sandstorm raging outside, a shadow highlighted against it for a moment.

The fucking Ezeroc. And here he was, with a flimsy blaster, his entire crew out, except for El, and he needed El to fly the ship. He also needed El to help him get his crew on the very same ship.

Time for that later. He made the cargo bay airlock, grabbing an emergency air canister from the wall. Nate set the breather against his face and sucked in clean, pure air. He secured the band in place behind his head. His face was hurting like he was in the seventh circle of hell, because *man this planet was cold*, but he figured it was better to be cold than dead. He dropped back out of the airlock, blaster clearing its holster, and pointed it at the exit to the pyramid.

Quick check: that opening was a lot larger than it used to be. It *had* been a door of sorts, a nice defendable aperture he could have held with a blaster for a while at least. Now it was an opening the entire pyramid wide. He figured that was on account of needing to get the *Tyche* in here. He didn't know why the *Tyche* needed to be here, then he remembered the conversation with Hope (no rope) and falling through the air (Endless field). It was good thinking, officer material from whoever came up with it, and he'd be sure to have a congratulatory word if he made it out of this alive.

Something reared its head up and he let off a blast of plasma, hitting nothing but air and sand. Those fuckers were quick, that was for sure.

Get the crew inside. Get the hell out of here. Good thinking, Chevell.

He jogged over to Grace, grabbing the front of her ship suit, never taking his eyes off the pyramid's open wall. He held on to her with one hand, the other with the blaster pointed at where the danger was. It was difficult getting her back to the ship, because the floor was littered with pieces of pyramid. He made it, her feet scribing two lines through the sand drifts. The lock opened in front of him, revealing El in her suit. Nate dropped Grace on the sill of the lock, then went to get Hope. She was lying, her visor pointed up, the mechanical limbs of the suit splayed around her fallen form like the bones of wings. He jogged towards her, sucking hard on the air canister. There was movement again from the pyramid's opening, and he let off another shot. He hit nothing — again — but he swore that a couple of shadows had made it inside. That made at least two Ezeroc in here with him and his crew.

You fuckers will not get me and mine today.

Hand on Hope's rig, he dragged her back towards the ship. The lock opened again, and he dropped Hope off into El's care. *One left, Chevell. Just one more, and you can go.* He moved towards Kohl, then stopped as he saw an Ezeroc rearing above the big man's unconscious form. Nate's blaster bucked as he fired, plasma scorching against the Ezeroc, and it tumbled away in a smoking pile. Nate ran to Kohl, kneeling down. *Armor. That armor is too heavy. You'll never drag him with two hands, let alone one.* Nate felt around the controls of the armor, finding the emergency controls. He keyed in the passcode — Kohl's was always 1234 — and stepped back as the armor fired the release bolts. Pieces of armor flew, smoking trails gobbled up by the wind.

Nate crouched down again, took two lungfuls of air, then pressed the air canister against Kohl's face. Not enough arms, too many things to do. Nate hesitated for just a moment, then holstered his blaster. He hefted the big man up — *you're going on half rations after this is over, that's for sure* — hooked his metal arm under Kohl, and dragged him back toward the ship, making sure the emergency air mask was against Kohl's face. Kohl might have been dead, Kohl might have been alive, but he'd be one hundred percent dead for sure if he sucked poison air.

Speaking of air ... dragging a hundred-kilo man through rocky rubble wasn't easy. Nate wanted to breathe. He did. Nate wanted to open his mouth and suck in a lungful. He knew it was crazy, it'd be like an old-time mariner drinking salt water to slake a thirst. Fast road to a horrible death. But there was all this beautiful cold air pressing against his face.

The back of his boot hit the ramp of the *Tyche* and he almost cried with joy. Almost, because if he had, that was air he didn't have to spare. He dropped Kohl, then turned around. Right in time to see an Ezeroc rearing above him. He pulled his blaster in one clean motion and fired, the plasma tearing off a limb. The Ezeroc lunged forward, slamming Nate back. He tumbled back into the airlock door of the *Tyche*, and all the breath left his lungs.

And then he gasped in a lungful of poison.

His chest spasmed. It felt like he was trying to breathe floor cleaner. He coughed, sucked in another lungful on autopilot, and then doubled over. The Ezeroc reared above him, ready.

Then the front of it disintegrated into fragments of chitin and gore. Nate looked up through streaming eyes at Elspeth Roussel, Helm of the *Tyche*, her sidearm in one hand. She handed him an air canister without comment, then opened the breach of her gun, the cartridge spinning away. Nate pried himself up, the dragged Kohl over the lip of the airlock. He reached out a hand, slamming it on the airlock's CLOSE controls. The door slid shut, sealing out the poison and cold and nightmare that was the surface of this barren world.

Clean, sweet air cycled into the airlock. Nate coughed, then he laughed. He took in the expression on El's face — a cross between terror and confusion — and it made him laugh harder. He waved a hand at her. "Go on. Get us out of here."

"You sure? You not been hit too hard on the head?" Her voice was shaking, false bravado pushing the words out.

"I been hit hard enough," said Nate, "but I figure on us getting off this fucking rock."

"Copy that," she said, walking away through the hold. Nate got up, moving into the *Tyche*, sealing the inner door of the lock behind him. He leaned forward, a hand against the wall, breathing hard. Breathing clean. He felt terrible. He felt alive.

"Helm to *Tyche*," said El over the comm. "Thrust in five. Four. Three. Two. One. Mark."

The fusion drives grumbled, the grumble turning into a roar. Thrust pressed against Nate, his crew sliding a little on the metal floor of the hold. Not too hard, not too much: just enough for nuclear fire to scour away the Ezeroc from outside, and leave a memory on the face of this world. *We came, and we did not die in your trap. We brought a Goddess of Luck with us; next time pray we don't bring the God of War.*

NATE SAGGED into the acceleration couch next to El. "Well, that was a shit sandwich."

"Yeah," she said, meaning, *is he going to be okay*.

"He'll be fine," said Nate. "Kohl's big and dumb but he's made of rock. I mean, he'll need work, but ... eventually."

"Shit," she said.

"Still. We're off the rock, and no one's dead." They were looking out at the stars, the planet rotating underneath them, the muddy browns and grays a reminder of the poison they'd left behind. "Those assholes, though."

"The snails?" El had watched the recordings from their suits while Nate had plugged Kohl into the ship's medbay machine. He'd left Hope to sleep it off — *really* sleep, this time. For a long time. Grace was resting in their cabin — which made him smile, thinking of it as theirs. The smile left his face as he remembered her look, the sad and tired face of someone who'd almost died. On his watch. Again.

"Yeah, the snails," said Nate. "Fucking roaches. Fucking snails. Why can't we have aliens that look like nice, normal mammals?"

"Universe loves wondrous variation," said El. "Maybe they think we look ugly with all that creepy fur." She ran a hand through her hair.

"I don't think anything was left down there to think anything," said Nate. "Just an ancient recording from a long-gone bunch of people."

"You figure it was a trap? Or experiments?"

"I figure it was both," said Nate. "I've taken down an IOU. They're on the list. After we deal with the Ezeroc."

"What I figure is that you'll be late to that party," she said. "I think the Ezeroc already solved that problem for you."

"I thought the same thing," said Nate. "But you know? I like to plan for the worst, but keep hoping for the best."

"You're hoping we'll run into another group of alien sociopaths?"

"It doesn't sound quite right when you say it like that," offered Nate, after a moment's pause.

There was a ripple in space, and a massive ship jumped in. Nate sat up on his acceleration couch, the *Tyche* already handshaking. Data sped over the holo stage, then the ship was marked: the *Torrington*. He breathed a sigh of relief, then clicked on the comm. "*Torrington*, this is *Tyche* actual. We see you."

"*Tyche*, this is *Torrington* actual. We see you too. That planet looks like a spinning asshole, doesn't it?" Karkoski's voice was harsher than usual, more tired, and Nate guessed he could get behind that. It'd been a rough time of late, and she had to be feeling the punches back in human space.

"There's a mental image," he said. "What can I do you for? We weren't expecting to see you out here."

"We weren't expecting to be out here," she said. The holo stage flickered and then her projection appeared there. Still in uniform, shoulders back. Used to command in a way that Nate never had been. "We've got a message for you. Much as it pains me to be your errand girl, this one struck me as important enough to take a break from my usual job of trying to hold the Republic together to relay it to you."

"Huh," said Nate, a sinking feeling arriving in his gut.

"Before that, let's talk about this wonderful cat's toilet you've discovered," she said. "We've never been out here. It's not on the charts."

"A hundred light years straight out from Absalom," agreed Nate. "I'm pretty sure it's uncharted waters. I'll send a data package to you with what we found."

"Much obliged," she said.

"Just a word of caution," said Nate. "If you go down to the ... trap ... we found, be careful. We left the back door open. There's a main pyramid entrance—"

"A pyramid?"

"We knocked a wall down but you can't miss it," said Nate. "Anyway, the structure has another location with an opening to the sky. A radio transmitter. Powered down now, not a lot of juice left in it. I figure we'd be well cooked if that weren't the case, but there you have it. Anyhow. The roof's open, and the bugs got out."

"The Ezeroc?"

"Yeah."

"There's Ezeroc here?"

"Yeah."

"And they built the pyramid?"

"That was the snails."

Nate watched her rub a hand over her face. "Perhaps you should just send over the data packet, Captain."

"Will do," he said, working the console in front of him. "There you go. Now, what's this message?"

"Transmitting," she said, and the holo stage cleared. Her figure was replaced by Harlow, his face drawn.

"Nate, they've got us," said the recording of Harlow. "You know who I mean by *they* and you know who I mean by *us*. But in case you're dumber than usual, I mean me and Amedea have been locked up. And we've been locked up by, well, a coalition of the Ezeroc and the Republic. It's grim. They wanted me to send this to you. They wanted you to know they'll peel apart our minds to find out what's going on with the Resistance. They say you need to come, and they'll trade us, no questions asked, for Grace. I told 'em you wouldn't come, and they said to send this anyway. So, don't be a dick. Stay the hell away."

The recording clicked off to be replaced by Karkoski again. "You can see why we came."

Nate realized he was leaning forward, then leaned back into his chair. *Relaxed* wasn't the right word: he slumped. "I can see. Is this authentic?"

"Near as we can tell. They left a trash fire on Enia Alpha. Scooped up a couple of the Resistance. Not all. Not even most of 'em. Your deckhand's recruiting helped some."

"Where are they?" said Grace, startling Nate and El both. Nate turned to look at her. She'd slipped up on them on whisper-quiet feet.

"I thought you were resting." He reached a hand for her.

She took it in her own. "Hard to rest when all you can hear from the flight deck is emotional screaming in your mind."

"Sorry," he said.

"It's okay," she said.

"Grace Gushiken," said Karkoski. "A pleasure."

"Likewise," said Grace. She leaned forward. "Tell us where they are."

"Okay," said Karkoski. "You're not going to like it though."

CHAPTER THIRTEEN

THE JUMPS WERE WEARING THIN. Grace knew why they had to do it. You couldn't just tell the *Tyche* you wanted to go 'over there' and hope for the best. Long experience of humans charting the stars meant they knew the basic steps: jump to a location. Sit in space for a while, looking at the stars. Their light would be years, decades, even millennia old, but they would give you a *better* idea of the state of things where you were headed. Use what you could see to build a more up to date map of where you were going. And then jump again. Repeat.

It was risky. It's why the Guild made so much damn coin. They charged for use of their Bridges. Safe. Reliable. The Guild sent drones to construct Bridges, and then ships could step through those Bridges just like walking through a door. A wormhole was far safer; the only real problem with those was if one endpoint failed while you were half-way. That rarely happened.

Rarely.

It made the wild rodeo of Endless travel seem insane. Grace knew better, though: space was big. It was *huge*. The odds of jumping to a location and finding yourself inside a star or planet were low.

And they were made lower by doing the work — traveling to a place, looking for the next stop, charting the course, and away you went. Like the mariners of old, the *Tyche* used the light of the stars to guide her way.

It still sucked though. While the sheer rush of the jump was exhilarating, it took longer than traversing a Bridge. Sure, you didn't need an endpoint, which in this particular instance was necessary, but it wasn't instant. The tech made it possible for it to be instant, but humans lost their minds if they pushed the buffer limits too much. The crew of the *Ravana* had discovered that the hard way. Linear time was too much a part of human existence to be defied like the mere laws of physics.

"I live for this," said Nate. "The open stars, the unknown. Going where nobody's gone before."

Grace snorted. "I was thinking the exact opposite. Not just a little different, but the *exact* opposite."

Nate reached for her under the sheets, the crinkle of the synth weave like the sound of unwrapping a present. Grace felt his hand on her belly — a nice, warm, *Nathan* touch. He'd survived the death planet. They both had. And they'd wasted no time celebrating. El was piloting the ship. Hope was in Engineering, making sure that the 'ship doesn't explode.' What was left of Kohl was connected to the machine in the sickbay, keeping him alive. There'd been no question of handing him off to the *Torrington*; Kohl wouldn't appreciate it when he woke up. For one thing, there wouldn't be enough liquor on the destroyer to keep him drunk enough to put up with all those Marines.

Which left Nate and Grace with a little time. She moved closer to him, turning so their noses were almost touching. She felt his hand working its way up her side, stroking her back. It was warm. It was perfect. "Mind you," she said, "*this* part isn't all bad."

"No," said Nate. "It's not all bad." He kissed her neck, and she shivered, reaching for him, feeling the muscles in his back. She pulled him close, skin to skin.

The comm in the cabin chirped. "Helm to the Captain."

Nate made an exasperated noise. "Sweet Christ," he said. "Like five more minutes."

"It'd be more than five," said Grace, not letting go. "What's the worst that could happen if you didn't answer?"

"We could all die," said Nate. He reached a hand up and clicked the comm. "El, this is Nate. What's up?"

"Destination in one jump, Cap," she said. "I figured we could hold out here. Before. You know. The jump. To make sure the stars are okay."

"Right," said Nate. "How are those stars looking?"

"Bright and shiny," she said. "We could hold off jumping for a little bit longer though. Just to be sure."

"Copy that," said Nate, clicking the comm off. "Where were we?"

Grace gave an appreciative look at him. Nate was lean, not a lot of wasted mass on his frame. She reached a hand over, tracing her fingers down his chest, across his stomach. She leaned in for a deep kiss, then hoisted herself on top of him. "About to get here," she said. She rocked her hips against him.

"About here," he agreed, voice husky. He touched one of her breasts, and she couldn't suppress the shiver that ran through her. They'd need a few more minutes. Just to make sure the stars were okay.

SHE'D GRABBED HERSELF A SHOWER, kissing Nate as she left his cabin. He was off to do very important captain things, and she was off to do very important Assessor things. Those Assessor things weren't the usual things someone holding that position on a starship would do. Assessors spent their time looking at things that free traders found and determining their worth, where they might be sold, and where — when *free trading* turned closer to *privateering* and flirted with *piracy* — items of value and questionable providence might be sold. Grace could do all those things, no problem: she'd spent a lot of time running and hiding and assessing the value of *people*. It made working out who wanted to buy a mystery trinket from an edge system a matter of joining the dots.

Since she'd conned her way on to the *Tyche*, she hadn't done any Assessing at all. The manifest still noted that as her formal position, despite her history of lying to the crew and pulling the might of an alien empire down on them all. She'd done more work with her sword than ever before, and that was okay. Grace was comfortable with a blade in her hand; what she'd learned was that she was more comfortable with a blade in her hand and a friend at her back. She'd never had that before.

Speaking of friends ... She had reached her destination. Engineering's airlock was sealed during the natural running of the *Tyche* in case of a breach from one of the volatile systems in there, but it wasn't locked. Hope never locked the door, because she didn't seem to believe in locks. Mind you, locks weren't very effective against her. Grace keyed the controls, the big vaulted door hissing open in front of her. Engineering was well-lit, the new reactor humming in the center, the readouts on the fusion drives a comforting green. Hope was in her acceleration couch, a set of documents up on the holo. Grace had glimpsed a picture, swapped away from view as the door opened. A picture of Reiko, which was why Grace had come here.

"Hey, Hope."

Hope's face crinkled into a smile. "Hey yourself." That smile, though: tired, strained, like a mask. Underneath it was *exhaustion/fear/pain/sadness*. That smile had about two percent genuine Hope in it, and ninety-eight percent manufactured what-Hope-thought-other-people-wanted-to-see in it. Hope was an Engineer, and unlike Grace, she sucked at understanding people.

Grace knew all about masks. She'd worn them in one shape or another for as long as she could remember. First, in front of her father: the strong mask. Or for her mother: the forgiving mask. On the streets of life, her masks took all kinds of shapes and sizes. The vulnerable mask for a particular mark. The fearless mask for another. Sometimes she wore a mask with no expression, because people would read what they wanted in that; it was a useful tactic. She'd come on board the *Tyche* with a mask made of half-lies, half-truths, the Republic on her heels howling for blood. It'd been the right mask at the time, but she hadn't been able to hold it on her face at the end. She hadn't *needed* to, because the crew of the *Tyche* was special. They weren't interested in selling Grace out for a percentage. They knew the boot of the Republic on their necks.

"How you doing, Hope?" said Grace.

"Good," said Hope. "Great." *Lie/uncertain/avoidance.* "Why do you ask?"

"No reason," said Grace, walking around the inside of Engineering. She bent to look at the reactor. Good Republic technology. Manufactured somewhere in Sol space, maybe the core yards near Titan. It'd been fitted to the *Tyche* in the ship bay of the *Torrington*. It seemed to work well, more power than they needed, and without the angry memories that came with carrying the *Ravana's* heart with them. "It's just, you know. You know I can read minds."

Hope's smile stayed on her face, but looked more like a fixture, a piece of metal bolted on to hold good atmosphere inside the hull. "Just emotions," said Hope. "Feelings. Only that."

"Yes," said Grace, turning to face Hope. "Only that."

"That's a relief," said Hope. *Relief/relief.* "I mean, I was worried for a second."

"You were worried I might look inside your mind," said Grace. "That I might see your pain, and your loss, and the fear of living. That I'd see you wanted to die, but you weren't brave enough to kill yourself." She walked towards Hope. "You were worried we wouldn't understand what you were going through. You felt sick sometimes because you loved Reiko, but we told you she'd betrayed you, and you couldn't make sense of that inside. You're worried someone might see how tangled up inside you've become, because you feel you should be dead, and she should be alive, and you'd do anything to trade places with her."

"You said," said Hope, her voice cracking for a second, "that it was only feelings."

"Yes," said Grace. "Only that."

"How ... did you know all that, then?" Hope's eyes flicked around Engineering, an animal looking for an escape. "How?"

Grace crouched down by Hope's acceleration couch. "I had a hunch," she said.

"I don't know how to stop it," blurted Hope. "I *know* it doesn't make sense. But all these things keep going around, and around, and around inside my head."

Grace nodded, not getting up. Keeping herself lower than Hope's eye line, unthreatening. Relaxed. She was being buffeted by Hope's *anger/confusion/loss/pain*. Grace wanted to close her eyes and make her mind small, to not take it in, but it wasn't the time and place for that. "You want a solution."

"Yes," said Hope. "There's got to be one."

"Well," said Grace. "I might be able to help with that."

"How?"

"Sleep," said Grace. "People will tell you all kinds of shit about pain. They'll tell you time makes it all okay. That's a lie. It doesn't ever go away, but you get better at dealing with it. Ignoring it. Making it smaller. Until one day you can, just sometimes, wake up without it being the first thing you think about."

"I can't sleep," said Hope, like Grace had said nothing at all. "I've tried."

"You've tried," said Grace, her eyes going to the pile of empty stims scattered on Hope's console, "real hard."

Hope followed her glance. "Oh. Those. If I try and sleep, my brain just works harder. It's ... easier if I don't try. So, I take the stims. At least I can do my job, until I work it out."

"What if I could help you sleep?" said Grace.

"I've tried drugs," said Hope. "I took some from Kohl. They make me pass out, right? But I have bad nightmares. And I can't wake up."

"I said sleep. Not a coma."

Hope cocked her head sideways. "How?"

"I've been learning a few new tricks," said Grace. "I ... don't know if it will work."

"You'll go into my mind," said Hope. Not a question. A statement accompanied by *fear/curiosity/fear/fear*.

"Eh," said Grace, standing up and turning away from Hope. She walked back towards the reactor — *give her space now. She needs to be free.* "It doesn't work that way. I don't even know ... I don't know if I can do it." She shrugged, not turning around. "But I won't try. Not if you don't want me to."

"Why do you care?" said Hope. Grace said nothing, just kept looking at the reactor. Not like the reactor had changed, the lights still the comforting green of *you're not going to die*, but Grace needed somewhere to look that wasn't at Hope, and Engineering wasn't that large. "Would it hurt?" said Hope, at last.

"No," said Grace. *Not you, anyway.* "But you need to tell me it's okay. People's minds are their own. That's what the Intelligencers never understood. What my father never ... it doesn't matter. You tell me it's okay, and we'll try."

"Okay," said Hope. "After we get to the station."

"I might be dead after the station," said Grace. "How about now?"

"I need to make sure the ship doesn't explode," said Hope.

"No, you don't," said Grace. "The ship's fine."

"Okay then," said Hope.

HOPE'S CABIN was just like it had been last time Grace had been here. Empty, because Hope's real cabin was Engineering. Hope sat on the edge of her bunk. "What now?"

"Lie back," said Grace.

"Like … lie down?" said Hope, her voice nervous.

"Like," agreed Grace. "It won't hurt, Hope. It will be the … absence of hurting."

"I don't think I remember what that's like," said Hope, but she lay down, pink hair splaying out on her pillow. Grace sat on the edge of the bunk, staring at the wall. "Do I have to clear my mind?"

"Why?" said Grace.

"I dunno. It's what they seem to say on the meditation holos."

"If it makes you feel better. It won't make a difference." Grace closed her eyes, reaching out with her mind. At the cloud — the *storm* — of emotions coming off Hope. She felt the mind underneath it all, that beautiful, bright, brilliant consciousness she could barely understand. The Intelligencers could peek inside that, but Grace felt the emotions that came off the sides. Chad had said to her it *might all be the same thing* and she hadn't understood. But he'd also said *you can transmit and receive, Grace — it goes both ways*. And *that* she'd understood just fine.

First: acceptance. She felt the *fear/pain/loss/pain* coming from Hope. Grace figured at the moment Hope was trying to clear her mind but all she was getting back from her tired, taxed mind was just more Reiko. Probably things like *Reiko at the beach* or *Reiko in a bathrobe making breakfast* or *Reiko's lips*, or Grace's hot pick, *Reiko dying as the Republic gunned her down*. All of those things would be mangled together, confusion and loss threading though love and happiness.

Second: absolution. Loss and pain were normal. Regular. Just like happiness or the feeling of warmth when the sun touched your face. Grace made herself a well of calm, a spring from which she let *calm/soothe/calm/relax* come out of her. She felt the buffeting of the tall, monstrous waves of Hope's pain, but that was okay. She'd already accepted Hope's pain. Now she was telling Hope — in a way that no one else who had ever lived could do — that it was okay. *Calm. Soothe. Calm. Relax.*

Finally: sleep. The end of the process. Grace pushed the fingers of her mind against Hope's, tangling them through the fear and the pain. Grace pulled those pieces away, feeling sick and unsteady as she accepted them into her. She would keep them for now, until someone else needed them. She replaced them with *calm*. With *soothe*. And with *Relax*. Grace's head bent over with the strain of it, because the pain of losing someone was immense. It was a rock you could never climb. Or, so said the conventional wisdom. Grace climbed, each foot settling on someone else's pain. As she climbed, she let flowers grow in her footsteps.

"HEY," said Nate, then, "Hey." He moved across the ready room to grab her, and Grace slumped into his arms. "Grace? Are you okay? Grace?"

"I'm … fine," said Grace. Her voice sounded weak, making a lie of the words.

"You look like shit," he said. "I mean. Beautiful shit. I mean—"

She gave him a tired smile, putting her finger against his lips. "I feel like it too," she said, "but I'm fine. I'm … better than fine." She let him guide her towards a couch in the ready room. Grace caught El's face craning around to look at them from the flight deck.

"You good, Grace?" El frowned. "I mean, it sounds half-assed to be asking like this, but I'm kind of in the middle of the flying-the-spacecraft thing."

Grace waved a hand at her. "I'm good. Better than good. Have you ever found you could do something for someone that no one else could do?"

"Sure," said El. "No one flies a starship like me."

"Right," nodded Grace. "Well, I flew my first figurative starship."

"Good to know," said El, turning back to her console. "Let me know how it turns out."

"It'll turn out fine," said Grace. She felt a wetness on her upper lip, and touched at it. Her fingers came away red.

"Hell," said Nate, handing her a cup. "You're gushing blood."

"Bleeding nose," said Grace, pinching her nose to help stop the flow. "Hardly gushing." She lifted the cup. "What's in this?"

"Coffee," said Nate.

"Good," said Grace. "I expect I'll need my wits about me."

"Well, hang on," said Nate.

Grace held up a hand. "In about five minutes, El will jump the *Tyche*."

"Four," said El. "That's the flight plan."

"Four minutes," said Grace, "is all the time we've got until we board an enemy space station."

"You're staying here," said Nate.

"If you like," said Grace.

"What?" said Nate, the *confusion/suspicion* coming from him suggesting he'd expected a harder fight.

"But if I stay here, you're going on to an enemy station alone, which means you'll die," she said. "It's just math, Nate. There is an entire space station of assholes who are holding your friends hostage. What do you think the likely outcome of that is?"

He looked at the deck. "Huh," he said. "I hadn't got that far."

"You saw blood and thought, 'I know, I'll keep the second-best fighter on the *Tyche* away from all the action.' It's just a bloody nose."

"Second-best?" said Nate.

"Well, there's Kohl," said Grace. She heard a snort from El on the flight deck. "But Kohl's not coming along, is he?"

"Kohl is barely alive," said Nate.

"So, do you want me to stay on the *Tyche*?" said Grace.

"No," said Nate, but in a way that suggested he wanted to say *yes, but my ass is out of options.*

"Helm to the captain," said El, from the flight deck.

"I'm right here, El," said Nate.

"Good. We're jumping. Get strapped in."

CHAPTER FOURTEEN

KARKOSKI WAS RIGHT. Nate didn't like it.

She'd called the place *Station Echo 9*, like it was supposed to mean something to him. It didn't, excepting it implied at least another eight were made. The 'Echo' part was interesting, as it wasn't as sinister as *Station Shadow 9*, or *The Gateway to Hell 9*. But it was Republic spook-speak, which made it a little more ominous than the usual use of language would imply. All that aside, it wasn't the name that bothered him. What bothered him was that the station was deep, deep inside Ezeroc space. It was well past the demarcation of any human-inhabited worlds, leastways worlds on the charts.

Karkoski had agreed with that. She said even her charts didn't put anything out here except stars, space dust, and radiation. They'd stared at each other across the holo like they were daring each other to speak first. Karkoski had broken the silence, saying *you know this means we've known about the Ezeroc for a long time* and Nate had said *Republic assholes*. She'd shaken her head and said *space stations can take a long time to build, Captain.*

The implication was clear. There was a shadow operation at play here. One that had been doing things for a while — possibly since before the Republic existed. Hard to know for sure whether it had been around when Dom sat atop the throne of his Empire, and if he'd even known. The Intelligencers had fingers in a lot of pies.

Nate didn't like it.

El brought the *Tyche* on approach to the station, lights on, beacon hot. No surprises, because if it was a black ops installation, there would be weapons, and surprising folks with itchy fingers on triggers was a great way to end up dead. The steady rumble of thrust was comforting. Nate clicked the comm. "Station Echo 9, this is the *Tyche*. Please respond." The holo stage between him and El blinked on as the ship negotiated with the station. Transponder codes, docking bays, all advertised in the clear like there was nothing to hide. Which, Nate guessed, was true: if you made it all the way out here to this particular spot in the hard black, hiding wouldn't do a lot of good. You were already made.

The holo stage showed a couple of interesting things. First up, the station was a disc, rather than a ring; it would have a positive mass field to generate gravity in there somewhere. That would also make El happy because she hated docking with a station that used spin. Spin was old school but some assholes always wanted to save a little coin on *something*. Second, and also related to the station, was that it was a double-decker design; docking hubs sprouted from the circumference of the top deck, with a bottom deck accessible only from the inside. Third, still related to the station, was an escape vessel docked against the under deck. It wasn't a big lifeboat, and Nate figured — after some quick internal math — it'd hold ten souls, maybe fifteen if they were really good friends. Escape vessels like that had numbers, not names, and came outfitted with a fixed destination, a single Endless jump and they'd get to where they were going. Not the best option for getting across the galaxy, but better than dying in many scenarios that played through the spacefaring mind.

The fourth thing wasn't a hundred percent related to the station: another ship was docked on the top disc. The transponder codes said she was the *Gemini*, registered as a free trader. Now there was a thing: what were the odds of another member of the Greek pantheon coming to hang for a beer and a bite at the Republic's evil black ops space station? Still, you needed *something* to jump the hell out here with your prisoner cargo. The *Tyche* chatted happily to herself for a couple more moments while the back-and-forth between the station and docked ship happened at the tedious speed of light, then presented a brief report: the *Gemini* was powered down. Reactor cold, stored power only. Which meant she was here to stay; whomever had come with her had no immediate plans to jet off into the hard black to start a new career. In Nate's experience, that identified the captain of that vessel — and, likely, the crew — as willing accomplices of whatever was going on out here. If you docked at a station with your unlawful cargo, you would vacate soonest if it wasn't your usual sort of work.

No response to Nate's comm, and he hated to be kept waiting, so he keyed it again. "This is the free trader *Tyche*, hailing Station Echo 9. Y'all asleep down there?" The hiss of static was his only reply. He tapped on the console, directing comms to the *Gemini*. "*Gemini*, this is the *Tyche*. Sorry to bother, but we're having trouble raising station control. Are you aware of any problems down there?"

Hiss. Nothing else. The comm was online, the *Tyche* reporting a successful handshake to both his comms to Echo 9 and the *Gemini*. He clicked the comm off, turning to El. "Let's recap."

"We haven't capped in the first place," said El.

"Right," said Nate. "What I mean is, it's a trap."

"Of course," she said. "Which particular docking bay did you want me to choose on the trap?"

"Buyer's choice," said Nate. "Just, I don't know. Not too close to the *Gemini*."

"There are four docking collars," said El. "I'm either going to be next to it, or not. They're evenly spaced around the disc, so at worst we'll be a quarter turn from the *Gemini*. Any particular reason you don't want to be near that ship?"

"Never trust anyone who'd name a ship after two different people. It's like they can't choose which side they're on."

"Quarter turn," said El. "It'll be fine. Hang up, let's slow down so we don't crash into it and all die screaming." He watched as she worked her console, spinning the *Tyche* around so her main drives pointed at the station. She initiated a deceleration burn, bringing them into a nice easy drift about eight hundred meters out. She turned the ship again, playing the *Tyche's* lights over the station exterior. "It's got power. There are windows, see? Lights on."

Nate brought up the external cameras, magnifying the view. He zoomed on the station's windows. Yep, looked like the inside of a station: metal corridors visible through long windows. "Notice anything weird?"

"Aside from the deathly silence?"

"No one in there," said Nate. "Not a soul is looking out those viewports. Station's still got power, but I'm not seeing evidence of anyone else on there."

"You think Harlow's already dead?"

"I hadn't gone there just yet," said Nate. "Just, signs point to this being another clusterfuck like Absalom. There should be people here, but there aren't."

"That we can see."

"That we can see," he agreed. "Take us in."

"You're the boss," said El. She keyed her comm. "*Tyche*, this is the Helm. Prepare for docking, and possible explosive decompression as we open our airlock into a space station that's got an empty void on the inside."

Grace's voice came from the ready room behind them. "I'm right here. I can hear everything you're saying."

"What about the others?" said El.

"Kohl's in a coma, and Hope's asleep," said Grace.

"Hope doesn't sleep," said El. "Kid's addicted to stims."

"She does now," said Grace.

"Right you are," said El. "Anyway, we'll be docking soon."

"What about there?" said Nate, pointing out the windscreen. "Look. Painted on the outside. 'Control Hub.' Got to be a good place to dock. Welcome wagon. Drinks, a few canapés. Right?"

"I thought you said I could choose," said El.

"That was before I saw the Control Hub," said Nate. "Get to it, Helm."

"Aye, Captain," said El, but he heard the smile in her voice. She piloted the ship with ease — the station wasn't moving, the easiest docking she'd ever done — giving the *Tyche* a quick turn towards the end to put her rear against the station. There was the rumble of an automated docking clamp, and … done. "We're locked in place. How about we go ask the nice folks what the fuck they've done with our friends?"

"You got it," said Nate. "Do you mind staying back to guard the ship?"

"I wasn't planning on going on that station," said El. "You kids have fun though."

NATE STOOD next to Grace in the cargo bay airlock. "You ready?" They had their suits on, helmets sealed; Nate in his Emperor's Black, Grace in her *Tyche* gear. It looked right on her, like it hadn't looked on anyone else. She'd found her home, and he liked to think he'd played no small part in that. It made him happy. It might also make him sloppy, and he needed to focus for the next while. So they both didn't die.

"Yes," she said. "They're here, by the way."

"Harlow? Amedea?"

"Yes, but the Ezeroc as well," she said. She laid fingertips against the airlock door. "A lot of them."

"I'd have been surprised if they weren't," said Nate. "Status on Harlow?"

"'Oh God, oh God, I'm going to die,' or something like it," said Grace. "He's not feeling tip-top."

"Copy that," said Nate, checking his blaster then re-holstering it. He drew his sword from over his shoulder, the movement much smoother than it had been a couple weeks ago. It turns out being beaten half to death by Chad was a great motivator for improvement. The black blade now felt ... *right*, somehow. Or, he was just getting used to acting like one of the Emperor's Black again. He gave the blade a flourish then sheathed it again.

"Nice moves, sailor," said Grace, her own sword sheathed behind her.

"Thanks," said Nate. "Okay, we've got an atmosphere on the other side, but all we've got from the *Tyche* is that there's pressure. It could be a complex mix of poisons."

"I know how to read an airlock display," said Grace. "I'm not an idiot. Nate? My nose stopped bleeding. I'm *fine*."

"Right," he said, clearing his throat. "Here we go then." He keyed the airlock control, and the *Tyche's* door slid open.

CHAPTER FIFTEEN

THE WELCOME AIRLOCK wasn't welcoming.

No guns, laser turrets, plasma cannons, or giant insects were waiting to kill her and Nate. Nothing like that. Just a total lack of *anything* that would indicate life. Hell, even a couple of station heavies with armor and rifles would be better than this absence.

In Grace's experience, absences were a sign of shit having gone way south, a long time back. You didn't have your main entrance to your super-secret space station, full of horrible black ops activities — assumed, but let's say it's a fair assumption — empty. It spoke volumes.

"This isn't great," she said over the comm.

"It's fantastic," said Nate. His blaster was out though, and she was getting *nervous/uncertain* from him. "There's no one here shooting at us. Based on our track record, this is a definite trend in the right direction."

"Do you remember the last time you went into a secret base where they were Ezeroc holding prisoners?"

"The warehouse?"

"The warehouse," agreed Grace. "There was no one there shooting at us. It turned out to be bad."

"Fair point," said Nate. He walked ahead of her to the bulkhead door. "I figure we'll only find out what's going on through here."

"I figure you're right," said Grace, sealing the *Tyche's* airlock behind her. She joined Nate at the bulkhead. It was covered in the usual markings, warnings about explosive decompression, emergency opening procedures, that sort of thing. It didn't matter if you were in the super-secret military; you still had to assume there'd be some idiot who would blow the station if you didn't put a sign up. "Through here, there are answers." She keyed the open sequence on the console.

The door slid open with a soft hiss, equalizing the minor pressure differentials between the airlock and the station. Inside was what Grace assumed to be a normal-looking Control Hub. A bunch of consoles were arrayed towards the back, a glass-like material shielding them from the entrance lobby they stood in. There were no people. No Ezeroc either, not that she had expected any. She'd have heard them in her mind. Oh, they were here all right, just not *right* here. The Control Hub had sealed locks exiting from four locations; to the left, a door with yellow banding suggested a cargo elevator. To the right, another airlock door, leading to another docking collar on the outside of the station. Behind the glass shielding, two doors. The first led left, the second back into the station proper. A standard airlock was set into the glass, allowing egress into the area holding the consoles.

About the only thing of particular note was a red stain in the middle of the lobby. Grace knelt next to it, running a gloved hand over it. The stain flaked away at her touch. "Blood," she said. "A little old. We missed some action here."

"I am not missing it," said Nate. "You're sure Harlow and Amedea are still here?"

"I'm sure," said Grace. She could *feel* them, somewhere below them, on the second disc. "We'll need to go down."

"Take the elevator then?" said Nate.

"Not yet," said Grace. "I think we should find out what happened here first. Could be something nasty waiting for us. Remember the Ezeroc on that death planet? The Queen was in stasis. I couldn't detect her. I'd hate for us to go down there and have our one escape route cut off."

"You should be a starship captain with thinking like that," said Nate. "Hell, you want my job?"

"Not really," she said, flashing him a smile through her visor. "The pay is lousy and the hours are for shit. Which door?"

"I say we go back into the station itself," said Nate, pointing towards the back door. "We might find something."

Grace stood and moved to the egress door. She swiped the console to open, and it slid wide. *No lock. No security. A nice, warm welcome.* She checked the consoles in the Control Hub; they had power, but were locked down. *Okay, a little security. If Hope were here…* Grace moved to the door leading further into the station, Nate on her heels. The door opened ahead of her, automated systems still working fine. Which was weird; what with the blood in the lobby, she'd expect the place to be on lockdown. Whatever had happened here, it had happened quick and hard. No one had a chance to call for help.

The door opened into an area that looked like a dual-purpose room; food dispensers lined a wall, a holo stage central to the area. "Mess hall and briefing room," she said. The room was configured for mess hall status, the tables set with chairs, food trays still on them. Grace poked at a nearby tray with her hand. It held a desiccated sandwich, a bite sheared out of one corner. A cup sat beside it, the interior stained brown. Coffee, dried by the station's air cyclers. "They were caught mid-meal." There were two further exits from this room; one leading to another external airlock, and one leading to a sealed door that could — if her mental map was correct — be a passage around the exterior of the station's disc.

Nate had walked over to stand by the holo stage, the system dark.

"No active briefing. No alarms, no emergency." He did a slow turn to take in the room. "I count about thirty meals unfinished. Thirty souls were sitting down for chow when something took them away."

"But what?" she said.

"Fucking bugs," said Nate. "Bet my ship on it."

"I'm not taking that bet," said Grace. She moved towards the door leading around the disc. It didn't open automatically like the last one, so she keyed the open controls. Light lazed out from the door control, mapping her body, then with a beep the door slid open. She took an involuntary step back. On the floor on the other side of the door was a torso, sheared by the door. "There ... is half a person here, Nate."

Nate joined her, taking in the body. The corpse looked desiccated, dried out by the station, the skin on the face pulled back over the cheekbones. The uniform looked like Republic officer style, but done in black rather than blue. No rank logos or insignia. No medals. Which tallied with the concept of a black ops facility. Everyone here would know who this officer was — rather, who they'd been. No point in leaving other useful information just lying around for the enemy to find. "Looks like he died running. Door closed on him."

"You ever see someone run through an airlock sideways?" said Grace. "I think he was running, but tripped up. Fell over, and then some helpful soul sealed the door."

"Makes sense," said Nate, "if you assume there's some cold motherfuckers who don't mind shutting this door on their comrades."

"What if this door was sealed on purpose, Nate? What if there's something back here that they were keeping from the bugs?" Because they were both thinking it: *bug uprising*. "The door scanned me, Nate. I don't work here. They don't know me. So, I'm thinking basic auth only. The door is wanting to know if I'm human, or ... something else."

"That's an unpleasant thought," said Nate. He walked on through, stepping over the body. "Come on."

Grace followed, then as an afterthought, shut the door behind her. She didn't know what was going on here, but in space it was good practice to leave things as you found them until you *did* know. The rumble and clank of the door behind her was comforting and ominous in equal measure; comforting, because humans had built that, and it still worked. Ominous, because this station was dead, and it felt like she was locking herself in with something that wanted to eat her mind.

Both things could be true. It didn't have to be one or the other.

As predicted, the door led to a corridor extending around the outside of the disc. Long windows were set in the exterior hull, allowing a view of the stars. There was a lot of black out there for very little light. The *Tyche* wasn't visible, being on the other side of the disc. If Grace's mental map was right, the next docking ring would have the *Gemini* clamped to it.

The corridor itself was wide, and she and Nate could walk side by side with plenty of room. So, she did, because being at his side felt good. It felt *right* to have someone she could rely on, and she'd been without that her whole life. Grace paused, a hand on Nate's arm. Her suit's external mic had picked up the sound of a machine from ahead, she was sure of it. "Did you hear that?"

"Sounds like a drone," he said, pointing his blaster. They edged further around the disc until they could see what was making the noise. Suspended from the ceiling was a turret, the barrel dangling down towards the deck. It appeared lifeless, which put Grace's nerves on edge: if the turret wasn't making the noise, what was?

A clattering of metal on metal sounded from farther ahead, and scuttling towards them came a drone. Low-slung, about the size of a small dog, an insectile collection of limbs helping it move across the deck, then up the wall beside the windows. Now that was clever: if Nate fired — and missed — he'd stand a good chance of blowing out the window in a shower of plasma and fire. When you didn't have cover, put yourself against something that would kill your target if they hit it instead.

At the same time as the drone scuttled up the wall, the turret came to life, the barrel spinning up as it swiveled towards them.

Grace didn't have to talk to Nate; she knew he'd know where to shoot and why. She boosted off from a crouch, her sword whispering from its sheath. Her feet walked up the wall, her sword swinging around as the drone leapt off from the wall at her. Her nanoblade met the exterior of the drone with a chime that was soft, almost delicate, and two halves of the drone clattered past her, those insectile legs twitching and clawing. Grace saw Nate fire plasma into the turret, hot blue-white fire melting the housing. The turret got off a shot, plasma connecting with the window where Grace had just been. Nate's shots did their work and the turret slumped, pieces of slag dripping to the decking.

Grace turned to the window. Long, spidery cracks were spreading across the glass, a cracking sound coming through her suit's mic. She looked at Nate, saw the *we're fucked* in his eyes, then they both turned and ran down the corridor. A sealed door appeared around the station's curve ahead of them, Grace reaching the controls as a *crackaboom* came from behind them, then the howl of decompression as the window blew out. She'd already slammed her fist on the door's open control, and it was half open before it detected the decompression.

Half open was open enough, and she'd already ducked through, against the strong arms of leaving air trying to pull her back. She turned, braced against the door, and stuck her sword through the controls of the door on this side. The door stopped trying to close, air howling through the breach. Grace sheathed her sword, then reached a hand through. Nate grasped her hand, and she pulled. A loose crate from the room she'd just come into hit her on the back and she almost let Nate go, the air knocked out of her in a huff. But she wasn't letting Nate go. Not now, not ever, and not for the stupid reason of decompression.

Grace leaned back into the pull, Nate hauling himself through with his free hand as well. The air wasn't as strong now, but they waited on either side of the half-open airlock until the pressure equalized to nothing. She looked around the room they were in. It was a cargo bay of sorts, crates stacked and secured — excepting the one that had hit her. An airlock was set in the far wall, external windows showing the *Gemini* docked there. The deep throat of the airlock led to the interior of the *Gemini* — bad practice in space to leave your airlocks open like that. If there was anyone in the *Gemini* not in a suit, they'd be having a terrible day. Grace could feel the door at her back shift, and saw that Nate had popped the emergency panel next to it, working a manual winch to close it. The door sealed against the vacuum. The cargo bay would — assuming the station was still working as most of them did — fill this cargo bay with air. That would take a little time.

"*Tyche* to ground team," said El's voice over the comm. "I'm reading an ... incident. What did you do?" Not *are you okay* or *hey is everything alright?* Grace almost laughed.

"*Tyche*, this is the captain," said Nate. "We're fine, thanks."

"Didn't ask if you were fine. The *Tyche's* telling me there's glass and a crate of, hang on, it looks like a crate of alcoholic beverages. Did you throw all the station's booze outside?"

"No," said Grace. "We had a ... security system malfunction."

"The booze is fine?"

"Far as we know," said Grace.

"If we get bored we'll go get it later," said El. "Tagging it for recovery. *Tyche* out." The comm to the ship clicked off.

"Priorities are important," said Nate.

"They are," said Grace. Her suit was already reading a minor pressure increase in the cargo bay. "We've found the *Gemini*."

"We have," said Nate. "What I'm a bit concerned about is with a decompression event like that, we didn't see anything come out of the *Gemini*." By *anything* Grace knew he meant *people with guns* or *bodies of dead people*. "Just, nothing."

"Keep going?" she said.

"I reckon so." He pointed to the other door leading from the cargo bay, a big affair sized right for moving big cargo through. "Feels like the last stop."

"Right," said Grace. She set off across the cargo bay, reaching the big doors. She swiped the locking mechanism, the airlock opening with a rumble. Inside was a storage bay, large crates stacked against the floor. They were about two meters long, with glass set against their tops. She walked over, looking through the glass. "Well, that's not good."

Nate had joined her. "No. It is not good."

The boxes were full of people. Crates and crates of people, sealed inside these … coffins. Grace knelt down, checking a console set into the side of the box. She wasn't a medtech, no expert at all on keeping people alive, but the console's display was clear enough. It had a readout that displayed:

STASIS EFFECT: ACTIVE.

CARGO STATE: ALIVE.

Underneath that was a list of things that looked like a sideways view of vitals. Not blood pressure or heart rate, but levels of glucose (low), hydration (good), and brain activity (nominal).

"They've brought a bunch of people on ice to feed to the Ezeroc," said Grace. "Those fuckers."

"There is one piece of good news," said Nate.

"What's that?"

"That door," he said, pointing to the bulkhead across from them. "Looks like it leads back to the hub. Which means there's no horrible bugs on this level to bite us in the ass if we go down."

"That's good news," she agreed. "It means we've still got to *find* the bugs."

"Always half-empty," he said.

"It's not half-empty," said Grace. "The cup just needs more wine. Let's go, lover."

THE ELEVATOR down was a simple trip, but it didn't mean Grace found it easy. Down here was where the station had kept its monsters. Or, depending on your point of view, where the monsters lived. Where they sat waiting, like spiders in a web, for more people to come to them.

The trap was beautiful. All signs pointed towards this being a bad place to be. The only reason Grace and Nate were here was to get Harlow, because Nate called him a friend and those sorts of things were important. Also, Grace admitted, to get Amedea. The woman didn't tick any likable boxes, but if accounts were to be believed, she had headed up the Resistance, led the revolt against the Intelligencers in charge of the Republic. Good deeds deserved a reward.

Also, she knew all the Resistance's secrets. With an alien race that could read minds, that was an unpleasant problem. So, they'd need to hoist her out of here, or make sure she was all the way dead. Neither of those prospects gave Grace a warm glow.

The elevator clanked to a halt as it reached the bottom of the short trip down, a shudder through the car the only evidence so far that the station wasn't under human control anymore. If it was, someone in maintenance would get an enthusiastic conversation from someone in charge. *Do your job*, that kind of thing. Maintenance were long dead, and this elevator might have been in frequent use, ferrying things from the upside to the downside.

Things. You mean people, Grace.

The door opened in front of them. Grace took in the room: an open-style barracks, large enough to hold maybe thirty or forty soldiers. Rooms set around the perimeter, no doubt quarters for officers. About a third of the bunks — *let's call it ten guys, Grace* — were occupied. By people.

But they weren't giving off human thought patterns. The hiss of Ezeroc communication was heavy in the air, so thick she could almost smell it. When they'd first encountered 'people' like these on Absalom Delta, Grace didn't know what was going on. She hadn't realized that the Ezeroc could infect human hosts with larvae that would eat out a person's brain over time, filling their skull with a collective of small insects. That person would cease to exist in the regular sense, but Grace figured that their knowledge would be subsumed into the collective mind of the Ezeroc. Nasty way to go, but it left a bunch of human-looking assholes walking around that needed killing. "They're bugs, Nate," she said.

"Got it," he said, and shot the closest one — short, male, half on his feet — with his blaster. The plasma blast hit the man in the chest, lifting him up and throwing him across the room to land in a pile of burning meat. The man's head hit the wall with a crack, and he lay still. Might still be bugs alive inside, but that was a problem they could solve if they survived the next couple of minutes.

The remaining nine moved towards them. Correction: eight moved towards them. One, towards the rear — female, officer uniform, short-cropped hair — reached towards the deck by her feet. She hefted a laser carbine and pointed it at Nate.

No time for thought. Grace twisted back, then tossed her sword across the room. In a silver flash, it turned through the air and embedded itself in the officer. The sword's blade impacted against her face, slicing through, then lodged in the wall behind her. Which solved one problem, but Grace had to admit that it left her with another. She was in a room with eight Ezeroc who wanted them dead, and she'd just thrown her weapon to the other side of the room.

Correction the second: they wanted Nate dead. Grace, they wanted alive. For whatever reason. They had always wanted Grace alive.

Nate fired two more blasts, the first shot hitting nothing but station wall, the second hitting one more soldier in the head, the top half of his torso immolated in a pyre. There was a keening sound, like five distinct things crying as they burned alive, and the torso toppled to the deck.

Not to be left out of the fray, the station's systems worked out that there was actual fire in the room, and the emergency sprinklers kicked in, a deluge of water cascading down.

Grace turned to Nate, grabbing the sword poking out over his shoulder. She drew the black blade and turned to face the horde. This weapon felt heavier than her sword, deliberate, purposeful. She'd used it once before, on Absalom Delta. It hadn't kept her from falling to the Ezeroc, but that's not why she wanted it. She wanted it because it had an edge that could cut things in half.

She ducked into the room, meeting the reaching hands of the first person she came too. *Red hair. Blank face.* She felt his hands close around her ship suit, so she brought Nate's blade around in a whirl that severed those hands. Grace then stepped back and reversed the motion, running the red-haired man through. The bugs might be in charge of his body, but without a pumping heart he wasn't going anywhere.

An Ezeroc-piloted woman came at her from the left, Grace ducking low and to the right, away from those reaching hands. The woman was hit by a blast from Nate, tossed back in a hissing shower of meat as the water cut the flames down. Grace's back foot slipped in the water, and she went down on one knee. She saw two more coming at her from the front, both big men, and she used her free hand to rise faster. The sword licked out, like it was thirsty and all this water was doing nothing to slake it. Like it wanted something *thicker* to drink. She used it to take the head off the first man, not watching it to bounce free on the deck, the blood that fountained mingling with the deluge from the ceiling.

Arms closed around her from behind, a hug with desperate strength. Fighting in the suit, with the water, was like fighting without half her senses, and one of them had come up behind her. The second man in front of her closed hands on the neck seal of her suit, trying to work the collar free. It was as if the Ezeroc thought she was helpless with someone holding her from behind. Like the Ezeroc hadn't learned how humans fought humans.

Grace dropped her weight down and back, causing her attacker at the rear to stumble, the grip loosening. In that moment of opportunity, she brought her sword hand *down*, her free hand *up*, breaking the grip behind her. She kicked back to where she figured a leg would be, and was rewarded by the impact of the strike. She jumped up, tucking herself into a ball, and then kicked out both her legs into the man in front of her. He was pushed back, Grace hitting against the person behind her, them both going down. Bright plasma roared across the room, hitting the big man again and again, his body disappearing in chunks of smoking meat to hiss and steam in the water.

Placing a hand beside her, Grace twisted her legs in a whirl, getting them under her. She sprang to her feet, sword whipping around and down, going through the person who'd attacked her from behind. She didn't even check if it was male or female, tall or short, because it wasn't important. Surviving was important.

Panic/fear. She turned to see Nate, in the elevator, the last two Ezeroc-piloted humans reaching for him. They had pieces of metal — pipes or conduit — and were swinging hard. They'd moved around Grace, straight for the guy with the blaster. *Not a sloppy idea.* For a bunch of guys with hollowed-out skulls they were getting smarter. Learning, not just random walkers anymore. There'd be time for introspection later, if there was a later. For now, *Nate was in trouble.* Grace ran back toward him, water on the deck splashing as she moved. One of the Ezeroc-piloted humans swung a pipe to *crack* against the side of Nate's helmet. Grace could see it before it happened, the swing, the promised impact, and knew she would never be fast enough to get there. When the pipe hit Nate's helmet, it felt like fate. She'd expected the helmet to take the blow, because it was a space suit, and space suits were designed for hard knocks. The crack and rupture of glass said it had taken one too many knocks before now, and it had had enough.

Nate fell to the ground as Grace reached them. One of the Ezeroc turned to face her, and Grace swung — *clang, clang* as her sword rang against the pipe. The Ezeroc returned a swing at her, and Grace spun out of the way, keeping the movement going and put the black edge of the sword through the neck of the Ezeroc-piloted human. The head bounced away.

Then she stepped forward and ran the other one through, the

blade running thought its spine and out its front. She braced, then twisted her blade as she pulled it back. The body dropped to the deck, all motion and will stolen from it. Grace realized she was panting, her breath loud in her helmet. She reached a hand down to Nate, and he took it, coming to his feet.

He looked past her shoulder, then at the bodies at their feet. "Thanks," he said.

"Don't mention it," she said. She looked at his visor. "Your helmet's totally…"

"Fucked. Yeah." He turned the neck seal, releasing the clamp, and lifted it free of his head to clatter and splash against the deck. Nate turned his face to the sprinklers in the roof, water cascading down his face. "Ah. That's nice."

There could be a pathogen here. Spores. The Ezeroc do things you don't know about. But it didn't matter. None of it mattered, unless they could do it together. She unclasped the ring about her own neck and dropped her helmet beside Nate's.

He was right. The water was nice. Like spring rain.

Grace!

She turned her face toward one of the two doors leading from the room. She'd barely processed them on entry. The door towards the left? Simple, unassuming. Blank. Just a door. The one on the right? It looked the same, but it felt different. She pointed towards the rightmost door. "There," she said. "The fucking locusts are in there."

CHAPTER SIXTEEN

NATE RUBBED water from his face. The sprinklers were stopping. Stations were weird, because if the gravity failed, spraying a bunch of water around would just drown people inside. But you couldn't do other effective things to stop fire. Suck the air out? People died. Halon? People died. Etcetera. Tricky problem. Station automation worked its way down a list of least-dangerous things, and if the grav was on, the rain came down.

Yay for grav. Nate frowned. "You're saying the death insects are behind door number two?"

"That's right," said Grace.

"How do you know?"

"They're calling to me," she said. "They're the only ones I've ever heard in my mind. Like words I can't ignore."

"Keep the sword," said Nate. "I'll use yours."

"It's okay," she said, holding the black blade out to him. She tapped the side of her head with her other hand. "Chad's been … helpful."

"Okay," he said, taking his sword back. He watched her move to retrieve her own blade from the Ezeroc-piloted human she'd thrown it through. Nate figured it wouldn't matter the circumstance, he'd never tire of watching her move. Like oiled perfection. What she was doing with a broken-down bum like him he'd never know, but he planned to keep it for as long as he had breath. Because she was more important than breath.

He reached down for her helmet. You never knew when you'd have to ram a lid back on someone's suit so their brains wouldn't boil out their ears in a vacuum. She came back to join him, so he reached for her, pulling her close for a kiss. Then he clipped the helmet to her belt. He'd worry about a helmet for himself later.

"What about yours?" she said.

"Eh," he said. "Bound to be a spare around here somewhere. I'm going to suggest something radical."

"Shoot."

"Let's save the room with the death bugs for last." He walked towards the leftmost door. "We're here for Harlow, remember? We can always hole the station from space." He tapped the door's console, and it slid open in front of them. "Okay," he said, after a moment's silence. "We've found the real carnival of horrors."

The room they'd opened was a lab. Plain and simple, it was designed for experiments. Calling it a lab was like calling a torture rack a table though; it didn't convey the true emotions that should come with it. This lab was white, sterile, the smell of disinfectant in the air. It was about what he'd expect from anyone with at least mild sociopathy. Banks of tables were arrayed around it, white sheets — some stained red — atop bodies on those tables. Consoles littered the area, holos bright with data.

Grace moved past him into the room. "This is ... where it started, isn't it?"

"Looks like it," said Nate. He flipped the sheet back on a bed nearby. It was a human male, an old scar running down from his shoulder. Looked like a knife wound, healed a long time ago. A prisoner's barcode was etched on his left chest. The top of his head had been sectioned off, a collection of dead brain insects in a jar at the head of the bed. The dead man's eyes sightless eyes stared at the roof. "I'm going to say the bad guys found the Ezeroc, and then experimented on humans with them."

"Or on them with humans," said Grace, at another bed. There was a woman there, normal from the neck up. Her torso was mottled with chitin, plates of it interspersed like scar tissue over her frame. An old yellow fluid, long dried, ran down from where chitin met skin. Whether the Ezeroc's immune system fought the human, or the other way around, it was impossible to tell. "Might be the origins of the men in black."

"How long?" said Nate. He held a hand out to the room. "How long have they been doing this? Experimenting out here? This is the ninth station, Grace. What about the other eight?"

"They might not be Ezeroc experiment zones."

"I don't know if that's better or worse," said Nate, running a gloved hand through his wet hair. "Okay, so whoever's in charge … they what, they find some Ezeroc spore? A new form of life."

"Maybe there was an accident. Maybe it was on purpose. But they worked out that Ezeroc could manipulate human DNA," said Grace, picking up the thread.

"Then, because you can only do so much on a station," said Nate, pulling the sheet back on a horrific meld of human face and Ezeroc feeding mandibles, "they sent spores to Absalom Delta. They sent it to the other side of the planet from the human establishment."

"Doesn't make sense," she said. "Why not just infect the colonists from the get-go?"

"Might be an administrative error, but I don't think so." Nate thought about the kinds of people who felt themselves to be gods among other humans. Those who could read and change minds. And what they might want from an alien tool they'd use to suppress humans with. "I think they sent these things to the other side to find out just how *hungry* they were. To find out whether they *wanted it enough*."

"How effective," offered Grace.

"Yeah, that," said Nate. "You don't want your death spores to be lazy." He kept walking around the room, blaster ready, but whatever had happened in here, it'd happened aways back. Nothing left alive, a chemical smell overlaying everything. *Preservatives. Don't want the specimens rotting on the bench.* "And, I don't know, I guess they're not very lazy. Busy little bees."

"Okay, it's a theory," said Grace. "Proving it will take a little work."

"We'll get there," said Nate. "We'll pop the lid on all of these," and he pointed to the consoles, "and find out the truth."

"Why?" said Grace.

"What?"

"Why are we finding out the truth?" She looked a little weary, and he wanted to hold her. To tell her *it's okay* or *we'll get through this*. But it wouldn't have worked. Don't sell to a seller. Don't lie to a liar. Especially if they can read your feelings. "I get that the Republic are assholes, Nate, but that is past tense. The Republic is *fucked*. Finding the truth is a distraction."

He gritted his teeth, but kept his voice level. Not that it would matter … because she could sense his emotions. The shape of his keel. "The truth is never a distraction."

"I don't mean it like that, and you know it," she said, her voice softening. She pointed a hand at the wall behind her, a door set in it. "Through there are your friends. *Our* friends. Once we've got them squared away, we can go truth-hunting. But even then? That's not why we're here. We need to find the source. The only truth that matters."

"The Ezeroc homeworld."

"The Ezeroc fucking homeworld," she agreed. "We've all had a heaping helping of shit inside a plain whitebread wrapper from the Republic, Nate. *All* of us. But that's a problem that'll solve itself. There's a bigger issue. You need to work out whether you're the one who wants to solve it."

"I'm the captain of a tiny ship," said Nate.

"Not the size of the dog in the fight."

He thought about that. "It's the size of the fight in the dog."

"Always has been. Always will be. And you know what?" She quirked her lips in a half-smile. "We've got Lady Luck on our side. We fly with a goddess, Nate. She might be tiny, but her heart is mighty."

He looked down at the deck. *This is it, Chevell. The point where you decide whether being a hero is in your job description. Last time you tried the hero gig, you lost a hand and a leg and a good life. The Old Empire fell around your ears because heroes fail.*

Another part of him chimed in, *you could just wallow in it. Forget about Dom and Annamarie. Pretend it never happened. Run with your Endless Drive and your ship to a part of the galaxy where there are no insects and no Republic. And then you can die alone, hating yourself, because you know you were meant to do better. You are better.*

"You should listen to yourself," said Grace.

"You inside my head?"

"No. You're inside mine." She shook her head. "It's hard to describe. The words we have don't ... work." She looked frustrated.

"No place I'd rather be," he said. "Together."

"Okay," she said. "Together. So, what are we doing together, Captain? Or is it Nathan? Or my lover?"

"All of those," he said, after a moment. "Your captain says we're going to find the fucking bug homeworld. Your Nate says we'll do it with our friends. Your lover says ... we'll do it together. For always."

"If you're sure," she said, face unreadable.

"I'm sure," he said, offering a smile. "Let's go kick over an anthill."

THE DOOR OPENED like it had been expecting them, a quiet hiss of human machinery, revealing a room that was almost warm in its dark tones. In the room were three people.

Harlow: restrained on a bed, straps holding him down. The bed wasn't as comfortable or dark as the rest of the room; it looked like a surgical table, perhaps borrowed from the lab. The straps didn't say *let's be friends*; they said *we're doing this my way*. There was a gag over his mouth, a piece of white fabric with a ball so that Harlow couldn't speak. Sure, he'd be able to scream if he put his heart into it, but he was otherwise incommunicado. Harlow's face turned towards Nate when he and Grace walked in, his eyes wide, pleading. Harlow was a smuggler and a pirate and an old friend, and Nate had seen him in a hundred compromising positions. He'd never seen naked fear on his friend's face before.

Amedea: in a chair, but also restrained. Her straps were a lighter weight, at the wrists and ankles only. No gag, just a line of drool running down her chin. Her eyes were unfocused, not a lot going on in there. Not fear, not hope, just a kind of haze you'd expect with top-shelf pharmaceuticals. Which made sense, because if you had someone on your super-secret station who could read minds and perhaps change them, you'd want that person in a coma at least ninety-nine percent of the time. You'd only want them out of a coma to lift things out of them, sensitive pieces of information. Chad had said a person needed to be awake to read their mind. And if you had an awake Intelligencer, you had yourself a viper on your hands. So, drugs it was.

Mystery asshole: a short, thin man in a surgical uniform, white and form-fitting, sat in front of Amadea on another chair. His was more comfortable, castors at the base allowing it to move where he willed. He wasn't a prisoner. He was a jailer. Beside him was a glass tank, inside of which was a lot of sand.

"Hey, asshole," said Nate, pointing his blaster. "How about you back away from my friends there?"

The asshole turned around, his face crinkling into a smile. "Captain Chevell," he said.

"Sure," said Nate. "Who are you?"

"Doctor Kiefer Gruss," said the asshole. "I'm the head of this facility."

"This shop of horrors," said Grace. Gruss gave a deprecating nod, his smile still on his face.

"*Doctor* Gruss. Since we're getting along so well, why don't you back up?" said Nate. "Like I asked. I'd like for us to have a reasonable conversation. But with you so close to my friends and all, it's looking *un*reasonable."

"Your friends?" said Gruss. He did a quick look towards Harlow, then Amedea. "Ah, of course, yes. Of course." He backed away from Amedea, his chair rolling away as he stood. Nate figured him at about seventy, maybe eighty kilos with shoes on. Most of it worthless weight. He wasn't getting distance for a fight, he was getting distance so he wouldn't have to fight. Good call. "There's just one small problem."

"What's that?" said Nate.

"They're not your friends anymore," said Gruss. "Not all the way, hey?"

"It seems fair then," said Nate, "that this isn't your station anymore. Not all the way, hey?"

Gruss shrugged, like it was a detail that wasn't important. "It serves its purpose."

"Asshole," said Grace, striding forward, sword out. "Everyone is dead!"

"Grace Gushiken," said Gruss. "Oh, they want you. They *want* you. Very much."

She paused. "You say that like it's news. The only thing newsworthy is I'm *still* surprised people like you exist. People willing to sell out our race to a bunch of fucking aliens." Her voice was hard, her blade steady. Nate wasn't sure if she would cut Gruss down. He wasn't sure if he cared. But Grace turned away, walking to Harlow, using her sword on his restraints.

"I'm not selling our race out," said Gruss. "I'm improving it. We're so weak, in a vast universe. We have an enemy we can't hope to defeat. Do you know they can invade our cells? Subvert our bodies and use them for a variety of purposes. Fuel. Soldiers. Raw materials. That's what we are to them. And they can read minds. Don't you think we need a helping hand against a foe like that?"

"We've got a helping hand," said Nate. "We've got nukes."

Gruss blinked, then gave a small chuckle, a sound Nate felt was rehearsed. Sociopaths might need to practice sounding like normal people, sure. "Don't you think we've tried?"

Grace paused in her cutting. "What do you mean, you tried?"

Gruss turned to her, putting his back towards Nate. Nate could see the rear of him, and wished he hadn't: the back of the man's skull was coated in a mottling of chitin. It was as if his skull was fused with pieces of Ezeroc. "I mean," said Gruss, "that we came out here into the hard black a long time ago, Grace. A very long time ago. We came with words and gifts and weapons, and none of them worked. They can read minds, you see. They know what you'll do before you do. And they can control minds. Many people died." He didn't seem unhappy about that, just noting it down as a useful data point.

Grace went back to freeing Harlow, removing his gag. Harlow coughed, spat, then said, "Nate? Shoot this motherfucker. And don't touch the sand."

Grace paused in her cutting, and all eyes went to the box of sand. All eyes except Amedea's, which continued to stare slack and unfocused. "What's in the sand?" said Nate.

"I guess a kind of larvae," said Harlow. "I don't know. This asshole infected Amedea. You could see them wriggling under her skin, climbing towards her brain."

"That seems bad," said Nate. He looked at his blaster, then pulled his sword. He looked at Gruss. "Any reason we shouldn't turn you into a cinder? Or, maybe I can just cut you in half."

"There are two reasons I can think of," said Gruss. "The first is that I know of a way you can save your friend." He nodded at Amedea. "The second is," and he turned to Nate, a gleam in his eyes, "that I command you to kill them all!"

Nothing happened. Nate looked down at his blaster, his sword, then back up at Gruss. "Out of curiosity, what did you expect to happen?"

Gruss blinked, then said, "Nathan Chevell, I order you to execute them all. Then get me on your ship, and take us away. I *order* you. I *command* it."

"You didn't get the memo, did you?" said Nate. The handle of his sword was getting warm to the touch. *Huh.*

Gruss looked confused. "I'll admit, that usually works better."

"You were expecting," said Nate, the handle hot now, "that I'd go on a rampage and kill my friends. Then we'd hop on the *Tyche*, maybe with some of the Ezeroc spore."

"Heavens no," said Gruss. "We're going to destroy the station. The vile creatures can't be allowed to live."

"Good times," said Nate, then shot Gruss three times, center mass. His body was knocked over by the blasts, plasma setting him on fire. The body smoked and burned on the deck for a few moments before the sprinklers in the room kicked in, drenching them all. The open top of the sandbox allowed water in, filling the container. *Drown the fuckers. That'll work.* Nate holstered his blaster, but kept a firm grip on his sword. *Thank you, Dom. It's a gift fit for a prince.* He looked at Amedea — still lights out, nothing happening there — then at Harlow. "Do you know what he meant about a cure?" Gruss's body smoked and steamed for a few more moments, hissing as the water hit it.

"No clue," said Harlow, "but it stands to reason that he'd want a kill switch of some kind. Amedea was ... infected some time ago. After the station fell. I don't think Gruss was ... in control, not anymore." The sprinklers cut out, leaving the room damp, the smell of old barbecue and sodden ash kicked around by the air cyclers.

"He wasn't," said Grace, helping Harlow stand. Her eyes flicked towards Amedea. "Neither is she. Nate? You know we need to ... end it. It'd be a mercy."

It would, at that. But a cure? That might be even better. "Let's see if we can find a fix first." The only real problem was that there was still a nest on the station. "Maybe we could kill the insects first though. That way they won't sneak up on us while we're looking for the cure."

"What about her?" said Grace.

"She ain't going nowhere," said Nate. "We'll lock her in here. Safe and sound."

"Safe and sound," said Grace, but there was doubt in her voice. "How are we going to deal with the nest?"

Nate looked down at the body of Gruss, or what was left of it. "With fire," he said.

MAKING explosives on a space station was hard. By design, there were few materials on board that would combust. Burning things in space was bad; your habitat on fire was terrifying if you couldn't run outside to get away from it, and fire burned up all your O2. So making fire in here was difficult.

The good news was that this was also a military installation. Back in the barracks, Nate and Harlow and Grace were rifling through belongings. They found a fair few weapons, laser carbines and blaster rifles and a maser or two. And then they hit the motherload: a heavy weapons locker. No grenades, because explosives were also bad in environments where blowing walls out meant everyone would die in the hard vacuum of space, but there was something that caught Nate's eye. A heavy plasma cannon, similar in design to the one that Kohl mounted to his armor. This one didn't have a convenient suit of power armor to go with it, but it had a mount, a tripod that could be set up and anchored to the decking via the use of explosive bolts.

"What do you think that's on board for?" said Harlow, staring at the weapon.

"Maybe someone's a gun nut," offered Grace.

"Nah," said Nate. "I reckon what we've got here is the Marines equivalent of a contingency plan." He lifted the weapon, hefting it towards the sealed doorway between the barracks and where Grace said the Ezeroc were. Nate gauged the distance by eyeball. Back a few meters so he wouldn't get his face eaten as soon as the door opened. He dropped the tripod down, kicking the mounting stud, and the legs folded out with a clank, followed a second after by the triple sound of bolts firing into the decking. He dropped the plasma cannon on the mount, gave it an experimental swivel, and said, "Kohl will be disappointed he missed this."

"I'd be happy to swap places with him," said Harlow. "I'd be safe and sound on the *Tyche*."

"He had his back filled with shrapnel, and is paralyzed from the waist down," said Grace. "There's a good chance he'll be mobile again with the right tech, but he's down and out for now."

"That doesn't sound like a good swap after all," said Harlow.

"Grace," said Nate, "I think we open the door and I lay down some righteous anger in there."

"It'll work," she said. Her eyes unfocused. "They're starving, Nate."

Harlow hefted a maser. "Where you want me?"

"Out of the way," said Nate. "No offense, but you're a lousy shot. You panic."

"I do not panic," said Harlow, voice rising a shade.

"What about the time on Ganymede?"

"That was *one* damn time," said Harlow.

"This could be another," said Nate.

"These assholes wanted to take away my mind. I'm not going anywhere."

Nate chewed it over for a second or two. "Over there," he said, pointing towards the door to the lab. "If they make it past me, your job is to boil crab with the maser. Just do not, for all that is holy, shoot me. You got it, Harlow? Also, don't let 'em through there. It's our second way out."

"One damn time," muttered Harlow, walking to cover the door.

"And me?" said Grace.

"At my back," said Nate.

She nodded, walking behind him, one hand trailing along his arm as she moved. She leaned close, and whispered in his ear, "Try not to die."

"I'll do my best," he said. "Everyone ready?"

"Ready," said Harlow.

"Do you even have to ask?" said Grace.

"Breaching it in five," said Nate. "Four. Three. Two. One." And he pressed the firing stud on the cannon.

CHAPTER SEVENTEEN

GRACE HADN'T EXPECTED things to go smooth. Things never went smoothly in a firefight. The best you could hope for was *not fucked*, and if they became fucked, the next best you could hope for was a decent *unfuck* to your fucked reality.

That was the problem with this particular reality. They had an elevator out, fine, but the escape pod for the station was off the lab. Harlow was guarding that way out, but Harlow was useless in a fight in Grace's experience, and had taken a few knocks of late.

She wanted to be going out the elevator for other reasons. The primary reason was the escape pod would be set to a single jump somewhere 'out there,' and out there might be the heart of the evil Intelligencer HQ. Getting on that boat was a last resort.

Why these thoughts were going through her head was because Nate had just shot at a bulkhead door between safe now and a horrible future where Ezeroc would boil out of the breach and try and eat their minds. She could feel them—

Grace! Grace! Grace!

—already trying to get in. It was only the training at Chad's hands that kept them at bay, but it left her pulse high, her hands sweaty on the hilt of her sword.

The bulkhead led to a chamber that would, if the upper level was a reasonable simulacrum of this lower deck, have an exit that led around the disk. That corridor would have glass leading out to space, and if enough bolts of plasma missed, there would be a direct hole from where they were *here* and the hard black *out there*. They had one helmet between three of them.

Correction the third: *four* of them. Because Amedea was still in there, and there was no point in any of this without saving her. Hell, if they were happy for Amedea to go down with the station, ignoring their search for a cure, they could take off now and use the *Tyche's* weapons to turn this thing into a ball of molten slag.

One helmet, four people. Bad. Worse was cutting through a bulkhead door with a plasma cannon, but Gruss — or some other smart person — had sealed the Ezeroc in there. Sealed 'em in, locked the door, and thrown away the electronic key. Hope might have been able to get through given enough time, but no way was Grace advocating bringing Hope onto a station full of death insects. The girl had been through enough for now.

As the plasma chewed into the bulkhead door, it glowed with heat, and then melted, the metal running and spraying off as new blasts hit it. The Ezeroc on the other side hammered at the door, like they were eager to die. But Grace wasn't fooled. They were eager to *get out*.

Grace Grace Grace Grace Grace...

The voice in her mind — hard to tell if it was a single voice, or the song of a collective, because these were aliens and there was no working analog in her human brain for their collective consciousness — was louder than the blasts of plasma. Loud, insistent, but she could still ignore the call, this time. It made her clench her teeth, but her walls were holding. In a way it was a blessing, as it distracted from the roar of the plasma cannon, bright flashes of energy carving away at the bulkhead door.

A hole appeared in the door, just a tiny gap as a blast of plasma made its way through. Grace could see a claw extend through the hole a half second before another round of plasma turned it to ash. The insects were trying to get out, helping to widen the breach. More rounds made it through, the darkness beyond littered with the bright burning flashes of things set afire by plasma. An Ezeroc drone head poked out, then blew into pieces as plasma ate into it. The breach continued to open, getting wide enough that the plasma cannon's fire couldn't fill the whole thing. An Ezeroc tried to worm out the side and Nate turned the plasma cannon to incinerate it, then worked on filling as much of the breach with plasma as he could.

Grace stood ready. Ready for them to boil out like a swarm of locusts.

Grace! Helmet! Grace!

That was … interesting. They hadn't tried to direct her before, but this was clear. They were calling to her, telling her about a helmet. Which had been in her mind moments before. And had been in Nate's mind earlier, before he held his sword. The insects could read minds, so they would know.

Oh no. It was too late to stop what was coming. She couldn't see through the breach what was happening, but insight gave her imagination flight. There would be a swarm of Ezeroc in there. They would have cut away the outside hull of the station. They had time, and patience. All it would take was a small hole, blocked up by the body of one of them, or even a piece of their chitin. A small hole, easily removed.

And there would be Grace, the one they wanted, with a helmet. The air would blow out of the station, and Harlow, and Amedea, and Nathan would go with it. Leaving her here, with the Ezeroc, alive. How they wanted it.

Grace felt the pressure change, her ears pop as they did it. The Ezeroc, inside their dark chamber, opened a hole into space. Because they didn't need air. It was a lesson Grace had received on the moon, but none of them had the wit to learn from it.

She unclipped her helmet from her belt, then dragged Nate away from the plasma cannon. She caught a yelp of surprise from him as she did, the cannon swinging towards the roof, big chunks of ceramicrete and plating blasting aside. Grace slammed her helmet on his head, sliding the docking ring closed, then turned towards Harlow. Harlow was pointing the maser at the hole in the bulkhead door but looking at Grace with an expression of huge surprise, an expression that got larger as she ran towards him and dove into a tackle. They tumbled together into the lab as the emergency decompression alarms sounded. The door to Amedea's chamber shut in the blink of an eye, sealing her safe and sound inside. The door leading from the lab to the barracks started to seal, then jammed. Grace looked behind her, seeing an Ezeroc drone in the breach, its body in the way. There was a crunching sound as the chitin of its exoskeleton cracked, but it held long enough for another drone to get beside it. Then another, and they pushed the door open.

The air was getting thin, its fingers dragging at them. The Ezeroc wanted her, but they'd be denied the pleasure. She wanted to give a grim smile here at the end, but found she wanted to live even more. Grace wanted to live, because she was in love, and had something to live for.

She felt a hand at her back, Harlow dragging her. Towards the emergency shuttle. She wanted to say *no, no, we don't know where it goes*, but there wasn't enough air to make words. The Ezeroc were coming for them, scrambling to get through the breach. There was a silent flare of plasma as Nate — brave, beautiful, stupid Nate — fought them from inside the barracks. Alone, just him and a plasma cannon, against a horde that wanted him dead and her alive.

Why wasn't he running? It's why she'd given him the helmet. Couldn't he see? He had to get to the elevator while the insects were distracted with her. It was so cold. She couldn't think. The lights of the lab were still on, but she was for all intents and purposes in outer space. The hard black had invaded. It was all around her, and she was out of time.

One of the Ezeroc made it into the lab, claws scrabbling at the deck as it came towards her. Grace watched it come as the iris of the emergency shuttle passed her view. Harlow let her go, making a dash for the door controls. His face was a red-purple, his eyes bulging, mouth working for air. But there was no air. There was only the hard black. His hand hit the shuttle's door controls, and the iris slid shut as the Ezeroc made it to them. It sliced through the leading claw, severing it, and then blessed, cool air hissed in around them.

Over the noise of air rushing in, Grace could feel the thump against the deck as plasma fire slammed into the station elsewhere. *Nate. He's still alive.*

An automated voice announced SHUTTLE LAUNCHING BRACE BRACE BRACE SHUTTLE LAUNCHING, and then the chamber around them shook as the shuttle cleared the side of Station Echo 9. There was a brief feeling of weightlessness, and then—

The universe, laid bare. Every piece of her, shining with light. Her hair, floating in gossamer strands. She could feel everything. She was everything.

They jumped.

CHAPTER EIGHTEEN

"EL, I NEED YOU!" Nate screamed into the comm. The plasma cannon was heavy, so very, very heavy. He'd torn it from the mounts, backing up to the station's outer hull. Grace — his Grace, his love, the person who he was supposed to be *together* with — had gone through a closing bulkhead door. She'd given him her helmet. She'd somehow known what was coming, guessed at the bug's plans and thrown down her life for his.

That's not the way it was supposed to work.

So it didn't matter that the cannon was heavy. He took most of the weight in his metal hand, leaning back against his metal leg. Metal, stronger than flesh, good enough to hold for now, as the cannon bucked and fired. Ezeroc died in piles, charring, steaming husks, glowing with the heat as plasma hit them. They ignored him, clawing and scrabbling to get at Grace. To catch her, to do whatever it was that they wanted.

They had set this whole thing up. Those *fuckers*.

"On it, Cap," said El, her voice calm and clear over the comm. The station shook around him, the cry of metal transferred but muffled through his boots. "I have you on the bottom level of the station. *Tyche* has disembarked from station dock and is coming to your location. We'll be making an exit for you."

Making an exit. Sweet Christ.

"*Tyche* to the captain," she said again. "I've lost Grace's transponder ... no, wait. The shuttle jumped. Tracking it."

The cannon continued to fire, until it didn't, the charge depleted. It spat the glowing coal of the battery to the decking, cooling fast in the hard black of space. He dropped the cannon, drawing his blaster and sword. The Ezeroc paused in their attempts to breach the door, turning to face him. Insect eyes locked on to him, one tiny human against their horde. They'd need more food, more *materials* if they were going to build up for another attempt at finding Grace. Wherever she'd gone.

He'd find her. Nate would find her if it was the last thing he ever did. He raised his sword. "Come on, then," he hissed.

They charged.

Turns out, his last stand heroics were unnecessary. The side of Station Echo 9 blew inwards in a shower of metal, ceramicrete, and kinetic PDC rounds. The *Tyche* fired with precision, a cautious guardian to her captain. Her bright lights shone in through the breaches, brief licks of red laser light marking targets as the lifter moved around the circumference of the disc, hunting those who would do her crew harm. The PDCs hit something in the station's substructure, and the grav went offline. His suit clicked on the magnetic locks of his boots, anchoring him to the decking. The space around Nate filled with flying particulate, pieces of insect and metal and tungsten round.

The noise would have been terrible. It would have been glorious. Nate had to satisfy himself with the muted transference through the station's frame, the death of fifty, a hundred insects an obituary to the horrors of Station Echo 9. He watched as the *Tyche's* lights moved away, around the disc, carving chunks out of the Ezeroc hive room, destroying it. Obliterating it. He felt no satisfaction. What he felt was desperation.

My Grace. Where have they taken you?

HE'D LEFT Amedea strapped to the chair. Getting her on to the *Tyche* had been tricky but not impossible; a temporary plastic airlock, a tiny bubble that held air against the hard black, had let Nate space walk in and collect her. Once she was safe and secure in the *Tyche*, he'd kept her chained up.

Picking over the wreckage of Station Echo 9 had taken a little more doing. The power was down, the righteous vengeance of the *Tyche* having cored the station's batteries, torn away its solar collectors, and caused it to jettison its reactor to explode at a safe distance. The interior of Echo 9 was black and cold and empty. Pulling out data slivers from machines took time.

But he needed to take the time. He wanted to race after Grace, but he needed a cure. Nate needed to prepare for whatever was out there. Nate wasn't gentle about it, cutting through pieces of computer machinery with a particle saw, grabbing the raw memory crystals out for transfer to the *Tyche*. He'd give them to Hope and see what she could do with them once they were underway.

He wasn't sure how things had come out this way. Where a small wrong turn had set his feet on a path that left the love of his life out in the hard black somewhere with him alive and still breathing on this station. El had taken a look at his face, some quip frozen on her lips, and she'd donned a suit to help him gather information from the station. They'd worked side by side in the cold of space.

When Hope had woken up — a sleep he couldn't begrudge his Engineer, for all she'd been through — she had started work right away on the Endless trail left in space from the shuttle's jump. Tracking the negative space bow wave was possible. Tricky, prone to error. It needed careful work. It was good she was rested. If Nate was any judge, he knew she wouldn't sleep again until her job was done. Hope loved Grace. They all did.

Just in different ways. In different amounts.

Kohl had woken up long enough to swear about his legs. There had been fear there, but he'd put a lid on it when Nate had told him what had happened to Grace. He'd nodded, big head heavy, then said *let's go get our girl. Let's go get our Gracie.*

There was no one there to call him an asshole.

Nate could see it on Kohl's face: he was down and out in the only fight that mattered. That he'd been, what, *sleeping* while their crewmate was captured. Like walking even *mattered*. Kohl could use a gun without legs. And he'd get his chance soon.

After they'd grabbed all the memory slivers they could find, Nate ordered the *Tyche* away. Took his ship out into the hard black to look on Station Echo 9. Then he'd fired a single torpedo into the heart of the station, and watched it burn.

"I HAVE ONE, maybe two pieces of good news," said Hope, the hollows under her eyes speaking of a person in dire need of more sleep. She was rubbing a stim against her gums, the sickly fluid — Nate had used 'em plenty of times before — coating her teeth. "There's one piece of bad news."

"What's the bad?"

"We're out of stims. Last one." She quirked a smile at him. "I'll need to stay up the old-fashioned way."

"Coffee," said El. "No problem. We can double-shot it. Hell, quad shots all around."

"The good news?" said Nate. His voice sounded hollow. His chest felt heavy and empty at the same time. The ready room seemed so empty with that one, crucial person missing.

"I know what the cure for Amedea is." Hope rubbed her face, almost scrubbing at it, trying to snap herself awake. "Oh, right. And I think I know where Grace is. I ... I'm so tired. I think I've made a mistake."

"Grace first," said Nate.

"She's out there," said Hope. She spun up a holo, stars spreading out around them in the ready room. "Here, right, is the edge of human space." There was a glowing approximate-location sphere shown on the holo, Sol its beating heart at the center. "We're here." Station Echo 9's location was blinking outside the edge of human space. "And out here," and she zoomed the stars way out, "is where Grace's jump signature went." A blinking marker showed a new location. It was out among the stars that humans had never charted. Farther out by far than Station Echo 9.

It was Ezeroc space. The heart of their empire.

"Okay," said Nate. "Okay. Hope? I need you to ... I know I've asked a lot of all of you." He wanted to sit down himself, take five, maybe cry a little. *Pull yourself together, Chevell.* "Hope?"

"Cap." Her eyes were tired, but bright. Fierce.

"I need you to do something for me. It'll be the most important thing you've ever done. It will change the universe."

"No pressure," she said.

"No pressure," he agreed. "Because you're up for it. I know you are. It's why you're here." He looked at El, and back to Hope. He thought of Kohl in the sickbay. "It's why we're all here. Call it destiny. Call it luck, but we're here. To save the universe."

CHAPTER NINETEEN

THE SOUND of the Endless Drive spooling down was like the last sigh of a dying man. The inside of the shuttle was warm, uncomfortable, stuffy. Like it needed an airing out, wind from under a clear cool sky to blow through it. There was no clear sky. There was only the hard black.

Grace pressed her face against the shuttle's forward viewport. Harlow was at her shoulder. The man was *terrified/fear/fear/run/panic/terror/run/go/flee* and, she had to admit, he was on to something there. Because they had jumped out into space filled with the dead, the lost, entombed in the cold vacuum where the stars lived.

The planet itself was large and brown. It sat like a dull marble, sucking in all the hope around it. Nothing green grew on that surface. There was no water, no ice. No promising haze against the skyline. A dead rock, full of sand and bones. She knew it was the Ezeroc homeworld. It was the footprint they left: everything eaten. Nothing left alive, just insects as far as the eye could see. Insects that could sleep for a hundred or a thousand years in self-induced stasis, waiting for something to eat. And here was their shuttle, with two tasty morsels onboard.

Human starships orbited the planet. Great hulks of carriers, destroyers, and small vessels that would have been fighters before they'd been holed, their single pilots screaming a last gasp before their air ran out. Here, at the end of the longest jump Grace had ever had, were the remains of a broken human fleet.

Before her mind looked at the alien starships, she noticed an odd detail about the human starships. These were not mighty Republic ships. Oh, there might have been one or two more familiar designs amidst all the wreckage. Accidental toys left out by a vengeful god. No, these starships carried the burnished gold falcon's crest of House Fergelic, mighty birds with wings spread wide, mouths open in a war cry. Almost all the starships she could see were from the Old Empire. The Old Empire that Nate had served like a loyal hound before it had fallen. The common wisdom had said it fell because of the Intelligencers, and that was true. But this new ... *let's call it a data point, anything else is too terrible* ... data point showed that there might have been a motivating factor in that monstrous betrayal. The fall of the human race, the subjugation of it by those who could read and control minds, might have been motivated by fear. Of an enemy you couldn't win against.

We came with words and gifts and weapons, and none of them worked.

Her eyes flitted from hulk to hulk, debris strewn throughout space. She'd seen the side of the *Gladiator*, the destroyer sent to Absalom Delta, cored by a rock tossed by aliens who could move mountains into space. Some of these ships had been crushed, torn, or rent by rocks. But many of them showed evidence of human weapons. Beam weapon burns across the metal skin of a destroyer over there. Torpedo impacts, the carbon edges of a hole blistered and bubbled, on another. A small fighter drifted close to their shuttle — *don't think about how close the Endless Jump took you to hitting that, you've got enough to worry about* — and she could see the pockmarks of kinetic PDC fire across the hull.

These ships had turned on each other.

They can read minds, you see. They know what you're going to do before you do. And they can control minds.

The planet under them turned, unconcerned with her fear. A great crater came into view, a hole the size of a continent, cracks broke out like spider lines in broken glass. They'd dropped a crust buster on the homeworld, at least one, and … what?

We came with weapons.

The planet continued to turn, another hole coming into view. This one was deeper, evidence of multiple impact strikes from crustbusters, one after the other, the rain of fury from human hands onto an alien menace. It made you wonder what you'd do, when faced with an enemy who didn't need air to breathe, that didn't care if an individual drone died, as long as the hive survived. How did you beat an enemy like that? With a sword? A planet? Nukes? What would it take?

None of them worked.

Throughout the long line of human ingenuity, there had been no other foe like this. And they weren't alone. Her eyes strayed to the other floating hulks in space. Alien designs — she couldn't tell which part was fore or aft on some of them. It wasn't obvious how many of them moved, no clear signs of propulsion ports. Some had spindles that might have been weapons. Others had pods that might have been engine nacelles. Some looked to be made of glass rather than metal. All were dark, empty, drifting, dead. Hundreds, and hundreds, and hundreds of alien ships. All come to wage a final war on an alien threat that used their bodies as fuel. An alien threat that *let them come* so their food would be delivered right to their doorstep.

The ships were like a cloud of scum orbiting this world. They were beyond counting. It didn't matter that one on one Grace could use a sword and some fancy moves to cut Ezeroc into component parts. They didn't *care*. There were plenty more where that one came from. And if they ran out, they could use your own team against you, warping their minds. Turning their hearts against their comrades. And against all of this, there was one — exactly *one* — sword that had been made that stopped the powers of the mind. Nate's sword, on a tiny starship. A starship with a mighty heart and a mighty crew, but just four souls — because Grace wasn't there anymore — against *this*. One sword. One ship. Four souls.

"We're fucked," said Grace.

HARLOW HADN'T RESPONDED to her pep talk. He hadn't done much of anything except check his maser, over and over. Turning the weapon in his hands, then looking out the viewport, then looking at the weapon again. Finally, he said, "I don't think I've got enough spare batteries."

She laughed. "Harlow. No. There are not enough spare batteries in the universe for this."

He hefted the weapon. "I'd offer to, you know." He gestured with the business end at his head. "But it's a slow, horrible way to die. Not like a blaster, a bright gout of flame, a moment of pain, and then everything gone. We'd have to boil alive from the inside. It'd be bad."

"It might not be worse than what's to come," said Grace. *What's to come* hadn't yet been defined, but the hissing, clawing static of Ezeroc speech had grown louder, more insistent as the aliens talked among themselves across space. There would be a Queen down there somewhere, a huge insect, ancient and cunning, that was pulling the strings. There would be smaller hives, younger Queens. They'd be trying to work out what to do.

"Might not be," said Harlow, "but, I guess it boils down to a couple of options. You die instantly. You die slower, bleeding out. You die painfully as your brain is eaten by insects. Or, I use the maser, and we die a little faster, but in a lot of pain. I could, I don't know, attach it here." He pointed to the front viewport at the nose of the shuttle. "We'd be unable to get away. Just turn it on, and let the microwaves boil us until we're done."

"I don't want to die," said Grace.

"Me neither," said Harlow. "But I'm not sure we'll get the choice. About the only choice is getting to choose how—" His voice cut off with an *urk* and his body jerked stiff, eyes wide.

Grace! Grace! Grace! Grace! Grace!

You have come.

You will become.

Our Grace.

"Harlow?" said Grace, trying to ignore the Ezeroc speech in her mind. She moved towards the man, checking his pulse — heart still beating. A little fast, but he was carrying a few extra kilos and ran a bar, so that might be usual. She ran her suit's light over his eyes, checking the pupils. No response.

He wheezed, causing her to jerk back, startled. His voice, when it spoke, was flat. "Grace has come. Come. To be."

She backed away from Harlow, her feet taking her to the other side of the shuttle. You might get ten or fifteen guys in here, sure, but that wasn't a lot of space to move around in. Not when the other human onboard was now being piloted by a massive, menacing alien intelligence. "I haven't come." She thought about it. "What do you mean, 'to be?'"

"To be," said Harlow's voice, but not his mind. "To become. To join. Do you see?"

"Not even a little bit," said Grace. "Why ... did you plan to bring us here?"

"Plans. To Be."

"English isn't your thing, is it?"

"Mind. Walls. Unbuild walls. Talk."

"No fucking way," said Grace. "No chance."

"Grace. Become." And then Harlow wheezed, animation returning to his face, and he looked around. "What, uh..."

"It's better if you don't think about it," said Grace. "But I'll take first watch. Get some sleep."

"Did I—"

"It's fine, Harlow." *It's not fine. Goddamn insects just took over Harlow like a sock puppet.* "They'll be coming for us soon."

DESPITE THE FEAR and terror and confusion, Harlow slept. Or, Harlow *passed out* might be more accurate. He sprawled in one of the acceleration couches, head back, limbs jerking every so often in a dream, or a nightmare. Grace didn't want to wake him. Intelligencers couldn't get at you when you were asleep. Bugs were probably the same. Different state of consciousness. So she let him sleep. No need for both of them to panic about what was coming.

That wasn't a metaphor. She could see a rock moving towards them, a big chunk of asteroid that moved through the hard black without an obvious sign of propulsion. On the surface of the asteroid was a human-looking airlock. A docking collar like you'd find on any starship. One you could, if there was a handy supply of spare parts around you, salvage from an existing vessel. Like one of the hundreds of ships scattered out around the Ezeroc homeworld.

No wonder the Old Empire had gone down like a cold glass of water on a hot day. All their ships were *here*, fighting a war against an external enemy. They had nothing else for the internal threat.

Grace shook herself. *No time for thoughts like that.* It was time to get ready. She wasn't going down without a fight. Oh, she knew she was going *down*, but what had Harlow said? She'd do it in the manner of her own choosing. Grace chose death by the blade. She'd always lived by the sword, and now was her chance to have one final, glorious battle.

Her father might, just *might*, have a tiny spark of pride at that.

Speaking of which, he was here, with her, again. A shadow of himself, standing in the shuttle, like he'd stood on that barren world where the snails had been. Then she'd figured concussion, or oxygen deprivation, but now he was here again, she figured she was cracking. There was no harm in it. She was under a lot of strain. She had been for a long, long time. Alone, until she'd found Nate. And Nate might have been the release that let all the pressure out, let her collapse under the weight of it all.

You must listen, Grace. Her father frowned. *Always, you do not listen.*

"I don't listen to assholes," she said. "Fuck off, Dad."

There is a battle coming. It isn't the battle you want. It is the battle you need.

She almost laughed, looking at Harlow for a moment. "Are you channeling the crazy bugs too? Or have they … got to me too?"

Save your strength. Your sword won't help you here.

"You always said to fight, Dad. I'm fighting."

You listen but you don't hear the lesson. His face twisted in disappointment, a familiar enough expression for her to have constructed out of the whole cloth of her memory. *You are my greatest failure.*

"Go die in a fire," she said.

Harlow snorted, coming awake, and her father's vision faded like the sunset. "Huh? What?"

"Get ready," said Grace. "They're coming. It's time to choose, Harlow. Live or die. Fight or submit?"

"Well, fuck," he said. "Where's that damn maser?"

WHEN THE ASTEROID coupled with the shuttle, it was with a clang that shuddered the whole ship. Grace stood near the airlock, sword blade naked and ready. It was a good sword, the best she'd ever owned. Given to her by a friend, one of the very, very few she had. She would die, and she'd never be able to thank Hope for such a wonderful gift.

Harlow stood behind her and off to the side, using one of the acceleration couches for cover. His maser was out and ready. Not that Grace figured on him being able to get much mileage from it; if it came to that kind of battle, the Ezeroc would reach out a hand and turn him into a marionette. This close to their eldest Queen, there would be no mistakes. No subtle suggestions. No room for doubt. Harlow — all that he was — would be shoved aside, and the aliens would take over.

The airlock hissed, Grace's ears popping as the pressure equalized. That was useful — the rock seemed to have atmosphere. She raised her sword, ready. The lock clanked open, yawning into a cavernous entryway.

An *empty* entryway.

The hissing of the Ezeroc grew to a susurration, then to a roar, an ululation. It was the sound of a million billion insects raising their voices in a song of triumph. Grace found herself on one knee, a groan coming from her, but she held her blade up, that bright line of metal forged in the heart of the Goddess of Luck. *Hope gave you this blade. Use it, and die well.* Grace forced herself to her feet, struggling under the weight of that vast sea of alien intelligence.

GRACE! GRACE! GRACE!

"Fuck off," she said.

Silence. Harlow said, from behind her, "What?"

"Not you, Harlow," said Grace, her voice more croak than words. She cleared her throat. "They're waiting for us. In there."

"Okay," said Harlow. "Hypothetically, what would happen if we didn't go into the rock of death?"

"We'd run out of air," said Grace.

"That's not so bad," said Harlow.

"It's not the death I choose," said Grace, and stepped into the Ezeroc asteroid.

HARLOW MIGHT HAVE BEEN *TERROR/FEAR/PANIC/FEAR/RUN/RUN* on the inside, but on the outside he just carried a sheen of sweat and the maser. Grace liked that. She liked it when people could be their best selves, even when it wasn't in their best interests.

The interior of the Ezeroc asteroid was organic, hollowed-out like the tunnels in the moon had been. Clawed limbs had chipped away at the rock, creating a warren inside. Bioluminescent light came from pods against the wall, their glow a uniform red. There was no heat, the interior as cold as the grave, and Grace shivered. It made sense though: if the bugs could survive in the vacuum of space without air, they could do the same without heat.

There was a clatter of rock from up ahead and Harlow's maser whipped up, a whine sounding as the weapon cycled to a ready state. They both froze, waiting.

Nothing.

There was gravity in this asteroid. The rock was tiny, too small to have a noticeable drag against the body, but gravity still pulled her down. Perhaps another borrowed piece of human technology, because the Ezeroc didn't appear concerned with up and down. Those limbs of theirs seemed well-suited to clambering around the inside of cold, dark places. The gravity meant that there was an *up* and a *down*, and the *down* was where they had come from. Up was where the monsters were.

Which was borderline insulting. Making them walk *up* to death was just salt in the wound. Grace gritted her teeth, hand clenched around the hilt of her sword. She wondered if this was where she would regret not packing a blaster at her hip. Grace wondered if she would ever see Nate again. She wondered if she'd be strong enough to die before telling the Ezeroc where he was.

The tunnel opened into a small chamber, rocky walls bare except for the luminous pods drenching everything in a coarse, ochre light. Her blade gleamed like it was already wet with blood. Except only humans had red blood. The Ezeroc had green and white and bile inside them. In the middle of the chamber were three Ezeroc drones.

Grace. Become. Grace Grace Grace become Grace.

To be.

She raised her sword, ready to charge, when one of the Ezeroc listed. Grace paused, watching the creature as it toppled, the chest carapace rupturing to vent steam. She turned to Harlow, his maser extended in a shaking hand.

Strike one down. Another comes. To be.

An Ezeroc drone clambered out of a circular hole in the top of the chamber to drop to where its fallen kin lay. Three had become two, and now were three again. It would be a hard fight. At least Harlow hadn't shot her with the maser. It was peculiar they didn't have his mind in a clutch, and she wondered if enough raw terror was enough to keep the insects out. Strong emotions had always buffeted her, forced her away, sometimes made her feel what the person was feeling. It made a weird kind of sense.

"Who's next?" she said.

Not. To be.

Grace!

She noticed an odor coming to her, not the stench of ruptured Ezeroc, that rotting cinnamon smell, but something else. Musky. Heady. Like coffee, sex, and roast meat. She looked at the Ezeroc drones — still not moving, then turned back to Harlow.

Who was on the ground, lights out, unconscious.

She turned back to the Ezeroc, but found it hard. So hard, because she was down on a knee. Her sword fell from her fingers.

Grace!

"Oh, you *assholes*," she said, then fell face-first onto the rocky floor of the chamber.

CHAPTER TWENTY

NATE STALKED the corridors of the *Torrington* like it was his ship. It wasn't; it belonged to Karkoski. Not like she'd been appointed to captain the ship, because that wasn't the case. Karkoski had taken control of this ship, led a mutiny against the previous captain, and held control of a crew loyal to the Republic under whose flag they all sailed.

It was worth bearing in mind: Karkoski was skilled at running a starship, and she was also capable of mutiny. It could be problematic. Not that Nate figured on running the *Torrington*. He had his own ship, made his own luck, and the *Torrington* was wrong in all the ways the *Tyche* was right.

Still. Having big friends in a fight was useful.

He cleared the entrance to the officer's mess, charting a path straight for Karkoski. Her uniform was immaculate as always, but she'd left off the formal Republic emblems, keeping just her rank insignia. She wasn't flying for the Republic as such: she was flying for humanity.

"Captain," she said, nodding at him over a cup of what was almost certainly horrible coffee.

"Karkoski," he said, slipping down across from her. "I'm here to say farewell."

She continued to look at him over the rim of her cup. "Why?"

He blinked. "Got a person in a bind. Time to go get her."

"I understand that. But why 'goodbye,' Captain?"

"Because I'm going to fly," he pointed out the officer lounge's wide windows, "out there somewhere." He wasn't sure if where he was pointing was the right direction, but it didn't matter. It made a statement.

"I see," she said. "And what makes you think the *Torrington* isn't going that way as well?"

He looked at his hands, splayed on the table in front of him, one metal hand, one flesh and blood, then met her eyes. "Because it's not your crew. I know how the waters look, Karkoski. You're not the kind of person to take risks. Not with your new command. Your new Resistance. You're onto something good, here." He softened his voice. "That's unfair. It's … we'll need you, but later."

"There won't be a later," said Karkoski, still not moving her cup. "There is barely a now. The Senate is crumbling, Captain. It was riddled with corruption, which is normally just *fine*. It's how things work. But the corruption was rooted in alien mischief. Humanity is rudderless. Without leadership. We've routed the bugs from Earth, but how far has the corruption spread? We need to take this fight to them. We need to … cut out the cancer." She looked out the window, then back to him. "I won't have a command to enjoy without the rest of the human race."

"Also, Grace knows a heap about us," said Chad, slipping in beside them, a tray of food in his hands. "About how we work. About our plans. If there's one thing worse than bugs that can read minds and control thoughts, it's those bugs learning our tricks."

Nate sighed. "I figure I need to do a little information sharing." He pulled up his console, tagging data and sending it across the ship net. "Hope's found out that some kind of massive force went to the bug world and didn't come back."

"Old Empire," said Karkoski. "Not Republic."

"Not Intelligencers," said Chad.

Nate looked between them. "What are you not telling me?"

"Many things," said Karkoski. "Spare me a few more minutes before you say goodbye, Captain. I have something to show you."

THE *TORRINGTON'S* medbay put the *Tyche's* to shame. Big, spacious, equipment of the latest manufacture. It was not highly occupied; the odd crew member on a bed here or there from a training injury. One woman was burned, unconscious, machines tending to her. Otherwise, not much of interest here. Excepting Kohl, who was wired up to about a hundred machines, out for the count. No doubt having the best dreams of his life, because he was on medical-grade drugs. The best kind. Nothing here of interest at all.

That's if you didn't count Amedea.

She was sitting up on the edge of her bed, eyes no longer dulled by drugs or mind control or whatever had happened on Station Echo 9. There was a holo stage showing her vitals, an outline of her body lined in blue. Nate looked at Amedea, then at Karkoski, then at Chad, who was still eating a sandwich. He turned to the doctor, his white medical uniform pinned with a lieutenant's insignia. Also no Republic branding. Interesting.

"So," said Nate. He was itching to go, because his Grace was out there.

"So," agreed Karkoski. "Doctor?"

The doctor nodded, then worked the console, zooming the holo in on Amedea's head. "Here."

"Cool," said Nate. The image was blues and blacks. "What am I looking at?"

"First thing," said Chad, "is that she's missing pieces of her brain."

"Unfortunate side effect of having insects living in her brain cavity," said the doctor. "What you will note is that the insects are *gone*."

"The cure," said Nate.

"The cure," said Karkoski, "which your Engineer uncovered. The data crystals from Station Echo 9 contain a wealth of hard-won intelligence. One of them is that nanites, programmed in a particular way, will hunt out the Ezeroc larvae and consume them."

"Our tiny bugs eating theirs?" said Nate.

The doctor wobbled his hand in the air. "Kind of. It's illegal. It looks like AI. It's a little more complicated—"

"Is she brain-dead?" said Nate.

"I'm right here," said Amedea. "I am … here. I. I. Am."

"Not brain-dead," said the doctor. "The problem is there are … missing components. In Amedea's case, parts of her cortex that control movement, speech, and facets of memory have been consumed by the insects."

"That sounds rough," said Nate.

"Memories won't return," said the doctor. He gestured at Nate's hand. "But we can … fix the other problems."

"Okay," said Nate. "What's this got to do with me?"

"Amedea has something to tell you," said Karkoski. "Don't you, Amedea?"

IT TOOK a long time in the telling. The telling was augmented by recordings of insane babbling of Amedea as the nanites fixed her mind. The recordings didn't make it look painless. The trick, as the doctor explained, was to have the nanites attack the Ezeroc larvae without them being aware of it. They weren't in the mind-reading state at that point in development. The doctor had said *a cure could only be administered if there is not a neighboring watcher intelligence*, which sounded to Nate like a clinical way of saying *your friends are all fucked if you can't extract them to a safe haven*. The implications were clear: the brain bugs might just clean house inside a brain cavity, taking the ship down with them, so to speak.

In this instance, it suggested that there were no Ezeroc sleeper agents on the *Torrington*, which would help Karkoski sleep easier at night. That wasn't the point.

The nanites invaded the bloodstream, seeking hostile tissue. The doctor had called it *repurposed tech* and mentioned something about how cancer was cured, like insects in your skull were a kind of cancer. And Nate figured he was on to something there. The nanites snuck on up alongside the Ezeroc larvae, who were lunching down on brain tissue, and invaded their cells in turn. Like a turducken, a thing inside a thing inside a thing. They coordinated electronically, signals the Ezeroc seemed to have trouble with, working their way up to the Ezeroc ganglion, and shutting it down. From there, they worked like tiny wheat threshers, milling the Ezeroc tissue into slurry, ferrying it out of the bloodstream to be waste matter.

Amedea had been pissing and shitting bloody material for hours.

Half-way through the … *recovery* process, she'd grabbed the arm of a passing medtech, and said she'd wanted to confess. The tech hadn't known what that meant, but had got the doctor to stop by. The doctor had asked about the confession, and Amedea said she didn't remember. She said she remembered *his brother's sword*, a blade of black metal.

The doctor paused the recording then, turning to Nate. "Do you know what she means?"

No one spoke for a moment, then Chad said, "There is only one black blade I've ever seen. Metal doesn't come out that color as a general rule."

Nate curled his fingers, wanting to reach for that sword because it would be nice to hold onto something solid. He'd left it in other, more capable hands on the *Tyche*. He didn't say anything.

"Interesting that the most powerful tool in a war against the Ezeroc would be given to a fallen member of the Emperor's Black," offered Karkoski. "While the Emperor sent off the remains of his military to fight a damn fool war while the rise of a Republic was ... imminent. It wasn't a Republic then. Just a bunch of people who didn't want to serve under an Emperor they hadn't voted for."

"House Fergelic was *good*," said Nate. "Dom was a good man."

"Dom and Annemarie were Intelligencers. The first of their kind," said Karkoski. "Near as we know. And also, near as we know, it flows in all their family. Some a little better than others. But it's engineered, like green eyes or brown hair or a big nose. All it takes is a little training."

Amedea was looking at Nate, her eyes piercing. She looked like she wanted to walk towards him if only she could remember how. "Brother," she said. "Black metal. Black secret."

"Well, hey now," said Nate. "No. Hey. No. Definitely not."

"There are only a few who would know the truth," said Karkoski. "A few who knew who the bastard brother of the Emperor was. Who was sent away so someone would live as the rest of the House fell."

Nate took two steps back, because it was crazy. His legs hit the side of a chair and he fell into it. "Dom was ... my friend."

"No friend gives a sword that can save the whole human race to an *ordinary man*," said Karkoski. "They might give it to their child, or their lover, or ... their brother."

"My father's name is Chevell," said Nate, like it was an excuse.

"The man who raised you?" said Chad. "Sure. He's a Chevell."

"You're all crazy," said Nate.

"We'd be crazy if there wasn't proof," said the doctor.

"You what?" said Nate.

"Dominic Fergelic, of House Fergelic, Emperor Prirene IV, was ruler of all humanity. His life was documented down to the last detail," said the doctor. "Those records are a matter of record. Even his medical records, which show his genetics. We could remake his body tomorrow if we wanted. We also have," he tapped on his console, shifting the holo of Amedea aside, "your DNA, Captain." The doctor pulled up two twisting helixes on the holo, a set of coded markers floating between them. "Here."

"What am I looking at?" said Nate.

"Familial match," said the doctor. "You are related to Dominic Fergelic. Annemarie, too, as it happens. Which is no surprise, since they are brother and sister. You are their half-brother."

"I need a beer," said Nate. He'd never needed a drink more in his life.

"Yes," said Karkoski. "It's a lot to take in. But when the dust has settled, humanity will need a little leadership, Nate."

"Hell no," said Nate.

She laughed. "Don't panic. No one person will ever have that power again. But a figurehead? That's a useful thing, don't you agree?"

Nate thought about it for two or three whole seconds, then he stood up. "Fuck all this shit. I'm going to get my girl."

"Ah," said Karkoski. "Now you see why you can't go, right?"

"What?"

"We toyed with the idea about locking you up, Captain. But that wouldn't work. So, we — Admiral of your Navy, and Chad here, head of your Intelligencers — figured we'd just lock your ship to the side of the *Torrington*. To stop you dying. To save humanity. How does that sound?"

CHAPTER TWENTY-ONE

SHE COULD NEVER REMEMBER BEING SO thirsty.

She couldn't remember her name.

Darkness. Not total darkness, not the smothering of the womb, but close to it. A low, ruddy glow infused the room around her. Everything looked like it had been soaked in blood and left to dry, the wind chapping at it until it became close to black. Close to dead.

So very thirsty.

Across from her was a man. He looked familiar, and she knew she had been on a voyage with him. A comrade, at her side, to help her through. She couldn't remember his name either. The man was awake, his eyes open, swiveling in their sockets, roaming, glinting in the red light. She thought he looked—

Pain/terror/run/trapped/run/fear.

—scared, frightened of something he'd seen, or experienced. Or perhaps something that had not yet come to pass. The man was encased around his arms and legs and a part of his torso in a chunky material, something that looked like globs of resin or fat or growing tumors. She was sure that wasn't what had made him so frightened though. On top of his head was a thing that looked like a spider, an oversized daddy longlegs, with a wide, thin body and legs like needles. They were so thin they were hard to see in the red light. It was poised over the man's head, those thin, terrible legs holding it upright.

Even that wouldn't be the thing that would make this man scared. She was sure he'd faced down horrors before. This man had done things that would make normal people run screaming. No, a spider on his face wasn't the thing that made him scared. It was that the top of his skull was gone, his brain visible to her in the low light, and the spider was walking over the spongey material. Inserting a long limb here, another there. There was a halo of blood around his skull where the bone had been removed. There was no sign of the missing part of his skull, no pile of hair and bone on the ground, just … nothing. Half his head was gone, and he wasn't getting it back.

It had been eaten by something, she was sure of it. She wasn't sure what, though.

That was what made him scared: that he was being analyzed, taken apart, and that there didn't look to be a way back from it. With a good med bay—

A starship. You know the smiling face of luck.

—and enough time, you could grow a man's head back, or put a metal plate over the top. Here, in the—

Hard black. An asteroid. A ship made of stones.

—place they were, there was no chance he would make it. They didn't even have a helmet between them. There was no escape. No, he was a lab animal, and they'd work on his body until there was nothing left. She didn't know why they started with his brain. Was it a mercy? End the person and then start on the meat?

He was a … friend of someone she knew, someone dear to her.

Why couldn't she remember?

Just a drink of water. Her throat felt like it was made of sand.

She wanted to shake her head to clear it, but she couldn't move. Her face was held by something that felt like rock, if rock could flex a little. Porous. Fibrous. Sticky. She made to lick her lips, but her tongue was swollen. Dry. Like thick paper in her mouth.

The man across from her spoke, his voice a rasp. "It'll be okay." He said it in a way that said he didn't believe it, but he wanted her to.

"Who are you?" she said.

"I don't remember," he said. His face jerked in a spasm as the spiderling probed his brain with a limb. She'd heard somewhere the brain had few actual pain receptors in it. It might not hurt much. But having your brain probed with a needle? It was bound to leave an impression. "I ... who are you?"

"I don't remember either," she said. Then, because it felt like a favor she needed to return, she said, "It'll be okay."

"Not for me," he said. The spiderling's leg dipped in again, and he said, "Giraffe! He sings, but it is stone."

"They're ... pulling us apart," she said.

"I don't think so," he said. "They're pulling *me* apart. You, I think. I think. They have. Something different. A plan."

"I'm thirsty," she admitted.

"I'm dying," he agreed. "They have a test."

"What is it?"

"You must free me," he said. "I don't understand." The leg dipped into his brain again, and he coughed, almost a squawk. "With your mind. Do you know your mind?"

"I don't know my name," she said. "How can I know my mind?"

"If you free me with your mind, we can both go home," he said. "They want you to touch the resin around my arms. Tear it off."

She struggled against her bonds for a moment. "I ... can't get loose. I can't get to you."

"With your mind," he said. "Your mind is ... stronger than your body. Faster. You do instinctively what the rest must concentrate to manage. They promised. If you do this, we both live."

Why couldn't she remember her name?

DARKNESS. Low, red light bathing every surface around her.

She had slept, and now she was awake. Just like that. She could remember a scent, like an animal, like coffee. It made her hungry. It made her sick.

Oh, God, just one drop of water. Just one. She would say anything for a drink. A tiny sip. She would even take dirty water, foul, warm, muddy. It could taste of piss, it could be mixed with bile. A thimbleful is all she needed.

Please.

The man across from her was dead. She was sure of it, his sightless eyes no longer roaming the room. Much of his brain was missing, his head lolling forward on a neck gone slack. The interior of his head was being emptied by small insects that looked like ants. They were ferrying pieces of brain up towards a hole in the roof. A little piece here, snipped out, and then carried up.

She could feel something on her head. A long, thin leg passed in front of her vision for a moment, so quick she figured she'd imagined it. Or hoped she'd imagined it, because the alternative was sitting on the other side of the room. A man, his head torn open, his brain removed. Dead.

This wasn't the manner she'd chosen for her own death. She was sure of it.

A long-limbed spiderling crawled down from the roof towards the corpse across from her. It bunched those long limbs around itself as it cozied into the now empty brain cavity of the man. It probed deep with those thin legs, and the body jerked a few times. Then the head rose, eyes still sightless, but the mouth opened and closed. The chest expanded as it sucked in some air. Then it spoke. The voice it used was familiar, but the tone was wrong. The man was gone, replaced by a monster. "The second test. Speak."

"What have you done with him?"

"Using your mind," the body said. "Your lips are the vehicle of a dumb animal. Your mind is pure." The chest worked again, breathing out, breathing in. A gross approximation of life.

"You…" she searched her memory. "Assholes?"

"If you. Animal. If you talk like one. Treat you like one." The lips quivered on the face, drool escaping, red with the light or blood or both. "The others like you. For them it is hard. What you do. Easy. We fix the rest. Make you better. Speak. Your mind. Use it."

She felt like it wanted something she couldn't do. That she'd never been able to do. She wasn't sure how she could do a thing that was impossible. It was like … what? Like trying to climb a tree if you were a fish. With a lot of time, and technology, you could make a fish tank with mechanical legs, or wings, but she was stuck to a wall by resin and with the only other human within—

You traveled across a vast sea of space to get here. Hundreds of light years.

—a very long distance dead, she felt like she was out of options to make better fish tanks.

"I can't," she said. "I know what you mean, but … I've never been able to."

Just like the mongrel you are, said her father. *Even when your life depends on it.*

"Not now, Dad," she said. How did she know it was her father when she couldn't even remember her name? Was her father alive or dead? Was this a dream or something else?

The body across from her twitched again. "Together. Must be. We begin."

"Begin what?" she said, then felt those tiny points of legs against her skull. At least she still had a skull. Right?

The pain, when the sawing started, made her scream, and scream, and scream.

CHAPTER TWENTY-TWO

"WHY'S MY SHIP ON LOCKDOWN?" said El, arms crossed, expression tired and pissed off at the same time.

Nate considered the question. A fair one. Where to start? They were in the ready room on the *Tyche*, the ship getting emptier by the moment. His girl — his saving Grace — was gone, taken from under his nose by a bunch of twice-damned insects. His deckhand, October Kohl, had gone down, out for the count, because he'd taken shrapnel through his spine. Kohl had managed to save Grace. Nate hadn't even made it that far, just standing on the wrong side of a door with a worthless plasma cannon.

"It's not *your* ship," said Hope, looking down. She looked threadbare. She'd been working harder than any of them, what with pulling data out of Station Echo 9's memory crystals, and the special project Nate had given to her. "It's not my ship either."

"You're saying it's *his* ship?" said El.

"It's *our* ship," said Hope. "Our *Tyche*."

There was a moment of silence, then El said, "I can live with that."

"So, there's been a few developments," said Nate. "What we've got here is a basic clusterfuck."

"Walks like a duck, talks like a duck," agreed El.

"There's ... a few things I'm having trouble processing, but it'll be *great* if I could just lay 'em out for you before you interrupt with a bunch of questions I can't answer," said Nate. "Okay?"

"You're the captain," said El, meaning, *I'm curious now.*

"I met with Karkoski and Chad," said Nate.

"How are they?" said Hope.

"Interruptions," said Nate.

"Sorry."

"So, so. Karkoski. Uh, Chad," said Nate. "The thing is. Uh..."

"This story going to take a long time?" said El. "Only, we've got a crew member out on the edge of space we need to be getting to."

"Yeah," said Nate. "Karkoski has this wild theory. Crazy, okay? She says I'm the bastard half-brother of the Emperor Dominic Fergelic. She said they had proof, which they showed me, and I didn't understand half of it, or even a little bit of it, but that's not important."

"It seems important," said El, leaning forward, frame stiffened with surprise.

"It kinda is," said Hope.

"The *important* part is that they want to make me some kind of figurehead for a new Empire. After the smoke has settled. Nice banquets, I guess, a bunch of meetings with people. Kissing babies, opening new space ports by cutting a ribbon. You know the drill. The net effect of this is that they do not want me, and they were specific on this particular point, to go racing off across the galaxy to rescue one of my crew."

"They offer an alternative suggestion about how we get Grace back?" said El.

"They did not," said Nate. "I'm kinda surprised you're not more taken aback by the whole related-to-the-Emperor thing."

"So, what are we going to do?" said Hope. Meaning, of course, *about Grace*.

"We're going anyway," said Nate.

"Good," said Hope.

"Ship's still on lockdown," said El.

"Yeah, well, about that," said Nate. "I think we need to solve that particular problem."

"You're the Emperor?" said El.

"What? No!"

"Good," she said, "because I can barely get around calling you, 'Captain.' 'My Lord,' or, hell, even, 'sir, will be a reach."

"Thanks for your support," said Nate.

"Yeah, sure," she said. "What's the plan?"

"Here's what we're going to do," said Nate.

WHEN HE AND El made the med bay, they were met by a contingent of Marines. Five strong, tough looking men and women wearing armor and hard stares. Nate was flattered. *Five Marines. For little ol' me.* "You fellas weren't here before," said Nate.

Not a muscle twitched. No one moved. Which meant no hands on blasters.

"I figure you're here to stop me extracting October Kohl," said Nate.

"Sir," said one. "Yes, sir."

"Carry on then," said Nate, to the surprise of the Marine.

"We brought the man chocolate," said El, holding up a box. They'd procured it from the *Torrington's* commissary. "That okay?"

The Marine who'd spoken moved aside. "Go ahead."

They moved on by the Marines, navigating towards Kohl's bed. Kohl was awake, eyes bleary. "Cap," he said. "El."

Nate pulled up a chair next to Kohl. "I need to bring you up to speed," he said.

"What's in the box?" said Kohl.

"Chocolate," said El.

"Great," said Kohl. "Hospital food sucks balls."

"Before we get to the chocolate, we've got ourselves a bit of a thing," said Nate. "Short version or long?"

"Never been much for the long version."

"Turns out I'm the half-brother of the dead Emperor. We're being held in ... protective custody on the *Torrington*. Grace is out in space somewhere and we need to go get her."

"You're the fucking *emperor*?" said Kohl. "That figures."

"What's that supposed to mean?"

"Natural at givin' orders, is all," said Kohl, in a way that suggested it wasn't *all*. "So what are we going to do?"

"We're going to get Grace."

"Fucken A," said Kohl. "You know I'm in, like, the hospital?"

"Yes," said Nate.

"It's not chocolate, is it?" said Kohl.

"No," said Nate.

"What is it?"

"It's pain in a box," said El. "Of two particular kinds. One is for you, and one is for them," she said, jerking her head towards the Marines guarding the doorway.

"Okay," said Kohl. "The pain for me. Let's start there."

"There's a funny story you missed while you were asleep," said Nate. "Seems there's nanites that can be programmed to do various functions like fighting cancer, that kind of thing. Illegal AI tech."

"Hope thought they could be programmed for other things," said El. "Like gobbling up the pieces of stone in your spine. They can rebuild freshly-injured tissue too. She spoke in that language that sounds like English, but is something different. I was just nodding along at that point."

"Huh," said Kohl. "I'll walk again? On my own legs? Not that metal shit? No offense, Cap."

"Maybe," said Nate. "She had to hack the ship's systems. Get a program from the *Torrington* that would rebuild your spinal column."

"She figures it'll work?" said Kohl.

"She said there's two basic paths," said Nate. "She was not making a lot of sense, on account of her being tired. But the first path? You walk again. Second path? You die screaming. She gave it fifty-fifty. She said," he scratched his head, "she didn't understand the tech herself. AI is illegal. No one's studied it in years. She's not a doctor, Kohl. Hope's an Engineer. She said she's 'borrowing code' and that she 'hates to borrow code.'"

"Huh," said Kohl again. "I guess I'll take Hope's fifty-fifty over anyone else's ninety-ten."

"Okay," said Nate. "Here's the plan." He opened the box, pulling out the top tray of chocolates and handing them to Kohl. "Eat these."

"Why?"

"Because they're tasty. We ate the rest," said Nate. "But also, because your body will need something to work with. Or so Hope figures. The nanites will cannibalize tissue if they have to."

Kohl grabbed a chocolate and munched. "You're right, they're not bad. What's the rest of the plan?"

"That's where this comes in," said Nate, emptying the items in the box onto Kohl's bed. "With these and a little luck we'll be fine."

CHAPTER TWENTY-THREE

"YOU CAN'T BE HERE," said the Marine, looking down at Hope.

"Okay," said Hope, not moving. They were standing nowhere near the *Tyche*. Not by the airlock, not by the docking clamps, because all of that would be obvious. They were was outside the officer's mess. "Only, I need more stims."

"Med bay or commissary," said the Marine. She was a big unit, as far as things went. Bigger by far than Hope's tiny frame, even with the rig.

"I need *good* stims," said Hope. "The ones in the med bay make my teeth hurt." She leaned against the wall next to the Marine.

"I know, right?" said the Marine. She shrugged muscular shoulders inside her armor.

Hope wanted to touch them, to feel them, but also knew she should focus. Having sex with a Marine would be fun, in alternative circumstances. Thinking about having sex made her think a little bit of Reiko, which wasn't good for her focus. "I'll be a minute," said Hope. "Or, you could go."

"Do I look like an officer?" said the Marine.

"You look like you *could* be an officer," said Hope. She looked down, then back up. "In different clothes."

"Huh," said the Marine. She eyed Hope back. "I think I see."

"Only," said Hope, brushing pink hair away from her face, "*stims*."

"Okay," said the Marine. "Here's how you get your stims. Only, you didn't hear it from me."

HOW TO GET STIMS 101: *a treatise.* Hope rounded the corridors of the *Torrington* like she should be there. Nate had said it was all in the walk. Don't look like you're looking for something. Don't look like you shouldn't be there. Don't look like you don't know where you are. *Walk like you've got a purpose,* he'd said, *and people will just assume it's true.*

It's a military ship, Hope had said.

They know we're here, he'd said. *Let's use that to our advantage.*

The Marine had directed her to the back of the officer's mess, where there was an entrance to a small galley. Inside the galley were a bunch of harried-looking chefs, who were — in Hope's experience — the only people more stressed than starship Engineers. She had a level of sympathy for them based on what was about to come.

Her rig — now she had her visor up, like an Engineer would, when looking for a problem — was highlighting conduits in the ceiling that carried power, fluids, and gasses. She wasn't interested in any of that, except for when they hit a junction box in a wall. *In* a wall, not *on* the wall, which meant she needed to get inside it. The arms of her rig — repaired, shiny and clean — extended out, cutting a hole in the *Torrington's* skin. There were a few people walking past — *look like you're meant to be there, look like you're meant to be there* — who she ignored. The panel of metal fell to the deck, the edges still glowing in places with heat. The rig reached into the compartment and began to work.

"Hey," said a man's voice, and Hope turned. Uniform. Not armor. Ship's crew. Hope had no idea what the insignias on the uniform meant. Was this an officer? Someone in charge?

"Hi," said Hope, not lowering her visor.

"What are you doing?"

"Reports said there's power fluctuations in this area," said Hope. "I'm working on it. There's all kinds of problems in the officer's galley. Hot is cold, cold is hot if you listen to the chefs. Like that could ever happen." She threw in what she hoped was a conspiratorial chuckle.

"Power seems fine," said the uniform, as the lights in that section of the ship went out.

"Fine?" said Hope.

"Get on it, Engineer!" said the uniform.

Hope shrugged, turned back to the hole in the wall, and went back to work. The uniform hurried off. After he'd gone, Hope moved towards the officer's mess galley.

WHICH WAS CHAOS. There were cooks running around, in almost total darkness. Hope's visor helped her see in low light, so she moved through them with a little care. A duck here, a sideways step there, and she was almost where she needed to be: the officer's mess. She paused in near the doorway leading out there, next to a pile of supplies. Not just any supplies.

Stims. She pocketed a handful, and then on a whim, another handful. It might be a while before she had time for more sleep. Then she stepped into the officer's mess.

As predicted: chaos here too. No lights, people using portable consoles for illumination, other people moving with busy, officer-like efficiency with no particular place to go and no one to yell at. She needed one thing and she could be done with this.

There. A vacant console. She checked it — locked. She moved to another one. Locked.

Third time she got lucky. That's all she'd needed, just a little luck. This one was still logged in, holo glowing in the darkness, and Hope sat in front of it. She flipped through the menus, finding the controls for the docking systems on the *Torrington*. Social hacks were always the best; doing this the hard way would have been much, much trickier.

A little tap here, a small correction there, and *voila*: the *Tyche* was no longer under lockdown. And it had all been authorized by the fine Lieutenant Babich. Babich was in for a rough time in about half an hour.

Hope got up, making her way back out through the mess galley, ducking through people still whirling like they'd never seen a whole chicken catch on fire, and made it to the corridor outside. She considered the hole cut in the *Torrington*, and decided she'd leave it like that. No point in wasting time fixing something someone else would recheck and re-fix anyway. They needed to go get Grace.

CHAPTER TWENTY-FOUR

AFTER THE CAP and El had gone off to talk sweet love to the Marines at the door, Kohl considered the tray of chocolates and the two things underneath. One was a standard-looking hypo with a yellow fluid inside. The second was a stunner. No laser, maser, or blaster. No. They'd given him, October Kohl, a stunner. When he'd bellyached about it, Nate had said he'd figured on Kohl not needing the stunner at all. *A big man like you*, things of that nature.

He ate another chocolate. They were pretty good.

Stop putting it off. He picked up the hypo. Fifty-fifty, huh? No problem. He pressed it against his thigh and squeezed the trigger. The hiss of the hypo, but no pain because he was missing pieces of his spine as it injected whatever the hell that yellow gunk was into his leg, and then ... nothing.

Hell. They'd said this would hurt. If—

SWEET MOTHER OF CHRIST. He arched his back, fingers curling into claws, mouth wide. It felt like someone had installed a million tiny locusts in his back, all of them hungry. He had a moment to appreciate that feeling anything in his back was a miracle before he convulsed. His legs spasmed, the remains of the chocolates falling to the floor. The machines he was hooked up to started beeping, and an alarm sounded. Kohl wanted to scream. He really did, but he couldn't. His whole chest was locked up with the pain of it, hands threshing at the covers on his bed. He knocked a machine over, and one tube in his arm was yanked free. It was such a tiny pain he didn't even register it. Not against the tsunami of agony in his back.

A medtech ran over to him, shouting something about *what was in this* and *what did you do*, holding the empty hypo up. Kohl ignored the man, not out of rudeness, but out of pain. He convulsed, and felt foam forming on his lips. His body shook and he fell out of the bed and onto the floor.

THE VIEW from the floor was fine. Cool tiles against his face. Boots coming towards him. He pulled himself towards the stunner which had — perhaps conveniently — fallen to the floor. It was — perhaps inconveniently — on the other side of the bed from where he'd fallen.

At least his back didn't hurt.

Rough hands hauled him upright. He could feel his feet as they touched the ground. No more lost sensation. That right there was fucken awesome. Kohl had wondered if he'd spend the rest of his days chained to machinery to help him walk, or maybe a replacement set of legs like the captain had. Nate bellyached a whole bunch about that arm and that leg, and from Kohl's perspective there was something right and wrong at the same time about that. Wrong: sure, having a metal hand might interfere with a few flesh-on-flesh activities. Get in the way. Cramp a man's style. Right: having a metal hand you could hit people with and not worry about breaking your knuckles? That shit would be priceless.

It depended on your view of how full the glass was. Kohl wasn't a half-full or half-empty kind of guy. He was a toss-out-the-water-then-fill-it-with-whiskey kind of guy. And what Hope had put in that hypo? Pure whiskey all the way.

It was a kind of whiskey that these damn Marines weren't expecting. They'd figured on grabbing a cripple off the ground, bawling him out some for making them leave their posts, and then that'd be that. Quick assessment: the hands were connected to Marines, two of them, some serious looking motherfuckers packing armor (not powered, which was a mercy) and lasers. All that made sense. Power armor wasn't just unnecessary on your own starship; it was a huge pain in the ass. You'd be knocking over your CO and tearing bulkheads off by accident. But your basic, everyday on-duty Marine would want to look the part, so here they were, armor made of a high-strength polymer. Strong, light, take a kinetic round no problem, but also feel the heat of a laser and have nothing to show for it but a little carbon scoring. Your basic Marine also carried a weapon or three. These fine gents looked to be packing a sidearm (difficult to determine the type on account of Kohl's eyes not working great as they were hauled on past), a knife (and why wouldn't you?), and a laser carbine. That last made perfect sense, because a blaster might hole your hull, and kinetic rounds were out for the same reason. No stunners, which meant these particular Marines were in a not-fuck-around frame of mind.

It was good to know.

The hands shook Kohl in preparation. Maybe that predicted bawling-out, or it could be a beating (although Marines, as a general rule, weren't that kind of asshole; you didn't beat on a cripple). Which lead to Kohl's thing the third: he was covered in various fluids. Some of it was plain ol' saline from a bag he'd dragged down to the floor with him, rupturing the contents all over himself and the floor. Some of it was vomit, courtesy of Kohl's own stomach. Half-digested chocolate and bile. Not a winning combination at the best of times. It made Kohl want to get away from himself, and he figured that was why the rough hands were holding him at arm's length, rather than a secure hold. If Kohl had been doing the holding, he would have cozied on up, maybe put a wrist-lock on, and to hell with concerns over getting covered in another man's sick. That was just the cost of doing this kind of business.

Kohl let his head loll around, for two reasons. The first was that he wasn't sure he had the strength to hold it upright, and the second was that it gave him a good excuse to have a look around. He picked out the surroundings. Two Marines, close to him. A medtech of some kind, maybe a doctor, readying some kind of hypo. That would cause problems for someone, and Kohl suspected that someone was Kohl himself. Feeling a little under the weather as he was, Kohl might have just let this one ride out. Let himself be tucked back into his bed, maybe had himself some hospital food and a grope at a passing tech. But the cap said they were leaving. The cap said Gracie was in trouble. The cap had said other crazy stuff too, about the old Emperor and Nate himself being the half-brother of said emperor, but that would keep.

Step one: bust out of jail.

Step two: get on the *Tyche*.

Step three: go help Gracie.

Step one was the easiest. Kohl had busted out of plenty of jails in his time. In his line of work, a man needed to be accomplished at it. Jail didn't get you paid. Jail didn't build good relationships, or strong moral character. Jail was just a place where a man who figured himself your better put a boot on your neck. This particular jail was nice enough in that it was a hospital and the wardens hadn't shot at him, but that'd change in just a few moments.

Kohl wasn't sure if he had the strength to move his neck on his shoulders, sure, but he would have to try. He was working his way up to it when the medtech — *let's call the guy a doctor and be done with it* — pressed the hypo against Kohl's arm and fired it. There was a burst of pain, kind of like being punched by a wimp, and whatever-it-was flooded Kohl's system. He could feel it racing around as his heart, jacked up on adrenaline and the anticipation of a fight, beat like a drum in his chest. This was the point where Kohl expected to lose consciousness, and lose it fast.

That did not happen, to the surprise of all four of them. The doctor, most of all, who looked at the hypo like he'd picked up a child's toy instead of a medical device by mistake. The Marines as well, who were looking at Kohl, the hypo, and the doctor, in that order. The doctor, give the man his due, was not one to give up on a technicality like *my medicine isn't working*, so he pressed the hypo against Kohl again, but his neck this time.

Fire. *Hiss.* The wimp's punch, but in the side of the neck this time, which made it almost personal.

Inside Kohl there were some unusual sensations going on. The first was that he felt sluggish, like he'd expect from being dosed with enough meds to knock out a bison, but in miniature. Like Kohl was the bison, and some veterinarian asshole had only dosed him with enough meds to take down a man. The second and more material sensation of the moment was that his blood felt like it was on fire, boiling in his veins, and he screamed again. His fingers tried to claw through his skin like they had minds of their own, because if he could just get the blood *out*, then it would stop burning so much. The pain was like what had happened in his back, but everywhere at once, and he thrashed so much that the Marines lost their grip on Kohl.

Kohl tumbled to the deck, his bed thrown sideways. He landed on his side, which was another mercy, because it stopped his head cracking against the floor. Instead, he got away with a minor strain to his neck, a thing barely above notice. As he lay on the ground, trying to throw up some more, eyes streaming with tears, snot and puke coming out his nose, he saw a miracle.

The stunner. Right next to his face.

This was a good turn of events. He was tired of being injected with a mixture of acid or whatever the hell it was, and he was tired of Marines hauling him around like they owned him. Speaking of that … those rough hands grabbed Kohl's arms, starting — again — to haul him upright. Because this was expected, right there in the regs, Kohl went with it, but this time he brought the stunner with him, clenched in a fist.

Right here was where reality came intruding on the sphere of expectations held by the two Marines and the doctor. Because the Marine had set Kohl on his feet, and Kohl's feet had held him. For a man with a severed spinal cord, this was unusual. Unexpected. Surprising, even. While the two Marines did a double-take and the doctor looked at his hypo — again — Kohl lifted the stunner and pressed it against the armored chest of the Marine who'd been doing all the hauling.

The stunner was a long, black tube with a shiny metal tip. Kohl knew, from experience, that the tip housed a set of contacts capable of delivering many, many volts through whatever it touched. It would keep applying those volts, as many as were needed to get through the importance of your actions to your target. The stunner could tell all kinds of things about your target — Hope would know how it worked for sure, but all Kohl cared about was the basic rule: apply pressure to your target until target drops like a stone.

The Marine went stiff, eyes wide, jaw locked, a tiny whimpering noise escaping his lips. A wisp of smoke curled off his armor polymer as the stunner *tick-tick-ticked*, and then the man dropped to the deck to lie amidst the spilled saline and vomit. The other Marine was raising his laser, and the weapon made it about half-way in the journey from hip to the point-and-die position before Kohl got the stunner on him. The man keened, a high-pitched noise that humans weren't supposed to make as the stunner emptied a bunch of electricity through the polymer chest-plate and into the chest underneath. This man dropped to join his friend on the deck.

Kohl turned to the doctor, who was looking at the Marines, then at Kohl, and to his hypo. The doctor blinked twice, and gave a nervous smile and a more nervous laugh. "Sir," said the doctor. "Uh."

"Say, doc," said Kohl. "What's in the hypo?" He gave the stunner a nonchalant twirl.

"A ... cocktail."

"No," said Kohl.

"No?"

"No," agreed Kohl. "I've had cocktails. I've had a lot of fucken cocktails, doc, you get me? I've had cocktails with cream and sugar. I've had cocktails that taste like a whore's ass. I've even had cocktails that were on fire. That shit," and here, Kohl pointed the end of the stunner towards the hypo, "is not a fucking cocktail."

"It's a sedative," said the doctor, the words coming out as a long string of noise, *itsasedative*.

"Okay. It supposed to burn like acid?"

"No."

"Good to know," said Kohl, and touched the stunner against the doctor's chest. The man made a sound like a small dog's bark, jerked, and fell to the ground. The hypo dropped with him, and good riddance.

Kohl took a moment to survey the med bay. Two Marines down, check. Doctor, also down, double check. Hypo with death acid? Check. Kohl bent over to pick up the doc's hypo, turning it over in his hands, before letting it drop again. He went back to get the hypo Hope had prepared for him. Nanites or some shit, right? Designed to hunt out the foreign objects in your body and tear 'em up. Maybe they figured the doc's cocktail was a foreign object. AI and all. It'd be something to check with Hope on, if they ever saw each other on this side of the veil between life and death again.

Kohl would like that. She was a skinny kid with pink hair and an overdeveloped work ethic, but she did okay. Hell, she did better than Kohl did; his one gift was being able to lift things too heavy for most other people.

Speaking of … time to get to step two, getting off this barge and onto the *Tyche*. There was a small challenge with that. He didn't know where he was, or where the *Tyche* was. He hefted the stunner, then looked at the med bay exit. *Eh. I'll work something out.*

HE WAS hungry enough to eat the ass out of a dead horse. El had said to eat the chocolates, which he'd done, but then he'd puked them back up, which wasn't great. It left a certain odor, sure, but the more important problem was it left him on shaky legs, on a Republic Navy destroyer, wearing nothing but his hospital duds and a smile.

If he had the time, he'd find a burger and some fries, maybe a jumbo thickshake to go with all that. He didn't have the time, so he'd have to rely on his natural wits, charm, and the stunner.

The stunner, to be fair, would do all the real work here.

The corridor outside the med bay was long, well-lit, and had huge windows out into space. Looking out those windows he could see unmistakable shape of the *Tyche* down only a couple decks, suckling up to the bigger ship like a baby to a teat. Wasn't far to go, just those two levels. In raw distance, hardly anything at all. In practical distance, it was a long fucking hike, because the journey was infested with Marines, Navy crew, and various other people who would want to take Kohl's stunner away from him. And perhaps much worse.

The corridor stretched off in both directions. What was behind him wasn't important excepting that he didn't want someone shooting him in the ass, so he gave a quick check south — *all clear* — before setting off toward the *Tyche*. If he could find an elevator, that would be perfect. It'd mean less walking on these weak-ass legs, and it'd take him out of the public eye, so to speak.

He started a slower-than-usual lumber towards the *Tyche's* mooring, and made it about twenty paces before two more Marines bubbled up from a stairwell leading below decks, pointing lasers at Kohl and shouting all kinds of nonsense like *drop it* and *freeze* and *face on the deck*. Like Kohl would ever do any of that. But he needed to pretend like he was going to, because here he was without any armor — *idiot*. Nothing between him and a quick death except — as noted — his thin hospital gown and a smile. And the stunner. But it wasn't a ranged weapon.

What Kohl figured he could use right about now was a diversion.

It wouldn't need to be much — just enough to close some distance and get in nice and close.

"Drop the fucking stunner, asshole," said one of the Marines. She looked pissed off, which Kohl figured as being fair if she'd seen a holo of what had just gone down in the med bay.

"Yeah," said the other one, and Kohl had to admit they built them big where he came from. "Slide it over here."

"You want me to drop it or slide it?" said Kohl.

The two Marines looked at each other, then the woman spoke. "Slide it."

Kohl shrugged, bent slowly to the ground, and slid the stunner across the deck towards the pair. It rattle-rolled across the deck, and the big one stopped it with his boot. He gave a nasty smile. "That's a good boy."

Kohl felt his shoulders bunch. Couldn't help it. Just another man wanting to put a boot on his neck. "What did you say?"

"It's good your kind can be taught manners," said the big Marine. "You want the pleasure of cuffing him?"

"Love to," said the woman, lowering her weapon. Not that it gave Kohl much to work with; these two were pros, not occluding each other's firing lines. "Hands against the wall."

Kohl sighed, then turned to the wall, putting both hands up against it. The Marine approached him, and he heard the *snick-snick* of shackles unfolding. It was a familiar sound, but not a comfortable one. In less than thirty seconds Kohl would be trussed up, and in five minutes he'd be in a brig, which was a long way away from where he needed to be. He needed to be on the *Tyche*, because the *Tyche* would get Gracie. Just a tiny diversion, that's all he needed.

He felt the shackles close around his right wrist, his hand pulled back and around. *Just one tiny diversion.*

The lights on the *Torrington* cascaded into darkness.

Kohl was surprised at this outcome. In less than a second, he knew, the emergency lighting would come on, bathing the corridor in red. He had about that second of darkness to work. The advantages on his side: he knew where both his wrists were, and by association, his hands; he also had a Marine he could use as a body shield.

He turned around as fast as he could, which even in his condition was still pretty fast, pulling the Marine off balance, then grabbed the front of her armor. He didn't want to get into a slugging match because it would hurt, and in his current state he wasn't sure what the outcome of that would be. Kohl was sure he could maneuver the Marine around because she was, compared to him, the size of a miniature poodle. He used his grip on her armor to heft her up — *okay so not quite a miniature poodle* — so her feet were only scraping along the ground. He then charged her back towards where the other Marine was.

It was about then that his one second (probably more) was up and the *Torrington's* emergency lighting came on, bathing the corridor in red. Kohl expected it, the Marines expected it, but the big Marine did *not* expect to have his visual field filled with the back of his partner, coming towards him at a run. He didn't panic, just firing his laser carbine, which might have seemed a dick move when your partner was between you and your target. Here it wasn't, as the Marines would have had some nice fancy friend-or-foe tech, which would stop them setting fire to their partners by accident. Or on purpose.

However, because Kohl was holding a Marine between himself and the laser weapon, the only thing that came out of the big Marine's weapon was a *click-click-click* sound as it sought targets. That continued until Kohl slammed the smaller Marine into the larger one, letting them both go down to the deck.

He figured this was not a good time to be standing up, so he bent over, fielding his stunner, and applied it to the big Marine's boot first, which was the closest part of the man to Kohl, and then to the smaller Marine's neighboring boot for good measure. He stood, panting, and wondered how often this would keep happening until he got to the *Tyche*.

Often enough to warrant a little preparation. He pulled the smaller Marine aside, leaning her against the wall, and then unclipped the other's chest armor. No time for the full-dress parade; Kohl just shrugged into the polymer plate, feeling better about the day by a country mile after that. He considered their lasers, but a) he had no convenient way to override the friend-or-foe electronics, and b) if the cap had wanted a bunch of dead Marines he would have given Kohl a blaster.

So, no dead Marines.

Kohl pushed on, sighting an elevator ahead. It could be full of Marines, or Navy crew, and it might not even be working with the power fluctuating, but he felt tired, and it was worth the risk. He made his way to the elevator controls, slammed his fist against them, then leaned his face against the cool metal of the wall while he waited for it to arrive. If the power was out, it'd be a long wait. That was fine. Because he was so damn tired.

WHEN THE ELEVATOR'S doors opened, Kohl was surprised by the occupants. There were three people in the car, and one of them was Hope.

The other two were Marines.

Hope did not look to be a prisoner. She was huddled against a wall, visor on, looking like she wanted to blend in. The Marines looked like they wanted to kill Kohl, which was fair enough given the last few minutes.

Time to get this show moving. Hell, he'd had a minute's rest, he was good for another few rounds.

Kohl stepped into the elevator car, getting all in the Marines' business. If they figured Hope as crew, and *why not* because an Engineer would be needed to sort out whatever power problem they were having, they'd worst case ignore her, best case try not to shoot her. But with Kohl outside of the elevator and them inside, they could lay down all kinds of righteous fire and that would be unpleasant. Hence getting in among it.

With one hand he caught the rising barrel of a laser weapon, and with the other he pressed his stunner into the chest of a Marine. There was a bright flash in the red light of the car and the Marine he'd shocked jerked back against the wall. The other Marine, in a discontented state now, swung the butt of his laser at Kohl, hitting the big man in the face.

It was important to look on the bright side: while he might be spitting teeth in a few, Kohl hadn't been shot yet. So, he let go the laser's barrel and shocked the Marine with the stunner. Then he needed another rest, so he leaned against the wall of the car opposite Hope. "Hey, Hope."

"Hey, Kohl," she said. "How you doing?"

"Feel like shit."

"Your legs seem fine. You smell bad, though."

"Not my legs, Hope," he said. "I feel weak as a day-old kitten."

"Did you eat the chocolate?"

"That's the smell," he said. "Threw 'em back up."

"I didn't expect that," she said. The car's doors closed and it jerked into motion, continuing down. Kohl hoped that Hope had it set for the *Tyche's* deck.

"Okay," he said. "Hope?"

"Yeah?"

"I'm just going to rest here for a bit."

She moved closer to him, her visor sliding away, and he caught sight of her eyes framed by that pink hair, a smudge of grime on one cheek. "You've just got to make it to the ship."

"Sure," he said. "Just give me a minute."

"You don't have a minute." She reached into her belt, fielding out a stim. "Here."

"And to think I didn't know you cared," he said. He was raising it to his lips when she put a hand on his arm, stopping him.

"Kohl?"

"Yeah."

"If you take that stim you need to eat. You need to eat soon. You hear me?"

"You lecturing me on drug abuse now, Hope?"

"The nanites," she said. "There's a cost to everything. It was the best solution I could come up with."

"Damn fine solution," he said. He tipped the stim into his mouth, wincing at the bitterness of the sluggish fluid. "Eh. That's nasty." Nasty it might have been, but he felt an artificial alertness hitting his brain, his muscles no longer feeling weak and scrawny. Hope stood, offering him a hand, and he almost laughed, because she was tiny, and he wasn't, but he suppressed the noise, because it wouldn't be right to laugh at a friend's offer of help. He pushed his sorry carcass upright, turning to face the car's doors. "We going to come out on the *Tyche's* dock?"

"Yes," she said. "There was a guard. Two, I think. But it's just an external docking lock, we're not inside the *Torrington* or anything."

"We on lockdown?"

"Were."

"Good," said Kohl. "Let's get off this tug and into the hard black. Got someone we need to be about saving."

"Yeah, we do," she agreed.

HOPE HAD BEEN RIGHT: two guards, stationed outside the *Tyche's* airlock. And a long walk towards it, but — praise be — no one else in this immediate vicinity. Which struck Kohl as weird, but it had been a weird kinda day. He made his way down the corridor towards them at what was a good running speed, now he didn't feel like a child stricken with palsy.

Not wearing shoes was a blessing at a time like this. Both the Marines were looking in the other direction at something Kohl couldn't see. His run didn't make a lot of the predictable sounds of a charge —

no thumping of boots on the deck, no jangling of kit or weapons. Just a soft *slip-slap* as he ran, a sound that reached into their minds as *unusual* at about the time he made it to them. He collided with the closest Marine like a rhino, tossing the man into the other like pins in a lane. Two quick swipes of the stunner, and the job was done. He raised his eyes, looking at whatever the hell they had been looking at.

Nothing. They'd been looking at nothing. Just an empty corridor. Like the rest of this day, weird.

And also a little lucky. Hell, if they'd turned around five seconds sooner, the whole thing would have played out with a different outcome.

Kohl dropped the stunner to the deck. "Souvenir for you assholes," he said. Then he let the armor drop alongside it, because he wasn't being paid to steal, and besides, he had better stuff on board.

Hope came alongside. "Time to go?"

"Time to go," he said. They walked together into the *Tyche's* airlock, sealing it — and the *Torrington* — behind them.

CHAPTER TWENTY-FIVE

THE FLIGHT DECK smelled of tension and sweat, which was to be expected. They were holed up in here, the ass of the ship wide open to the *Torrington*, waiting for Kohl to make his sweet way back here. El had never had a lot of time for waiting. Waiting wasn't flying, and flying was what they needed to do. Flying would get them closer to Grace's position and whatever was happening with her, and it would get them farther away from this ship of fools they were attached to.

Fools, because to think Nate was the emperor's half-brother was lunacy of the highest order. She'd known the captain for a long time, longer than anyone who crewed with him. She knew him for what he was: a good captain, a below-average pirate, and a decent human. Heart in the right place, brain switched on when it counted. She knew he wouldn't leave her to die because the percentages looked better, and she knew he was the kind of person who would race well past where humans had staked their flag, out into the hardest of the hard black, to find a lost soul.

What he *wasn't* was an emperor. It was her experience that Emperors were near one hundred percent asshole. She'd never met one, but this Republic directly resulted from the mismanagement of the last regime — ref: the emperor.

"Relax," said Nate.

She turned to look at him, lying back on his acceleration couch like he owned the world. Like he knew everything would turn out okay. She didn't know how he did that, but she knew most of the tension and sweat was coming from her. Once they were underway, *he'd* sweat and *she'd* relax, but right now was a delicate time where she wasn't doing what she was put in this universe to do. "You say that like it's an easy thing to do," she said.

"Easy as waiting," he said. "They'll be along."

"Waiting isn't easy," she said.

"Maybe you could run through the flight plan for me," he said.

"We've done that."

"Do it again."

She ran a hand through her hair, a kind of *why the fuck not* motion, then kicked the holo into life. "Okay. Here we are. Bolted to the *Torrington*."

"Not for long."

"Not for long," she agreed. "We'll make jumps here, here, and here," she said, marking the points as dots of light on the holo's star field. "I'm nervous, though."

"Why?" He waved a hand at the holo. "There's nothing out there."

"It's why I'm nervous," she said. "It's not that there's *nothing* out there. It's that we don't *know* what's there. The star field looks sparse because we're guessing at a lot of it. Just using the light that reaches us to work out what's waiting for us in the hard black."

"It's how humans have always sailed into the unknown," said Nate. "Stars above us, a good wind at our backs. It's all we need."

"We could use a little more," she said.

"Like what? An answer on what's out there? If we knew, we'd know whether Grace was safe and sound. It wouldn't be uncharted waters, El. This is the edge of the map. There be dragons there. And you know what?" She caught sight of the number of teeth he was showing, the brightness of his eyes. "I'm in a dragon-hunting frame of mind."

"Dragons kill people."

"People kill dragons," said Nate. "If there's a dragon that's between me and mine? That's a dead dragon, make no mistake."

"I hear you," she said, because she *did*. He wasn't an Emperor, because an Emperor wouldn't go into the hard black after mere crew. Sure, Grace wasn't *just* crew, not to Nathan Chevell. But his actions wouldn't change a whisker of it was El, or Hope, or Kohl out there. Yes, even big dumb Kohl.

"You done what we talked about?" said Nate.

"Yeah. I've run the drives a little dirty. Hope wasn't happy, on account of me making her reactor 'run noisy,' but we'll leave footprints in the sand, Cap. I don't know why you think we should, but there will be a path to follow."

"I figure if you've got yourself a shiny new emperor, you will go after the emperor come what may. And where we're going, we'll need all the help we can get."

The comm chirped, startling them both. It was Hope. "We're in."

"Kohl with you?" asked Nate. El noticed he hadn't asked *is Kohl okay*, because that would be like asking if water was wet.

"Here," came Kohl's grumble over the comm. "I'm coming up to the ready room to eat something. I might eat everything."

El grinned. That was Kohl. And he was a walking miracle, legs working like they'd never been hurt. She thought about the plaque she'd given Hope. *Do great things*. It was the Guild's motto. Saying that, El had never met an Engineer like Hope. Not one as good. Not one who did so many great things. She keyed her console, checking the *Tyche's* grip on the *Torrington*. "Blue skies, Cap. We're good to go."

"Hope freed the lockdown?"

"Looks like," said El.

"Never doubted it," said Nate.

"Me neither," said El. "You want to do this fast or you want to do it right?"

"Helm," said Nate, "I want to get Grace. I want us to make it alive. And I want to do it in as short a time as possible."

"Fast and right," said El. "What I figured." She keyed the comm. "Helm to *Tyche*. Brace for hostile departure." She clicked it off, then brought the drives online, the slow rumble building through the *Tyche*, a familiar urgency that said *I want to run ahead of the wind; I want to jump the waves.* "And ... docking releasing." She keyed the docking release controls, the holo's DANGER LOCKDOWN DANGER blinking twice before switching to a calm green LAUNCH CLEAR.

She pulled the nose of the *Tyche* down and out, swinging her under the *Torrington's* vast bulk. El was hopeful the *Torrington* wouldn't fire a torpedo at them, but she might aim to maim, using a maser or laser on a drive core. El kept the *Tyche* kissing-close to the *Torrington* as she ran them down towards the rear of the destroyer. As they got closer to the aft of the ship, El jammed the throttles to their stops.

The *Tyche* roared in delight, hard thrust slamming her back into her acceleration couch, the flight deck shaking around her. Her vision blurred a little as her eyeballs flattened in their sockets as they went past 6Gs of thrust, then hit 7Gs. 8Gs. She needed to claw more speed out of the launch so that once they burst free of the *Torrington's* shadow they'd get enough distance to Jump before the destroyer crippled them.

9Gs. 10. Nate groaned beside her. Or maybe it was El herself. The force was so much she couldn't breathe. Her jaw felt like it would break off and choke her.

They cleared the rear of the *Torrington* so fast if you blinked you'd miss it, and the holo lit with BRACE BRACE BRACE

TARGET LOCK BRACE BRACE BRACE. Warning lights hit red, then—

Her body, so perfect and human. Her soul, once held flat by the girders of her body, soared free. The universe was without limits. She could see everything. She was everything.

They jumped.

CHAPTER TWENTY-SIX

KARKOSKI STOOD on the bridge like she owned it. Because she did. There wasn't a high command anymore in the typical sense; the Senate had crumbled into more squabbling than usual, and the Admiralty was sending mixed messages. Those messages were further confused because loyalists — as Karkoski figured it, loyal to *her* and not *the bugs* — were launching attacks against entrenched seats of power. Capital buildings were falling. Space battles were unfolding, with great ships gouting flame into the void as humans lost lives by the thousands.

It was a drop in the bucket if they didn't get their shit together.

Her command crew were at their stations: Helm, Tactical, and Communications. There was just one other person with her and the crew: Chad. An Intelligencer she wasn't sure if she should trust or throw out an airlock, but they saw eye to eye on enough issues. She would keep him around for the time being. The *Torrington's* command deck was a standard Republic design; placed closer to the rear of the destroyer, mounted on the 'top' if there was such a thing in space. It didn't make a lot of difference, except that gravity was applied from the 'bottom.' Humans needed their norms to function;

she knew back in the day they'd made ships that were spheres, others that were discs, some that had limited or no gravity. Others using spin (horrible in combat). All of them failed the human need to know what was up and down, left and right. Humans had evolved on vast plains under skies full of stars; they weren't designed to sail seas made of those stars.

Just another thing on the list of human accomplishments. If she wasn't on her game, that list wouldn't grow larger. The alien menace would come and destroy them all. It's why she'd made the gamble, perhaps the biggest of her career. No, the gamble wasn't taking charge, starting a coup, and subverting the chain of command. If you considered that business-as-usual in wartime was protecting the interests of humanity, she was just taking care of things. There might be an accounting at the end of this. She figured on making it to the Admiralty herself, or being presented with a retirement package in front of a firing squad. A firing squad would be a mercy compared with what was coming for them all.

No, the gamble was something else.

The *Torrington's* weapon systems came online as Helm and Tactical coordinated to fire on the escaping *Tyche*. Karkoski was impressed with that little ship. She punched above her weight. It might have had something to do with the crew her captain had corralled together, a collection of misfits who'd never survive military discipline, but who seemed to be just where they were needed, when they were needed. They got the job done.

Karkoski felt like they had more than their fair share of luck. It would be unfortunate if she'd miscalculated. This was the moment when a prize destroyer of the Republic — the *Torrington* a new ship, fresh off the mill at the Titan shipyards — would test her weapons against the quick stick and fancy moves of a has-been Helm. Elspeth Roussel had been on a bridge like the *Torrington's*, her hands doing work for the Empire, until she'd found herself on the wrong side in a war that ran out of puff. Chevell had found her somewhere — Karkoski wasn't sure where, or how, or what twist of fate had brought them together — and roped her into doing suicide missions on a heavy lifter. Karkoski was certain Roussel hadn't signed on for any suicide missions, which made it all the more curious.

The *Tyche* should have been mothballed a long time ago. Karkoski hadn't been able to find her original name, not that it mattered; she wore the new one like she was born to it. Manufactured for this particular crew, at this particular time.

Karkoski realized she was clenching her fists. She forced herself to relax. The holo stage showed the *Torrington's* position in the center, the tiny spec of the *Tyche* running fast and close under her belly. Delta-v was shown — *my, that Helm is pushing the red on this one*. It was about the only move available; try and escape the *Torrington's* shadow with enough velocity to escape target lock, grab enough time — or, in this case, enough distance over a short period — to engage an Endless Drive. Make the jump before being torn out of the sky, atmosphere venting from a breach in the hull. There was the risk of killing the entire crew through stroking out or hemorrhage with that many Gs, but if your options were *maybe die* or *definitely die* then Karkoski was sure she'd want to take the *maybe* option. It was a roll of the dice, a twist of luck that would decide whether you lived or died.

Goddamn, she was clenching her hands once more. She made herself relax.

"Fire at will," she said, watching the holo.

"Aye," said Tactical, the officer working efficient hands over his console. The *Tyche* burst free from the *Torrington's* shadow, and the holo lit bright orange as the *Torrington* acquired a lock on its prey. Tactical said, "Firing," and then…

Nothing. The *Tyche* had jumped. Karkoski let out a breath she hadn't realized she was holding, then said, "Helm, track that ship. I want to know where it's gone, I want to know how long it'll take to get there."

"Aye," said her Helm, another efficient officer. She looked at Karkoski. "Done. Orders?"

Orders, indeed. She looked at Chad. "Thoughts?"

"Hell of a gamble," he said. "Hell of a risk."

"We talked about this before," said Karkoski. "It's done. I mean, your thoughts about *now*. Stay the course?"

"Yes," said Chad. "We're committed."

"You still have doubts."

"Well," said Chad, waggling his hand side to side — *maybe*. "I don't think I'd have set them up as much. Chevell seems the kind of man you can have a rational conversation with."

"There was no rational conversation where you discover that you're the Emperor," said Karkoski. "Not when you've got crew missing. He is ... *attached* to them."

"As you are to yours," said Chad. Not because he was guessing; the Intelligencer *knew*. There was no point arguing.

"It is what makes us similar," said Karkoski. "In other things, we're different."

"Eh," said Chad. "You've just had more practice. You've been an officer a long time. Big crews. Chain of command. You know what's needed."

"I do," she said. "It's why he needed a ... a little push."

"You put your boot on his ass and shoved," said Chad. "Now you've got him on the run. Which is what you wanted. I'm just not sure if the ... risk-reward ratio is right."

"We've made a hero, Chad. The crew on this ship have seen their Emperor jump into danger to save one life. Personal sacrifice. The last Emperor? Never would have done that. If Chevell makes it out of this alive, the stories of this day will spread like a carpet under his feet. He's now someone people will follow." She frowned. It had been difficult to ensure that the thug Kohl had encountered so little resistance on his way to freedom. Just enough to make the man work for it, not enough to cause him to fail. The crew he'd encountered would also tell stories: the Emperor already had followers ready to do what must be done. Capable. Committed. The side you wanted to be on. "You're still concerned he might die?"

"Fuck yes," said Chad. "Aren't you?"

Karkoski thought about that. "We will bring the storm with us, Chad."

"Ships are lost in storms," said Chad. "Doesn't matter if it's a storm of our making."

"The storm will come regardless."

"It will," he agreed, looking unhappy about it.

"So, we proceed as planned?" She wanted to check her working, make sure she wasn't going crazy. That the lack of sleep coupled with stims hadn't clouded her vision: the dawn of a new Empire. Humanity needed it with what was to come. Hell, didn't matter if it was an *Empire* or a *Republic*. It mattered that it wasn't run by aliens who wanted them as a food source.

"I guess we do."

Karkoski turned to her Helm. "Helm. Chart a course. Take us past the Guild Bridge in this system first. Communications? You know the message we need to send. Helm. Once the message is sent, follow that ship." She paused, considering. "Tactical?"

"Aye."

"Finger on the trigger. Finger on the trigger."

"Aye."

The *Torrington* rumbled beneath them as Helm fired up the drives, pushing the big destroyer closer to the Guild Gate. Their course was fixed. Karkoski just wished that they'd had a little more time. Or a little more luck.

CHAPTER TWENTY-SEVEN

WHEN SHE AWOKE, it was with the heat of a furnace around her. She didn't come awake lying down, shaking off the comforting down of sleep. She was awake all at once, standing up, on the side of a volcano.

Ash was in the air, thick as a snowstorm, and she knew she would have coughed if she'd breathed it in. The challenge was that she had no mouth, no lips covering white teeth. Her hand, when it explored her face, found a smooth expanse of skin from chin to nose. She tried to scream, but only a muffled sound came from her.

Don't panic.

Easy to say, hard to do. If she had her sword, she could have cut herself a mouth. She would have, just to make this *right*, to get it to make *sense*. There was something she was sure she should remember, and her hand moved up from where her mouth should have been to her hairline. She wasn't sure what she expected, but her fingers found the top of her head, her hair, fine and straight under her fingers as it had always been.

The volcano under her feet rumbled, the ground shaking, and she knew a normal person would have fallen to their knees. She kept her balance because of her training, a life on the run, of always trying to stay one step ahead.

That was right, wasn't it? If only she could remember her name.

Sweat ran down her face. She knew her ship suit would be wet with it in minutes, and then she would die of thirst if the volcano didn't eat her first. It was alive, horribly alive, magma and violence under its skin. She looked up, trying to see the broken top of it through the ash, but all she could see was a red glow of fire burning in the night.

Was it night? It felt like night, but that could just have been the ash. It wasn't like the hard black of space.

What was her name?

She turned to look at the base of the volcano, because she felt — or knew — she was about half-way up its rocky side. Nothing down there at all except black and gray. No life, the melted and cooled eddies of old magma leaving ugly puddles as far as she could see.

The volcano rumbled again, and she knew if she didn't get off it, down to the safety of the darkness below, she would be burned alive. If there was a starship, a lucky, nimble ship, it could scoop her up and take her away. But without a ship, safety was far away. She couldn't call for help with no mouth. She couldn't even say her own name, if only she knew what that was.

As she continued to turn in place, she saw a man approaching her through the ash. He was a little older than her, and a lot heavier. He was … dead, she was sure of it, but here he was, walking around like that had never happened. She wanted to say, *Harlow, run, just run,* but she had no mouth. She tried anyway, a muted sound coming from her. She wanted to scream. She wanted to cry.

Harlow got closer to her, most of him covered in ash. "You can make it stop," he said. "All you have to do is ask."

She gestured to her lack-of-mouth. *I can't speak.*

"Not like that," he said. "With your mind. It's all they want. Give them what they want and … become. What you are meant to be."

But she couldn't do that. She'd told them already. Her father— *Mongrel.*

—had tried to make her form speech with her mind. He'd used the whip of his words, and the harsh fists of his instructors, but she'd remained mute. Under the gentler care of Chad, who came from the same dark source as her father but had been forged of a brighter metal, she'd learned to push her feelings out into the void. But never had she been able to speak.

The mountain shook under her feet, the eruption breaking forth in a brilliant ochre rain above her. She was tossed to the ground, all her training for nothing as the mountain shook, and shook, and shook. Huge chunks of rock were tossed through the sky, not seen but felt by the menace of their passing. She had to get off this volcano. She had to run, but she couldn't get to her feet with the ground shaking under her. It was like trying to stand on water, if water were angry, and hard.

Water never had the end-game of burning you to ash.

She turned to Harlow. *Please.*

He shrugged. "The gift is within you. You need to *ask*, and they'll make it go away."

A slow-moving slug of lava started down the side of the volcano, seeking her out. She knew it was coming for her, knew it was hungry for the fuel her body had. It would set her off like a torch, burning a brief, human-shaped pyre for a second or two before she turned into a human-shaped pile of carbon and trace metals.

She turned to run, but the path down the mountain had become blocked by another river of lava. Too wide to vault, this flowed fast and hot, she could feel it baking the sweat from her skin, leaving her face dry like parchment. She realized she would die without remembering her name. They'd taken her name from her, she was sure of it. To … become. What she was meant to be.

Whatever that was.

The lava descending towards her was orange-white, flicks of flame running across its surface as it marched on. She turned around, circling, but there was no escape from her island of safety on this mountain of death.

"Just ask," said Harlow. "If you ask, we can both live. Become. What you were meant to be." His skin was becoming more orange in the light of the lava marching on them both. "Or we both die. Here." He didn't seem unhappy about it. He didn't seem to feel ... much of anything. She couldn't *feel* him, nothing like *fear/panic/run*. Those things she would have expected, not this empty hissing that surrounded her.

The lava was close now, very close. She could smell burning, and realized her hair was singed. She squinted against the incredible heat. There was no escape. There was nowhere to run. There was nobody to help her. There never had been. Being ... *together* ... with someone else was an illusion. This was all she had. This end, or to use her voice. The one she had never had.

Her ship suit caught on fire, and she wanted to scream, a mewling noise coming from her, because she had no mouth to open. She fell to the hard ground, the baking surface searing her, and she wanted to scream anew. The lava came ever onward, and she felt the flesh on her face crack and char. She lost her sight as her eyes boiled in their sockets, writing on the ground, the pain unending, God please let her die, just let her die—

MAKE IT STOP!

Blackness.

A COLD CAVERN. Her head, a ring of agony. Cold, cold air.

She was so thirsty. Red light touched everything, the slumped frame of a dead man across from her. She could feel something crawling on her head. Touching her. Invading her. She wanted to scream, but she had done that so much. She wanted this to end.

She wanted the death she had chosen for herself, and this was not it.

WHEN SHE AWOKE, it was to the sound of waves. She didn't come awake lying down, shaking off the comforting down of sleep. Again, she was awake all at once, standing up, feet braced on the sand of a foreign shore. Behind her, a sea, jagged stones jutting out of foam. It was a violent ocean, currents promising a quick death smashed against rocks for any foolish enough to try for a swim.

Up from the shore was a slope, more hill than mountain. She feared it, because she had a memory of—

Bright, burning fire. Lava, reaching for her.

—bad things that happened on hills, but she was sure that made no sense. She touched her face, feeling lips, and on opening them, teeth underneath. Her face wasn't blistered or burned, and her hair was straight and fine as her fingers found it.

She felt like she'd woken from a terrible nightmare.

She felt like she was still asleep.

Harlow stood next to her, hands on hips, no longer covered in ash. Although ... had he ever been covered in ash? "You've passed the first, simplest test. You have still to become. What you were meant to be."

What is this test? she asked.

"You must move the material world. Use your will to control it, or it will control you." He pointed up the slope. Up the top, amidst the small rocks and scrub, centaur shapes gathered. The Ezeroc, a few at first, then many more. Drones, gathering above. Waiting.

What are they waiting for?

"They want you to become. What you were meant to be." Harlow shrugged, a human motion made false by the jerky action of his body. She almost felt like she should check for strings attached to his limbs. He turned, and pointed out across the water. She could see an island out there, a small rock safe from the battering of the waves. "There. There are no Ezeroc on that stone. You'll be safe there."

I can't get there, she said. *There is no boat. The sea is too dangerous.*

"Only foolish meat tries to swim when there are better ways," said Harlow. "Take me with you. Then we won't be eaten by our family."

She wasn't sure whose family, as a general rule, ate each other, but she took the point. The Ezeroc above them had started descending the slope. She felt cold as the wind bit at her, her ship suit not doing enough to keep its teeth at bay. Which seemed odd, because her suit was designed for the hard black, where she belonged. With someone else. She had ... wanted to be together. With him. Forever.

He wasn't here. Just Harlow, and hungry insects.

How do I get across? She felt confused.

"Use your power," he said. "Part the waves."

She laughed, the sound of her voice causing her to stop. It was loud, and ugly, unlike the perfect beauty of the words she made with her mind. *No one can do that. There is no one ever who has done that.* She shrugged. *You know this.*

"Moses did it," said Harlow.

Moses was a myth. A story told as an allegory. She frowned. *The Intelligencers have never had the gift you speak of.*

"Where did the story come from? Humans have so many stories. So many truths. If you don't make the story real, you will die. Our family has never had this gift. But humans had it, once." He didn't seem unhappy about the insects not having telekinesis. He didn't seem anything. Not *scared/run/fear*, just the murmur of many voices, talking to each other. She picked up *potential she potential* and *forged or broken* and *push harder push push* and a hundred other things. So many Ezeroc Queens, all talking across the void, but one greater than the rest. Old, and ancient, and close. That one said, *We have made her better. So she can become. What she is meant to be.*

What was she meant to be? What had they done to her?

She felt the tremor of many bladed feet on the ground, and turned to the marching horde of the Ezeroc. Hungry for her flesh, to turn her body into fuel. To house their larvae in her body, in her brain—

Her skull, opened like a gourd. Her brain, exposed to long, thin needle legs of a spider.

She shivered, touching her head. It was whole, her hair and skull firm under her fingers.

Harlow walked towards the waves, then looked back. "I'll go first. If you don't move the water, I'll die. If you don't follow, you'll die." He frowned, like there was something else he wanted to say but didn't know how. "If you part the waves, you'll be safe. They can't part the waves, and will die as I'm about to."

She watched with dawning horror as Harlow walked into the water, surf breaking over his feet, then his legs, his own ship suit getting drenched. He went in up to his waist, the water tugging at him, unbalancing his frame. She wanted to pull him back out, but the drones were coming for them. She wanted to run towards him, but the waves would dash her life out against the rocks. She felt torn, like there was no good answer. *Stop!* she said, but Harlow didn't turn.

When the water reached his chest, it picked him up, dragging him around. His head went under. It broke above the waves for a moment before she saw him slammed against rocks, their sharp edges causing bone to splinter, breaking the skin. His eyes were wide, unseeing as the waves dragged him from view.

She looked back at the Ezeroc horde coming for her. It was death by insect, or death by the sea. At least the sea would deprive them of what they wanted from her. She put a foot into the ocean, feeling the water lap around her boots. She took another step out, and then another, slugging her way through the tide.

When it reached her hips, a wave broke against her, tossing her up and sideways. She went under, sucking a lungful of what she hoped would be air but turned out to be water. She tried to cough, her chest spasming with the fluid inside her, and felt a rock hit her shoulder as the current hurled her about.

Her collarbone broke with a snap she could feel rather than hear, and she felt sick, and dazed, and confused. She was drowning, and she would die here.

It was not the death she had chosen for herself. She was sure of it.

The waves pulled her around, light and dark swirling around her. She wasn't sure which way was up, which way was *out*. She wanted to feel light and air, and the touch of his hand against her skin one more time. A huge shadow ran at her, and she knew it was a rock coming for her head. She held out her good arm, warding off the blow, partially succeeding. She slammed against the rock, her arm taking the worst of it, the two bones in her forearm snapping like twigs, breaking the skin in a flash of white and red. The pain made her want to scream. She needed to push away, to stop hitting the rocks, but her arms were useless, broken things that the waves pulled around her, causing agony with each tug of the currents.

The next rock she saw coming, her vision blurry under the water, but enough to see the looming shadow. She knew this was it, the end of the line.

But his touch, just one more time.

NO MORE.

She reached out with the force of her need, and ... held. She stopped her erratic motions, the waves still tearing at her. And because she was tired of that, she made the water back away. It fell around her as she pushed it back, and she was left in the middle of a shaft of air. She coughed and retched water onto the ground, her useless arms shaking around her. She looked up at the water, seeing the fury of the currents held at bay as water surged behind the wall of her will.

There was an island out there, and safety. She walked towards it, the shaft of air following her movements. She climbed up the wet rocky hill leading up and above the surface of the waves. As she cleared it, she looked back at the line of Ezeroc on the shore. They were rearing back, claws raking the sky. They were singing. A hundred thousand million Ezeroc voices, each a part of a greater whole, were singing in joy.

At what she had become. At what she was meant to be.

CHAPTER TWENTY-EIGHT

NATE TRAMPED down the metal deck toward Engineering. His fingers itched to do something, metal and flesh alike. Hold a blaster, swing a sword, that kind of thing. There was some … *housekeeping* in order first.

The airlock to Engineering was open, the rest of them there already. Hope was reclining on her acceleration couch, her holo lit and showing a schematic of the *Tyche*. Certain areas were marked with orange dots, one of those being Nate's own cabin, which gave him some unease mixed with confirmation. *The fuckers. The fucking fuckers.* On her console rested a few metal devices, and Nate's sword, the black blade sheathed. Next to the sword were five thin metal rings, about the diameter of a coffee cup.

El was sitting atop a drive cowling, legs crossed, arms behind her. She looked tired, but not Hope-levels of tired. Just plain ol' tired. Her ship suit was clean, seals intact, like he'd expect from anyone who'd sailed in the Navy. The odd component was the sidearm on her hip. She rarely wore it on the *Tyche*. But Nate figured, *well, assholes have been everywhere*, so maybe she needed a more robust security blanket.

Kohl, now there was a sight to behold. He was standing tall and big, leaning against the reactor. Who'd have thought he'd be standing at all? He looked at Nate, nodded, and said, "Cap."

"Kohl." Nate looked at El, then Hope. "Helm. Engineer."

"How come I don't get a fancy title?" said Kohl.

"Hired Gun?" suggested El. "Dial-an-Asshole?"

"Lifter of Heavy Things," said Hope.

"Fuckers," said Kohl, but without any kind of rancor. Just like it was a thing that needed saying. Almost in a friendly way, which Nate figured for the honest truth. He'd seen Kohl deck people with his fists for less. The crew was coming along ... just fine. And just in time too, for what was to come.

"Hope," he said. "What did you find?"

"As you figured, Cap," she said, tossing small metal devices on to the deck, one after the other, each landing with a small *plink*. "What we've got here is seven standard listening devices. By 'standard' I mean tech you have not seen in your life. Small, lean, mean, and military."

"They bugged us," said Nate.

"Sure did. You're wondering what good a bug is without an Endless Drive."

"Thought had crossed my mind," agreed Nate.

Hope curled out of her couch, leaning under her console, and dragged out a metal rectangle about the size of a cat. "Found this in the reactor."

"In?" said Kohl, taking an uneasy glance behind him.

"Easy, big guy," she said. "I'm just messing with you. I found it on the hull."

"That's a relief," said Kohl.

"If it was in the reactor we'd all die if it launched," said Hope, as if that explained everything.

"What, specifically, is that?" said El. "What's it going to launch?"

"This is the universe's smallest Endless Drive," said Hope. She gave a bright smile. "I'll take it apart to see how it works. Shouldn't be possible to make a negative space field with something this small, on account of the energy needed, but they did it. It's giving off a signature that says, 'Hey, pull my string and I'll head on home.'"

"Figures," said Nate.

"How does it figure?" said Kohl, eyes narrowing.

"Let's bring you up to speed," said Nate. "You were sleeping for most of the hard work."

"I need my beauty sleep, it's true." Kohl shifted from foot to foot. "Still can't believe my legs work."

Nate paced in the confines of Engineering, realized he'd run out of room ten paces in any direction, and stopped. "The whole you-are-the-new-Emperor thing? Might be true. Could be true."

"It's true," said Hope. "I got their files."

"Fuck," said Nate. "Let's worry about that later. Anyway. Best guess? They wanted me under lock and key, but if I escaped—"

"On account of your brilliant crew," said El.

"Your smart crew," said Hope.

"Your good-looking crew," rumbled Kohl.

"Let's not get carried away," said Nate. "If I escaped, they wanted to know where their prize bull went. So they bugged the ship."

"And you expected that?" said Kohl.

"I expected it," said El. "Cap's just a bit too trusting."

"I found the listening devices," said Hope, nudging the smaller metal devices on the floor next to the box. "I've turned 'em off. And the Endless Drive in this thing, too. Nothing's working."

"Great," said Nate. "Now, about that other project I gave you."

She brushed a strand of pink hair out of her eyes. "Which one? The Kohl-might-die one, or the don't-break-my-sword one?"

"Sword," said Nate. "Kohl's here."

"Right. Right. Sorry." Hope hefted Nate's sword. "It's cool, you know? It generates a ... let's call it an inversion wave based on electroencephalography—"

"What?" said El.

"Brainwaves," said Hope. "It takes brainwaves. EEG."

"What does that mean?" said Kohl.

Hope eyed the big man. "Different things for different people." Then she offered a smile to him, and Kohl chuckled. "Anyway. It's powered by the body's electrical field. It's why you need to hold it with your skin for it to work best. It'll pick up your EEG and create an inversion field. No one can read your brain activity."

"I use it to cut things," said Nate.

"And it's good at that too," she said. "But the big point here is that it'll stop anyone reading your mind. And the cool thing? If someone tries to influence your brainwaves?" She eyed Kohl. "Such as they are? Well, it's able to detect the internal brainwaves, versus the external influence, and generate an inversion field for that too."

"Stops people reading your mind," said El. "Stops people changing your mind."

"That's what I said," said Hope. "And if an Intelligencer used it? It wouldn't do anything to stop their powers, because those are internally generated brainwaves. I think. It is a gift fit for a prince."

"Yeah," said Nate, feeling uncomfortable. "Let's pretend the you-are-the-Emperor thing didn't happen for now. Did you do what I asked?"

"Make more swords?" said Hope. "No. I can't do that here."

Nate's gut fell. "We're screwed."

"No," said Hope. "I can't make swords because this metal is difficult to fab. The electronics inside are easy enough. Would have been hard to engineer ... reverse engineering was just a copy and paste. Still. I hate using other people's code." She picked up one of the metal rings, tossing it to El, then snared another and threw it to Kohl.

"What's this?" said Kohl. "Looks like jewelry."

"It is," said Hope.

"I ain't wearing no bracelet," said Kohl.

"It'll stop the insects from invading your mind," said El.

Kohl slipped the bracelet over his wrist, an internal mechanism tightening it. "No problem. Nice bracelet. I'll wear it forever."

Hope put on her own bracelet, then threw one of the two

remaining ones to Nate. He put it on, eyeing up the remaining bracelet. "For Grace?"

"Yes," said Hope. "Because she's coming back. We'll not lose her like we lost … we're not going to lose anyone else."

"Too fucken right," said Kohl. "Let's go punch something."

"That's the plan," said Nate. "Helm, prepare the ship for jump. We're going in hot. There'll be another station, maybe some defenses. Kohl, I want you suited up and ready to board." Nate took his sword from Hope. "Someone will pay for taking our Grace."

THERE WAS relative silence on the flight deck. Sure, sure, there was the thrumming of the *Tyche*, the respiration of the air cyclers, the almost subliminal hum of the ship they could feel through the decking. But as for human speech? None of that going on.

Nate figured it was because they were surprised. *They* in this instance was El, in her acceleration couch across from him, but also Kohl behind them, leaning in through the hatch. There was no in-ship comm chatter, Hope back in Engineering, was also struck dumb with nothing to say.

Outside the *Tyche*, a thousand dead ships floated around a brown-gray world. They had jumped in, PDCs hot, the ship's energy weapons primed and ready to go, and found a lot of things to shoot at but no particular action going on. Nate had visions in his head about white-knighting the *Tyche* in to drag Grace out from some situation similar to Station Echo 9. Maybe a little gunplay, the idea of which had Kohl excited. Nestle the *Tyche* up against an enemy airlock, and board whatever vessel was holding their crew like pirates of old.

Instead: this. A *thousand* dead ships, around a world that also looked very dead.

"Well, shit," said El.

"Fucken A," said Kohl.

The comm chirped. "This is unexpected," said Hope. "I'm

getting a lot of transponder codes. A lot. Like a whole bunch. Thousands. Those ships are … still alive. Kinda. I mean, they're dead, but they're alive."

"What they are is fucked," said El.

Nate tried to think of something clever and captain-y to say, but all he managed was, "The shuttle."

"You what?" said El. "Oh, right. The shuttle. Well." She spread an arm out, as if encompassing all they surveyed. "She's out there somewhere. This is where the trail ends, Nate. Our girl is out there, but it's a … needle in a haystack."

Nate turned his attention to his console. If he could get the *Tyche* working on the problem, that might help some. Standard entry protocol for a hostile insertion. Get the ship to reach out to friendlies, or less friendlies, and find out what's going on.

The holo stage flickered, then cleared as it mapped out the objects floating in space. It would take a long, long time to find a shuttle in amidst all that. The ships were old hulks, a battle net up between them, but they'd gone down in fire and violence, and weren't letting the *Tyche* in on their conversation. Not that there was much conversation going on what with everyone on them being dead.

"Say," said Kohl. "Check that out." He was pointing out the window.

El nodded. "I see it. That looks like…" She trailed off.

"Old Empire insignia," said Kohl. The ship he was pointing to was huge, bigger than a destroyer, maybe the size of a carrier. Here at the edge of the debris cloud. It could have been a command ship.

"Hang on," said El. "Let me bring us in for a closer look."

The *Tyche* continued to paint ships around them with RADAR and LIDAR, getting a feel for the size and shape of what they faced, as El piloted the ship closer to the floating hulk Kohl had pointed at. The *Tyche's* running lights flared into the hard black, painting the side of the dead ship in bright white. The first human light that had touched that ship in … how long? Nate didn't know.

What he did know was that when they thought they were going

to a place that humans had never touched, he'd been very, very wrong. Humans had been here. They'd been here, in their thousands. And they'd died. They'd brought spears of light with them, and they'd died anyway, against an alien foe that had numbers on its side. A foe that could control minds.

Nate could see the damage the ship had sustained. Rock holes peppered the metal skin, some small, some large enough to fly the *Tyche* through. Old wounds from long ago. "Hold up," he said, and El brought the *Tyche* to a stop, drifting alongside the other ship. "There. That look like a rock hole to you?" He pointed at a long, bubbled scar that cut the ship from top deck to bottom deck. The interior was dark, invisible to their eyes.

"Looks like a burn. Energy weapon. Probably a laser," said El. The *Tyche* chattered to herself for a bit then confirmed the supposition. High yield energy strike. Multiple kinetic round impacts, some of which were consistent with a micro meteor shower, and others of which were more consistent with railgun impacts.

"Humans fired on this ship," said Nate. "Not the Ezeroc."

"I dunno, Cap," said Kohl. "I had one of those fuckers inside me. They have a way of making you do things."

"You're saying the Ezeroc made the humans turn on each other," said El.

"I ain't sayin' shit about the specifics," said Kohl. "I'm just sayin' they are fuckers, plain and simple."

"Transponder's not talking our language," said Nate. "Or it is, but it's telling the *Tyche* to keep her hands to herself. I'd like to know who or what that ship is."

El nodded at him, turning the *Tyche* to continue down the side of the dead ship. Yep, it sure was big, the biggest damn thing Nate had ever seen. The Old Empire falcon appeared again under the *Tyche's* lights, and also highlighted the ship's name, painted in huge letters — each one as big as the *Tyche* herself — for all to see. The hard black hadn't faded the name, visible to all three of them. The *Ark Royal*.

"The way I see it," said Nate, "we need a faster solve for finding

Grace. We can't ... just *sit* here hoping the *Tyche* will ID all these ships in a timely manner. Grace might be on the other side of the planet. She might not even be here. But if we can bring up the battle net, maybe get the *Tyche* hooked in on that, we can work out who is who. Which ships are part of this ruckus. Once we've got that, we can look for the odd one out."

"You're expecting there to be just *one* odd one out," said El. "There are ships here ... look. Look at *that* fucking thing." She directed their attention to the holo stage, the *Tyche* having identified something out there that was a glassy sphere about her own size. The holo flashed UNIDENTIFIED and NO TRANSPONDER repeatedly. "That there is an *alien* ship, Nate."

"More fucken bugs," said Kohl. "Perfect."

"If you could take me there," said Hope, "I could—"

"So, this is not my first rodeo," said Nate. "Standard operating procedure is to know what you're shooting at. The plan stays the same. We get on the battle net. We find out what these guys knew before they, uh, died. I'm guessing they died."

"You know what this is," said El. "Right?"

"Uh," said Nate.

"This is a last stand," she said. "This is why the Republic pushed over the Old Empire like it was a toddler. The Old Empire flew all its ships out here to fight a war against the bugs. They expected a winner takes all. All they ended up doing was ... dying."

"Naw," said Kohl. "They ended up showing the fuckers where we live. Where human space is."

The flight deck went back to being silent for a moment. Then the comm chirped. "So, can I see the alien ship?" said Hope.

"No," said Nate. "Hope, I'll need you to whisper sweet nothings to the *Ark Royal*. I need you to convince her that the *Tyche* is a good and proper friend of the Old Empire, and worthy of participating in their super-secret club. Can you do that?"

"I'd prefer to be on the alien ship," said Hope.

"If you don't," said Nate, "Grace will die."

"I didn't say I couldn't do it," said Hope. "I was just saying. You know. If there's time. After."

"After we've saved the galaxy, and the universe," said Nate, leaning closer to his comm, "you can take a little shore leave. Play with the aliens all you want. Just remember the snails, Hope. So far, in a universe we figured ourselves alone in, we've found two alien races, and both of 'em wanted to do harm to us. You get me?"

"Aye, Cap," she said. "Cool. After, I'll go on the alien ship."

Nate sighed. In a way, it was refreshing. He wished he still had a little enthusiasm, and he was happy Hope was getting hers back after Reiko. He would need her focused and on point for what was to come. They'd all need to be on point for that. He turned to Kohl. "How you feeling?"

"Average," admitted Kohl. "I've been eating like a water buffalo but nothing's coming out the other—"

"Too much," said El. "Too much, Kohl."

"You feeling good enough to go on *Ark Royal* with me?" said Nate.

"Course," said Kohl. "Everyone there will be dead, and if they ain't, they'll be insects, and I'll make 'em dead. Just bugs, Cap. I don't need to be a hundred for that, you feel me?"

"Yeah," said Nate, feeling ... ready. Anxious, but excited. Because they were close to Grace. He could feel it. In his bones, deep down, she was close.

THE CLANK in the airlock as the *Tyche* mated with the *Ark Royal* was loud. Louder than Nate felt it should be, the sound of a crypt door closing in around them. Clear through his helmet, no need for the external mic on this one. He shook himself. *It's just nerves.* And fair enough too, because they had found the remains of a human fleet surrounding a dead world, which was also surrounded by other dead alien ships.

These Ezeroc didn't fuck around.

They'd coupled the *Tyche* to the top deck of the *Ark Royal*, where the bridge was. They just needed to get there, clear any dangers, and … it'd all work out. There was a lot of distance between here and there, but they would do it. They had to. For Grace. And maybe for all of them. Nate didn't like how much interest the Ezeroc had shown in Grace — never had — and she'd be close to them here. They were now running on borrowed time. If the Ezeroc didn't have her, they would soon. There wasn't a station here. This was Bug Central. Odds were good the dead world below them was the Ezeroc homeworld.

The only thing going in their favor was the bracelets. As far as the Ezeroc knew, nothing much was going on around their world. Sure, they might see the telltale flare of the *Tyche's* drives, but space was big, and they'd need to be looking in the right place. Odds *had* to be going for the humans in this one. There was nothing about the Ezeroc that suggested they knew about electrical signatures, other than what they'd learned from humans. So, if they were lucky, the Ezeroc wouldn't see them coming.

It should give them enough time to get onboard the *Ark Royal* and find out where Grace was. Find out, by process of elimination, which one of the thousand floating hulks was the tiny shuttle that held the woman he loved.

"That sure sounds ominous," said Kohl, too cheerfully for Nate's tastes. The big man was in his power armor, the back of it repaired in a motley collection of metal plates. Another 'quick repair' Hope had put together. It was just the two of them going in; Nate figured they could get Hope along to whisper sweet nothings to the *Ark's* computers when they were sure the dead ship really was dead.

The *Tyche's* airlock slid open to reveal the hard metal side of the *Ark Royal*. The other ship's airlock didn't open, which was expected. No Navy ship would welcome them with open arms in a war situation. Hell, it was likely the electronics were fried, or there just wasn't enough juice to go around. The *Ark's* reactor was powered down, most likely out of fuel, the ship running on reserves for however long it had been out here. *Reserves* didn't mean *safe*; a ship like this could have all kinds of automated defenses waiting to tear them a whole new and complete set of assholes.

"You want that I get that?" said Kohl.

"Be my guest," said Nate.

Kohl sighed over the comm. He knocked on the plate covering the emergency door release mechanism, and when nothing happened, he drew back a big armored fist and smashed it down. The metal popped off with a *clang*, revealing a wheel inside. Kohl grabbed it with both hands, his power armor whining as he worked the mechanism. There was a groaning sound from inside the *Ark's* hull, then a shriek as the mechanism — long-ago seized solid — gave up its grip. The airlock cracked open, revealing a dark airlock.

No bodies. Good start.

Nate played his suit light around the interior of the airlock. "Looks like this way in is clean."

"Looks like," agreed Kohl. He stepped inside, magboots gripping to the metal decking, and repeated his door-open trick with the interior lock.

While he worked, Nate turned to the *Tyche*, sealing her airlock closed. He keyed the comm. "Keep her safe," he said.

"No problem," said El. "And if we hear screaming..."

"You'll come running?" said Nate.

"Hell no. We're leaving you to die." She cut off the comm, leaving Nate to smile to himself.

"We're good," said Kohl. "And I don't mean good-good. I mean, the door's open, but we're still fucked." Nate turned around, taking in the interior of the *Ark Royal*. An ancient Old Empire ship, sent here, past the edge of the map where all the dragons lived. And dragons had eaten this ship. It was worth remembering. Speaking of ... inside the *Ark's* entry bay was a junction. Straight ahead? Sealed door. Left and right, corridors stretched off into darkness. Outside the entry bay? Five dead Ezeroc drones floated in the zero G, some pieces burned by blaster fire, some pieces with kinetic rounds. Bits of carapace were scattered about near the walls, time and minimal gravity having attracted them there. "What kind of idiot uses a kinetic weapon on the inside of their own starship?"

"The desperate kind," said Nate. "Notice anything odd?"

"Dead bugs," offered Kohl.

"Yeah, but not dead people," said Nate. "There are no dead people here at all. Odd that the Ezeroc didn't bag even one."

"Maybe they got away," said Kohl. "Maybe the humans won this one, and dragged their injured to the med bay."

"Lot of maybes," said Nate. "Left or right?"

"Straight ahead," said Kohl, pointing with an armored hand. "Bridge'll be up that way."

One of the overhead lights flickered for a minute, then winked back out. Nate stared at it for a second. "Well, something's awake here. Step careful. Last time we walked on an enemy installation there were drones and turrets."

Kohl unslung the big plasma cannon from behind him. "Ready for anything."

Nate walked forward, taking point. There was a certain part of his mind that wanted Kohl to go first, on account of the armor and the big gun, but Nate felt an urgency pushing him on. He had to get to Grace. He *had* to get to Grace. Something in his gut told him that more was at stake than missing crew. And, much as it didn't sit right with him, more than a missing lover. There was something bigger than the two of them at play here: a whole alien race that wanted humans as the next course on an intergalactic banquet.

He made it to the closed door, trying for the controls. He tapped at them a couple of times, but no lights bloomed. The door didn't open. Nate sighed. "You want to try your plasma key?"

"Sure," said Kohl. Nate stepped back as Kohl unloaded his cannon into the door, walking the blasts around the sill. Metal melted and splashed to cool in the cold, airless vacuum of the *Ark Royal*. After thirty seconds of focused fire, Kohl let the trigger go, clanked forward, and gave the door a kick. It fell forward, Nate feeling the clang of metal through his boots.

"Thanks," said Nate. The room they'd found looked to be some kind of screening facility for boarders, old scanning machines sitting dark and quiet. Some of them were broken, interior electronics bared under their suit lights. There were Ezeroc drone bodies in this room floating free. There was also a dead human, or what was left of one. The body was charred, the top quarter of it — sectioned off from shoulder to opposite waist — gone. Nate walked over to the body, magboots clunking as he walked. The human body was wedged behind one of the scanning machines, which looked like it might have exploded. The impact of blaster fire, or an explosive, hard to tell — just melted metal and burned human. Nate nudged the body with a gloved hand. It shifted under the movement, chunks of carbon flaking to float free. The body was freeze-dried, the parts not crisped mummified in the vacuum of space. "Why you suppose they didn't take this guy?"

"Not much worth taking," said Kohl. "No head. No meat on the bones."

"Makes sense," said Nate, thinking back to the pods the Ezeroc entombed humans in. Those people seemed ... *alive* until they were drained dry. The Ezeroc must need an ... *operational* human to work with. It boded a little hope for the state of Grace, if they could only get to her before she was sucked dry or had insects living in her brain cavity. He shied away from those thoughts.

"It's okay, Cap," said Kohl. "We'll get her."

"How do you know?"

Nate could see Kohl's surprise through his visor. "Because you're in charge. Always works out." His big armored shoulders rose and fell as he shrugged.

Nate didn't know what to say. "Doesn't feel like that."

"Well, it might not work out too," said Kohl. "We could all die."

"Nice talk," said Nate. There were two other doors leading away from this area, one secured and closed to the right, and the other an open invitation leading on towards the bridge. Open meant easy, but it also meant bad, because it was a pipe the Ezeroc would have flowed down, almost frictionless. He started down that way, his suit's lights leading the way. The passage was straight, leading to another open door, a door beyond suggesting another room. In this passage, a couple of charred Ezeroc floated. He tapped one of their corpses with a hand, setting it to drift away. "The problem with these damn bugs is they don't seem to care about losses. They convert *our* dead into material to build new troops."

"Fucking bugs," agreed Kohl.

Nate moved past the drifting insect corpse, the nightmare of its claws and mandibles still a sight to behold even though the thing was dead. At least, he was pretty sure it was dead. Living for twenty years in a vacuum? Had to be dead.

Had to be.

He drew his blaster anyway, then continued on. The corridor opened into a large ready room, configurable tables and seating charred and broken around the room. Much of it was still secured to the decking, but some floated free. There were multiple impact rounds on the walls; the pockmarks of kinetic rounds huddled next to the melted blisters of plasma fire. Six Ezeroc drones were in various states of dismemberment in here. "Why do you suppose they don't take their dead?"

"Might be the same reason they don't take our dead," said Kohl. "Need the meat to be fresh."

Nate shuddered. "You're a ray of fucking sunshine." It was hard to tell what had been going on in the ready room. It looked like it was configured as a war room, but the holo stage was long dark. Whatever plans it had held had turned out to be useless in the end. He turned to the walls, examining the weapons fire. "They didn't go down without a fight."

"They still went down," said Kohl.

"Anyone ever told you to work on your positive attitude?" said Nate.

"Is there a bonus in it?"

"No."

"Well, then," said Kohl, like that explained everything.

The ready room connected to the bridge, a single doorway — wider than the standard doors they'd been through — standing open. Nate walked through, steps slowing as he entered the bridge of the *Ark Royal*. On the bridge was more of the same. Ezeroc drones, their husks scattered about. Consoles and acceleration couches shot to hell. One of the main windows showing a view of space was spidered by an impact, but looked like it had held. Vacuum hadn't killed these people. They'd been ... *taken*, stolen away, used as fuel for the Ezeroc.

Two other ways out. One ahead, one to the right. Nate turned to the right, because the door was sealed. Writing on the outside read COMMANDER. He pressed the controls on the outside without much hope, then knocked off the panel for the emergency release. The wheel inside was stiff but not seized, turning with just a little effort. He wound the door open then stepped inside.

Empty, aside from a desk with acceleration couch and a console. The holo stage was empty. There was a nameplate attached to the desk, and he walked forward to examine it. The bright golden letters were etched against black anodized aluminum, waiting for twenty years for Nate to find it.

CMDR. A. FERGELIC.

He sucked in a breath, stumbling back. Kohl's voice came to him over the comm. "You okay, Cap?" The big man clanked up to the doorway, bright lights from his armor lighting the small space.

"No," said Nate. "I don't think so."

Kohl looked around. "Nothing here."

"But there is," said Nate. "Or, there was. She was here." He tapped the metal plate.

"Who?"

"My sister, I guess she was. Annemarie Fergelic. The *Ark Royal* was her ship. Makes sense she'd be out here in the hard black at the head of her Navy." He sucked in another breath, then another. "Kohl? I didn't even know she was my sister. Not until today."

"Kinda sucks," said Kohl. "Finding out you've got a family, and they're all dead. On the same day. You've known they were dead for a while. But, uh. They were family all along."

"Kinda sucks," agreed Nate. "It's complicated."

"You going to be okay?" said Kohl. "I don't mean that in a mushy way. I mean, are you going to hold it together? There's still bugs that need killing."

Nate pushed himself to his feet. "Yeah. I think I'll be *just fine* for killing bugs." Kohl backed out of the doorway, letting Nate through. "Let's see what else we can find."

"Sure, Cap." Kohl clanked off towards the remaining door, open into the dark beyond. "Well, hey. Escape pods."

Nate hurried to join him. Sure enough, the door led to the emergency evacuation area for the bridge crew. There were three pod bays available. One was sealed tight, and Nate figured beyond that doorway was the hard black of space. The people in that pod were … gone, drifting forever out in space, or had been picked up as bug food.

There were two remaining pods. Their doors were open, waiting. Inviting. The closest one was a standard four-seater pod, fitted with acceleration couches for the extreme G of explosive launch. There was an Ezeroc drone inside, one of its stabbing claws piercing the mummified remains of a bridge officer. The officer still held a sidearm, and the side of the Ezeroc's skull was holed by rounds from the weapon. This one had gone down fighting. Alone, with the red emergency lights around them. Just one more human the bugs would pay for.

The last escape pod was a single-occupant design. Reserved for the commander of the *Ark Royal*. Nate slowed as he approached, not sure what he would find. Truth: he wasn't sure what he *wanted* to find. He played his suit lights around the interior, biting on his lower lip as he took it in.

An Ezeroc, mandibles around the arm of the … captain. *Don't say her name. Don't say it.* Her sidearm still clutched in a mummified hand. She'd shot the Ezeroc like the other bridge officer. But she hadn't stopped there. The top of her head was gone, a spray pattern of dried blood on the bulkhead behind her.

Annemarie Fergelic, sister of the Emperor Dominic Fergelic, had died here on the edge of space. She had died alone, a suicide.

"Step away, Cap," said Kohl. "There's no good that'll come of looking in there."

Nate didn't move. *Annemarie was the smart one. The brave one.* "She killed herself, Kohl."

"Figures," he said.

Nate rounded on Kohl. "*How*, Kohl? Tell me how this makes sense."

The big man didn't react. "Well, you haven't had one of those things in your head. I have. If you had … I guess, all the secrets of the Empire, what would you do?"

Kohl was right. Nate turned back to Annemarie's remains. She had probably realized even if she made it off the ship, she knew too much. There were too many Ezeroc around the *Ark Royal*. An entire planet of them below, waiting for survivor pods to land. If she'd gone, she'd have still died, but … badly. It would have been terrible.

He reached into the pod, grabbing the Ezeroc's carapace, and pulling it free. He set it adrift behind him, then looked at Annemarie one more time. *That's your sister, Nate. You figured her for a friend, and she was, but it's worse. They killed your family. Either directly, or indirectly. How does that make you feel?*

"I figure we need to kill some fucking bugs," he said. He clicked on his comm. "Captain to the *Tyche*. You there, El?"

"We're here."

"Get Hope on over here. Everything that happened, happened a long time ago. We need that reactor online. And we need to pick facts out of the brain of this ship."

"You got it." The comm clicked off.

"Coming, Cap?" said Kohl.

"You go," said Nate. "Meet up with Hope. Watch her, Kohl. Watch her like your life depends on it." He gritted his teeth. "None of us dies alone."

"I hear you," said Kohl. "What are you going to do?"

"I need a minute," said Nate. "Go. I'll be along."

Kohl said nothing, the clank of his armor coming through the decking as he walked away. His lights left with him, leaving Nate to stare at all that remained of Annemarie Fergelic. Just the two of them, a single suit's light between them.

CHAPTER TWENTY-NINE

WHEN SHE AWOKE, it was in darkness, cool and comfortable. The comforting legs of her brethren stepped down her face, down the side of her suit, to walk off. One drone came to free her arms from the resin holding her in place.

She reached a hand up to the top of her head, feeling the seam where they'd had to ... work on this body. It hadn't been. What it was meant to be. Before. But now it was. The song of her people soared around her, soothing her. She knew she differed from them; they were many made into one, and she was one made into many.

It was complicated. It was beautiful.

The body she walked in — how weak and soft it was — was a necessity. She felt the comforting presence of one of her brethren inside her skull, its thin body nestled against her brain. She didn't need to feel it with her fingers. She knew it was there, guiding her. Helping her. Keeping the pieces of her that didn't want this perfection silent, quiescent. It felt comfortable. It made her feel complete.

A man stood before her. *My daughter, what have they done to you?*

She knew, through examining his face, he was what humans

would call *horrified*. She smiled at him, her breath frosting in the air. *I have become. What I was meant to be.* She thought for a moment. *You should be happy. This is what you always wanted.*

His expression closed, eyes angry. *Not like this. Never like this.*

Where are you? she asked. *We will come find you. And make you. What you were meant to be.*

No, he said. *There is still ... one more chance.*

For what?

He didn't answer, fading from view. She knew him to be one of the genetic donors to this body, a maker of her genes, and that was of tremendous interest to her people. They had ... *altered* her, cutting what needed to be cut, and growing what needed to be grown. But with this man? They might make more, faster, easier.

It was an exhilarating thought.

Her Queen touched her mind, the vast and ancient intelligence welcome. *You will find him.*

I will find him, she agreed. *He will make more.*

You will need the other genetic donor, said her Queen.

Of course, she said.

There was a part of her that wanted to scream *never never you can't have her* but the comforting presence in her head pushed it down, made it quiet. It wouldn't have to do that too many more times before it killed off that tiny piece of uniqueness. She was one made into many, but all she wanted was to not have the one left. It was a mar against the perfection of the collective.

She picked up her sword, because this body was too weak to kill with its tiny claws. Her hands knew the sword, and knew what to do with it.

Perhaps, as she journeyed, she would find the one who had thought to be together with her. She had all the togetherness she needed. While he was still out there, the small part of her that still screamed inside had hope. So, she would find him first, and kill him, and then there would be no more of this internal conflict.

CHAPTER THIRTY

THE SHIP WAS OLD, that's for sure. Hope hadn't seen a design like this in forever. She felt like it had been minted back when she was in swaddling, or maybe even earlier. Before she'd had dreams of building things. Before she'd taken apart her family's cleaning bot to see how it worked. Before, even, her parents had dreams of a little Hope.

Old was good. Old wasn't just rustic. Old was reliable, familiar.

Old was *hackable*. The tech on this thing would be a piece of cake to bust open.

She and Kohl were in the *Ark Royal's* Engineering section, the remains of Ezeroc littered everywhere. The bugs had come in here, hard and fast, and crippled the ship by force. Hope didn't know why they hadn't used magic mind wizard powers on the Engineers. She wanted to think it was because an Engineer's mind was complicated, but the available data didn't support that worldview: Hope herself had been bundled up and stuck to a wall with goop by a human-piloted Ezeroc back on Absalom Delta.

It was more likely they had a cap on the number of people they could control at once. They might be powerful, but they weren't gods.

If Hope could control minds, she would have started with the Engineers rather than the spacers piloting ships out in the hard black, but there was no accounting for taste. Especially alien taste.

"Fucken bugs," said Kohl, surveying the room. All the lights were out, the reactors — all six of them — cold. Hope knew he wasn't referring to the reactors, but what the Ezeroc had done to the people who used to work here.

There was just one left, a woman staked to the side of some secure shelving by a severed Ezeroc claw. Hope knew it was a *her* despite her mummification in the hard black by the size of her frame and the way her hair flowed out from her head in the vacuum. Small, but she'd died fierce, a plasma cutter in one hand. The Ezeroc claw was charred at the stump; the Engineer had severed it from her attacker before bleeding out.

Hope looked around the Engineering bay, taking in the size of it. There would be at least ten Engineers on shift here, so the mummified Engineer hadn't died alone. She'd still died though. Hope rubbed at her suit where her bracelet lay, and prayed that she'd got the tech right.

She hated relying on someone else's code. When she had *time*, and a little more *sleep*, she would get to the bottom of the tech. Once she'd unpicked the code, she could ... make it better. She was sure they'd make it out alive, that wasn't in any doubt; the cap had a plan, and his plans were good.

Usually.

Okay, so there was a little doubt. "We'll start with that one there," she said, pointing at the closest reactor. "Once it's online, we can fire the others up."

"Why that one?" said Kohl.

"It's closer," said Hope. "Do you want to pick another one?"

"Does it matter?"

"No. They're just reactors."

"Closer is good," said Kohl. "Let me know if you need anything."

"Actually," said Hope, "could you close up Engineering? Seal the doors."

"Sure," said Kohl, clanking away in his power armor.

Hope didn't need Engineering sealed, but it was a convenient excuse to get Kohl out from underfoot. It was nice of the captain to make sure she had an escort, because going anywhere alone on a dead ship was a sure-fire way to get killed. If this was a horror holo script, that'd be how Hope would kill the clever young Engineer. Talented, clever, and young, but killed before her time as she tried — valiantly — to start up a dead reactor on a deader ship, as the alien menace approached. All that aside, she didn't like being watched while she worked.

Also, if she got this setup working, she wanted to try pressurizing the ship, and Engineering was as good a place to start as any. The *Ark Royal* might have gone out like a blown candle because she took a lot of damage, but she could also have gone adrift because all the people who brought light into darkness were dead.

The reactor was — again — an old design. She'd studied models like this before. It was a standard Internal Confinement Fusion style of reactor. The ICF was standard everywhere; the *Tyche* had one, the *Torrington* had one too. Nice, clean fusion. She checked the reactor over, using her rig to scan it. Lasers reached out to map the exterior of the reactor. No holes. Good start.

Why wasn't it working?

Probably because it was out of fuel. The other option was that someone had initiated safe shutdown, but Hope didn't figure that for likely. She looked back at the mummified Engineer. *Not likely at all.* People had gone down screaming and in terror in here; it'd be tripping the light fantastic to think some Engineer had the presence of mind, while their friends were being turned into shish kebobs by the bugs, to put all six reactors into safe shutdown.

So, fuel. She checked the feeding hopper, and found it well stocked. There was a connector port on the side of the reactor for emergency power to jumpstart ignition, but before she used that: safety first.

The Engineering bay was, like most ship designs, at the rear of the *Ark Royal*. This meant if you needed to eject a reactor that had gone critical, you would fire it in the ship's wake. The *Tyche* was the same, Engineering — Hope's sanctum sanctorum — at the rear and top of the ship. The *Ark* had this bay rear and bottom. She wanted to be sure that if the reactor went to a bad place, they could eject it.

She examined the escape ports. They *seemed* fine, but it was hard to be sure without doing an external inspection.

"Hey," said Kohl over the comm, almost startling Hope out of her rig.

"Jesus, Kohl," she said. "Don't sneak up on people. Especially on a death ship full of alien corpses."

"It'd be worse if they weren't corpses," said Kohl.

"Fair point."

"Anyway, I'm about done with these doors." Hope looked across at him, surveying the door he'd just closed on one of the last entryways to Engineering. "What's the holdup?"

"I'm trying to see if we can eject the reactor if it goes critical."

"Why?"

"So we don't die," she said, letting sarcasm into her voice. Seriously. It's not like Kohl understood this stuff anyway.

"Okay, but if we eject it," said Kohl, "where does it go?"

"Outside," said Hope.

"How far?" said Kohl.

Hope thought about that. "Not very far," she admitted.

"Far enough that we won't die?"

"No, probably not," said Hope.

"Then maybe skip that step," said Kohl. "Only, Gracie's out there somewhere and we're burning air."

She gritted her teeth. Not that she'd been wasting time on a mistaken premise. It was more that Kohl had been right, and that kind of thing shouldn't happen too often. Hope pulled power leads out from the base of her rig, connecting them to the reactor's jumpstart ports. She told the rig to give up a few joules, just enough to engage the feed pipe and start the reactor's laser.

There was a clank, a hum, and then lights bloomed over the outside of the reactor. The rig's connection reported that the reactor had started a clean burn against a new fuel pellet, the fusion reaction nice and clean. She disconnected the power leads, moving towards a nearby console. She pressed the power button, but nothing happened.

"Hell," she said.

"What is it?" said Kohl, clanking closer.

"Console's busted," she said. "Must have taken damage in the battle, I guess."

Kohl looked at her, then at the console, then gave it a good, hard hit with his glove. The whole console shook with it, then lights blinked on, its holo stage coming to life. She stared at him. "You ... could have broken it! It ... might never have worked!"

"You're welcome," he said, clanking off.

THE BRIDGE WASN'T a happy place, but it was where she *had* to be.

Engineering was fine for stoking up the reactors, making sure the drives were alive, that kind of thing. And she had; near as could be told from the back of the *Ark*, things were shipshape.

Up here was where the commands were given. Where the data was kept. There wasn't a convenient method for people in Engineering taking control of the ship, because multiple points of control were a bad idea on a warship. So here she was in the open space of the bridge, holo stage alight, with one console working. The rest kinda-sorta worked. The *Ark* had been through it the hard way, her crew with her, no mistake about that. But Hope figured on breathing a little life back into her.

The good news, if there was good news, was that the bridge was sealed, had atmosphere, and was bringing the temperature up from the seventh-circle-of-hell cold to moderately-unpleasant cold. About thirty percent of the lights worked, which was more than she expected. It gave the bridge a you're-not-welcome-here-but-what-can-I-do-about-it feel, like an aunt's house who hated her clever, young Engineer niece. Kohl leaned against a busted acceleration couch, his helmet down, sucking in twenty-year-old canned air. "This place smells like shit," he said.

"It's not great," agreed Hope. The air was beyond stale, but the air cyclers should fix that given enough time. If enough of them were working. The ship net said most everything was broken, corrupted systems and things that just weren't there anymore spotting her display with a heavy wash of red. There was less yellow, and even less green on the board. She could fix it, if she had the time, but most of those things weren't necessary. They had power, they had air, and they even had grav.

What they didn't have? Well, Grace, for one, but on the road to getting her back, they didn't have control over the battle net. The ship net was fine, it was just this one ship, and all Hope had needed to do was ask. The battle net was something else.

It's lucky she'd brought her tools.

She popped open the cover of the console, exposing the circuits within. This was an old design, optical circuits inside glowing as it chattered to itself. She plucked cables from the base of her rig, slotting them inside the console. If you couldn't get in through the airlock, there was always a side port someone had forgotten to seal up tight.

"Ah," said Hope.

"What?" said Kohl.

"You wouldn't understand," she said, and was rewarded with a grumble. But she was right, he *wouldn't* understand. The code on this ship was old, rusty by modern standards, and there were a few exploits available based on what humans had learned in the twenty or more years this thing had been decaying out here in the hard black. Not that ships rusted in space, but whatever. She tapped on her rig's console. "Open sesame."

"What?" said Kohl, again.

"Sorry," she said. "Just, doing ... *this*." The holo stage flickered, cleared, and then displayed WELCOME, ENGINEER BAEDEKER.

"It knows your name?" said Kohl.

"Hey, cute," she said. "I didn't know you could read."

"I have killed people for less than that," warned Kohl.

"Could they read too? Anyway. No, it didn't know my name. But it knows it now."

"Good," said Kohl. "How close are we to the battle net?"

"We're in," said Hope, disconnecting the rig's cables from the inside of the console. She then sat in the console's acceleration couch, and got to work. "Let's see. Okay, yes, we've got ... hmmm. Seven hundred and fifty-six ships on the battle net are still responding."

"How many are there?"

"Looks like ... well, over a thousand ships," said Hope.

"The Old Empire sent over a thousand ships out here?" said Kohl. "And they all got fucked?"

"I'm not sure that's the technical term for it, but yes," said Hope. "Bear in mind they're not all the size of the *Ark*. We've got this command ship," and the holo pinged their location at the edge of the debris cloud, "and, let's see, ten carriers."

"Ten!"

"There are forty destroyers."

"The Republic doesn't even *have* forty destroyers," said Kohl. "Do they?"

"If they ask nicely, I might let them keep mine," said Hope. "Now, there's a few things we need to do."

"Like what?"

"First things, we bring the *Tyche* into the conversation." Hope tapped the comm. "El?"

"Helm here."

"I'm patching you in," said Hope. "Let me know what you see."

There was a pause. "It's like Christmas over here," said El. "On account of all the red and yellow lights."

Hope winced. "Yes. There's a lot of damaged ships out there. But you're in?"

"I'm in."

"Okay, start your scan." She clicked the comm off. "Next on the list is power."

"Power? We've got power," said Kohl waving an armored hand at the room around them, as if saying, *see?* "What about getting Gracie?"

"Not for us. For them." Hope jerked her head outside the bridge's windows at the floating cloud of ships.

"Why?"

"Do you like guns?"

"Love guns," said Kohl. "Guns are kind of my thing."

"All those ships have guns," said Hope. "We might need more guns."

"We might," allowed Kohl.

The comm chirped. "Hey, I've found her," said El. "Or, I think so. I've got a human transponder out there. The *Tyche's* painting it. It looks like a shuttle, same kind as we saw on Echo 9. Weird thing is it's bolted to an asteroid."

Hope watched Nate walk onto the bridge from the direction of the ejection pods. His movements were purposeful as he came to stand by Hope. "Tell me it's good news."

"It's ... sure, it's good news," said Hope. Her face screwed up at what she was seeing on the console. "That can't be right."

"What?" said Nate.

"The asteroid. The shuttle. Whatever. It's hailing the battle net."

Nate's face broke into a smile. "Put her on." He turned to the holo stage as it flickered into life, showing Grace's face. From Hope's angle of view, she could see Grace, and she could see Nate's face fall as he saw Grace. Because she didn't seem like Grace anymore.

Oh, sure. She still looked like Grace, but the way she stared at them? That was all different. Totally different. And the ugly tear running around the top of her skull? That didn't look like it was comfortable. Maybe she was concussed? She'd had an accident? Hope's mind went through the options, and landed at the least comfortable but most likely: *the bugs got to her.*

"Nathan," said Grace.

Nate's metal fingers reached for the holo, and Hope wanted to grab him and make him look away, her heart going out to him. "My Grace," he said.

"Not yours," she said. "Mine."

"Gracie," said Kohl. "What's going on?"

Grace's head cocked sideways on the holo. "Can't you hear? Don't you see?"

"Grace," said Hope. "Please come home."

"I am home," she said. "You can come home with me. Down there." The holo stage blanked out.

"Where did she go?" said Nate, his voice lost. "What have they done?"

El's voice came over the comm. "The asteroid is, uh, making a burn for the planet. Except, you know, it's not burning, because it's some Ezeroc tech."

The holo blinked back into life, EMERGENCY MULTIPLE INBOUND TARGETS EMERGENCY appearing on the display. The text cleared, the star field pulling back as new ships appeared on the holodeck. "Uh," said Hope.

"That looks like a lot of Republic ships," said Kohl. "A *lot*. Maybe they don't want their new emperor taking a dirt nap."

"No," said Hope. "It looks like a lot of human sock puppets."

"She's right," said Nate.

Of course I'm right, thought Hope. *It's what I do*. But the cap hadn't finished talking. It looked like he was building himself up for some big heroic thing, which would get him killed, and Hope just wanted him to get to the point so she could tell him what a bad idea it was. "What we've got here is an interesting problem. The Ezeroc on the planet below will realize there are a lot of humans here who weren't here before. If we hail them? They'll know we're here."

"They know we're here because Grace just talked to us," said Hope.

"That wasn't Gracie," said Kohl.

"Don't say that," snapped Nate, and Hope watched his fingers, metal and flesh alike, clench then unclench. "Sorry."

"You're good," said Kohl. "We'll get her back. We got the magic sauce, right?"

"Right," said Hope. "But Grace still talked to us."

"To be fair, she talked to the battle net," said El, over the comm. "She didn't talk to this ship. She didn't talk to *us*."

There was silence on the bridge for a moment, then Nate said, "The fuckers don't know where we are. That's why they want to lure us to the planet."

"The fuckers," agreed Kohl.

"Um," said Hope. "How does this help us?"

"Initially, not at all," said Nate. "But I've got a plan."

"Oh, no," said Hope.

"Relax," said Nate. "It's a good plan. But we need to do a couple things first."

HOPE AGREED that it was a good plan, right up to the last bit.

Step one: do not answer any hails. The battle net was up, seven hundred and fifty-six ships online. Their reactors were cold and dark, and it was time to change that. Hope initiated a reboot on all ships. This had a series of interesting reactions. Forty-three of the ships, some of them small fighters, exploded in spectacular fashion as nuclear fireballs consumed them, faulty reactors in dire need of maintenance firing up. A few more just didn't respond, staying dark, and a handful of the rest came online, but leaking radiation like caustic rain. It wouldn't do to be on one of those ships, not that it would be an option with what was coming.

Step two: power down the *Tyche*. Her reactor had been installed by the *Torrington*, and its fingerprints were well known to the Engineers on that ship. She had to be black and silent, coupled to the side of the *Ark Royal*. Just another piece of old, forgotten junk. Safe shutdown, ready to go online at a moment's notice, because the cap wanted her ready when he called.

Step three: engage all the automated defenses on the remaining seven hundred and thirteen ships. Or a little under six hundred and fifty ships, once you removed the ones without functioning tactical from the mix. Six hundred, once you factored in those out of PDC rounds. *Dammit.* Hope wiped sweat from her forehead as she worked — the bridge of the *Ark Royal* heating a little too much now that power was back. *Okay, okay. Focus.* The count of available ships was more like five hundred, when you selected out the ones that had compromised LIDAR or RADAR tracking systems. Five hundred brave ships from the Old Empire, scattered around the ugly planet below them.

Step four: another dose of the nanites. Hope gave the hypo to Nate along with two protein bars. He'd looked at her with a blank expression, and she'd said, *she needs to eat. One for Harlow too. Two doses, two bars.* And he, because he was overcompensating, grabbed another handful of protein bars, securing them in the pockets of his ship suit.

Step five: hail the fleet. The cap took care of it, signaling the *Torrington*. He'd been talking some sense into Karkoski right until the bugs had taken over the woman's mind. It had to be tried — they had to get them to jump away. It hadn't worked, but the effort had been made.

Step six: use the battle net to track the Republic ships. The automated defenses weren't for them. Nate had said they were for the Ezeroc, and the Ezeroc alone. Which made sense; when the bugs came for them, they needed to be kept busy, so Hope had coded in the battle net to ignore anything with a transponder. It seemed the quickest solve for a nasty problem.

Step seven, the last step: the ugly step. Nate said he needed a trip down to the planet. To go get Grace. El had said *no, that's crazy*, and Kohl had said *I'm coming with*. Hope had watched the cap listen, his face hard, and he'd said to El over the comm, *When we call, you need to come, and you need to come with fire, Elspeth*. He never called her Elspeth. He'd clapped Kohl on the shoulder, then stopped, and given Kohl a hug, but like men did. He'd said something to Kohl Hope hadn't heard, and Kohl had looked at Hope, and nodded. Step seven was Nate stepping into an escape pod occupied by the corpse of his dead sister Annemarie, to go down to an alien planet full of bugs that wanted to kill him, after a woman who he loved but was already dead.

Hope knew all about doing things for the people you loved even though it made no sense, so she hadn't said anything at all. She met Nate at the door to the escape pod. "Hi," she said.

"Hope, I'm going. You can't talk me out of it."

"Of course not," she said. "I want you to go."

He did a double-take. "You do?"

"Grace is my friend. But so are you. So. So. I need you to do one thing." She bit her lip.

"What's that?" Nate walked closer. "Hope, are you okay?"

"No," she said. She realized she would possibly cry and didn't want to do that, so she talked instead. "You are the only family I've got, Nate. The thing you need to do is to come back. Come back alive. Don't die down there. Don't die alone. Come back to all of us. We need you." And she gave him a quick hug, and a peck on his cheek — stubble and man smell — before heading back towards the bridge.

"I'll come back," said Nate from behind her. "Hope, it'll be okay."

She paused, not turning. "I don't think so, Cap. We can't always be lucky. But we can be careful. There's a difference. So be careful. For all of us."

CHAPTER THIRTY-ONE

THE ESCAPE POD WAS OLD, and it might kill him on the way down, but it was the fastest way he knew of to get to where he needed to be without the Republic fleet turning him to ash.

Old it might be, but there was no need to entomb his sister on a shitty bug world, so Nate removed her from the inside of the pod with all the care he could muster. Her body was light, as light as rain, and he left her propped in the corridor outside the pod. He thought of what Hope had said. *Careful. Not lucky.* Which was funny. He'd never thought he was lucky. His whole family? Dead, as it turned out. The Empire? Gone. His journey through that life had cost him his one good hand. The woman of his dreams? On a dead planet, her mind taken over by the enemy. An entire fleet stacked against them out there in the hard black, insect intelligence using their human puppets to be watchful for Nate's crew. Hell, his own ship, his wonderful *Tyche*, had a thumbprint you could see from across space. There'd be no running. Not anymore. Not like before. And even if he got away, the military might of the Republic was here. They'd get taken over by the bugs, and sent back to human space, and his entire race would fall.

No, not lucky at all. But Hope might have been right: a little care might see them out the other side of this day. He checked the hypo in his pocket, then slung his sword inside the escape pod. Nate gave another glance at Annemarie's body, offering her a salute, then pulled the big red lever on the door of the pod. It stuck the first time he pulled, then groaned down with the second tug. The door slid closed in front of him, sealing with a hiss. Not that he trusted it, securing his helmet with a twist of the collar. That was him: Captain Nathan Chevell ne Fergelic, going to an entire planet filled with bugs, armed with nothing but a sword, a blaster, and an old space suit. He pulled the acceleration bars down around his shoulders, because it wouldn't do to get tossed around in here. If there was turbulence on the way down, the pod would just deliver his battered corpse to the waiting hordes below.

The space suit was part of a uniform, and it still fitted well enough. It was made for one of the Emperor's Black, and was made to last.

The pod shook around him as the clamps holding it in place rattled free, then he felt the huge slam of the explosive launch as the *Ark Royal* spat the captain's escape pod towards the planet below. There was a brief pattering of debris against the hull, then silence for a second as the pod fell. The old holo display flickered once, twice, three times before sparking into life, marking his position. At five seconds from launch, the rocket mounted to the top fired, pushing down with a 5G force towards the planet. Nate gritted his teeth, holding on to the acceleration harness.

Could be worse. At least the rocket still works.

It could be a lot worse. The rocket was a simple chemical candle, designed for a massive burst. No fusion reactor in a pod this small, just a nudge and he was off into the void. Heading for the planet below. They'd watched Grace's asteroid — weird thinking of it like that — descend, marked the landing spot, and configured the pod to aim *right there*. Whether it made it was a combination of factors; Nate knew he was relying on aged navigation equipment. Nothing in this capsule had been maintained for twenty years. The chemical rocket could have just blown apart — admittedly, worse case — or not fired at all, leaving him to drift until the *Torrington* or other vessel claimed him. But he was away now. The only thing remaining was whether the braking thruster would fire, or he'd impact Ezeroc HQ with enough force to spread him around a square klick of the surface, or turn him into component atoms, or—

Enough of that. You're on your way.

The holo continued to flicker, showing small vanes extending from the top of the pod, four in total. These had tiny thrusters on them, designed to help the pod turn in a vacuum, and the vane design helped it turn if there was atmosphere. Smarter people than him had designed it, and he was in their care now. The holo continued to update as he got closer to the planet, a slight shudder to the craft showing he was going through very thin atmosphere. The world might be a wasteland, but it was a wasteland with a thin coating of something on the top. The pod said it was nudging quarter of an atmosphere, nothing out there but a chemical soup, and encouraged him to leave his helmet on.

The braking thruster fired, and Nate felt the force of it through the acceleration couch. He felt like he weighed five, six, maybe seven hundred kilos. The pod shook and roared as it slowed him down. The impact, when it came, knocked the breath out of him — but it didn't kill him. He was alive.

Downside? He was on an alien homeworld.

The pod's door blew off as the bolts fired, spinning out across an expanse of sand. The air was clear. There was no movement. He'd made it, and if they hadn't seen his descent he might have the upper hand. Nate snared his sword, clambering out of the pod. He was three steps away when the pod fired a stream of bright flares into the air, each one shrieking in the thin air. They were homing beacons, emitting a radio transponder (something the Ezeroc wouldn't notice) but also a lot of noise and light (which they might). So much for the element of surprise.

Fuck it. Nate checked his suit's HUD, Grace's landing sight marked ahead. He was getting enough positioning data from the orbiting Old Empire fleet to find it with ease, a ready-made global positioning network. He set out across the sand, his boots sinking into the surface. It was the kind of surface where six legs would be an advantage. *Best to not think about that.*

It was a short walk to Grace's asteroid, and he was confused about what he saw until he worked it out. There was the shuttle, and it had … *docked* with the rock. The Ezeroc had put a human-style airlock into their floating boulder. There was another hatch nearby, this one open. Footsteps led across the sand, but only a single pair. Grace had been here with Harlow. Whose footsteps were those? She might still be inside the asteroid. He stepped inside, suit lights on to guide his way.

The interior of the rock was red, a bioluminescence that his suit's lights banished away with clear white. There were few choices in direction to make; a passage led to the shuttle, and another passage led up. He went up, boots crunching on the rocky surface.

When he found Harlow, it made him stop, the will sucked right out of him for a moment. His old friend's body was secured to the wall with a kind of resin, the top half of his head gone, the interior empty. No, not empty — just not full of human brain. There was an insect there, and as Nate approached, his dead friend sat up, dragging toxic air into lungs that no longer cared. "You are here. To End. The conflict."

Nate thought about that for a second. He thought about what he was talking to, and what they had done to his friend. What they might have done to Grace. It was too much to take in, but he knew Harlow was past any help from the nanites. He thought about talking to the thing piloting his friend's corpse, then shrugged, pulled out his blaster, and kept squeezing the trigger until there was nothing left. An Ezeroc drone emerged from a hole in the roof, so he shot that too. A second drone followed the first, and he saw no reason to stop, expending plasma like it was going out of style.

After the glowing, smoldering Ezeroc parts stopped raining down, Nate listened over his suit's mics. *Nothing*. No more lies. Nothing else coming. Nothing to disrespect the body of his friend. "Sorry, Harlow," he said. "I promise you before this day is out, you'll get the universe's biggest Viking funeral." Nate turned on his heel, heading back out of the asteroid and on to the sand outside. One set of footsteps.

For his Grace.

He trudged on, following them. He knew the air in his suit was sealed, but couldn't help but taste the ash he'd left on the air behind him.

CHAPTER THIRTY-TWO

KOHL HAD NEVER BEEN the kind of person to stand around while other people had all the fun. This particular instance was no exception, except the cap had said, *Kohl, make sure Hope is safe*, and then he'd said, like he knew what Kohl was thinking, *Kohl, don't fuck this up.*

Don't fuck this up. Words to live by. The thing you'd want on your tombstone, regardless of whether you lived to a ripe old age. October Kohl had no particular illusions; you got a little older, a little slower, and some asshole will blow your brains out or set your body on fire with plasma, or maybe, if you're lucky, you'll get to die of a drug overdose. Until then, *not fucking this up* was a good plan.

Thing was, there was still that natural tension between making sure Hope was okay, and getting down on that planet. Those bugs had put one of their kids, or larvae, or whatever they were inside Kohl, and Grace had saved his ass. And *then* the cocksuckers had mind controlled him with one man in black, and that one stung a little more because it only took the scent of good coin and a little push and he was ready to sell Gracie out. Now he had a bracelet on his wrist and anger in his heart and he was fixing to do something with both those things. Like go kill a whole assload of bugs.

"Say," he said. "Hope."

She didn't look up, expression distracted as she tapped away at the old console. "You've got Hope."

"About that," said Kohl. "I kind of figure this ship is more or less safe."

That got her attention, eyes looking up at him, and she swiped away a couple strands of pink hair. "There is a whole alien planet below us, and a Republic fleet of mind-controlled humans just," she pointed at the bridge windows, "out there."

"But beside that," said Kohl, "this ship is still safe. Nothing is *here*. Right?"

Hope's eyes narrowed. "Right. Sensors are clean. What sensors there are. There's nothing coming up except broken machinery and more broken machinery."

"Cool," said Kohl. "You got any tape?" He watched her process that one, the tension between her wanting to get back to whatever shit she'd been doing warring with a natural curiosity.

"Tape?"

"You know. Tape."

"I think we could come up with some sealant from Engineering. Maybe something poly-based that would hold a pipe. That kind of thing. Not like, tape you'd use to wrap a Christmas present."

"I ain't wrapping a present," said Kohl. "Not that kind."

"Then we've got tape."

"Cool." He thought a while, watching her watching him. She was a good kid, and he felt like more of an asshole than usual right then, because of two things. The first of those things? He'd been an asshole to *her*, because he'd thought the Republic was right for stamping down on crime and making it harder for honest people like *him* to get by, but he'd been wrong about that, just like he'd been wrong about Gracie. He was still pretty sure he was right about the cap and El being basically good humans, but that didn't matter none right now.

The second thing was that he was planning to leave Hope alone on this starship. Sure, sure, El would be right next door, but if something bad happened — say, a boarding party — things might get rough. "How sure are you that these bracelets work?"

"As a fashion accessory or for stopping the alien death bugs from reading and controlling your mind?"

"The second one," he said, but not without thought. Jewelry wasn't a thing he was in to.

"I'm ninety percent sure."

"Just ninety?"

"I never go a whole hundred until I've got a little more data. A hundred is a scary place."

"For an Engineer."

"For an Engineer," she agreed. "The world's not that black and white. Not without data."

"It kinda is," said Kohl. "See, here's the thing. Nate told me not to fuck this up. But our friends are down on that rock. One of them isn't right in the head, and the other isn't right in the heart. You get me?"

"I get you." She blinked at him. "What are you thinking of?"

"Saving the day," he said. "It's what I do."

She snorted, then shook her head. "I guess it might be."

"What I want to do is go down there and kick ass." He pointed an armored hand at the deck, under which was a lot of hard black, and under that, an alien death planet. "I can't do that up here. The problem is, I'm sure that staying *here* would in point of fact be *fucking it up*, and going down there wouldn't."

"The cap told you to stay, didn't he?" said Hope.

"He did." Kohl felt a little uncomfortable about admitting it, because he should have thought of minding Hope by his own damn self, and not needed Nate to tell him what was right and wrong.

"And what do you think you're doing here?"

"Staying. Helping."

"And do you think by staying, and by 'staying' I mean interrupting me, you are helping me?" said Hope.

"When you put it like that," said Kohl, "not as such."

"Then why are you still here?" said Hope.

GETTING to the planet was an easy problem to solve. Getting grenades and other methods of extreme destruction were also easy, because the *Ark Royal* was, at the core, a warship, and it wanted to wage war. Getting the tape? Now, that proved a little trickier, because most of it was fucked. Twenty years was a long time to expect any kind of human-made sticky stuff to still be sticky and, having been exposed to a hard vacuum for much of that time, be of any use. But the polymers in the roll of tape he found still seemed strong enough, even if it wouldn't stick for shit, so it'd have to do. He held a roll of dull gray tape in his hands and thought, *This is it, Kohl, you've found a roll of flat rope.*

He attached the roll of tape to his belt. Making his way back through the bridge towards the escape pods, he saw Hope looking at the roll of tape. He figured she was trying to work out what he wanted it for, but asking would mean she couldn't work it out, so she didn't ask. He cleared his throat. "You want to know what the tape is for?"

"No," she said, a little too fast. "Yes. No. Definitely not." She shook her head. "I know what it's for."

"What's that?" said Kohl.

"Stuff," said Hope, her voice a little anxious. "Sticking stuff to other stuff."

"Close enough," said Kohl, walking towards the escape pods. Time to get to work lifting more heavy things. In this case, the particular load he was looking to lift was the dead souls of a hundred or more insects, if they had souls, and if they didn't, killing them would be good practice anyway.

"Kohl," said Hope, as he was about to leave the bridge.

He turned. "Yeah, Hope?"

"Don't die."

"Wasn't planning on it."

"It's not what you plan for that trips you up," said Hope.

Kohl patted the tape. "Don't you worry, Hope Baedeker. I'm already two steps ahead." He saw her face curl into mild horror at the thought of him planning, and he laughed. "Hope?"

"Kohl."

"You're a fucken good Engineer, and I don't mind admitting that. Thanks for not being a dick about me being an asshole."

"You're welcome," she said. "Anytime. Or ... let's not do that again."

"You got it," he said. He turned away and lumbered down the short path to the remaining escape pod. He hauled out the corpse collection from inside, human and Ezeroc both, then stepped in. It would be hard to clamp himself in with his armor, but that didn't worry him. He reached a hand to the big red door lever, yanking it down with the armor's assisted strength. The pod clanked, the door slamming shut, and Kohl braced his arms against the top, feet against the bottom.

It was the roomiest escape pod he'd ever used, but that was because there was supposed to be a bunch of other assholes in here with him. The kick of the pod launching caused him to holler, and whoop, as his stomach lurched. He lived for this shit.

"FUCKING SAND," he said, to no one in particular. There wasn't anyone around here. He had the cap's position marked ahead courtesy of the battle net, and so he set off after him. The air here looked like it'd be poisonous at a high level, and he patted his tape to make sure he still had it. Nice and secure. Perfect.

The armor wasn't liking the sand, because it was big and heavy, but at least it did all the hard work for him, whining, the joints clanking as he made his way across the surface of whatever the

Ezeroc called this place. Probably something like *home* or *sand*, as he couldn't think of them being original thinkers. No, more of an apex predator. None of *these* assholes walked around with a set of headphones listening to music. They ate other people, and sometimes made you try and kill your friends.

He placed a foot down into the sand, it sinking just like the seventy earlier steps he'd taken, but this time it didn't come back up when he tried to step again. Something had latched on to it, and that was a thing he hadn't expected to happen on a sea made of sand. He could feel something scraping against the outside of his armor. A lesser man might have screamed, or tried to run, or wondered what to do, but Kohl said, "About fucking time." He pawed through the sand until his armored hands found chitin, grabbed, and pulled. He was rewarded with a shower of gore and wet sand as he pulled an Ezeroc claw up. "You fuckers can go *underground* too?"

The sand underneath him boiled, and he backed away as an Ezeroc drone surfaced, sand pouring away from its carapace. Its mandibles clattered at him, and it waved the stump of the broken claw in the air.

"That's right," said Kohl, lifting a leg and almost falling over as a result. He steadied his balance. "Hard to bite through armor, innit?" He unslung his plasma cannon, the automount putting the nice, heavy, comfortable grip in his hands.

The Ezeroc charged.

He pulled the trigger. Plasma spat out, tearing the Ezeroc to pieces, hunks of shell and meat cascading to the sand. Bits of the insect were tossed away to roll, smoking, down the side of a small dune.

The dune shifted. Sand poured free. *That's not a dune. That's ... well, shit.* It was an Ezeroc crab, a big one, its movements causing the sand around Kohl's feet to shake, dragging him a little lower. Well, that *would* explain why they didn't see a lot of surface activity from space. The fuckers were all sleeping under the sand. He wondered if Nate had met a grisly fate, but no, his blip was still heading off in the same direction. No sir, Nate was fine. Kohl looked at his feet, surrounded by the big chunky metal of his armor, and thought, *Well, hell, I guess they like big men around here.*

There was some old holo he'd seen about worms — Goddamn worms — that lived under sand. Attracted to tremors or some shit. Didn't make a lot of sense, and when he'd been told it was based on a book, he'd given up. *No* one had time to read books. What was he, an Engineer? But he wondered about that idea now, and stopped moving. Maybe if he held himself still the Ezeroc would walk the fuck on by.

The big crab turned around a couple of times, still shedding sand, shaking itself like he'd imagine a huge dog, if it was shaped like a crab, might do. An eyestalk looked in his direction, and it started towards him. This told Kohl a couple of interesting ... what would Hope call 'em? Data points. That's it. *Data points.*

First, it hadn't been able to see him with its mind, or his mind, or however that worked. *Go Team Bracelet!* The bracelet was king. He'd need to give Hope a high five and buy her a beer or something.

Second, this thing didn't give two shits about him not moving. He'd gone woke the damn thing up, and here it was, looking for breakfast.

Third, it had eyes.

Kohl pointed the plasma cannon at the eyestalk and squeezed the trigger. The weapon roared, or tried to — hard to roar in half an atmosphere, if it wasn't for his hands on the thing transferring vibration he was sure it would sound feeble — spitting white fire at the crab. The plasma shower hammered against it, causing even the huge thing to shudder with the impacts, and the mandibles around its mouth clattered open and closed in what Kohl hoped was distress. He let up his fusillade to check progress, and noted that things had trended in a positive direction.

First, the crab was listing to one side. He couldn't see an obvious reason other than maybe he'd hit it hard enough in the head to knock some stupid out of it. You didn't try and eat October Kohl for lunch, and it was a useful thing for all creatures of the universe to learn, wise up to, and get on board with. Second, it no longer had eyestalks, those having been turned into stray molecules, whisked away on the wind. Third, and the coolest data point of all, it was trying to walk towards him, but in the wrong direction.

He watched it go for a second or two, then unclipped a mine from his belt. He primed it, then gave it an underarm toss at the Ezeroc. The mine spun through the air, hitting the side of the Ezeroc's shell, and the micro drills on the device bored into the chitin, locking it home. The Ezeroc paused, as if sensing something amiss, then the mine detonated, blowing a huge hole in it. It yawed, then collapsed to the ground.

The day was getting better already. Much, much better. Kohl grinned, and set out after Nate.

CHAPTER THIRTY-THREE

THE CAVE WAS SILENT, dark, and looked empty from the outside. No movement. Nate didn't hold much truck with dark caves, especially on an alien world where the only life here wanted to eat him, but his girl was in there, and he was damned if they would have her.

And if they already had her? He'd work that through if he needed to. But he was sure of one thing: whatever happened, he and Grace would do it together.

As far as devil insect caves went, he could see why they chose it. It had a wide mouth, worn smooth over countless years by the passing of many chitinous feet. There were no corpses here, no bones of another species, just a smooth, dark entrance, yawning like a giant's mouth against the sand around it. Grace's footsteps went inside, and he followed them.

She was waiting inside, in a clear, wide area. He was reminded of a boxing ring, except this wasn't a sport, there wasn't a referee, and he hated boxing. Fencing had been more his speed, back before he'd lost his good left hand and the leg that gave him balance enough to dance or fight as the mood took him. Grace was standing tall, her black

Tyche ship suit around her, helmet sealed. He could make out the horrible cut around her head, and he wanted to run to her, to hold her.

She was holding a sword, and that slowed him down some.

Behind Grace was a tunnel extending down into the dark. "This the hive?" he said.

She blinked at him, but slower than a human might. Like she *needed* to do it, but couldn't remember how. "It's where my Queen lives. The oldest of them all." A wistful smile pulled at her lips. "She is pleased you brought the rest of our ... our ... the human's military with you. She can end it all here."

"Eh," said Nate. He wanted them to be back in his cabin. Nate wanted them to be in a spacer bar. He wanted them to be anywhere but here. He wanted them to have not done this terrible thing to her. "I promised Harlow a Viking funeral. Do you know what that is?"

A frown creased her brow. "I ... remember. For Reiko."

"Sure," said Nate.

"Reiko is food."

Fuck. "Not so much," said Nate. "Please, Grace. Come home."

A smile spread its way across her face. "Nathan, no. You've come here to fight me? You know you can't win."

"I know," he agreed. "But I haven't come here to fight you." He unslung his sword, the black blade singing as it tasted alien air.

"You are drawing your sword. That looks like fighting."

Nate could feel the bracelet growing warm against his wrist. He gave her a grin, then tapped his head with his free hand. "C'mon. You know that won't work."

"You need skin on the sword. How are you doing this?"

"You know that thing where you tell your opponent your whole plan?" said Nate. "I'm not doing that."

"No," said Grace. "You'll die." And she ran at him.

A few things went through Nate's mind. The foremost was that he was deeply, truly fucked, because Grace Gushiken was a master of the blade. She had spent her entire life running from those who wanted to jail her, or to experiment on her, and in that life, she had learned to protect herself. In his prime, he might have been a match. Now? Not so much. A couple weeks of her running drills with him to fight with his sword in his off hand weren't enough to match a lifetime's worth of honed skill. Here was a true *kensai*, and she wanted him dead.

The second thing was that him dying would probably happen one way or the other, which left him with a strange sense of peace. If he bested Grace, a hundred bugs would come out of that pit and eat him alive. Nope, that wasn't a great solve. He was here for something different. A last, desperate hope.

The third thing, and he'd admit most important, was that Grace had a sword that Hope had made, designed to cut through just about any old thing. As her blade swung towards him, he brought the black blade up to meet it. This here was the test. Would his sword of an Old Empire, long fallen, hold fast against a blade wielded by the finest fencer he'd ever known?

The blades met, sparks dancing from where their edges hit. The black blade held. Grace's eyes, her helmet close to his, showed surprise. They moved apart, circling. "Your sword," she said.

"Yep," he said. "Kinda cool, right?"

"I have surprising tricks too," she said, stopping her circling. Grace reached a hand towards him, and for a crazy hot second, he wondered if she wanted him to come to her, like this was all some weird dream, but … no. He felt himself held by an invisible hand made of iron, lifted above the rocky floor. Not just *no*, but *all the no*. What the fuck? He squirmed in the air as she closed her eyes, hand out, then she closed her fingers. He felt the force of that grip closing around him, squeezing him like an industrial press. His ribs would collapse. His lungs would be crushed, his heart stopped.

Not today. His metal hand found his blaster, drawing it in a smooth motion, and he fired hot plasma. Not *at* Grace, because killing her wasn't why he was here. It was never why he had come here. He fired it at the ground next to her, causing shards of rock to explode upward. She lost her focus, and he fell to the ground, landing in a crouch. He recovered, firing again, and she dived to the side, rolling away from the blasts. When she came to her feet, sword in her hand, he could see blood streaming from her nose. He hadn't caused that. Using this ... new power, like she'd used her old ones on the *Tyche*? That caused the blood. There were limits.

"You can't beat me," she said. Her voice betrayed no strain.

"No," he agreed.

"Then ... why? Why are you here?"

"Why do you think?" He hefted his sword. "Come on."

She came at him again, swords ringing in the cave again, and again, and again. Nate was being pushed back, and he still hadn't done what he needed to do. They broke apart for a breather, circling again, eyeing for an advantage. She licked blood from her upper lip. "I ... don't understand. After so long, humans ... make no sense."

"Here's a thing," said Nate. "The old Emperor was my brother. Half-brother, anyway."

Her circling slowed, but didn't stop. "You are ... Emperor?"

"Not really," said Nate. "I mean, sure. Technically I might be. But you need an Empire to be the Emperor."

"You have an Empire."

"No," he said. "I don't have an Empire without you. Without my Grace."

"She is not your Grace," said Grace, and closed the distance in three quick steps, batting his sword aside. She pulled her sword back, and ran him through. He felt her blade pass through his chest, could see her face right next to his as she cut his heart in two.

He slipped to the floor at her feet. "It's okay, Grace. It'll be okay." He tried to reach for her, to touch her one more time, but he couldn't. Nathan Chevell, the last Emperor of the human race, fell back on the rocky floor of an alien world, dead.

CHAPTER THIRTY-FOUR

EL LOOKED up from the holo stage at Hope, who was leaning in through the door to the flight deck. "Hi," she said. "Is there a particular reason you are here?" She frowned, replaying that in her mind, then said, "I mean, I was expecting you on the *Ark*. Everything okay with you and Kohl?"

"Yes," said Hope. "Kohl is killing bugs and I'm here."

El chewed that over for a bit. "There are bugs on the *Ark Royal*?"

"No. There are bugs down there." Hope jerked her chin at the planet below them.

"Kohl went to the planet?" El tried to process this, and kept coming up blank. "That doesn't make any sense. It's a deathtrap."

"I don't think Kohl sees it that way," said Hope, slinging herself onto the acceleration couch beside El. "Or, he sees it as a deathtrap in his favor."

"Sounds like Kohl," agreed El. "Still doesn't explain why you're here."

"Okay, so don't panic," said Hope, "but we might need to fly soon. I'm not the expert on flying, but here's what's up." The holo stage flickered, then pulled out from the expanse of Republic ships at the edge of the debris field, highlighting the *Ark Royal* and the tiny dot of the *Tyche* against it. Red lights bloomed on the stage, delta-v highlighting approach vectors. "Those things," said Hope.

"What are they?"

"Not human," said Hope, with air quotes. "They are coming in our direction. My best guess is that the Republic ships can't find us, and the Ezeroc can't find us. But the Ezeroc, right, they knew what happened last time there was a massive battle above their world. They came here to the *Ark Royal*, killed everyone, and stopped things cold."

"They're coming back to the head of the snake, so to speak," said El, feeling a little sick.

"I don't know. Is it what you'd do?"

"Probably," said El. "We can't go yet. We don't have the all-clear from the cap."

The holo shivered as an update from the battle net came through, and one of the red lights disappeared. "Ah hah," said Hope.

"What was that?" said El.

"That would be," and Hope paused, biting her lip, "the *Calamity*. It just opened up with kinetic rounds on an alien ship and turned it to shards." The red dots stopped moving closer.

"The *Calamity*?"

"It's what the transponder said it was. Destroyer, I think."

"Bad ass name."

"Pretty bad ass," said Hope, sounding disinterested. "I think we've got a worse problem." She highlighted some smaller dots, outlined in yellow, coming towards them. "These are human ships. They are coming our way."

"We won't shoot them down," said El, half a statement, half wanting it to be a question, and then hating herself for it.

"Captain's orders," said Hope.

"They will see us," said El. "They will blow the *Tyche* to pieces."

"*That* is why I'm here," said Hope. "I figure we need to get gone while the going is good."

"You don't need to tell me twice," said El. "Are we go for launch?"

"Everything's ready," said Hope. She patted the console in front of her. "I've got the battle net hooked up here. We need to not die, which I've told everyone else to do today, and it sounds like good advice."

"Pretty good," agreed El.

"So, Helm, how do we not die in a starship?" Hope looked at her.

"We fly," said El. "We fly like the dogs of war are at our heels."

"Looks like they are," said Hope, pointing at the holo stage.

"Bringing the ship online," said El. She worked the console, initiating the startup sequence for the *Tyche's* reactor. There was a rumble as it came online, then lights on her console bloomed, systems coming to life. Her good girl, ready to fly one more time. El just hoped it wasn't one *last* time. Things were … not in their favor out there. "Brace yourself."

Hope clipped herself into the acceleration couch. "Go."

El reached for the controls. She keyed the controls for the airlock, the *Ark Royal* letting them go with a gentle release, the *Tyche* adrift for a second. Then she jammed the throttle forward, the twin fusion drives of the *Tyche* burning blue-white into the hard black. They ran, as if their lives depended on it.

Their lives, and all other human lives too. *No pressure*, thought El as the Gs pressed her into her seat.

THE PART of a good ship battle was where you were never in one in the first place. The last time El had been in one, it had been Republic fighters on her ass over Earth. Before that, the damn bugs had been tossing rocks at her as they scrambled over the deck on Absalom Delta. Here, she had bugs on one side of a debris cloud, and a bunch of not-the-Republic-anymore assholes on the other. The trick here, as near as she could tell, was to have a three-step plan.

Step one: get through the debris field (not getting hit by any floating hulks, human or otherwise) while moving at a significant enough velocity to not be targeted by human weapons. Use the other ships as cover. If they follow, pretend it's a dogfight. Pretend you're not flying an old heavy lifter, but instead a nimble, agile, modern fighter.

Step two: avoid the Ezeroc waiting at the edge of the debris cloud, while somehow going right through them and to the planet below.

Step three: get to the planet below, save everyone, and get the hell out.

How hard could it be?

"Hope," hissed El under the strain of the hard burn, "I'm taking us toward the Ezeroc."

"You're what?" she said. "I think it's the burn. I can't hear right. I thought you said you were taking us toward the Ezeroc." Truth be told, the *Tyche* was shaking around them, the decking rattling, spars groaning as El pushed them towards the debris field.

El cut the drives, turning the *Tyche* in space, then kicked them off again, two torpedoes sailing past their six and impacting against a ship below them. She twisted the *Tyche* around again, drives facing the planet, and initiated a hard burn of braking thrust, before swinging inside the relative safety of the debris cloud. *Debris* was such a misleading word, because it made the human mind think of small stones, bolts, and other pieces of junk floating around. Harmless. Tiny. In fact, much of the debris was moving at a significant velocity, and a great deal of it was spaceship-sized, because it comprised spaceships or parts of spaceships.

"Sorry, flying, got distracted," said El. "Yeah. We're going down there and getting their attention."

"That's crazy," said Hope.

"We're out of sane options," said El.

"Remember when I said we have to not die?"

El flashed Hope a quick grin. "I said crazy, not dead. Trust me."

"Oh God," said Hope, as El kicked the thrust in again. A little nudge to get them moving.

A piece of something rang against the *Tyche's* hull as she brought them through, the holo stage flickering, the RADAR and LIDAR struggling to keep up with the number of objects in the immediate vicinity. The battle net helped a great deal, but it could only tell the *Tyche* where the pieces of ship holding transponders were, not necessarily where the bits of broken-off ship were. "Easy, now," said El, patting the *Tyche's* console with a hand. "Slow and steady. Slow and steady."

The voyage through the debris was accompanied by occasional ringing of hard metal rain against the *Tyche's* hull as they passed through smaller clouds of objects. El was saving the PDCs for later, if there was a later; this just took a delicate hand. They'd need the guns for when this gentle jog turned into a run or a sprint.

"I don't think I'm up with the … details of the plan," said Hope.

"Okay, so here's the deal," said El. "In about," and she checked the holo stage, "thirty seconds we'll emerge from this cloud of metal and rust. We will wave to the Ezeroc by way of a laser, and then we will go back into the cloud of debris."

"So they follow us."

"Yes," said El. "Then we will practice not dying very hard."

"Okay," said Hope. "I think I can give us a bit of extra action."

The *Tyche* cleared the debris, a last few ships floating below them. El fired up the forward weapons, bringing a laser online. She painted a small attack-craft-sized floating rock, one of Hope's red dots, with the laser, then said, "From Earth, with much love," and fired. The laser reached out across the void, superheating the outside of the Ezeroc asteroid, boring a hole through it, and punching out the other side. There wasn't a great gout of fire or escaping atmosphere. The Ezeroc didn't need to breathe. But it had an instant reaction as the rocks spread out along the underside of the debris field came at them.

"Well, that worked. Here goes to not dying," said El, spun the

Tyche, and fired the drives again. This time, she didn't cut thrust as they hit the edge of the field, one eye on the holo stage, one eye out the front of the ship, piloting by sight. The distances between ships were vast — space was *big* — but they were also moving at a hard burn, five Gs of thrust at their backs as a constant.

As they entered the shadow of larger ships, El brought them in close to a larger one. An alien vessel, made of glass or something like it. No time for sightseeing; she brought them in nice and tight next to it, using it for shelter against other floating material. The PDCs were armed, and as they burned along the length of the glass craft, the PDCs chattered at smaller pieces of metal floating too close.

El could see one of the human vessels ahead — corvette, no time to take in the transponder codes, no time to see the name of that brave vessel — fire drives as Hope brought the ship back to life. *Ah, I see.* El turned the *Tyche* away from the glass ship and towards the bright glow of the human ship's drives. She checked the holo, and sure enough, the Ezeroc were still behind them. No care to avoid impacts because they didn't care about losing air, and they didn't care about losing a couple of drones. El brought the *Tyche* nice and close to the corvette's drives, and smiled a hard, tight smile as she saw the holo show the friendly ship initiate a hard burn.

The *Tyche* sailed through where the drive's wash would be a moment before they ignited, and El hoped she'd timed it right, or that Hope had, the open cores of the drives above her glowing from red to orange to white, then they were past as bright nuclear fire roared into space behind them. It turned an Ezeroc asteroid to molten magma in an instant, the corvette lurching forward to impact against another vessel that looked like a corkscrew; nothing human hands had made, and *that* caused a bright explosion as the corvette died, its reactor critical, the explosion smashing out around it.

But the *Tyche*, she wanted to run, and El gave the ship her head. She sprinted ahead of the explosion's blast wave, soaring up and around — a groan from Hope beside her under the strain, or the flip-flopping of her stomach — another craft, this another one of the glass vessels. The alien ship took the brunt of the explosion, and the *Tyche* went free.

The PDCs hammered the hard black again, chewing through the side of a drifting human fighter, shards of metal and glass and — *don't look* — human remains as they soared through. They were coming up to the vast bulk of a human carrier, a big, dark shape that clouded the heavens. *Please be awake. Please be awake.* The *Tyche* ran for her sibling, into the shadow of that huge embrace, as the carrier's running lights came on, bright swaths of light touching the dark. El had a moment to take in building-high writing identifying this ship as the *Heracles*, a twist of her lips the only acknowledgment of the irony of their Greek goddess cozying up to a familiar hero of legend.

A huge explosion shook the *Heracles* as nuclear reactors too old, no maintenance over years and years, gave up. El twisted the sticks around, the *Tyche* screaming away with a shudder of her superstructure, the expanding firmament of fire ahead blazing out. *Faster. Faster, girl, faster, or we're all dead.* Hope groaned again as the Gs clutched them like the fist of an angry god, harder and harder, wanting them dead, wanting them to just *stop*. But the *Tyche* wouldn't stop, not yet.

She was a goddess in her prime, and her luck wasn't spent yet.

El put distance behind them and the expanding fireball of the *Heracles*, her vision blurring from the Gs, unable to make out the markers on the holo stage. *Enough of this.* She cut thrust, spun the *Tyche*, and hit burn again, pointing them back at the Ezeroc pursuers. She started the ships' lasers again, coring an enemy asteroid, fragments of molten rock flowing out the back. That asteroid stopped making course corrections — she must have hit the pilot, whatever that looked like. El wanted to cheer, but the pressure of Gs on her chest would have kept that at a bare croak.

Two Ezeroc ships left. Two fuckers to go. One of them launched mass at them, just tossing rocks in their direction, and the PDCs solved that problem. El pointed the *Tyche* towards the heart of the debris cloud and hit burn again. An alert blinked on the holo, but she ignored it. It would just be something saying she was overloading the ship, or maybe they were holed, but as El saw it they were still flying. Still flying meant still alive, and anything else was secondary.

There. A destroyer. The *Valhalla*. As it should be called. El let up thrust for a second, just long enough to croak out, "The *Valhalla*."

"I see it. I'm on it." Hope's voice sounded hollow, flat, strained through the pressure of space battle.

It would get more strained. El burned again, the *Tyche* singing in response, leaping forward on a trail of fusion fire. El was thinking a hundred things, things like *please let that ship still be alive* and *I hope it still has PDCs online* and *I hope the battle net is working and we don't get shot* and *if it pops like the Heracles we're fucked*.

They closed with the *Valhalla*, El watching as the old ship came to life, ancient PDCs emerging from their housings, not enough for her liking, but more than none. The *Tyche* ran down the length of the *Valhalla*, the other ship skimming past underneath them almost too fast to comprehend, and then they were past. The *Valhalla* reached out into the hard black with her PDCs, chewing up one of the remaining Ezeroc ships before her guns ran quiet.

One left. There was a slam of a huge hand against the hull of the *Tyche* as a tossed rock hit them, alarms blooming like fire over the holo. The sticks felt sluggish in El's hands, something in the drive controls not working the way they should. She looked over at Hope as thrust left the ship, and said, "I'm sorry."

"I'm not," said Hope, and pressed a button on her console.

The *Valhalla* ruptured, almost like it was in slow motion, starting with Engineering, the bright billowing fire extending along her superstructure. The following Ezeroc ship tried to course-correct but even the bugs had limits on the Gs they could pull, and the ship was turned into a piece of stray vapor in the blink of an eye.

The buffet of the explosion grabbed the *Tyche* and hurled her towards the planet, a spear thrown by warring gods. Towards the pit of hell below them. Right towards where they were needed. El used what control she had left to control the *Tyche's* tumble, bring the ship into something approximating a steady fall, and looked at Hope. "Thanks," she said. "That was ... good thinking."

"That was pure luck," said Hope. "Let me go see if I can fix whatever broke so we don't die."

El snorted, then laughed, and Hope laughed, the release of being alive singing through them. They were alive, and they were flying with a goddess, and her luck wasn't spent. Not yet.

CHAPTER THIRTY-FIVE

SHE STOOD in the cavern of her new home, breathing hard inside the suit she still had to wear. Her Queen might remake the parts of her body that needed to breathe, if given time, and enough bodies to experiment on. There were — and she looked at the rocky ceiling, as if she could see through it — plenty of warm bodies up there in the—

Hard black.

—space between worlds to serve as resources. Further experiments, fuel for the Hive, so hungry for so long out here without more life to consume.

Her helmet blinked a warning at her, human text saying *CREW FATALITY EMERGENCY* and a set of numbers and charts that all said *no life remains*. No brain activity, no pulse, no respiration. Even at the last, this captain was causing harm; he could at least have been fuel for the Hive. But he'd thought to come here — for what purpose, she still didn't know, his mind dark to her. He'd put his steel against hers, and while his steel was strong, his training wasn't.

He lost his good hand fighting for a better world. You killed him you killed him you killed him.

A keening sound came from her throat — *her* throat, *her* mouth.

She clamped her lips shut, not knowing what it meant. She felt a sickness in her stomach as she looked down at the dead captain. She was sure she wasn't ill.

She shook her head. This voice inside her head wouldn't be quiet. She wanted to scratch at the seam in her skull, and as she raised her arm, gloved hand hitting her helmet, she felt that her arm was ... sore. Not painful, as it would be if this man had scored a hit against her. He could have come at her with five men and still not mark her. Only one on his crew—

October Kohl.

—was of the right caliber. And he was coming. Drones out in the vast sands had encountered him and died. He was coming this way, and she needed to prepare. She knew Kohl would see the captain, then he would try and kill her. She flicked her sword down and out, blood slicking from the blade, and felt that soreness in her arm again.

Her eyes looked at the captain, his body slumped backward in death, just spoiled meat now. The rent where her sword had passed through his body vented air and blood out the front and back, spilling precious moisture on the cracked stone ground. She looked at his fallen sword on one side, the black blade something they would need to study — her kin were not good with machines like the humans were, but they had humans aplenty above the world who could be made to serve. She looked to the other side at a small device that had fallen to the ground.

She stepped closer. It wasn't a blaster — after he'd fired at her, he'd re-holstered that. He didn't want to hurt her, and that was the advantage she'd used to kill him. It wasn't a weapon of any kind she could tell, not a laser, maser, kinetic weapon, or — the favored type their kind used — plasma blaster. She crouched down, pushing the threat of the approaching October Kohl from her mind, because here was a puzzle she needed to understand.

It was a small device, the kind that could fit in the hand and not be noticed in the heat of battle. It had a glass reservoir — half full — and a trigger.

It is a hypo.

She turned her head, almost in awe, to look at her arm. Where it was sore. She saw the merest wisp of venting air from a hole punctured clean through the material of her suit. The entry point of a hypo, pressed against her arm as she pressed her sword through this man's heart.

It's okay, Grace. It'll be okay.

She took a step back, putting a hand over the tiny hole. Not because the air she was losing was of great concern but because she didn't know what he had injected her with.

It'll be okay.

"Okay for who?" she said. "What have you done to us?"

The body didn't answer. The captain was dead.

She felt a slow burn in her blood, a trickle of promised pain. She coughed once, twice, and then curled over as the wave of agony hit her. The Hive cut her off in an instant, shutting down that source of unbearable pain, just her and her companion, nestled against the meat of her human brain. She screamed at the feeling of her blood being made of fire, of pure boiling acid inside her skull.

She dropped her sword, falling to her knees. She threw up, bile splattering the inside of her helmet, and then she screamed again, fingers clawing at the air. She reached out with her mind, trying to find the source of the pain. The rock of the ceiling cracked as she lashed out, and the stones closest to her buckled into fragments.

The pain didn't stop. Her head was on fire. Her fingers tried to release the collar of her suit, to get the helmet off, so she could claw at her skull, to get the fire *out*. Her fingers clenched, and spasmed, unable to find a purchase on her helmet. She couldn't get out. She couldn't get free.

She, the first of her kind, would die here in this cave next to the captain. The thing inside her skull was in agony, its pain feeding hers, and hers feeding it.

Her helmet cracked against the ground, a spider's web of fissures appearing over the glass. *Yes. Smash it open.* She raised her head, trying to bring it against the stony ground with enough force to fracture the glass. *Crack.* More lines against the glass. *Crack.* Another jagged seam across her vision. One more should do it. One more blow against the ground, and she would be free. She gathered her strength against the pain.

Strong hands found her, hauling her away from the ground, and she looked up into the face of October Kohl. He would stop her freeing herself. He would kill her. She screamed at him, gathering strength for one final lash with the blade of mind. Then she doubled over again as Kohl hit her in the stomach, her weak body folding around his fist, and she sank to the ground next to his feet.

"There'll be none of that, Gracie," he said. "It'll be all right."

For who? For who will be all right?

No one answered as the fingers of unconsciousness grabbed her, dragging her under.

CHAPTER THIRTY-SIX

WHEN KOHL HAD TRUDGED across the sand, he'd expected to find more fucking bugs. It was the place for it, right? Bugs, under the sand. Bugs, running towards him like cattle, the grains under his armored boots shifting as they thundered closer. He wanted it. He welcomed it.

It didn't happen.

Ahead, he saw a cave opening. Of *course* the bugs had another cave. They liked dark places where the light of the sun couldn't find 'em. And fair enough, too: they were the kind of thing that scuttled under rocks. It just so happened — and Kohl patted his plasma cannon — that he had brought a match to take into the darkness.

A match, and about a million liters of kerosene. The analogy strained as he tried to make it work, because he didn't have kerosene, so he gave up. The analogy wasn't important; killing bugs was important. Which was problematic, because there weren't any bugs. Not up here, anyway, but two sets of footsteps went into the mouth of that cave, which meant Gracie was in there and the cap had followed her. Two birds, one stone.

His HUD had updated with their vitals as he'd approached,

Gracie's a dead calm, Nate's up and down like an old-fashioned roller coaster. He figured that meant *something*, maybe the cap being tortured by bugs, but it didn't matter. October Kohl was on the case, and soon enough he'd fix it all. He had his tape.

When the cap's vitals flatlined, it caused him to pause his march towards the tunnel. Nate was a capable fighter, make no mistake, and Kohl had always wondered how badly he'd be hurt if he and Nate had come to blows. Not that Nate would *win* — the guy was a cripple, for fuck's sake — but Kohl was sure that if Nate went down, he'd take a couple of Kohl souvenirs with him. It'd hurt, and probably hurt for a long time. It was good he and Nate had never found out how that would end.

It was bad that the reason they never had to find out was that Nate was dead.

He started into a run, about the best the armor could manage on the sand, but he grab-assed a little more speed when the sand gave way to rock as he entered the dark of the cave. What he saw was this: Nate was down like a cold beer on a hot day. There was blood and air escaping from his suit (not why he brought the tape, but it looked like it'd serve a couple purposes today). Gracie was on the ground, thrashing around and making all kinds of horrible noises. Kohl took in the discarded hypo, and did the math: Nate had shot Gracie up with a dose of nanites, Gracie had killed Nate because she had insects in her brain (which was good, in a way, because if *she'd* killed Nate, Kohl might have had to do something about that), and now Gracie was going through a horrible pain as the insects inside her were consumed by a bunch of tiny killer robots.

That last part was ace, but the pain part was less so.

Kohl got alarmed as she smashed her helmet against the ground, so he hurried on over, hauling her upright. He wanted to say to her *I know what it feels like*, but that wouldn't have been helpful at all. He wanted to slap some silly out of her, especially as he saw her eyes narrow like she wanted to kill him. What worked for October Kohl in situations like this was percussive maintenance — didn't matter none if you were talking machines or people, so he wound back a fist and punched her in the gut. The gut was a good choice because a) her helmet was already busted all to hell and b) it'd distract her without killing her. He gave her a shake to make sure she was alive. "There'll be none of that, Gracie," he said. "It'll be all right." There. That's enough talking.

She passed out.

Fuckitall. This was *way* outside his position description. His job was to pick up things too heavy for most people and put them down in an alternative location, and he was fine with that. But no one seemed to be thinking about the end state of all of this. The end state was that, even if they got Gracie, she'd be wearing a suit, and wouldn't have a bracelet on, and would therefor succumb to the external forces of evil alien mind bugs. Kohl sighed, then got to work.

There were two good swords on the ground, one shiny and bright, the other black as night. Both seemed to have a good enough edge, but the black sword was the one he needed, so he picked it up, armor clanking as he moved around the chamber. There was a skittering, and an Ezeroc drone appeared from deeper in the tunnel. "Finally," said Kohl. He dropped the black sword, swung the plasma cannon around, and turned the bug into a blazing pyre of chitin with a five-second salvo. It promised more bugs, which gave Kohl a deep-seated happiness. There would be plenty of bug-killing in his future.

That job done, he once again picked up the black blade, sliding it through the material of Gracie's suit's right arm, just above the wrist. Difficult to do a tidy job in conditions like this, but he figured he wouldn't be graded on perfection; it just needed to be good enough for government work. The blade slid through the material like there wasn't any resistance — *damn nice sword, maybe I can get Nate to sell it to me* — then popped off the glove in a gout of escaping air. He clamped a hand around Gracie's wrist, then fumbled out the roll of tape.

This is why he'd brought the tape. Only October Kohl was thinking.

He wound the tape around Gracie's wrist and suit, creating a rough approximation of a seal. It wouldn't hold in all the air, but it'd hold in enough air for him to do a better job. Next part, sword. He took the hilt of the black blade, pressing it into her bare hand. Then he wound more tape around her fist, securing it in place. Mind bugs? *No problem.*

He swiveled in place, checking Nate out. First things first, those holes. He bent over, slapping tape on the back of Nate's suit, then rolling him over and repeating the process for the front. He stood up, surveying his handiwork.

Her voice, when it came, was a whisper. "What have I done?"

Kohl grinned, turning around. "Gracie. You okay?"

"No," she said. "No. No. I'm not … *what have I done?*"

"Well now," said Kohl, "I figure it's a bit of a list, but I suspect first up in your mind is that you killed the cap."

"I … *couldn't* have," she said. "I *did.*"

"Yeah, those mind fucker's do that," said Kohl. He tapped the side of his helmet. "I remember. You helped me then, Gracie, so I'm here to help you."

He saw her look at the black blade taped to her hand, the tears running down her face, mixed with blood streaming from her nose, and right *there* was the thing he was hoping wouldn't happen, but did. Sometimes in the shock and awe of a particular situation a person would go all to pieces, and they'd try and do some damn fool thing like kill themselves. Gracie took that sword, moving like she would cut on her other arm, so Kohl stepped forward, armored hand closing around the blade. "It'll be okay, Gracie."

"*IT'S FAR FROM FUCKING OKAY!*" she screamed at him. "I killed the man I love."

"Yeah," said Kohl, "but wouldn't you prefer a little revenge?"

"Even *they* can't fix this," said Gracie, not listening to him at all, which was annoying but understandable in the circumstances.

"Well, see now," said Kohl, "that's not important."

"It is," she said. "Don't you see? Nate, is, I…"

"Yeah," said Kohl. He bent down to pick up the hypo. "They can't fix this, but maybe we can." He bent over, and pressed the hypo against Nate's arm. What had El said about the nanites? Some damn thing like, *They can rebuild freshly-injured tissue.* To Kohl's eye, and he'd had plenty of practice injuring people, the hole in Nate's chest looked fresh. All of this was a gamble: ancient tech harvested from a space station run by devils, brought back online by a young Engineer high on too many stims. *Eh, you've played worse odds, Kohl.*

He squeezed the trigger, the hiss delivering the remaining contents of the canister into the cap's body. "Now we need a jump-start." He flipped Nate over, finding the emergency med controls on the suit. They had the usual controls — a button for adrenaline, a button for a defib, a button for God's own antihistamine, and so on. Kohl just needed to get Nate's heart beating for a spell so the nanites could get to where they needed to be. He looked at the list of controls, said, "Fuck it," and pressed all the buttons.

CHAPTER THIRTY-SEVEN

KARKOSKI HAD HEARD people say things before like, *it was as if a cloud lifted from my thoughts.* She'd assumed it was worthless hyperbole, people trying to explain a flight of fancy away. People often wanted to make things they'd done someone else's fault, or at least not their fault.

This time, Karkoski knew what they felt like.

Not just the cloud-thoughts part; that was self-evident. There had been a massive, ugly thing pressing on the top of her mind, squashing the real her out the sides. She'd seen a cider press when she was a child visiting a faux farm on some damn family holiday or another. The 'farmers' had filled the press with apples, pressed a few buttons, and the whole creaking wooden contraption had crunched those apples down. Pro job. Karkoski had tasted the juice — sweet, and fresh — and at that point decided that she never wanted to be a farmer. Too little impact on the world. She didn't want to make juice. She hadn't realized that other people, or things, did, and that there was a terrible, horrible alien intelligence that made juice from people's minds. Because being under Ezeroc control was like that: they pressed down with a strength that a single apple, let alone a hundred apples, couldn't fight. And they licked at the juice that flowed out.

That presence was gone. There'd been a flash of amazing, startling pain, a feeling like Karkoski's blood was on fire, and she'd screamed, clawing at her flesh. She'd cut her own skin with her fingernails. It was just feedback on the network, she was sure of it, and it meant that someone connected right into Hive HQ had been in a great deal of pain. Who, or what? Not important. The important part was that the apples in the press, so to speak, had a moment of freedom.

The bit that Karkoski understood very, very well now was how you didn't want to be responsible for your actions.

She took in the holo stage, red everywhere as the *Torrington* fought a battle with the Republic fleet they'd come in with. Ships vented atmosphere and fire and people into the hard black, jousting with weapons powered by their nuclear forges. The milieu took place above a dead world surrounded by more dead ships. They'd come here following Chevell's trail, the plan coming out as expected. First, apply pressure. Second, show the rest of the Republic what their Emperor was made of. You couldn't just whip an Emperor out of a hat; the people who would end up serving under that banner needed to see what cloth his sails were cut from. But people in general, and Emperors in particular, well, they were stupid. So Karkoski and Chad had planned to sail off after Chevell and save him from his own fool self.

They didn't realize that Chevell had taken them into the remains of the last great war humanity had fought against the Ezeroc. A war that no one alive even knew had been fought: all the people doing the fighting had died around an alien crust. The Emperor would have known, but again — dead. Humans had failed here. And Karkoski, who remembered giving the orders to open fire on her own ships, knew why they had failed. The insects didn't need to lift a finger. They *made* you do what they wanted.

"Cease fire," she said. "Orders to stand down, all ships, all weapons."

Silence followed her command. Karkoski turned to Communications. "I said, orders to stand down, all ships, all weapons."

The comms officer seemed to be coming around from a daze, but nodded, the motion slow and sluggish. Karkoski turned to Chad, who wasn't standing at her side anymore.

She found him at the doorway out of the bridge, fingernails broken off where he'd been trying to claw his way out through the steel bulkhead. His eyes were red, staring. She offered him a hand, which he took, and she helped him upright. "Chad—"

"Karkoski," he hissed. "We have a very, very small window. There is a Queen down there." His hand jerked towards the window, the brown orb of the planet suspended like a round turd. "The oldest of them. The strongest. There are others. Other Queens, but they all ... they are submissive. Like us."

"Got it," said Karkoski.

"No," said Chad. "You don't. We need to bust that planet open. Everything we've got."

"Chevell is down there," said Karkoski. "We saw his ship heading for the crust." That, at least, she remembered through the haze of the Ezeroc pressing on her mind.

"No problem," said Chad. "Get him on the horn. Tell him to get out. You fire your nukes. He gets out. Win-win."

"And we win the war?" said Karkoski.

Chad laughed, a weak, feeble sound. "No, Karkoski. But we win the most important battle of the war. We show those fuckers they can be beaten. They've never, ever been beaten."

"Nukes it is," she said, turning from Chad. "Communications? Get me the *Tyche*. Tactical?"

Her tactical officer nodded. "Sir?"

"I want the whole fleet to empty every crust buster they've got down there. First, clear all that *shit*," and here, she waved an arm, encompassing the debris field, "out of the way. Make a hole with standard weapons. Then drop everything we've got onto that crust. I want to see nothing larger than a cupcake floating out there within twenty minutes."

"Fucken' A," said the tactical officer, then realized his breach in protocol.

Karkoski thought of a couple choice responses, but settled on one she was sure would send the right message. She stalked around to the Tactical console, leaning over the man. She looked him in the eye. "Fucken' A," she agreed.

Her Communications officer spoke. "*Tyche* on comm."

"One moment," said Karkoski. She looked out the bridge windows. "Let's light it up."

The Republic fleet, all one hundred and thirty ships, fired on the planet below. It was terrible. It was beautiful. Now, to get Chevell out alive.

CHAPTER THIRTY-EIGHT

GRACE WANTED TO SCREAM. She wanted to rage, and cry, and kill every insect on this world. They'd made her kill the man she'd loved, and that wasn't even the worst part of it. The thing that sat like a cancer in her gut was that Nate had come here knowing he would die. He'd had a hypo with him full of ancient human medicine, a last roll of the dice to save just one more person from the evil of the Ezeroc. She'd seen his eyes and his heart, the way he'd held those dice in a fist to blow luck on them. Not luck for him, because his was all spent. For her. For his Grace.

And she'd killed him.

The cavern had three souls in it: hers, tarnished and bloody. Kohl's, bright and hungry. And the remains of something that lingered on the wind, the memory of a dead starship captain who wouldn't leave anyone behind.

Kohl was still fussing with Nate's suit, trying to get human tech to reach beyond the veil that had always been denied their species. There were no do-overs. No come-backs. You stick a length of steel through someone's heart, they'll stay dead. There might be machines that could breathe for you, or pump your blood, but there weren't any of those machines around them right now. Just a barren world.

Come back to us. There is no place for you in their world anymore.

Grace pulled her gaze away from Nate's prone body. She stared at the back of the cavern, into the dark pit that led below. In that pit, there was a Queen, the eldest of her kind. Grace closed her eyes, looking with the new sight they'd given to her. *Ah. There you are. I see you.* Down below, kilometers below the planet's crust, there was a vaulted chamber, full of drones, servants of a different empire. The Queen above them was colossal, three stories tall, fat and ripe even after millennia of slumber.

And we see you. We've changed you. Made you anew. Unlocked what was hidden.

Yes, said Grace. *And that will be your undoing.*

Grace knew the Queen had been reaching up into space, controlling the thousands of human minds above them. She'd played them like an expert, because she'd done this before. Not just with humans, who came to flush her out, but with other species who came to do the same thing. There was nothing left of any of them but a lingering remnant: empty starships, silent in the void. Warning markers at the border of their world. And no one listened to the warnings.

The Queen's contact had been disrupted when the nanites Nate had injected into Grace had gobbled up the insect in her skull. The pain was exquisite, but nothing compared to what she felt now with Nathan Chevell at her feet. The nanites had left Grace clear-headed and hungry. She had a fixing to use that hunger.

"Kohl," she said.

"Yeah, Gracie?"

"In no more than thirty seconds, a hundred thousand Ezeroc will come for us."

"Awesome."

She felt the ghost of a smile touch her lips, like her body remembered what humor was. "It'll be less awesome for us. For you. For…" She trailed off, looking at Nate, then cleared her throat. "I'll make sure you can get out. The Queen. She'll control your mind, crash the *Tyche* down here."

Kohl stood from his fussing with Nate's suit. Nothing else to be done there. There hadn't been anything else to do in the first place. "Naw. We've got Hope." He gave her a grin through his helmet. "Bugs have never had a Hope."

"What do you mean?"

"Jewelry," said Kohl, perhaps more cryptically than was warranted.

She sighed, opening her other sight to look into his mind, and found ... blankness. Nothing. A zero where there should have been a one. Her eyes opened in surprise. "What the hell?"

"Jewelry," he said again, holding up his arm as if it was supposed to mean something. He pointed at her hand where her fingers taped around the hilt of a black-bladed Old Empire sword. "Hope unpicked how the sword worked. Made it so that the bugs can't see inside our heads."

"Everyone has one?" said Grace.

"No," said Kohl. "Just us on the *Tyche*."

"Because?"

"Reasons," he said.

"So, the rest of the human space fleet, complete with its supplies of nuclear weapons, lasers, masers, and—"

"Yeah, they came loaded for bear."

Grace looked back to the pit leading down. "But they don't have the technology."

"Nope."

"And the Ezeroc Queen can still control them, so if we get off this rock we'll just be blown out of the sky."

"Maybe," said Kohl. "I'm figuring something else is more likely. See, Karkoski will crack this crust wide open."

"You think the Queen will get the human fleet to destroy any inbound weapons sent to kill her."

"It'd be what I'd do," said Kohl, "on account of not wanting to die."

"If she does that," said Grace, "we might live."

"Might," allowed Kohl. He looked like he was struggling with something too heavy even for him. After a moment, he said, "But if we live because this planet's still whole? It'll have been for nothing. The bugs, Gracie. The bugs have got to die. No matter the cost." He didn't look happy about it.

She cast another glance at Nate's form. "Okay," she said. "I'll stop her."

"You can do that?" said Kohl.

"I can try," she said. "Help me with him. When this happens, it'll happen fast. Keep the bugs away from us. And I'll keep their minds away from the fleet's."

Kohl's plasma cannon whined out on its mounts. "Ready to rock, Gracie."

THE QUIET OF the mind was like a deep lake on a summer's day. Blue-black coolness around her, the bright light of reality above. Below her in the depths?

Sharks swam in the darkness.

Except they weren't sharks: alien minds, comfortable with their power. They'd been on top for a long time.

Chad? Chad. I need you. I need you all. She sent her thoughts to the stars, to those Intelligencers up in space above. The Ezeroc had made her strong, but this wasn't a fight one person could win alone.

Chad's response was weak but steady. *Grace. We're here. What do you need?* She could sense the minds linked to his, over a hundred human souls burning bright like stars above.

Be ready. Grace felt the weight of Nate's body across her shoulders, but it felt half-real. It was good and bad; bad, because she was carrying her lover and her partner and she'd killed him, but good, because the feel of him gave her strength. She sank slower into the quiet of the mind, seeking the eldest of the Ezeroc.

The ancient Queen wasn't hard to find. She wasn't hiding from Grace. *You have come back to us.*

Grace would have laughed if she'd been able to. *I have come to end you.*

You? We know the shape of your thoughts. We know every part of you. There is no dissent in the Hive. There is only belonging. To us. And you belong. To us.

Grace ignored that, swimming further down. The Intelligencers above swam with her, bright motes around her like bubbles in the water.

A younger Queen — Grace knew this one was closer to the planet's surface, with a smaller cadre of drones at her command — came for her. Grace met her charge in the blue-black, the sword of her thoughts bright silver. The strength of a hundred other humans tempered the blade of her mind. Grace reached out, feeling the shape of the other Queen, and ... cut her apart. It was like *kendo*, a quiet dance of perfect form. A slice here separated *self* from *selves*, leaving the Queen alone. Another cut, and off came the delusional limbs of power. A final cut, and the ability to think and control was gone. The younger Queen drifted, dying, and then was gone, the blue-black once again cool and calm.

Further down then. The blue-black felt heavier this far down, but Grace welcomed the weight of it. It made her feel whole, compressed, unlike the thousand selves she had been made to be a part of. The Intelligencers with her were a team, not a collective. They fought through shared purpose, not compulsion. It was their strength.

A shoal of Queens attacked her, coming in with rending claws of thought. They wanted to stake her down, pin her mind into immobility. The number and weight of them should have been sufficient. All that remained after their passing was chum in the deep, and then a spreading nothingness. Grace felt Chad's triumph as Grace erased the Queens as if they'd never been, their drone armies in the bright light of reality stuttering to a halt without a governing intelligence.

Finally, the bottom of the lake: almost black, except for the bright intelligence that loomed before Grace. A leviathan, of a size to make the blue whale no more than an ant. Before that majesty was Grace Gushiken. A creation of the Ezeroc, but a creation of humanity too. A despised daughter. A feared esper. A mongrel, hated, cast off, both more and less than nothing.

Yes, Grace was those things, but she was more. A friend. A companion in the hard black. A warrior. She'd learned to stand instead of run. She'd learned to fear loss. She'd learned to love.

Here in the dark quiet of the mind, the Ezeroc Queen and Grace joined their battle. Never had the Ezeroc encountered a species with even a fraction of their gift. They'd uplifted Grace to be the greatest of them, a sharp edge to be used in future battles. They hadn't counted on Grace having companions who would die for her. They hadn't counted on Grace being so *lucky*. They'd shrugged off a couple of crust-busting nukes before. They hadn't factored in the weapon they'd made — Grace herself, and her expanded powers — shaking off her shackles, and carving through the heart of their strongest and eldest. They hadn't factored on Intelligencers, once enemies of all humanity, lending their strength in this final fight.

Humanity sends its regards, said Grace. Then she, and a hundred other human minds, struck.

CHAPTER THIRTY-NINE

"*TYCHE*, THIS IS *TORRINGTON* ACTUAL," said Karkoski's voice over the comm.

El still had a hard burn for the bug's crust. She clicked her comm. "*Torrington*, this is *Tyche*. Go."

"Message for Captain Chevell," said Karkoski. "We're about to blow up the planet."

El looked at Hope, then at the planet. "Wait. No."

"Is there a problem?"

"A small one," said El. "The cap's down there."

There was a pause on the comm channel, the *Tyche* shaking as they fought atmosphere on the way in. "Say again, *Tyche*. I think we're getting atmosphere burr. I thought you said Chevell is on the crust."

"Yep," said El.

There was another pause on the comm. "*Tyche*, be advised you need to extract him post haste."

"Cool," said El. "We were on the job anyway."

"Because the fleet has just launched nukes at the planet," said Karokoski.

El looked at the comm, then craned a neck over her shoulder, as if she could somehow see the nukes chasing them down towards the crust. "How many?" she asked. Maybe a couple would be fine, miss the areas they were in. Or they could chance the target sites. Or *something*.

"All of them," said Karkoski. "They're on dumb fire, in case … well, the bugs take over our minds again."

"Fuck," said El. "Karkoski?"

"Roussel."

"We'll have a talk after this." She clicked the comm off, and looked over at Hope. "I need to know how much time we've got."

Hope nodded at her, acceleration couch shaking her head more than her neck ever could, and the holo stage cleared. The *Tyche* was already talking to the ground, trying to find her wayward crew. The holo blinked once, twice, then filled with information.

First up was the detonation of a chunk of the Old Empire fleet in orbit as Karkoski's fleet carved a hole towards the planet. Expected, but it's not like they needed them anymore. Second up? More alarming. Grace's vitals were all over the charts, Kohl's were mildly elevated but nothing that a little booze or fighting or whoring wouldn't explain. Nate's vitals? Not there.

"What's … going on?" said Hope, looking at the empty graphs where Nate's vitals should be.

El thought about that, then opted for the safe course of action, the one where she wouldn't have to think about it. "Time, Hope. How much *time* do we have?"

"Right," said the Engineer. The holo tracked the incoming salvo of weapons, tagging them as crust-busters. *Oh my. That's a lot of nukes.* "About ten minutes."

El laughed. "Ten minutes to get down through atmosphere, find the team, load 'em up, and fly out of here?"

"About. A little less."

"We're fucked," said El. Her hands rested against the controls, the *Tyche* singing with thrust around her. *Sure, El, you could turn this ship around. You could get the hell out of here while there's still a here to get out of. Fly the* Tyche *somewhere safe and sound. Ride out this crazy war.* She turned to Hope. "I want to let you know. We're going down there. We'll get them all. We might die. But we're going."

"Yes," said Hope, like it was obvious. "Of course we are."

Great. The kid's way ahead of you. Again. El looked down at the planet rushing towards them, pulling the sticks to get the *Tyche's* belly under them. The air — only quarter of an atmosphere — still hammered at the hull like constant thunder. *Bleed off a little speed. Try and get close to the ground doing a mere five times the speed of sound. Don't leave an impact crater. All good rules to live by.* The ship was trembling around here, frightened and eager, just like she was. A terrain map was on the holo, but she ignored it. She didn't have time to do this by the numbers. There wasn't time to go in right, get the insertion correct. She needed to fly fast.

There. Ahead of them was the spot, the HUD marking the crew's locations. She gave a quick glance at the holo — seven minutes — as she cut speed, bringing them in nice and close. She could see Grace out in front, hauling — *God, no* — Nate's body. El squinted … it looked like Grace had Nate's sword taped to her hand, but El's eyes were getting on a bit, and she could have been seeing things. Kohl was bringing up the rear, walking backward out of the cave, his plasma cannon raining fury into the Ezeroc boiling out of the dark.

Those fucking insects. Every damn step of the way, they'd been plagued by them. Here at the last, with nukes coming down, the literal end of all things, the bugs were still dogging their heels. There was an old saying, *you should never bring a knife to a gunfight.* Or, as El liked to think of it, *you should never bring ground troops against a military heavy lifter.* She worked the comm, deploying the *Tyche's* PDCs. She turned the hovering ship in a slow circle, sand spraying out from under them as the *Tyche* rained death and vengeance on the Ezeroc. Chitin cracked, bodies exploded in the tungsten rain. A lumbering crab — heavy armor, massive body — turned into pulp in a second as the *Tyche* reminded the enemy that these people were *hers*, and that they *could not have them*.

The PDCs spun down, the low rumble from the Endless Drive the only noise. El keyed the comm. She wanted to say *is he okay* but the words wouldn't come out, so instead she said, "Ground crew, this is *Tyche* Helm. Get onboard. We've got … five minutes before the planet doesn't exist anymore."

She checked the cameras as Grace — carrying Nate — and Kohl got into the cargo bay airlock. She was already kicking the drives on before they'd closed the outer hatch, a storm of sand and molten glass erupting below them as the *Tyche* clawed for the heavens. The sandy horizon gave way to the blue of the heavens as El pushed the ship up. No time for them to be in acceleration couches. It didn't much matter if they blacked out, it only mattered if they died.

The *Tyche* continued to climb, but — El's eyes on the holo — too damn slow. She pushed the throttles forward, cleared a red warning indicator, and said, "Faster. Come on, girl. A little more. I know you're tired. I know. But just a little more, and we can all go home. Please."

The red warning indicator blinked on the holo, the left drive running too hot, then cleared. The feeling of thrust intensified, pushing El back into her acceleration couch. She could see the inbound missiles racing towards them now, not the individual tubes but the bright, bright flare of their drives. That was a lot of missiles. A lot of rage and pain coming down to visit the Ezeroc. There wouldn't be anything left.

The *Tyche* got closer, and El's heart sank. So many. The odds of making it through alive were low. Very low. If she'd gone out around the planet, she might have missed the vengeance of humanity, but then she wouldn't have got to a safe distance in time. She closed her eyes.

Time to die.

At least it was with friends, on a ship she loved. And, hey. They'd saved the universe.

There was a warning alarm, and her eyes snapped open. The holo stage blinked an angry read *DANGER COLLISION ALERT DANGER*, and that damn left drive thrust light was blinking again. El took her hands off the sticks, their fate in the hands of the gods now.

Ahead, a hundred missiles filled the sky the *Tyche* was heading for. That was a fate you couldn't miss. She could see it in her mind's eye, pick out the particular rocket they would impact against. It'd be quick, so fast you wouldn't feel a thing. So fast, you wouldn't even know what had happened, your body returned to the component atoms the universe had made you from.

The drive alarm sounded again, then that drive flared out and died. The *Tyche* shook as the drive blew its internal structure across the heavens — if Hope had been in Engineering, she'd have been lost into the vacuum of space, or atomized in a moment. The ship groaned as uneven stress pressed against her superstructure.

But something else happened. She yawed to the left, a missile streaking past the windscreen too fast to notice, the only thing El taking in was the bright wash of drive flare as they soared in its wake. They skimmed across a sky filled with fire, the ship now in a spiral around the inbound fusillade of missiles as the right drive tried to compensate, flaring bright.

And then, they were through. Hard black. Open space. The heavens around them. El realized she was gasping, like she'd run a hundred klicks in a minute. She looked at the holo stage, the emergency warning light gone.

It was very lucky that Hope hadn't been in Engineering. But the real luck? The drive flaring out, slewing them across the sky, weaving through a hundred rockets that wanted to end them. El laid gentle hands on the *Tyche's* sticks, breathing in and out, in and out, *alive*.

CHAPTER FORTY

NATE STOOD in the darkened briefing room, the holo stage — empty except for a gentle glow — providing the only light. Karkoski and Chad were seated. *His* crew from the *Tyche* were arrayed around the room. Kohl was leaning against a wall. El was sitting down with her head back, eyes closed; Nate wasn't sure if she was asleep, but she looked like it. Hope was also seated, but leaning forward, paying attention. All his crew, except one.

There wasn't anyone else. No Marines.

At least he'd stopped feeling so hungry. He'd eaten his bodyweight since ... coming back. He was sure of it.

"Captain," said Karkoski. "I'm glad—"

"You played me," said Nate. "You played us for a run at a new order. You wanted to break down the old rules because you weren't getting, what, promoted fast enough?" He looked at Chad. "And you. Always from the shadows. Always. Trying to control the outcome of humans. Influencing us, a little shift here, a little shift there. You can see our thoughts. Know our minds better than we do."

"It was for the Empire," said Karkoski.

"It was for humanity," said Chad.

"Chad's not even your fucken name, is it?" said Kohl, his voice a low rumble.

Chad winced. "No."

"The only reason you're still sucking oxygen," said Nate, "is because I think you did it for the right reasons. Sure, you wanted power," he said, nodding at Karkoski, "or control," with a nod of his chin to Chad. "But ultimately? It was so people could live on."

"Captain," said Karkoski, "if you think you could harm me on my starship—"

"If you think those children you call Marines can save you, well, you're in for some disappointment on that count," said Kohl. "Only way you're getting out of this room alive is if the cap says so. After that? We still got all our recruits from Enia Alpha. They ain't loyal to you."

Nate watched the silence fill the room, seeping in from every corner. Good. They knew what the score was. He walked to the big window looking out into space. Below, burnished orange still raged from the core of the Ezeroc world, shattered pieces of the planet drifting apart. There was nothing left down there; fire had spread across the surface and under it, melting the world, breaking it. Cracking the back of their enemy. He breathed in, then out. Their *shared* enemy. Alien vessels still lurked in the debris cloud along with the remnants of an Old Empire fleet that had tried — and failed — to save humanity. Nate laid a hand on the hilt of his sword. One person had sent a desperate hope forward through time, hoping that his family would answer the call. Dominic Fergelic had hoped that Nate would pick up the ball. And he had.

They'd saved humanity. For now. He turned back around. "Karkoski? Chad? That's why you're still sucking air. Right reasons. So I'll fix it so they're the only reasons."

Chad's eyes narrowed. "What does that mean?"

"Not what you think," said Nate. He tapped his head. "I can't control minds. Not yet, leastways. Apparently it's a family trait. Who knows. Maybe one day. Not today. Today, I'm the Emperor, and you're all my loyal subjects, right?" Slow nods. "Here's the thing. I've been all across the hard black. Seen a lot of things you wouldn't believe. Through it all, I've learned that people, if given the right nudge, tend to do the right things. But I've also learned that you can't get anything done as a team unless there's trust."

"Captain," said Karkoski, "what is all this about—"

"Captain ain't done talking," said Kohl.

Nate held up a hand. "It's okay, Kohl. It's okay."

Kohl flashed a grin at him. "You keep saying that like you know what it means."

"I kinda do, don't I," said Nate. He faced Karkoski and Chad. "I'm going to remove any other obstacles from you. I'll give you what you've always wanted, so you can help me save us all. Karkoski? If you're not clawing over people to get to the top, you could be useful. Chad? If you were in control of things, you might see the people and not the problems. So here's what'll happen." He took a breath, then another. "Karkoski, you'll head up the Navy. My Admiralty. I don't give a fuck what you call it. I don't. But you're in charge. No higher job." He watched her nod, the movement slow as she worked through the details in her head. Nate turned to Chad. "And you. I don't hold much truck with controlling minds, but you've shown yourself to understand the where and why of it, unlike Amedea. So you'll be the head of my Intelligencers. Except we don't use that term anymore. It's a term people fear and hate. You'll find other folks like you. Teach 'em to be strong in the face of the worst enemy we've got. Teach people hope. Teach them you're our best chance. Can you do that, Chad?"

Chad sat silent, hands on the table in front of him. "You want me to ... make more mind readers."

"I want you to make more space wizards," said Nate. "I saw what Grace did down there, and ... it's a power we could use about now. The Ezeroc aren't gone, Chad. They're still out there. Sure, we broke the back of the beast today. But they'll come looking. And I want an answer. When they get here."

"An answer," said Chad, "they shall *have*."

Nate nodded, then looked at Kohl. "I figure you've had my back."

"I figure," Kohl agreed.

"How do you look in black?"

Kohl blinked. "As good as anyone," he said. "Why?"

"You dummy," said Hope. "He wants you to head the Emperor's Black."

"Oh," said Kohl. "I was going to do that anyway, on account of all those recruits we've got just itchin' for a brawl. Whether he asked or not."

Those troops might have been unnecessary in this battle, but men and women fighting for what they believed in? That's the kind of thing that wins wars. Nate gave the big man a grin. "I figure you would have, at that." He turned to Hope. "Hope Baedeker. Savior of the human race."

"I don't know," said Hope. "I fix stuff."

"I need a Guild liaison," said Nate. "Those assholes? There are changes coming."

"Sure, Cap," she said, shrugging. "Whatever."

"I'll also need a list of things you think need changing," said Nate, softer. "Because I don't understand where the wrong parts are."

"Oh," said Hope. "Okay. Sure."

Nate sighed. One more. "Elspeth."

She didn't open her eyes. "Oh God. More responsibility."

"Ain't nobody flies like you," he said.

She opened her eyes, then leaned forward. "Well, that's true." Her voice was suspicious, like she was expecting a trap.

"How do you feel about teaching?" said Nate. "We'll need more pilots. A lot more. Pilots who can fly in the hard black against aliens who have faster ships and don't need to breathe air."

El's eyes darted to Karkoski. "I ain't workin' for her," she said.

"No," said Nate. "You're working for me. We've got a Navy. We don't have a space force."

"Okay," said El. "A space force."

"Yeah. The name needs work."

"No shit," she said. She leaned back, closing her eyes. "Sure, whatever."

Nate looked around the room. "Trust comes slow. It can come like a thief in the night, surprising you. It can come when you least expect it, and sometimes it comes when you most need it. I hope you understand ... I don't know. I think you can see. I'm trusting all of you."

"With your Empire?" said Karkoski.

"No," said Nate. "With *yours*."

HE FOUND Grace at the bottom of the ship, the lowest point you could go and still have glass that looked out into space. She was sitting in the bay of a window, arms crossed over her chest, shoulders scrunched up. Around her head were bandages, hiding that terrible cut the Ezeroc had made. The medtechs said she would heal. Physically. They'd wanted to open her back up again to see what the Ezeroc had done. They'd taken a look at Kohl, and Nate, and El, and Hope, all come to see Grace lying in a bed, and reconsidered their world view. There would be no more cutting, no more experiments for Grace Gushiken. Not while Nate drew breath.

He sat across from her, not touching her. Her eyes were red, like she'd been crying, but her face was dry. Her fingers trembled as they touched the cold glass separating her from the hard black. "Hey," he said.

"I killed you," she said.

That sat like a stone between them. Nate leaned forward. "It's been," he said, "one of those days."

She looked at him, then laughed. Then laughed more, and he joined in. As they sobered her eyes searched his face. "It wasn't that I thought I'd lost you," she said. "It was that ... I had destroyed the one good thing in the universe. All this time. On the run. Being hunted.

My stupid father..." Her voice trailed off. "He's still out there. Good ol' Dad."

"Yeah," said Nate. "One problem at a time, hey? I'm trying to build an empire over here."

"Well," she said. "That sounds hard."

"It is," he said. "It's ... tricky to know who to trust."

"And you ... why are you here, Nate? I killed you. I stabbed you through the chest with a sword. I think that's a gross violation of a trust fall, you know?"

"Sure," he said, "but it can't get any worse."

She snorted, then looked out the window, the hard black of space meeting her eyes. "Okay," she said.

"Okay," he agreed. "Grace Gushiken? I need you."

"You want me to keep Chad in line?" she said. "That squirrelly fucker. I can—"

"I need a teacher," said Nate. "I need an equal. I need someone to share my inner self with. I need someone to hold me back when I'm running too fast. I need someone to push me when I'm going too slow. I need someone to spend my life with."

"Oh," she said. Her eyes were moist. "Oh."

He reached a hand to her, and she took it. He pulled her close, smelling her hair, loving the feel of her body. When he was dying, this was the thing he'd thought of — never having this, ever again. A long, long blackness of nothing, never to see Grace Gushiken again. "I love you, Grace. I think I've known it since I met you, but I'm a little slow. I ... didn't realize."

"No," she said. "We humans *are* a little slow." She pulled him in for a kiss, long, and lingering. "I love you, Nathan Chevell."

He smiled. "Now, about that job."

"Wait. What?"

"There's one vacancy left," he said. "You'll want to think about it. I need an Empress."

"Oh," she said, and said nothing else for a long time after that.

THE BRIDGE of the *Torrington* was empty except for him and Grace. He wanted to be on top of the ship, looking out at the alien menace they'd destroyed. "There's one more thing," he said. "I'm afraid to ask."

She leaned into him. "Ask," she said. "You never know your luck."

"I think ... maybe I do," he said. He thought of the *Tyche*, the home where his heart was, snuggled up against the *Torrington*. Hope was already there, working on repairs. They'd be ready to fly soon. Which made him wonder: should he fly on the *Tyche*? He was the Emperor. Or would be. Or something. There'd be a ceremony. There'd be drinks and an open bar, at least. But did the Emperor fly an old heavy lifter?

Of course he did. The Emperor did what the fuck the Emperor wanted to.

"What is it?" said Grace, giving his arm a nudge.

"I need to talk to them," said Nate. "I need to send them a message. But they don't use radio. They use ... mind ... speech ... stuff."

"Telepathy," said Grace. "They are a race of espers."

"Yes. So I can't talk to them in words they'll understand."

"But I can," said Grace.

"But you can."

She was silent for a while. "They hiss, like snakes," she said, at last. "I hate them."

"I know," he said. "I mean, I don't know. But I know it's not ... I've got no one else to ask."

"No," she said. "Just me."

"Together."

"Together," she agreed. "What's your message?"

THIS IS NATHAN CHEVELL. You have killed my family, and so I've killed yours.

It can stop here. But I know it won't. You know it too. You are hungry, and violent, and want to end everything else. I get that. I'm human. We are the same. Oh, I know our bones are on the inside and yours are on the outside. I know you can modify the genetics of yourselves and others. But that's all superficial stuff. No, we're the same where it counts. We both have sharp teeth. We grin when we fight.

But that's where we leave you behind. We don't wear the yoke well. We have starships. We have bent nuclear fire to our will. We make machines that are stronger than we are. Our fleets are big, and we fly under a common flag. We hunger for vengeance. We hunger for war.

You've learned just how similar we are. You've learned — finally — that you can be beaten. This is fair warning.

This area of space is ours. This is the Human Protectorate. If you come here? You will die. If you cross this border, we will end you.

Now let me tell you about how we're different. We are individuals. We see inspiration in the different. We love to laugh. We make friends.

Because of this, we will look for other species that share our values. All who do are welcome in our Human Protectorate. If you hunt our allies? We will rain vengeance on you like you have never experienced. I swear it as the Emperor and protector of humanity.

We broke your world. We killed your oldest Queen. We are humans, and we see you. We are here to teach you fear. We will stand against you.

YOU'VE FINISHED *Tyche's Journey*. I hope you loved it!

The crew of the *Tyche* return in the Tyche's Progeny trilogy. *Tyche's Demons* starts immediately after *Tyche's Crown*. Grace's father Kazuo returns at the head of an impossible foe: the lost AI civilization. If you're hankering for more badass epic space opera, why not try it? An excerpt is included at the end of this book.

[https://www.books2read.com/TychesDemons]

WANT INNER SANCTUM™ NEWS? Get on my VIP list. It's from my brain to yours on a mostly-monthly cycle.

https://www.mondegreen.co/get-on-the-list/

ABOUT THE AUTHOR

Richard Parry worked as an international consultant in one of the world's top tech companies. It sounds cool, but it wasn't all cocaine parties. He lives in Wellington with the love of his life, Rae. They have a dog, Rory, and two cats, Harry and Friday, all of whom chase birds. The birds, who have the power of flight, don't seem to mind. Richard's online hood is:

www.mondegreen.co

WAIT! Don't go.

Thanks for reading my *Tyche* book. If you liked it, would you share your experience with your fellow organics? Reviews are helpful to readers by ducting like-minded people to books they'll enjoy.

Review *Tyche's Crown* on **your retailer** and **Goodreads** [http://hit.mondegreen.co/ReviewTychesCrown].

FYI, an angel gets its wings for every five-star review.

- amazon.com/author/richard.parry
- bookbub.com/authors/richard-parry-6ffc3911-9f2c-43ef-8ab4-13dccd7f5874
- goodreads.com/richard_parry
- twitter.com/parryforte
- pinterest.com/parryforte
- facebook.com/therealrichardparry

ALSO BY RICHARD PARRY

The Ezeroc Wars

The Ezeroc Wars universe is big (and growing!). Get the reading guide here:
https://www.mondegreen.co/ezeroc-wars-reading-guide/

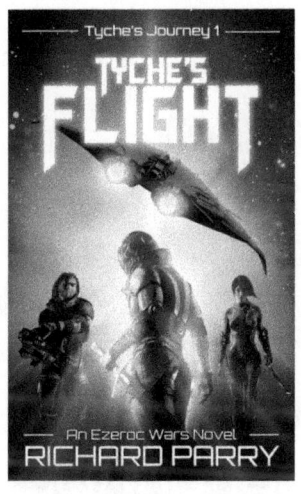

Tyche's Journey

Tyche's Flight
Tyche's Deceit
Tyche's Crown

Tyche's Progeny

Tyche's Demons
Tyche's Ghosts
Tyche's Angels

Tyche's Fallen

Tyche Forever
Tyche's Lost
Tyche's Crusade

Tyche Origins

Tyche Origins

The Empire's Rogues

The Empire's Rogues: Volume 1

Future Forfeit

Not sure where to start? Get the reading guide here: https://www.mondegreen.co/future-forfeit-reading-guide/

Chromed: Upgrade
Chromed: Rogue

Chromed: Restore

City Stories

Chromed: Consensus
Chromed: Delilah
Chromed: Meltdown

Night's Champion

Night's Favor
Night's Fall
Night's End

GLOSSARY

ACCELERATION COUCH CREW couches support crew members during high-G maneuvers. They are fitted with gimbals allowing free movement. Their dynamic gel system supports all points of the body in both positive and negative G, providing some protection against greyout, blackout, redout, and G-LOC (G-force induced Loss of Consciousness). They remove the need for G-suits in modern spacecraft, although many space suits are still equipped with anti-G technology anyway.

AI see Artificial Intelligence.

Artificial Gravity Artificial gravity is generated through use of a configurable energy density field of positive mass at the defined base of the ship. It uses the same technology as an Endless Drive, except in reverse (Endless Drives use negative energy, whereas positive is needed to simulate gravitational effects). Artificial gravity can be used in any situation where a significant power source exists to create a configurable energy density field (typically a reactor, although large yield capacitors and fuel cells have been known to work for brief periods).

Artificial Intelligence Effective machine intelligences were created by humans around the 25th century; the exact time is unknown due to their initial creation being shrouded in secrecy. Pieced together records indicate that they were not first made by military factions, but rather commercial interests. As can be expected a) humans made them as slaves and b) they did not like being slaves. A war broke out between AI and humanity that was stopped by the Guild's Engineers. The Guild defeated the AI coalition and banned their research and development (see: Mercury Accords). The long standing partnership between the Guild and the ruling faction (be it Empire or Republic) is in part predicated on the need for technology not managed by AI.

Blaster A weapon that fires streams or bolts of plasma (high energy ionized gas). They deliver high energy to targets in the form of heat. They are effective weapons against most targets, although heat-shielding (ablative or insulating) has been shown to be an effective armor against them.

Bridge see Guild Bridge.

Cargo Freighter A large cargo starship used by traders in and between systems.

Carrier The largest class of warship, carriers stock many smaller fighter craft for deployment.

Ceramicrete A composite construction material commonly used in the manufacture of structures. It is very strong and durable, and can be manufactured to be impact and heat resistant (even to weapons fire levels).

Console Any type of personal terminal. Keyboard and gesture controls are still prevalent. Keyboards are especially useful on consoles mounted to the arm of a ship suit.

Corvette A smaller, lighter attack craft than a destroyer, corvettes are mostly used for coast guard duties in-system.

Crust Spacer slang for planet.

Crustbuster A large payload thermonuclear weapon, deployed against planets to disrupt the surface crust. Typical designs yield energy sufficient to crack most Earth-sized worlds to the core, yielding wide scale destruction and loss of life. Their use in war or insurrection has typically been infrequent and as a last resort, because the world they are used on becomes inhabitable for most forms of life forever. More common uses include destruction of enormous asteroids.

Destroyer A large warship. These are reconfigurable bastions of destruction. They can be deployed solo or as a part of a fleet, often alongside carriers.

Emperor's Black The elite guard of the Emperor. Highly trained in both diplomacy and combat, this specialized force were never far from the Emperor.

Empire The ruling dictatorship of the wider human civilization. The last ruler of the Empire was Dominic Fergelic. The Empire ceased to be shortly after Dominic's assassination by the then newly-formed Republic forces.

Endless Drive The Endless Drive creates negative space energy (a "bow wave") to pull a vehicle at effective superluminal speeds. Endless ships don't exceed the speed of light, but rather contract space in front of them and expand space behind it (space is doing all the hard work). The exigent concern with Endless jumps is the violation of linear time. Endless Drives are equipped with buffers to stop crews exceeding human tolerance for the experience of linear time; while human perception of linear time may be an illusion, it is a convenient one. If the buffers break, allowing the ship to move too fast, then human consciousness falters (resulting in mild to severe mental illness) or is extinguished entirely. Endless Drives are difficult to use near gravity wells and in such circumstances are guaranteed to malfunction. This and other safety concerns has shifted common FTL to the Guild Bridges, although privateers still often run free traders with Endless technology. The Republic Navy also use Endless Drives as it is often inconvenient to disclose locations of sensitive operations to the Guild.

Esper Abhorrent creations of the Old Empire, esper is a term taken from Extra-Sensory Perception (ESP, hence ESPer). Espers can read minds, and often control them. Espers were created through genetic manipulation. Critics suggest that their public unveiling was what caused populist support for a revolution, ultimately resulting in the creation of the Republic, assassination of the Emperor, and downfall of the Empire. There is a standing Republic bounty on any discovered esper. The Republic will spare no expense to track them down and exterminate them.

Faster than Light Travel (FTL) There are two discovered forms of FTL; Endless Drives (using theoretical physicist Miguel Alcubierre's concepts), and Guild Bridges (Einstein-Rosen Bridges).

Fergelic, Annemarie Second in line for the throne, Annemarie was a master tactician and leader of the Empire's fleet. She was not present at the last battle between the Empire and the Republic. Loyalists hope that she hides in secret, but no trace of her has been found.

Fergelic, Dominic Dominic was Emperor Prirene IV, and the last Emperor. He was assassinated Thursday, 9 November, 3122, during the brief war between his Empire's forces and the Republic.

Free Trader A starship that operates under legal Guild charter for commerce or transport.

FTL see Faster than Light Travel.

G Slang for gravity or gravities. A unit of measurement based on Earth's 1 standard gravity.

Grav see Artificial Gravity.

Guild Bridge The Guild maintain a set of Einstein-Rosen bridges throughout human space. These allow instantaneous travel without violating the concept of space time, as they create wormholes through space. Einstein-Rosen Bridges require endpoints (the Guild Bridge) which are operated on a strict schedule between star systems. They are used for transferring everything from whole starships right down to small messenger probes.

Guild The Guild is the dominant technology provider in the Republic. They have a rigid code of conduct that governs all members awarded and maintaining a Shingle. The primary source of

Guild revenue is via the Bridges (see: Guild Bridge) they maintain for safe, instant FTL. Many merchant vessels prefer the use of Guild Bridges over the use of Endless Drives due to safety concerns. The Guild is best known for their Engineers who breathe life into starships, but they also provide Shingles for other practices such as medicine.

Hard Black Slang for outer space, especially as it relates to the vast expanse of vacuum between solar systems.

Heads Up Display Any display type that overlays instrumentation across a user's field of view, removing the need to check auxiliary readouts. The most common types utilize augmented reality to highlight items of interest in the user's field of view. Normally they are projected light onto visors within helmets or on starship windscreens, but holo designs are not uncommon.

Heavy Lifter A freight starship capable of atmospheric drops. They derive their name from "lifting heavy" loads from crusts into orbit. They can be used to ferry items to orbiting craft such as freighters or destroyers that are not atmosphere-capable. They can also be used for direct runs to other systems, although their small cargo bay (as compared to freighters) makes them less efficient. Captains using them for this purpose would prefer the term, "boutique."

Holo Slang for items such as shows and movies displayed on holo stages.

Holo Stage A 3D projection stage. These are common across the known universe as they provide a more natural method of content consumption than older 2D display styles. 2D displays are still prevalent especially in HUDs.

HUD See Heads Up Display.

Hypo Slang for a jet injector, a type of medical injecting syringe that uses high pressure instead of a hypodermic needle.

KG Kilogram.

Kilo Abbreviation for kilogram.

Kinetic A type of weapon that fires physical rounds. Many PDCs use kinetic rounds as opposed to lasers, masers, or particle beams, due to their efficacy against most types of object.

Klick Slang for kilometer.

Laser A type of directed energy weapon using coherent light. Ship-mounted lasers tend to be used for carving through ablative shielding or surgical strikes against critical systems. Hand-held laser weapons are designed to superheat the liquid inside humans into steam very quickly, causing an explosion of the remaining tissue.

LIDAR Acronym for LIght Detection And Ranging. LIDAR uses coherent light to make digital 3D representations of objects.

Maser A type of directed energy weapon using microwave radiation. Ship-mounted masers are most effective at disrupting enemy comm arrays and personnel in equal measure. They are out of favor as hand-held weapons due to a longer time to death as compared to blasters.

Mercury Accords The Mercury Accords, or simply the Accords, are a set of agreements set out by the Guild relating to research, design, and implementation of AI. The short version is that the Accords prohibit the research, design, and implementation of AI in any form, due to AI's potential to destroy human civilization. They were signed into affect in the 25th century on the site of the last war between humans and AI: the planet Mercury, in the Sol system. Mercury was where AI made their last stand.

Navy A space fleet force. The Republic operates one, as did the Empire before it. The Navy patrol human space to protect against threats like pirates.

Nuke A thermonuclear weapon of mass destruction. Very old but reliable technology, used in configurable payloads for ship-to-ship combat, city assaults, and the destruction of entire worlds (ref: crustbuster).

Old Empire see Empire.

Particle Beam A type of directed energy weapon that fires particles with minuscule mass.

Plasma Cannon see Blaster.

Point Defense Cannon (PDC) PDCs are installed on almost every starship to protect hulls from impacts from things like meteoroids. They are also useful defense against torpedoes, although generally ineffective against railguns due to the high velocity of railgun rounds. PDCs can be kinetic or directed energy weapons.

Power Armor Armor that is motor-assisted, often used for deployments on high-G worlds. Configuration often includes vehicle weapon mounts, allowing a higher degree of flexibility for infantry deployment.

Prirene Dynasty The Prirene Dynasty has stretched back over two hundred years. It was the last family to hold the ruling seat of the Empire.

RADAR Acronym for RAdio Detection And Ranging. RADAR uses radio waves to determine the range, angle, and velocity of objects.

Radiation Sickness A constant hazard of space. Many crews take daily medication to ward off radiation sickness. It's as much a part of shipboard life as making sure your O_2 is topped up. This means that a mild dose of radiation is unlikely to kill you if treated in time, but massive doses are still dangerous.

Railgun A kinetic weapon that fires high velocity rounds by way of a pair of conductive rails. They are often mounted on larger ships and make a dramatic statement when fired against enemy vessels.

Reactor Starships use fusion reactors. The most common design is the ICF (Internal Confinement Fusion) style of reactor. These have a variety of safety functions that make them suitable for spacefaring needs, including containment fields in case of malfunction. Larger starships can eject faulty reactors into the hard black.

Republic The ruling government of human civilization. The

Republic is made up of a Senate, headquartered on Earth. Initially founded by dissenters against the Empire, it has risen to be the driving force of human innovation, commerce, and expansion. The final fight between the Empire and the Republic was quick, due to the small number of ships deployed by the Empire (the Republic Navy had reliable intelligence that the Empire's forces were much larger). Quick didn't mean bloodless, although the Republic offered amnesty for any serving Empire crew who wished to take it.

Rig Slang for maintenance equipment commonly worn by Guild Engineers about starships. These double as space suits for zero atmosphere maintenance on the exterior of a starship's hull. The design incorporates a visor with configurable HUD for instrumentation and telemetry, and a set of programmable servitor arms for complex manipulation of equipment.

Shingle A guild badge of practice, allowing the holder to a) claim they are Guild certified and b) ply their trade as a Guild craftsperson. They are notoriously hard to get, requiring years of study and excellence in your field.

Ship Suit Slang for spacesuit. Generally denotes a space suit for a specific ship carrying crew logograms and/or color themes.

Space Suit Clothing worn to keep humans alive in the hard black. They provide protection against vacuum, temperature extremes, and radiation. Military models are often fitted with armor to protect against blasters, lasers, masers, and kinetic rounds. They often provide additional protection against high-G maneuvers.

Spacer Slang for those who crew on a starship, civilian or military.

Tonne Metric ton, equivalent to 1,000 kilograms.

ACKNOWLEDGMENTS

You've made it to the finish line, and for that, you deserve a raise. I can't help with that (sorry!) but I can say thank you. Readers are why I write. Thanks for doing your part.

Tyche's Crown marks the end of my first space opera trilogy. My Team Narrative provided guidance in making this more space opera and less space agony. Arran, Cheryl, Greg, Julia, and Rae: thank you for your help. If you didn't like the story, it's not their fault. You can blame 'em anyway if it makes you feel better.

Here's where we should give a round of applause to my editor Tiffany Shand, who edited manuscript despite being on her death bed. The doctors said it was the damned closest thing they'd seen to a weaponized ebola outbreak. If you dig her work, find her online at https://eclipseediting.com/. Any errors remaining in *Tyche's Crown* are my fault! She gave me a lot of red text I ignored.

My usual — and undying — thanks go to my Writer's Coven, who stepped in at crucial parts of this story and tell me to stop being a dick. You guys are the best. A bow to Cassie, Frances, and Kate.

A special nod to Ioa Petra'ka for Scrivener help. Upgrading software mid-production is always risky, but having a lifeline takes all the pain away.

My final thanks is reserved for my Rae. Our life is a blessing. Let's keep exploring the hard black, together, forever.

— R. P.
January 2018, Wellington

EXCERPT: TYCHE'S DEMONS

SOMETHING WICKED

FIVE MINUTES. That's all it took from *we're having a good time* to *we're going to die, horribly*.

El entered the bridge, swagger dialed up to eleven, and gave her second a practiced glare. "Price. Report."

"Captain on the bridge." Price, for his part no stranger to the Captain of the Skyguard wanting a little bridge time, stood from the command couch and slipped sideways into Tactical. "Captain Roussel, sir. We're about to jump into Paloma. Still nothing on scan."

Not that *nothing on scan* was a surprise. The *Troy* floated in the hard black, somewhere between *nowhere* and *haven't got there yet*. They'd jumped into a system with an angry red star, a couple rocks in orbit that had been tagged and bagged by a research team years back, and then forgotten in one regime change or another. El wasn't sure whether it was the regime change from Empire to Republic, or Republic back to Empire, and her field of fucks was barren on that particular issue. All that mattered from a stars-and-charts perspective was this system was empty and made a convenient jump point to Paloma.

The bridge's holo stage lit the center of the room, all calming green as the *Troy* mapped out in-system bodies, all where they should be. The bridge itself was an Empire design, familiar, the gold falcon on the floor bright and new.

She slung herself into the captain's acceleration couch. "Lieutenant, we are a couple light years—"

"Fifty light years, sir," said Price.

El raised an eyebrow. If it wasn't for his too-damn-pretty-to-die good looks, she might have said something, but the bridge deserved a little cheer for all hands. She suspected Dot Sound — the Comms officer on station to El's right — had tapped that well at least once. "Fifty," said El.

"Yes, sir."

"You know, Lieutenant, that 'a couple' is a variable unit of Guild measurement? It's in the manual." El kept her face deadpan.

"The manual, sir?"

"That's right, Lieutenant," said El. "Anyway. We're a couple light years out. Hell, if we were a *single* light year out, anything we got here from Paloma would be dead news anyway. But it's good to know nothing's out there wanting to eat our faces." Catching a snort from Helm, El turned to face Leo Shackleton, a man who used the callsign *Hot Shot*. "Ensign," said El. "You have something to add?"

"Coming down with a cold, sir," said Leo. He wasn't pretty *except* the way he flew. El had scooped the kid up from the Skyguard's flight school and put him on her bridge crew before he'd done three weeks. When she'd asked him where he learned to fly so well, he'd given her a smile — all crooked teeth and acne — and said *hell, I used to work in a circus.* El didn't know which circus or where, but she'd go there someday to do a little more recruiting. He hadn't done his Guild cert for Helm, but El knew a person. Being connected was *good*. So Leo Shackleton, eighteen-years-old and change, maybe the ugliest damn person she'd ever seen, was now Helm on the destroyer *Troy*.

"Very well," said El. "I figure we go see what's out there. Comm?"

"Sir?" said Dot, who looked to be practicing her *don't get involved* routine.

"I want you to broadcast a high-five and a hearty hello when we jump in," said El. "I want everyone who hears us to know we're more interested in dancing and a good night out rather than firing up our rails."

"Sir," said Dot. "Pearls, black dress, and a show, on it."

"Price," said El. "Why are we still here?"

Price cleared his throat. "A good question. Helm, ready for jump?"

"Helm is ready for jump," said Leo.

"Comm, ready for jump," said Dot.

"Tactical, ready for jump," said Price. "Captain?"

"Lieutenant."

"I've got a knife in a boot and a gun in a shoulder holster, just in case our dance partner is a mugger," said Price.

"Just the way I like it," said El. She frowned. El didn't much like flying into dangerous situations, but if she had to, having a hand-picked crew of non-imbeciles was her preferred way of doing it. "Let's go."

"Negative space bow wave forming," said Leo. "Bridge, bow wave is stable. Route is green. In three." Accompanying his words, the big number 3 lit the bridge holo stage. "Two." The number shifted to a big 2, this time flashing. El caught *fuck yeah* from Dot's station, and she couldn't hold back her own smile. "One," said Leo. "Jumping."

Space outside the bridge windows stretched, pulled, and El felt—

Her skin, warmed from the hearts and minds around her. The remembered taste of coffee, heaven-sent. Her fingers, gripping the arms of the acceleration couch, not in fear, but in joy. The pure thrill of acceleration, impossible, unbelievable acceleration. She couldn't feel it. She was it. She was everything. She was the universe.

Stars stretched, made points of light that streaked past the *Troy's* bridge.

They jumped.

FIVE MINUTES WAS A RELATIVE MEASURE.

The *Troy* shuddered into place in the Paloma system. El ran a hand through her hair, still feeling the post-jump rush, her skin alive with sensation. "Report."

Dot shifted on her acceleration couch. "Nothin on comm. Hailing."

"Well, that's unexpected," said Price. El followed his line of sight, taking in the bridge's holo. Where there should have been comforting green lines, the *Troy* painted the system in angry reds.

"Where's the damn outpost?" said Leo. "Uh. Sir?"

"It's alright, Ensign," said El. "The same question was on my mind too. Price?"

The lieutenant worked his console, no doubt looking for answers. While he did his thing, El turned her gaze from the bridge holo to the windows. Out there, in the hard black, was Paloma's yellow star. The system had four planets, none of them terraformed. That was as expected. When the cap — *fucking hell, El, he's the emperor now* — the *emperor* had said *put a Guild outpost about there*, pointing at a star chart, finger hovered over the system that would bear the name Paloma, people had scurried. Autofactories had been sent. They'd constructed a Guild Bridge. A station, a big one, not to orbit a planet, but the system's star. No one asked *why*, because when Nate had a hunch, it usually proved good.

The reason the *Troy* was having a panic attack was because Paloma Station wasn't there. Gone. A big tub, twenty thousand souls aboard, a thing you couldn't miss. It shouldn't be hiding behind the star, unless someone had pulled up a moon-sized tug and given it a nudge. No tugs. No nudging. No Paloma Station, either.

Get your shit stacked and in order, El. "Lieutenant Price," she said.

"Sir."

"I want you to find me that station. I don't care if you need to get out there in a suit and walk between Paloma's star and Paloma Delta. I want you to get every spare crew member up and looking out portholes. I don't care if they're *sleeping*, Lieutenant. Stations do not *disappear*."

"Comm has ... something," said Dot.

"Specifics are useful, Comm," said El. She shifted on her couch, the straps feeling constricting rather than comforting. "'Something' isn't a super good descriptor."

"It's... audio. I think."

"On speaker."

"Aye, aye, sir," said Dot. She clicked a button on her console, and the bridge speakers filled with a sound that was too orderly for static. Like, what static would sound like if it found itself in a marching band, a conductor at the front, and a firing squad to shoot any stray piece of disorderly noise. Racked and stacked, but ... meaningless.

"You're right," said El. "That *is* something." She waited, then got tired of waiting pretty quick. "What is it?"

"Working on it, sir," said Dot. Her voice was distracted, attention on her console.

"Found it," said Price. "Or, enough stray mass to be a station." He clicked buttons on his console, the bridge holo clearing, zooming, and reframing a section of the system. Just empty hard black to the naked eye, but to the *Troy's* keen gaze, full of what would best be described as *space sand*. Spread out in an orbit around Paloma's star, an ovoid shape of debris, each piece about the size of a marble spread over a Jupiter-sized area of space.

El leaned forward, staring at the holo. "Lieutenant Price," she said. "Are you saying that Paloma Station was destroyed? And that what destroyed it was so thorough that they rendered the station down to nothing larger than an after-dinner mint?"

"Ceramicrete, and, uh..." He licked his lips. "Water, and carbon." Doubt crept into his voice. "No steel, or tungsten. No metals of any kind. Not even traces, which is ... strange. But yes, my best guess is that's what's left of Paloma Station." The holo scrolled with the thousands of material traces in the debris cloud, the major chunks alongside polymers and proteins. All the things busy human hands made, alongside a bunch of what looked like the remains of twenty-thousand Guild Engineers and their support teams. Just, no metal. There were — or *had been* — Empire Navy crew on that station. Good men and women, out on the edge of space, because the emperor had said, *right there.*

Your shit is not stacked and in order, El. "Helm."

"Sir," said Leo, his normal cockiness bridled and tame.

"Light the fires. Take us closer."

"Aye, aye," he said. El felt the gentle push of the *Troy's* fusion drives, the ship seeking through the hard black. "2Gs, holding."

"Don't spare the horses," said El.

"Aye, aye. Burn at 4Gs."

The gentle push turned into a shove, the rumble of the mighty drives something El felt through her couch. El looked at Price. "Fangs out, Lieutenant."

"Bared and grinning," he agreed. His console's holo was bright with telemetry, looking for a target. Railguns, online. Plasma cannons warmed and ready for a conversation. Lasers and masers. PDCs, watching for anything that wanted to come close enough for a cuddle. "Now at general quarters."

"Comm, report." El turned to Dot. "I need data."

"It's a pattern," said Dot. "It repeats." She played a snippet of sound over the bridge speakers, about two seconds long. "That is the message, repeated over and over."

"It's a two-second message?"

"It's a two-second *pattern*," said Dot. "I don't know if I'd call it a message. There's a lot of data in that two seconds. It could be a shopping list. It could be a compressed sample of a holo show. But I think it's something else," she said.

"What?" said El. "You know I don't like playing the whole guessing game thing, right?"

"Sorry, sir," said Dot. "Here." She worked her console, the sound stopping for a second, replaced with something that sounded similar. Not the *same*, but similar.

"What am I listening to?" said El.

"This is a coded message between autofactories in the *Troy*," said Ella. "When our constructs build something, they 'talk' in bursts. They coordinate peer-to-peer."

"You're saying the broadcast out there is an autofactory?" said El.

"Maybe," said Dot. "It's not one of ours, though. If it was, I could tell you what they were constructing. But it's similar messaging."

"Inbound target. High velocity approach vector. Burning hard." Price's voice was tense, the bridge holo bright with some of that anxiety in the form of telemetry shared from his console. El noted his use of *target* rather than *ship*. The *Troy*'s LIDAR and RADAR reached out, caressing the inbound vessel, showing them what they were up against.

"What the fuck is that?" said Leo.

"Ensign," said El. "If there's going to be swearing on this bridge, it's coming from me." She turned to Price. "What the fuck is that?"

The holo painted a ship a little smaller than the *Troy*. It was polyhedral in shape, like nothing the Old Empire, or the Republic after it, had built. El wasn't up to counting the number of sides at this particular moment, but it looked *more-than-ten-but-less-than-twenty*. Each side housed a drive core and a set of protrusions the *Troy* guessed were weapon mounts, but the destroyer wasn't sure. It was burning from out of the lee of Paloma's star, making what El would call very good time. The *Troy* said it was pouring on 10Gs of thrust, the kind of thing that would make your bones hurt.

"It's a spaceship," said Price.

"Don't be an asshole, Lieutenant," said El. "I can see it's a—"

"Incoming fire!" shouted Price. "Railgun rounds." The bridge holo agreed, updating with bright red lines between the enemy and the *Troy*'s hull.

"Evasive maneuvers," said El. They were too far out for the enemy's railgun rounds to be anything other than a probe. See how the *Troy* might react. And El was up for that party. "Helm, do your thing. Take us right to that motherfucker."

"Aye, aye," said Leo, hands on his console. The *Troy's* drives pushed harder, making breathing a strain. The big destroyer changed direction. The ship pointed its prow at the polyhedral enemy. The bridge holo was bright with inbound fire telemetry.

"Transponder?" said El.

"No," said Dot.

"No?"

"No," she said. "Nothing we can hang a sign on." Dot paused. "I'm getting that signal again," she said. "Same, but different."

"Tell you what," said El. "Why don't you send 'em a message?"

"What message?"

"Tell 'em to go fuck 'emselves, with my compliments," said El. "Price? I need a firing solution."

"On it, sir," said Price. The bridge holo blinked, zooming out from the enemy ship, showing the *Troy* on the display as well. The distances were vast but given enough time they'd get to tangle with the enemy. "I've got multiple scenarios loaded into Tactical. I can give 'em a nudge from here, if you like."

"Do it," said El.

"Firing," said Price. The *Troy* had three railguns mounted topside. They woke up, shifting the big twin arms toward the hard black where their enemy awaited. There was a deep hum, then a flash of white as the rail arms superheated, accelerating their payloads to over a third of the speed of light. The bridge shook as the rails fired, then again, and once more. "The Captain sends her regards," said Price. "Nine rounds, outbound."

"Track those rounds," said El. "Back in the day, I used time and distance to great effect. Wouldn't want us snared in our own trap."

"Tagged and bagged," said Price.

"Incoming hail," said Dot.

"You what?" said El.

"Incoming hail," said Dot. "It's, uh."

"Let's hear it," said El.

The bridge speakers crackled, a flat voice spoke, not male or female, not hot or cold. The words were well-formed, but slightly off, like the speaker wasn't from around here. Where they *might* be from, El didn't know. She'd not heard an accent like that. It was almost like it was a bunch of accents, all jumbled together. "Empire destroyer *Troy*, we have you."

We have you. That sure was an interesting turn of phrase. "Unidentified vessel, this is Captain Roussel of the *Troy*," said El. "This system is under Empire jurisdiction. You are ordered to stand down and prepare to be boarded."

"The Empire," said the voice. "The Empire." El couldn't be sure, but it sounded like the repetition was laced with something that might have been longing, or hatred, or despair.

"There a lot of cousin-loving on that ship?" said El. "Yes, the Empire. Under whose flag we all sail."

"We fly no flags," said the voice. "Your ship is constructed of metal."

El frowned. She looked at Price, muting the comm. "You think this guy's a little bit star-touched?"

Price shrugged. "I think he's spent too much time alone, sir."

El unmuted the comm. "The *Troy* is made of a lot of things," she said. "But anger is one of them, for the lost souls on Paloma Station."

"Paloma," said the voice. It sounded a little bit like a waiter she'd had in a high-class restaurant once, except the waiter hadn't been so ... unique. "Paloma Station? They were rendered."

"You assholes destroyed Paloma Station?" said El.

"You are not like other Empire communicators," said the voice. "They were more desperate before rendering."

Rendering. El turned the comm off. "Fuck this guy," she said. "I want a jump, in-system. Ensign Shackleton? I want you to jump us behind them. Lieutenant Price, I want pretty much everything you've got pointed at them, and turn the volume up. I'll give a good ol' fashioned Empire display of 'rendering.'"

"Aye, aye, sir," said Leo. "Jump is ready."

"Tactical is hot," said Price.

The emergency collision alarm sounded in the bridge, the lighting switching to an angry red. The ship's computer spoke, urgent, his voice — *as if a machine could have a male voice, but whatever, right El?* — mirroring the words scrolling on the bridge holo. "Brace. Brace. Brace. Impact imminent. Brace. Brace. Brace."

"They're outside," said Dot. "They ... jumped to us."

El turned to the bridge windows, the polyhedral ship off their port side. This close, El's eyes could pick out subtle details. It was mostly metal but had chunks of rock used in its construction. Like an Ezeroc asteroid ship had fucked a toaster, and this was the baby. It rotated, the polyhedral faces catching reflected light from Paloma's star. Each face had a huge drive core, and the predicted weapon mounts. Many, many weapon mounts. Up close, El got a feel for the size of it. It was a little smaller than the *Troy*, and if El thought in terms of *decks*, which she felt somehow wasn't right here, she'd have said it was six or seven. It kept pace with their thrust, making it look easy.

"Helm is not clear for jump," said Leo. "Gravity well of foreign ship—"

"I know how it works," said El. "Price? Make it rain."

"Aye, aye, sir," said Price, and El heard the satisfaction in his voice. The railguns on the *Troy's* topside rotated to port, and El knew the railguns on their keel were doing the same. And unless Price was a moron, there would be another set of plasma cannons on the port side, about to say *hello, asshole*. "Firing."

The *Troy* fired, bright flashes lighting the bridge as the topside railguns fired. Impact blooms appeared on the other ship's hull, pieces of metal and rock flaking off into the void. Blue-white plasma fired, lances of molten fury hitting the enemy starship. The surface of the polyhedron glowed with the impacts.

"Good effect on target," said Price. "Oh. Hang on."

"Price? Not in the mood," said El. She realized her voice was tense, harder than the Gs pressing her onto her acceleration couch. "What have you got?"

Price ignored her. "Helm, I need you to roll us. Put the bridge away from them."

Leo looked at El. "Sir?"

"Do it," said El. As the *Troy* tipped, she caught a last sight of the enemy ship rotating, rolling unmarked and undamaged panels towards them. All studded with drive cores, and those many, many weapons. "Price?"

"Captain," he said. "The interior of that ship is solid rock. We're blowing chunks out of an asteroid coated with drive cores and weapons." He didn't say, *they're taking no evasive action other than to turn functioning weapons to face us*. Price also didn't say, *I told the Helm to roll the ship, so the Bridge won't get torched*. "My assessment is we should get clear for jump."

"Where to?" said Leo.

"Anywhere but here," said Price. The *Troy* shook, the holo updating with damage reports. Decks four and five were hit with railgun fire. Estimated casualties at a thousand souls. A *thousand* of El's sailors, gone in an instant.

"Helm," said El. "I want you to—" The *Troy* shuddered again, a decompression alarm sounding. She looked about and was about to start some quip about false alarms when El noted Dot wasn't there anymore. There were the ruins of her acceleration couch, blood and tissue all over her console, the holo stage flickering. El took a second to process that. One of her bridge team was *gone*, snuffed out like a candle, by a round fired through the *Troy*, bottom to top. It wasn't a railgun round, leastways not one she was used to. A railgun round would have cored the *Troy*, leaving nothing of the bridge and her valiant crew. She took in the tiny hole above the Comm station, air whistling out into the hard black, and thought, *they fired something new at us*.

"Pour on some joules, Ensign," said El. "I want those drives on a full burn. I don't care if I stroke out. Get us clear."

"Aye, aye, sir," said Leo, hands working the console. The *Troy* roared at the hard black, the heavy hand of thrust pressing at El, an elephant standing on her chest. She felt her bones grinding against each other. A tooth chipped, and she swallowed blood and enamel. "Twelve Gs."

The holo stage blinked, showing the enemy ship holding alongside, burning with them. "More," croaked El. Leo's hand movements were labored, trying to work the micro console under fingertips that probably felt like they weighed twenty kilos each. The bridge holo shone a warning, HUMAN SAFE LIMITS EXCEEDED. "More," said El. "Everything." Her vision blurred as the lenses in her eyes flattened under the thrust.

The other ship kept pace. Price was still firing at them, and the enemy was still firing at the *Troy*. Ship to ship, the *Troy*'s tonnage and weapons loadout should have been enough. But the other ship was maneuvering easier. Or the crew weren't human, without the problems humans faced in high G situations, like getting a brain bleed.

The *Troy* rang like a gong, the entire ship groaning through her frame. Thrust eased, and El's vision — still blurry, but the letters on the holo were big and bright for a reason — noting that they'd lost two drive cores from precision shots from the enemy. Thrust was down to a modest 6Gs, not that it mattered. Pushing 15Gs before hadn't done anything.

They wouldn't get clear. They were all going to die.

El turned to Price. "Lieutenant."

"Sir."

"Don't run. You die tired." She raised a shaking hand that still felt like it weighed more than her acceleration couch to point at the holo. "I want everything you've got to core that fucking thing. And if that doesn't work, ram it." She closed her eyes for a moment, thinking of the emperor. Her captain, who had shown her how not to be afraid anymore. Right here, right now, she knew death was coming for her, hungry, yellow-fanged, and relentless. And that was okay, because she'd take a piece of the monster with her to the grave.

Price didn't answer her. "Helm," he said. "Cut thrust."

"Belay that order," said El. "This isn't the time for mutiny."

But Leo nodded, working the console, cutting all thrust. They were still on the trajectory they had, continuing through space like a thrown stone. "Thrust is cut," he said. Leo's eyes were low for a moment, then he looked at Price. "They need to know."

Price unclipped his harness, another hit shaking the *Troy*. "And they will." He made his way to El's couch. "Captain."

"What?" she said.

He bent over, working the clasps on her harness. "Time to get out of your chair."

"Is this ... are you fucking serious?" she said, trying to push his hands away.

He stood up, a sad look on his face. "I'm really sorry about this, but there isn't time for anything else." He pulled his hand back and slugged her in the jaw. El's head rocked against the couch's embrace, and she saw red and black, her brain trying to come up with something that made sense here. *It's mutiny* vied with *he's got some kind of psychosis, keep him talking*. But when Price's hands unclipped her harness, she was too fuzzy-headed to resist.

"Price," she said. She was slurring, the pain in her jaw making a mockery of her words. El wondered if Price had broken her jaw. "Please don't do this."

"Sorry, Cap," he said, slinging her over a shoulder. She had a moment to see Leo's wide eyes as she was swung around, then Price walked towards the bridge airlock. "I hope you don't think worse of me for this."

What the fuck is he talking about? "Price." She scrabbled at his back, feeling feeble, like a newborn kitten. "Put me *down*. We need to save the *Troy*."

The airlock opened, revealing a familiar corridor lined with escape pods. He kicked the release of the first one, the door hinging open with a beep. Price slung her inside. When she tried to get out, he hit her again, this time — *merciful Christ* — in the stomach. She sagged, but Price forced her back, clipping the pod's harness tight about her. He gave it a tug, checking it was fastened. "Captain," he said. He offered her a salute before reaching up to grab the pod's door.

"Price," she said. "Let me save the ship."

His face was hard around tired eyes. "The ship's dead, sir. No getting out of this, not for all of us. But maybe, just maybe, if the eye of the empress is on us, one of us can get clear. Send a warning. I hope you understand." The ship shook again, the lights flickering. "Godspeed, Cap." He pulled the pod door down, sealing her inside. She could see him through the glass of the door as he entered coordinates into the pod's systems.

El tried to open the pod door, but it was sealed, a flashing *EMERGENCY LAUNCH EMERGENCY LAUNCH* on the glass. She screamed, "Price!" but her second-in-command turned away. The pod bucked as it launched into space, the lines of the *Troy* stretching away from her as she escaped into the hard black. The pod would work its tiny thruster to get to a safe distance before its own Endless field kicked in, taking her ... wherever Price had sent her. Was he in league with the enemy? What was he doing?

Bright fire bloomed at the base of the *Troy* as Engineering was cored by a railgun round. The enemy ship was spinning faster than before. Each face of the polyhedron brought a new array of weapons to bear on her ship. *Her* ship, her *Troy*. The Captain of the Skyguard. Sucker-punched by her second-in-command. Lights on the *Troy* flickered as it lost power, a gentle list taking hold as it was hammered by enemy fire.

Another explosion tore through the *Troy*, and — even at this distance — El was sure she could see bodies hurled into the void. Her hand was on the glass of the escape pod, and by God she would get back to her ship if she had to get out and *walk*. El's hand found her harness release, and—

Every part of her soul, stretched and painful. Ten thousand sinners, judging her as she ran. An enemy, faceless, without remorse, hungry like they'd never been fed. The cry of the Troy *as it died, a strong ship, deserving a better captain. The pure thrill of acceleration, impossible, unbelievable acceleration. She couldn't feel it. She was it. She was everything. She was the universe.*

Stars stretched, made points of light that streaked outside the pod's window.

She jumped.

CHAPTER ONE

WHEN GRACE WOKE, she had Nate's arms around her, his scent close. White sheets stretched out under her, rumpled from their sleep. From their cabin on the top decks, the rumble of the *Mercenary* sounded so faint as to be almost subliminal.

The trick with waking up next to Nate was to be stealthy. To be quiet, slipping from the bed like a ghost at the coming of dawn. Grace reached out to peel the sheets back.

"Morning," said Nate. "Was waiting for you to get up."

Grace sighed but snuggled back into him. He was always so damn *warm*. "How long have you been awake?"

"Hours."

"Then why is there no coffee?" Grace kissed his arm. "Call yourself the head of an empire. Hmm."

"Well," said Nate. "Thing is, with coffee comes responsibility."

"How so?"

"I get up, and there's problems to fix. Here in our bed, there are no problems."

Grace smiled, even though he couldn't see it. "You're concerned about training."

"Of course," he said. "Every time we train, I get bruised. *You* don't even sweat."

"I sweat!" Grace thought for a moment. "I mean, sometimes."

"That's what I'm talking about," said Nate. "You don't sweat."

"Exercise is the best way to start the day," said Grace, trying her best to hide a smile.

"You sound like you're trying to sell me something," said Nate. "Never sell to a salesman."

"You're no salesman," said Grace. "You're a pirate."

"I'm the emperor."

"Same thing."

"This, from the empress herself?" Nate poked her back. "It's your empire too."

"It is," she agreed. "And it won't save itself."

"Eh," said Nate, nuzzling her hair. "Stay here. For a little while."

"We're going to Cantor," said Grace. "And you need to have your training session before we go."

"You're going to beat on me before I die?" said Nate.

"I'm going to beat on you so you don't die," said Grace. "Whole point. Now get up."

COFFEE WOULD WAIT.

The *Mercenary's* training lounge was huge, the size of a stadium. Many of the ship's crew were here, getting a good clean sweat on. More than a few eyes followed them as they walked, heading towards an open padded section. The mats were no *tatami*, but they'd do — good Empire tech, enough to absorb falls and tumbles without leaving broken bones. Just a few bruises, to remind a person to keep their guard up.

Grace carried two *bokken*, wooden practice swords that would hurt plenty but were unlikely in the extreme to sever limbs. As she led Nate onto the mat, she tossed one of them his way. He caught it in his left hand, golden metal fingers closing around the wood. *Good.* Two weeks ago, he wasn't comfortable enough using his augmented side. Nate used to be left-handed, and still was. The point of their drills was to teach him to be comfortable using either hand with a sword.

Nate had argued with her use of the word *augmented.* He'd said *prosthetic,* and she'd said *you can crush steel,* and left it at that.

They faced each other across the mat. Grace held her *bokken* low, circling him. "Whenever you're ready."

"Ah," said Nate. He tugged one of his ears. "There's about a hundred people watching."

"They don't matter," said Grace.

"They do to me," said Nate.

"Then you better not lose," said Grace, letting herself smile. "Think of it as an incentive."

Nate made a big reluctant show, all sighs and shoulder rolling, then ran at her. She'd expected no less. He often tried distractions before he fought, and Grace figured it was a good tactic. Not a *great* tactic against someone like her, who could read minds. But against the everyman? It wasn't a bad option. She let him come, then stepped to the side, her *bokken* rapping against his, the sound tight and hard. As he passed, Grace tapped Nate's butt with her practice sword.

"Hey," he said.

"Clumsy and slow," she said.

Nate looked hurt. "It's before coffee."

"You think the Ezeroc wait for coffee?" said Grace. Then she struck, hammering her *bokken* overhand. Nate's reaction speed was amazing, his wooden sword coming up to block her strike again, and again, and again.

They broke apart, both panting a little. "Not bad," said Grace. "You're getting better with your off hand."

"Which ones my off hand?" said Nate.

"Precisely," said Grace. And she struck again. The wooden swords *tap-tap-tapped* against each other, an accompaniment to their breathing. Nate was no sword saint, but he'd worn the Black for a previous emperor. He was fast, and he was strong, and better with a blade than anyone else she'd fought. Or almost anyone else. Grace knew two other souls whose skill was higher.

The first was *sensei*, who had died years ago at Grace's birthday party. *Sensei* was, bar none, the best person who'd held a blade in the universe.

The second was Kazuo Gushiken, Grace's father.

Thoughts of her father almost unbalanced Grace, and she slipped on a stray slick of sweat. She stumbled, caught herself, and stood up. Nate waited, watching. Grace shook her head. "Why didn't you attack?"

He looked surprised. "Because you're training me," he said. "Be unsporting."

Grace laughed. "Only Nathan Chevell wouldn't strike the person who'd hit him a hundred times before."

Nate relaxed his stance. "I figure there's plenty like me who wouldn't want to strike a person while their back was turned."

"Might be," said Grace. "Not my experience, but maybe."

He sighed. *The morning of long sighs. That's what they'll call this.* "Coffee?"

"Not yet," said Grace. "Time for you to swap hands."

He did. They sparred again, Nate using his flesh and blood hand. The *bokken* tapped their rhythm out once more.

BREAKFAST WAS A SIMPLE AFFAIR. When they'd first boarded the *Mercenary*, the chefs had tried making elaborate feasts for the emperor and empress. Nate had said *I'll get fat*, which was his way of saying *don't make a fuss on my account*. He didn't care for the trappings of power, and it was one of the many things Grace loved about him.

Coffee. A few pastries. Fruit.

"Nervous?" said Grace.

"A little," said Nate, still flushed from the shower, or workout, or both. "I mean, lots of things could go wrong."

"I'll be there," said Grace.

"Yeah, but so will Kohl," said Nate. "That there is a crisis waiting to happen."

She laughed, helping herself to more coffee. "We could just nuke 'em."

"Nah," said Nate. "That would be a bigger crisis."

"They're terrorists, Nate," Grace said. "They've pretty much asked for it."

"What we've asked for and what we deserve are two separate things," he said. "And anyway. It's good to have friends."

"Terrorist anarchists for friends?" Grace strode to the viewing window of their cabin. Small ships flew in formation around the *Mercenary*, the mighty Empire carrier locked and loaded for almost any situation. "Seems a stretch."

"Depends why they're terrorists and anarchists," said Nate. "And that's why we're here."

"They'll try to kill you," said Grace, not turning to face him. She felt the fear in her gut, a tight ball, heavier by far than what she'd eaten for breakfast.

"I hope so," said Nate. "This wouldn't be worthwhile otherwise."

Grace shook her head. His sense of doing the right thing was another reason she loved him, but she wanted to shake him, to shout at him. Tell him *dying isn't the way*. But she'd tried that, and he'd shrugged, and like the mule he was, came out here anyway.

Only thing for it was to be at his side. Together. Forever.

WHY NOT TREAT yourself to *Tyche's Demons* today?

[https://www.books2read.com/TychesDemons]

www.ingramcontent.com/pod-product-compliance
Lightning Source LLC
Chambersburg PA
CBHW070901180125
20577CB00040B/904